G. J. Whyte Melville

Holmby House

A Tale of old Northamptonshire. Vol. 2

G. J. Whyte Melville

Holmby House
A Tale of old Northamptonshire. Vol. 2

ISBN/EAN: 9783337080136

Printed in Europe, USA, Canada, Australia, Japan

Cover: Foto ©Andreas Hilbeck / pixelio.de

More available books at **www.hansebooks.com**

HOLMBY HOUSE

A TALE OF OLD NORTHAMPTONSHIRE

BY

G. J. WHYTE MELVILLE

AUTHOR OF 'DIGBY GRAND' 'THE INTERPRETER' ETC.

IN TWO VOLUMES.

VOL. II.

ORIGINALLY PUBLISHED IN 'FRASER'S MAGAZINE'

LONDON:

JOHN W. PARKER AND SON, WEST STRAND.

1860.

LONDON:
SAVILL AND EDWARDS, PRINTERS,
CHANDOS-STREET.

LONDON:
SAVILL AND EDWARDS, PRINTERS,
CHANDOS-STREET.

CONTENTS

OF

THE SECOND VOLUME.

HOLMBY HOUSE.

CHAPTER I.

'THE TRUE DESPOTISM.'

'NEVER to bear arms against the Parliament!—
never to be a soldier again!—scarcely to have
a right to draw a sword! Ah, Mary! life would be
dear at such a price, were it not that *you* had offered
it; were it not that *your* will, your lightest word,
is omnipotent with me. But oh! how I long to
hear the trumpets sounding a charge again, and to
see the sorrel in headstall and holsters shaking his bit
as he used to do. He's too good for anything but a
charger. Oh, if I could but ride him alongside of
Prince Rupert once more!'

Half ashamed of his enthusiasm, the speaker's
colour rose, and he laughed as he glanced almost
timidly at the lady he addressed.

She was tending some roses that drooped over the
garden bench on which he sat. There was this at-
traction about Mary Cave that perhaps endeared her
to the imagination more than all her wit and all
her beauty—she was constantly occupied in some
graceful womanly task, and fulfilled it in such a graceful womanly way. Were she writing a letter, or

threading a needle, or engaged in any other trifling occupation, her figure seemed to take insensibly the most becoming attitude, her rich brown hair to throw off the light at the exact angle you would have selected for a picture, the roseate bloom to deepen into the very tint that accorded best with her soft winning eyes. It was not her intellect, though that was of no inferior class; nor her form and features, though both were dangerously attractive: it was *her ways* that captivated and enslaved, that constituted the deadliest weapon in the whole armoury of which, womanlike, she knew so well the advantage and the use.

As she pruned the roses and trained them downwards from their stems, shaking a shower of the delicate pink petals into the sun, she looked like a rose herself—a sweet, blooming moss-rose, shedding its fragrance on all that came within its sphere; the type of pure loveliness and rich, bright, womanly beauty.

He thought so as he looked up at her, and his heart thrilled to the tones of her melodious voice. It was all over with him now—

Inch thick, knee-deep, o'er head and ears,—a forked one.

She knew her power, too, and made no sparing use of it. They must be either slaves or tyrants, these women; and like fire, they make good servants but bad mistresses.

'You are better here than wasting your life in Gloucester gaol,' answered Mary, 'and you can serve the King as well with your head as with your hands.

Any man with the heart of a man can be a soldier; there is not one in a million that will make a statesman. Do you think I would have taken such care of you if I had thought you fit for nothing better than the front-rank of one of Prince Rupert's foolhardy attacks?'

She asked the question with an inexpressibly mischievous and provoking air. She could not resist the temptation of teasing and irritating him on occasion; she loved to strike the keys, so to speak, and evoke its every sound, at whatever cost of wear and tear to the instrument itself. He winced, and his countenance fell at once, so she was satisfied, and went on.

'If you cannot serve the King on the sorrel's back, do you think you are of no use to the Queen at her need here in Exeter? That poor lady, with her infant daughter, has but few friends and protectors now. A loyal and chivalrous gentleman always finds his post of honour in defending the weak. If you seek for danger you will find enough, and more than enough, in doing your duty by your Royal mistress— in fulfilling the orders, Major Bosville, that I shall have the honour of conveying to you.'

She laughed merrily and made him a grand courtesy as she spoke, spreading out her white robes with a mock and playful dignity. Mary did not often thus unbend, and he could not but confess to himself that she was inexpressibly charming so; yet would he have been better pleased had she been in a more serious mood too.

He rose from the garden-bench and stood by her,

bending down over the roses, and speaking in a low grave tone—

'I am ready, as you know, none better, to sacrifice life and all for the King's cause. Do me the justice to allow that I have never yet flinched a hair's-breadth from difficulty or danger. I desire no better fate than to shed my blood for his Majesty and the Queen. If I may not draw my sword with my old comrades, I may yet show them how to die like a Cavalier. My life is of little value to any one,' he added in a somewhat bitter tone, 'least of all to myself; and why should I be regretted when so many that were nobler and wiser and better are forgotten?'

It was a random shaft, but it quivered in the bull's-eye. She shot a sharp quick glance at him. Did he mean it? Was he too thinking, then, of Falkland? No! that pained, sorrowing countenance forbade the suspicion of any *arrière pensée*. Her heart smote her as she scanned it. She looked kindly and fondly at him.

'Are you nothing to *me?*' she said. 'Should not I miss you and mourn you, and oh! do you think *I* could do without you at all? Hush! here comes Lady Carlisle.'

In effect that lady's graceful figure, with its courtly gait and rustling draperies, was seen advancing up the gravel path to put an end to the *tête-à-tête*. Such interruptions are the peculiar lot of those who have anything *very* particular to communicate; but we do not take upon ourselves to affirm that Mary's quick ear had not caught the sound of a door opening from

Lady Carlisle's apartments ere she permitted herself to bestow on Humphrey such words of encouragement as made the June sunshine and the June roses brighter and sweeter than roses and sunshine had ever seemed before.

With his loyal heart bounding happily beneath his doublet, and a light on his handsome face that Lady Carlisle—no mean judge of masculine attractions—regarded with critical approval, he followed the two ladies into the antechamber of his Royal mistress, now seeking with her new-born baby an asylum in the still faithful town of Exeter, one of the few strongholds in the kingdom left to the Royal cause; and yet, alas! but a short distance removed from the contamination of rebellion, for Essex was already establishing his head-quarters at Chard, and but two-and-twenty miles of the loveliest hill and dale in Britain intervened between the stern Parliamentary General and the now vacillating and intimidated Queen.

It was a strange contrast to the magnificence of Whitehall, even to the more chastened splendours of Merton College, that quiet residence of majesty in the beautiful old town—the town that can afford to challenge all England to rival it in the loveliness of its outskirts and the beauty of its women. Exeter has always particularly plumed itself on the latter qualification; and many a dragoon of the present day, whose heart is no harder under its covering of scarlet and gold than was that of the chivalrous Cavalier in buff and steel breastplate, has to rue his death-wound from a shaft that penetrated all his

defences, when shot deftly home by a pair of wicked
Devonshire eyes. Of the pic-nics in its vicinity, of
the drives home by moonlight—of the strolls to hear
'our band play,' and the tender cloakings and shawl-
ings, and puttings on of goloshes afterwards (for in
that happy land our natural enemies likewise enjoy
the incalculable advantage of an uncertain climate
and occasional showers), are not the results chronicled
in every parish register in England?—and do not
the beadle at St. George's, Hanover-square, and
other hymeneal authorities, know 'the reason why?'

The Queen occupied a large quiet house, that had
formerly been a convent, on the outskirts of the
town. Its roomy apartments and somewhat secluded
situation made it a fitting residence for Royalty,
particularly for Royalty seeking privacy and repose;
while the large garden adjoining, in which the holy
sisters had been wont to stroll and ponder, yearning,
it may be, for the worldly sunshine they had left
without the walls, formed a pleasant haunt for the
Queen's diminished household, and a resort on the
fine June mornings of which Mary and Humphrey,
who were both early risers, did not fail to make
constant use.

Their duties about the Queen's person had of late
been unusually light. The birth, under circumstances of difficulty and danger, of a daughter, whose
arrival on the worldly stage seemed to augur the misfortunes that, beautiful and gifted as she was, dogged
her to her grave, had confined Henrietta to her
chamber, and precluded her from her usual interference in affairs of State. The instincts of mater

nity were in the ascendant, and what were crowns and kingdoms in comparison with that little pink morsel of humanity lying so helplessly in her bosom? Well is it for us that we cannot foresee the destinies of our children; merciful the blindness that shuts out from us the long perspective of the future—the coming struggles we should none of us have courage to confront. Could Henrietta have foretold that daughter's fate, bound in her beauty and freshness for a weary lifetime to the worst of the evil dukes who bore the title d'Orleans, would she have hung over the tiny treasure with such quiet happiness? Would she have neglected all besides in the world at the very faintest cry of the little new-born Princess?

We must return to Humphrey Bosville and Mary Cave, and the terms of close friendship, to call it by no softer name, on which they now found themselves. Since his rescue from imminent death by her exertions, his devotion to her had assumed, if possible, a more reverential character than before. To owe his life to a woman for whom he had felt a slight attachment, would have been an obligation rather galling and inconvenient than otherwise; but to owe his life to *the* woman whom alone of all on earth he had loved with the deep absorbing fervour of which such a nature was capable, brought with it a sensation of delight which was truly intoxicating. It was such an additional link to bind him to her for ever; it made him seem to belong to her now so thoroughly; it was such a good excuse for giving way to her most trifling caprices, and obeying her lightest whim. Come what might, he felt that they could never now be entirely independent of each other; so he entered the Queen's service immediately on his return to Oxford, giving up his commission in the royal army, and resigning his right to wear a sword, as indeed the terms of his *parole* enjoined, with as little hesitation as he would have displayed in jumping with his hands tied into the Isis, had Mary only told him to do the one instead of the other.

It was no small inducement either to serve his Royal mistress assiduously, that his situation in her household brought him into close and daily contact with his ladye-love. Probably at no period of his life before had Humphrey been so happy as during the few golden weeks of Henrietta's confinement at Exeter. To meet Mary day by day in the performance of his duty; to see her in every phase of courtly life, from the strict observance of etiquette to the joyous moments of relaxation, over which, nevertheless, the atmosphere of Royalty shed a certain refinement and reserve; to admire her ready tact and winning bearing in all the different relations of a courtier's life; and above all, to walk with her morning after morning in those happy gardens, feeling that she too enjoyed and counted on their half-hour of uninterrupted conversation, and was little less punctual at the trysting-place than himself; all this constituted an existence for which it was very seldom he repined that he had bartered his life's ambition, his visions of military distinction and renown. Mary, too, whose knowledge of human nature was far deeper than that of the generality of her sex, whose organization forced her to be calculating, so to speak,

and provident even in her affections, Mary felt herself day by day losing much of the hard, stern, practical force of character that had encrusted and
petrified her woman's heart. She was often surprised
in her moments of reflection (for Mary was a rigid
and severe self-examiner) to find how little interested
she was comparatively in the progress of the Royal
Cause—how satisfied she could be to remain idle week
after week at Exeter—how happily she could bask
away her time in the summer sunshine, wandering,
but not alone, through those shady gardens. She
was ashamed—yes, *ashamed*—to confess to herself
how often the image of a certain kindly, handsome
face, with its long love-locks and dark drooping
moustaches, rose between her mental vision and all
considerations of duty, loyalty, and interest—ay,
even between her deep sorrow and the memory of the
dead. Yet the shame had in it a burning, thrilling
happiness too; and though she threw up her haughty
head, and a scornful smile curled her full lips as she
pondered, she would not have had it otherwise if she
could.

But she ruled him, nevertheless, with an iron hand.
It is unnecessary to admit that the prominent and
chief fault in this lady's character was that destructive
quality which, forming, as it does, a principal ingredient in the noblest spirits, is yet perhaps the cause
of more sorrow and suffering than all the cardinal
vices (if such there be) put together—Pride, the bane
of that resplendent being whom the angels themselves called ' the Son of the Morning;' the awful and
eternal curse of him who made his election ' rather to

rule in Hell than serve in Heaven.' Pride was with
Mary Cave as the very air she breathed. It prompted
her to conceal and stifle, nay, even to mock at, the
better feelings of her nature; to grudge the man that
loved her the full and free confession to which, if he
deserved anything at all, he was fully entitled, and
which would have made him the happiest Cavalier in
England; to check and warp even his kind feelings,
overflowing as they did with a fond and chivalrous
devotion, that would have made a humbler woman's
heaven, that she herself would have felt it a weary
blank to be without; to embitter for him many a
moment that but for this would have been tinged
with golden hues; and to goad and madden him for
no fault of his own when most he needed soothing
and repose.

He too had his share of pride, which she never
seemed to acknowledge; but in his singleness of heart
he sacrificed it to hers, as he did everything else he
had. She never knew, and he would never tell her,
the long hours and days of grief that she had cost
him. If he was sad, he suffered uncomplaining by
himself. The kind look was always there to greet
her; she never read reproach in the fond, frank eyes.
She was his first love and his last, that was enough
for him. It was a brave, confiding nature, this young
gentleman's; simple and honest, and one that it had
been a pity to see delivered over to bitter disappointment, reckless guilt, and wild remorse.

He did not understand women, poor boy! God
forbid he ever should!

A council had been assembled, and the increasing

hopelessness of the Royal Cause had called up a rueful expression of dismay on the faces of the Queen's advisers as they stared blankly at each other. Jermyn had returned with but little encouragement from the King. Charles was hardly the man to see the shortest way out of a difficulty, and had been so accustomed to rely upon his Queen for advice and assistance, that when he found himself in turn applied to by his wife, he was more than usually helpless and undecided. The Queen's own advisers consisted but of the refuse of her party. Jermyn and a few subordinate courtiers were scarcely a crew to weather the storm when the ship was so crazy and the navigation so intricate. Goring's pregnant brain and reckless hand might have been useful now; but Goring was far away, drinking and countermarching in the West Riding of Yorkshire. Ashburnham had retired from Weymouth before 'the Coming Man,' whose Ironsides had ere this perfected their drill on many a stricken field. Prince Maurice had lost so many men in the siege of Lynn, he could show no front to the dreaded and determined Essex. The enemy was near, ay, even at the very gates, and what was to be done?

At this crisis, weakened in body and disheartened in mind, Henrietta's royal spirit gave way. The determination was arrived at to sue the Parliamentary General for mercy, and on the most plausible grounds of common courtesy and chivalrous forbearance towards a woman, to entreat Essex to tamper with his duty towards the Parliament, and to forfeit his own character by conniving at the Queen's escape. Like many another measure of policy, this step originated, not in the council, but in the bedchamber.

Supported by a few of her weeping ladies, the Queen came to the resolution of thus humbling herself before the Parliamentary General; and of those frightened and despairing women, among whom even Lady Carlisle had lost heart and courage, there was but one dissentient voice to this humiliating proposition. Need we say it was Mary Cave's?

'I would rather take my child in my arms,' said she, when called on by her Majesty to give her unbiassed opinion, 'and placing myself at the head of our garrison here, march at once upon Essex's headquarters. I would cut my way through them, or leave my body on the field. If we succeeded, we should make a junction with the King in the north, and maybe restore the *prestige* of the Royal arms; if we failed, 'tis but an honourable death after all, and one right worthy of a Queen.'

The old Bourbon blood rose for an instant to Henrietta's cheek, and she almost wavered in her purpose; but it ebbed back again chill about her heart as she thought of her helpless condition and her little crying child.

'It could not be,' she said: 'there was a limit to all things, even the courage of a Queen. No; she would send a flag of truce to Essex, and a message he could not refuse to consider. But whom to send? Which of her courtiers would undertake the task? Savage reprisals were now the daily custom of the war: the white flag did not always secure the life of its bearer. Who would risk himself in the lion's den?'

'Perhaps Mrs. Mary will go herself?' suggested Lady Carlisle in her soft, smooth tones. 'She fears nothing, so she says, but dishonour. She would be safe enough, methinks, with Essex.'

Mary smiled proudly. 'I have been in the rebel camp ere this,' she said, 'and it was your ladyship's self that bade me go; for that counsel I shall always feel grateful. Your Majesty has one servant at least that will be proud to execute your will.'

She glanced as she spoke to where Bosville, with another gentleman of the chamber, stood in attendance in the next room. The Queen smiled faintly and stretched her thin hand towards Mary with a gesture of caress.

'He is a *preux chevalier, mamie*,' she said, 'and would go to the death, I believe, for you or me; though I think I know which is the queen that owns all *his* loyalty. I have watched him often, Marie, and I *know*.' She nodded her head with something of her old playful air, but she sighed after she spoke, and relapsed into the melancholy silence that was becoming habitual to her.

Was she thinking that, Princess and Sovereign though she were, in the bloom of her beauty and the hey-day of her prosperity, she had never enjoyed such an unqualified dominion as was possessed by her undemonstrative waiting-woman, proud Mary Cave?

CHAPTER II.

' FAREWELL.'

EFFINGHAM had ere this made considerable progress in the favour of the party he had espoused. His knowledge of his profession, coupled with a certain reckless daring of temperament, had won him the good opinion of Cromwell, whilst his readiness of resource, deep reflection, and powerful intellect rendered him indispensable to Essex, Fairfax, and such of the Parliamentary Generals as cherished liberal views of policy and an unselfish desire for the liberation of their countrymen. He had fought his way in a short space of time to the colonelcy of a regiment of pikes, and was now advancing with Essex on Exeter at the head of some five hundred stout hearts, such as have made British soldiers from time immemorial the best infantry in the world. Proud of his command, conscious of doing his duty, rising rapidly in his profession and in the opinion of those who were in the fair road to guide the destinies of England, there was yet in Effingham's bearing a restlessness and a reserve that denoted a mind ill at ease with itself—an unquiet sadness that spoke of some deep anxiety—some bitter disappointment. His friendship with Simeon had grown to a close intimacy, and he seemed to derive much consolation and refreshment from the conversation of that stern enthusiast.

They were walking up and down in front of Essex's head-quarters at Chard—a square brick house in the centre of the village, from which the proprietor had been ejected with as little ceremony by the Puritan General as he could have been by any one of his noisy Cavalier opponents. They formed a strange contrast, that pair, as they paced to and fro, buried in deep discourse—the stalwart iron-looking soldier, with his tall figure and warlike air and dress, thus listening with such respectful deference to the soberly-clad divine, whose eager gestures and speaking countenance betrayed the flame of enthusiasm that consumed him, body and soul.

The guard was being relieved, with the customary noise and pomp of all military proceedings, not to be dispensed with even by the staid and sober Puritans; but the pair heeded not the clash of arms nor the clang of trumpets, and pursued their walk and their conversation regardless of aught but the topic which seemed to engross their whole attention.

'There is yet a black drop in thy heart, my brother,' said Simeon, in his deep impressive tones; 'there is yet one jewel left that thou hast grudged to cast into the treasury—and if thou givest not thine all, of what avail is thy silver and gold, thy flocks and herds, thy raiment of needle-work and thy worldly possessions? The daughter of the Canaanite is a fair damsel and a comely, but the children of the congregation have no dealings with the heathen, and she must henceforth be to thee as the forbidden food, and the plague-spot of leprosy—unclean! unclean!'

'It is hard,' answered Effingham, and his voice betrayed how bitterly hard it was—'it *is* hard to give up my only dream of earthly happiness—the one bright ray that has lightened my existence all these weary months—that has cheered me in the bivouac, and encouraged me in the field. I am not like you, Simeon; would that I were! I cannot hold to the future alone, and resign this world and all it contains without a pang. I fear I am of the doomed—predestined to guilt—predestined to punishment. Lost! lost!'

He shuddered as he spoke, and yet something of the old Titan instinct, the daring of despair that bade the sons of Earth confront the power of Heaven, in those old days when good and evil bore gigantic fruit here below—made him rear his head more proudly, tower above his comrade more erect and bold, as he seemed in his rebellious imagination to 'stand the shot.'

'Whom He loveth He chasteneth,' was Simeon's answer. 'I tell thee, brother, once and again, it is not so. Thy fight is a stern and severe conflict, but it has been borne in upon me that thou shalt be victorious; and to him that prevaileth is given the crown of glory. I have wrestled for thee long and earnestly, and I shall not fail. Thou art as the drowning man, whose struggles serve but to drag down into the depths the friend that would save him from perdition. I tell thee, watch and pray!'

'I can watch,' answered Effingham, bitterly; 'none better. Sleep seldom visits my eyelids, and my waking is sad and painful indeed; but I can *not* pray!'

It was even so. The stubborn human will might be bent and warped from that which was, after all, a holy and God-given instinct, though fanaticism and superstition might vote it folly and sin; but the poor aching human heart could not force itself to supplicate at the throne of Mercy for that forgetfulness which it felt would be a more bitter curse than all the pain it was now becoming inured to bear. Fallible sons of men! Simeon *felt* he was right; Effingham thought himself to be wrong. Both were arguing foolishly and presumptuously from strong human passions interpreted by fanaticism into revelations from on high.

George had struggled on wearily for months. In occupation and danger he had been striving hard to forget. He thought he was making sufficient progress in the lesson, when the sight of his old friend Bosville riding into Essex's camp under a flag of truce re-awakened all those feelings which he had fondly hoped were stifled, if not eradicated, and made him too painfully conscious that time and distance were not quite such effective auxiliaries as he had hoped.

The General had called in some of his principal officers to aid him in his deliberations; nor could he, according to his custom, come to any decision without the assistance of one or two Puritan divines. Caryl had already been sent for; and ere long a grim orderly trooper, who had been expounding to his comrades a knotty text of scripture with interpretations peculiarly his own, was despatched to summon Simeon to the Council, and Effingham was left to pursue his walk and his meditations alone.

He did not remain uninterrupted for long. A bustle at the door of Essex's quarters, the clash of arms as the sentries saluted their departing officers, and the roll of a drum mustering a regiment of foot for inspection, announced that the Council was over; and Bosville, who contrary to his expectation had found himself treated with all the respect and consideration due to the bearer of a flag of truce, advanced toward his old comrade with his hand extended, and a frank air of greeting upon his face.

He looked somewhat flushed and disconcerted too—a thought angry, perhaps, and a little discontented besides, as he cast a soldier's eye up and down the ranks of an efficient battalion of pikemen, and thought he must never measure swords with the Roundheads again; but he was glad to see Effingham, nevertheless; and the latter's heart leapt within him, for many reasons, to grasp a 'Malignant' by the hand once more.

'I thought not we should ever have come to this, George,' observed Bosville, half bitterly half laughingly, after their first greeting was over. 'When thou and I rode through Ramsay's pikes at Edge-hill side by side, and drove them pell-mell right through their reserve and off the field, I little thought I should live to see myself a messenger of peace fit to be clad only in bodice and pinners—for i'faith 'tis but a woman's work, after all—and thee, George, a rank rebel, openly in arms against the King. And yet, 'slife, man, were't not for thy company, I could find it in my heart to envy thee too. They behave well these pikemen—hey, George? Dost remember how close the knaves stood upon the slope at Newbury?'

Effingham smiled absently. He was chafing to ask a hundred questions of his old comrade; and yet, bold stout soldier as he was, his heart failed him like a girl's.

Bosville, too, was indignant at the ill success of his embassy; in the presence of Essex he had had the good taste and prudence to dissemble his generous wrath, but it required a vent, and blazed up afresh as he took the Parliamentary Colonel by the arm, and they strolled out of ear-shot of the listening escort, already under arms to conduct the embassy back to his own lines.

'There is no chivalry amongst thy new friends, George,' he proceeded, the blood rising to his handsome face. 'You can fight, to do you justice, but there's nothing more of the lion about you than his courage. And as for your ministers! men of peace are they? More like croaking ravens and filthy birds of prey. Don't be offended, George: I am like a woman, you know, now, and the only weapon I have to use is my tongue. 'Faith, my blood boils when I think of the last hour's work. Essex is a gentleman, I grant you —I always thought so. We have both of us seen him walk his horse coolly along his line under a raking fire from our culverins; and he received my message with all the courtesy due to the emissary of a queen. It was not much we required. A safe conduct for herself and child to Bath, or maybe Bristol, for her health's sake. She has suffered much, poor lady, and looks so thin and weak—so unlike what she was when we saw her at Merton, George, whilst thou wert *honest*. Well, he seemed to entertain the proposal at first! and one of his Generals, a stout bluff-faced man—Ireton, was it?—voted point-blank in her favour, with some remarks, I am bound to admit, not flattering to the stability of our party, or the efficiency of her Majesty's defenders. Had my position allowed it, I had taken leave to differ with him on that point, but I thought the bowl seemed to trundle with the bias, só I held my peace. Then his lordship turned to a spare pale man in a Geneva band and black cassock, and asked him what he thought of the matter. Was that Caryl? So, I wouldn't be in *his* cassock, when the charity that covereth a multitude of sins is wanted to ward off punishment from *him!* My hands were bound, so to speak, or no man living, minister or layman, should have applied such terms to my royal mistress. Jezebel was the best name he called her; and if blasphemy and indecency be religion, my service to Dr. Caryl! Goring hasn't a match for him among his " hell-babes" for piety! They seemed to believe in him devoutly, though, for all that; and I saw Essex waver as I can see *thee*, George, wince. Well, one ecclesiastic I suppose wasn't enough, for there came in another knave, without his ears too; would the hangman had done his work yeomanly when he was about it, and cut his tongue out as well. They asked his advice, man (grant me patience), as he had been a bishop! And what said the Crop-ear in reply? " Go see now this cursed woman," quoth he, " and bury her, for she is a king's daughter." And again—" What peace so long as the witchcrafts of Jezebel are so many?" The devil can quote holy writ, we all know; but it was well they turned me out, to deliberate with closed doors, for I was almost beside myself with passion.'

The Cavalier paused to take breath. His listener gazed at him wistfully, with a sort of pitiful interest.

'And what was the result of their deliberations?' he inquired. 'I see they came to a speedy conclusion, for the escort is waiting even now to take you back.'

'When I returned,' answered Bosville, 'the General looked grave and stern, I thought a little pained and grieved too. "Tell those that sent you, Major Bosville," he said, in a slow, deliberate voice, "that if her Majesty pleases, I will not only give her a safe-conduct, but wait upon her myself to London, where she may have the best advice and means for the recovery of her health; but as for either of the other places, I cannot obey her Majesty's desires without directions from the Parliament. We will not blind-fold you," he added, courteously. "You are welcome to take note, and report to their Majesties on the men and munitions of war that you find in my camp." So he dismissed me civilly enough. George, my mind misgives me, that I have come on a sleeveless errand.'

'It is even so,' answered Effingham, solemnly. 'The Truth is great, and it shall prevail. But tell me, Humphrey, of those you have left behind. We have but few minutes to spare, and perhaps we may never meet again, unless it be on a stricken field. What of those who were once my friends, who minis-tered to me in the house of bondage? What of

Mistress Cave—of Sir Giles Allonby—of—of—his daughter?'

For reasons of his own Effingham hesitated as he put the question, the latter part of which alone, for reasons of *his* own, Bosville thought worthy of a reply.

'Sir Giles is hearty and busy as usual,' he answered. 'He has raised a large force of cavalry, and is with the King. Mistress Grace is anxious and ill at ease. As far as I can learn, they say she grows pale and thin, and has lost her bright looks and joyous ways. God forbid she should be really ailing, for if aught should befal her, it would go nigh to break old Sir Giles's heart.'

He spoke without the slightest change of voice or colour, and looked frank and straight into his companion's eyes, which nevertheless refused to meet his glance. It was hard to say whether grief, or joy, or anxious fear was uppermost in Effingham's being at that moment.

'If you should chance to see her, Humphrey,' he said, with a quivering, broken voice, 'or to write to her mayhap, tell her that I sought tidings of her welfare, and Sir Giles, you know; and that—that—though I am a rebel, and a Roundhead and all, I have not for that forgotten them; and if ever the time comes that I can serve them, I will. Fare thee well! fare thee well!' he added, grasping Humphrey warmly by the hand as the latter mounted to depart. 'Would that thou, too, couldst be brought to see the truth; but God bless thee, lad! Forget not George Effingham altogether, whatever comes uppermost.'

He gazed wistfully after the horseman's retreating figure as the escort closed round their charge and disappeared. It was his last link with the old life that shone back in such glowing hues. A tear glittered on his shaggy eyelashes as he strode off towards his quarters.

'Weak! weak!' he muttered. 'Unworthy, unprofitable servant. And yet perhaps even now she is not lost to me entirely and for ever?'

Bosville was destined to bring with him sad dismay into the mimic Court at Exeter. Like all weak minds in extremity, Henrietta had fully persuaded herself that the last card she played must win her the game; that this extreme measure of entreaty and humiliation could not but produce the result she so much desired. When it failed, she was indeed at the utmost of her need. Indignation, too, mingled with alarm; and like some bitter tonic, helped to brace her mind into a sufficiently vigorous frame to come to some definite resolution. Impeached as she was of treason by both Houses of Parliament, this proposal of Essex thus to carry her into the very jaws of her enemies was almost tantamount to an insult; and the queenly spirit, not yet thoroughly broken, felt and resented it accordingly. The foe, too, was in far too close proximity to be pleasant. Exeter was no longer a secure refuge, and she must depart. But whither? To join the King without bringing him supplies of men or money, was but to clog the sinking monarch's efforts at extrication, and to drag him deeper and deeper into the slough of his difficulties.

No part of England was safe from the dreaded

Parliamentary army, numbering as it now did amongst
its formidable soldiery such tacticians as Fairfax, and
such strategists as Cromwell. There was but one
haven left, and that was her native country. We
may imagine the struggle in the mind of that proud
though vain and frivolous nature, ere she could bring
herself to return as a homeless suppliant, to the land
she had left in her maidenhood a prosperous and
queenly bride. She was altered, too, in her very
person, and this to a woman added no inconsiderable
ingredient to the bitterness of her cup. Sorrow and
anxiety had hollowed the fair cheeks and clouded the
brilliant complexion that in girlhood with fine eyes
and delicate features had constituted such an attractive countenance ; and the fresh bloom of her spring-
time had withered sadly and prematurely ere 'twas
May. It was with galling self-consciousness that she
used to avow no woman could have any pretensions
to beauty after two-and-twenty.

So the daughter of Henry of Navarre, and the wife
of England's King, must fly for her very life to the
sea-board of her adopted country, must embark from
Falmouth in a Dutch man-of-war, attended by sundry
lighter craft, to the speediest of which it might prove
necessary to entrust the destinies of a queen ; must
sustain the insult of being fired on by her own navy
—for Warwick's squadron, stationed in Tor-bay,
actually gave chase to the Royal lady—and must land
in poor and desperate plight on the shores of her
brother's kingdom, to seek the repose and safety
denied her in her own.

All these events, however, are matters of history ;

and except in so far as they affect the proceedings of those subordinate dolls whose strings in our puppet-show we have undertaken to pull, they will bear neither relation nor comment at the humble hands of the mere story-teller, who can only flutter to and fro *tenui pennâ* through the shaded gardens of Fiction, but dare not trust his feeble pinions to soar aloft into the dazzling sunshine of Fact.

Mary Cave followed her Royal mistress to the very shallop in which she left the British shore. It was but a small household she carried with her from England; and though Mary would fain have accompanied her, it was agreed that her talents could be more usefully employed at home, and that living quietly in retirement here she might still aid the Royal cause with all the energies of her astute and far-seeing intellect, whilst she could keep a watchful eye on the state of public opinion, and communicate constantly and unreservedly by means of their own cipher with Henrietta in France.

To one of the household, this arrangement was the only consolation for a parting which he felt far more painfully than even *he* had expected. By Mary's wish he had consented to follow the fortunes of his Royal mistress, who was nothing loth to retain the services of one who had already proved himself so willing and devoted; but it was with a heavy heart, and a foreboding of evil by no means natural to his temperament, that Humphrey took leave of his ladye-love on the morning of the embarkation at Falmouth.

He was saddened, too, to think that for the last

few days her manner to him had been colder and more reserved than it usually was. She had studiously avoided every chance of a private interview, had apparently wantonly and unfeelingly neglected every hint and allusion that he had ventured to make as to his wish of seeing her alone once more to bid her 'farewell;' and had shown, to his thinking, an amount of heartlessness and carelessness of his feelings which grieved him as it would have angered another.

Humphrey, though a young man, was no inexperienced soldier. He had assisted ere this at the scaling of many a rampart, the assault of many a beleagured town; yet it never occurred to him that the last efforts of the besieged are desperate in proportion to their extremity—the resistance never so obstinate as on the eve of surrender. The weak are sometimes cruel, and a stern front is often but the mask that hides a failing heart.

He was leaving the Queen's apartments to make preparations for her Majesty to go abroad. He walked moodily and sadly, for he thought he should not see Mary again, and he was wondering in his simple faith how he could have offended her, and why she should thus think it worth while to grieve him, when perhaps they might never meet again. Like a child unjustly punished, he was less irritated than spirit-broken. Alas! like many a brave and gallant man, he was a sad coward, if only attacked in the right place.

A door opened in the gallery of the hostelry honoured by the presence of royalty. Mary advanced towards him, holding out her hand.

'I am come to wish you good-bye,' she said in her kind, frank tones. 'I looked for you an hour ago in the gallery. Humphrey,' she added, her voice trembling as she marked his whole countenance flush and soften, 'I have used you ill. Forgive me. I did not mean it—at least I did not mean to make you so unhappy,' and she gave him ever so slight a pressure of that warm soft hand—that hand which only to touch he would at any time have given a year of his life.

He was a sad coward in some things we have already said. He bent over the white hand without speaking a word, but she felt the hot tears dropping on it as he lifted his head and tried to smile unconcernedly in her face.

They were both silent. Had any eavesdropper been watching them in that long gallery, he would have thought the gentleman a strangely uncourteous gallant—the lady a dame of wondrously stiff and reserved demeanour.

Humphrey spoke at length, scarcely above a whisper.

'It is no use,' he said. 'I am a bad dissembler. Mary, you know all. Only give me one word, one kind word of hope, before I go. I will treasure it for years!'

Again that faint, scarcely perceptible pressure of the hand he had never relinquished.

'The task must be accomplished first,' she murmured. '"Loyalty before all."'

He raised her hand to his lips, and imprinted on it one long passionate kiss. Either by accident or design a bow of pink ribbon which she wore on her sleeve had become detached. Somehow it remained in his grasp when she was gone.

The wind blew fresh off-shore, and the Dutchman made gallant way, whilst Humphrey stood on deck, and watched the dim headlands of his home with a strange wistful glance that was yet mingled with triumph and joy.

Had he not won his decoration? And was not his heart beating against the ribbon of his Order?

CHAPTER III.

NASEBY FIELD.

THE undulating prairie of rich grazing ground which stretches far and wide round Market Harborough was blooming a brighter green in the declining rays of a hot June sun, sinking gradually to tip the wooded crests of Marston Hills with gold. Beeves of huge proportion and promising fatness, all unconscious of the dangerous proximity of two hostile armies, grazed contentedly in the sunlight or ruminated philosophically in the shade. Swarms of insects quivered in the still warm air; the note of thrush and blackbird, hushed during the blaze of noon, was awakening once more from tangled hedgerow, leafy coppice, and deep woodland dell, dense and darkling in the rank growth of midsummer luxuriance. Anon the quest's soft, plaintive lullaby stole drowsily on the ear, from her forest home amid the oaks of Kelmarsh, or the tall elm-grove nodding on Dingley's distant hill. It was a scene of peace, prosperity, and repose. What had they to do there, those burnished headpieces and steel breastplates, flashing back the slanting sunbeams, and glittering like gold in all the pomp and panoply of war?

It was a goodly sight to see them, too, as they wound slowly along the plain, those stalwart troopers on their tall chargers, with their dancing plumes and their royal guidons waving above the track of yellow dust that floated on their line of march. To mark their military air, their practised discipline, their bold bronzed faces, and the stately form of their commander with his white moustache and his keen blue eye. 'Tis the vanguard of the royal army, now, in consequence of the King's counter-march from Daventry, forming its rear. These are the flower of Prince Rupert's cavalry, the survivors of the rout of Marston Moor—the remnant of Sir Giles Allonby's brigade—the swordsmen that will follow that daring old man, as long ago he trusted they would at Oxford, 'through and through a stand of pikes once and again on a stricken field.' They have fought, and bled, and conquered, and retreated since then. Sir Giles looks a thought older and more worn about the face, the beard is whiter and the locks thinner, but the spare form, the gallant seat on horseback, lithe and erect as ever.

See! a noble-looking Cavalier, followed by a toiling aide-de-camp, who has tired two horses to-day in attending the hasty movements of his chief, dashes up at a gallop from the rear. Sir Giles salutes him with military precision and an air of frank admiration he is at no pains to conceal. With all his recklessness, there is but one cavalry officer in the world, so thinks Sir Giles, and that is Rupert.

The Prince's words are short, peremptory, and to the point.

'Throw forward an outpost on Naseby village, Sir Giles. The scout-master reports no enemy within sight, but Fairfax cannot be far off—best to make sure. Send young Dalyson in command. I owe him a chance for Marston Moor—bid him double his picket and mind his videttes ! Good even to you !'

The Prince had already turned his horse's head to depart. Sir Giles hesitated; Dalyson was but a boy—bold as a lion, but wild as a hawk; his nineteen summers had hardly given him experience for so critical a duty, and though at Marston Moor, his maiden field, he had behaved like a hero, Sir Giles mistrusted the 'young one' might be out-manœuvred by some of those Parliamentary veterans ere he was aware.

'Lieutenant Dalyson is a very inexperienced officer,' hazarded Sir Giles; but the Prince, turning a deaf ear, was already on the gallop, and the old soldier knew his duty too well not to obey orders, at whatever cost to his own private apprehensions. With no slight misgivings, he gave the delighted young officer his instructions, lavishing on him all the stores of caution and experience he had to bestow. He called out, moreover, a grim, ancient-looking personage from his own especial escort, and accosting him by the name of Sergeant Dymocke, bade him accompany the party, adding in a low tone, 'I think I can trust *you* not to be surprised.'

It needed but the grim smile with which the compliment was accepted to identify our old acquaintance, who, having left the service of Major Bosville, temporarily, and under protest, during the latter's absence in France, was now doing a turn of soldiering to keep his hand in. He was yet too young, as he told the expectant Faith, to settle permanently in life.

Sir Giles, pursuant to his orders, held on with the main body for Market Harborough, whilst the party he had detached, striking into a sharp trot, made the best of their way for Naseby village.

The dews of evening were falling heavily, and the twilight darkening into night, ere they reached their destination. For the last mile or two, under the sergeant's influence, great caution had been observed, flankers thrown out, and an advanced and rear-guard detached from the little party, till, as Dalyson laughingly observed, 'there was nothing left to form the main body but himself and his trumpeter.'

Still there seemed to be no vestige of the enemy, the few peasants that could be questioned at that late hour were either too ignorant or too stupid to give any intelligence, and on arriving at the village, the young officer's first care was rather to refresh his men and horses, than to pry about in the darkness, looking for that which did not seem to exist.

In the Royalist army so many born gentlemen rode in the ranks as simple privates, that there was but a narrow line of demarcation drawn between officers and men. It was therefore no breach of etiquette, though it argued culpable negligence for the officer to dismount his party in the small hostelry at Naseby, calling for the best, after the fashion of Royalists, and making his men welcome as they dropped in after seeing their horses fed, and drew round the old oak table, which bears to this day the marks of many a wild carousal dinted on its surface. He would have unsaddled, had it not been for the expostulation of the sergeant, who with difficulty persuaded three or four of the troopers to forego their suppers and accompany him on his look-out.

The rest of the party were drinking 'The King,' or 'The Ladies,' or some such customary toast, when a couple of shots ringing through the still night air, within two hundred paces, and the warning of the trumpeter pealing out the alarum of 'boots and saddles,' startled them from their carouse. Alas! too late. Ireton's troopers were upon them. Dymocke and his scouts galloping in upon their comrades, would certainly have been shot by mistake had the Cavaliers been a little more on the alert. It was the sergeant's pistols that had given the alarm.

The Royalists, half of them dismounted, and all un-formed, were ridden down like sheep by the disciplined Parliamentarians. Such as accepted quarter were taken prisoners, but Dalyson paid for his negligence with his blood. He had doffed his steel morion and his breastplate. Alone, with his head bare and his buff coat open, he sustained the shock of the leading files and the points of some half-dozen thirsty blades. He was dead ere he fell from the saddle, and of all his followers not one escaped save the wily sergeant, who with his usual imperturbability, when he saw all was lost, turned his bridle and rode for his life. The darkness of the night and his own familiarity with the country (for in happier times he and his old master had hunted and hawked over all that wide champaign, till they knew it every inch) favoured his escape, and he set his horse's head straight for the old Hall at Lubenham, where Charles lay sleeping in fancied security.

That locality is celebrated for its exhaustive properties on the equine race. We question, nevertheless, if it ever witnessed a steed more thoroughly jaded and overdone, than the panting animal that shook its reeking sides at Lubenham gate, as Hugh banged and shouted at the fastened door to arouse the sleeping inmates of the Hall.

Though we dwell not habitually in king's houses, we take the privilege of the story-teller's ubiquity to peep at Charles Stuart in his humble sleeping-room at old Lubenham Hall.

The face on which the night-lamp throws its shaded rays looks careworn and anxious even in slumber. The *doomed* expression which he has borne all his life comes out more strongly now on the haggard brow and the features sharpened by suspense and toil. Yet, sleeping or waking, there is a certain trustful confidence on that face still, the inner light of a pure unspotted nature breaking through the clouds of vacillation and incompetency. That breast on which in its deep-breathing heaves a golden locket containing his Queen's hair, his Queen, who has forgotten him already, whom he has not seen for more than a year, whom he shall never see on earth again—that breast may and does ache with sorrow, but it knows not the sting of remorse. Not even now, though the perspiration starts upon his forehead, and his white hands clench themselves rigidly in the agony of his dream. And this was Charles's dream the night before Naseby field :—

He stood with Strafford in the condemned cell. The cell in his own royal Tower of London, which he had never seen, and yet it seemed strangely familiar in its hideous arrangements and its gloomy security. The minister sat in his splendid dress of state, yet there were handcuffs on the slender wrists under his lace ruffles, and the jewelled garter at his knee contrasted with the heavy clanking fetters of the condemned nobleman. He knelt before his sovereign, but it was not to plead for pardon or reprieve. Those entreaties were not to save Strafford, but the King. He implored his master not to trust to arms, at least, not now.

'To-morrow,' said he, 'I die on Tower-hill. I beseech your Majesty to accept the sacrifice. I give back your Majesty's generous promise of interference. I die willingly for the Crown; but I can foresee the course of destiny at this my last hour, and I implore your Majesty that mine may be the only blood spilt under to-morrow's sun!'

The royal impulse was stronger in the sleeping monarch at Lubenham, than it had been in his waking earnest in the day of power at Whitehall, and he seemed to strive with the futile efforts of a dreamer to unclasp the fetters of his councillor and his friend.

'I will save you,' quoth Charles, in his vision. 'Are these not my walls, my gaolers? Is not this my own royal Tower of London?'

And he beat with bruised hands and noisy blows against the iron door of the doomed man's cell. In the struggle he awoke, and the awe-stricken monarch, sitting up in bed to listen, with a pale, wet face, was aware that the noise of his dream was not entirely the work of fancy, but that an express with important information was even then battering for admittance at the door.

We pass over Dymocke's cool and concise report, as unmoved in the presence of royalty as when galloping for his life from Ireton's deadly troopers. The King, dressing himself hastily, and accompanied only by two or three startled gentlemen of his household, was in the saddle ere his informant had answered half his questions, and rode at a gallop into Harborough, to his nephew's quarters, where he summoned a hasty council of war to assemble on the spot. The early summer morning of the 14th of June was already breaking, when Rupert, Digby, Ashburnham, Sir Marmaduke Langdale, and a few others met to decide the fate of the Royal cause. The hot Prince, for all his haste and bold impetuous bearing in a charge, was no mean strategist, and contrary to his wont, counselled retreat. Digby and Ashburnham, reckless at the wrong time, opposed him strongly, and urged an immediate engagement. The King, flushed with the late news of Montrose's victory a month before at Auldearne, and prompted by his unaccountable instinct always to choose the most injudicious course, decided on battle. The gallant Rupert, perhaps for the first time in his life, made ready to go into action with an unwilling heart.

Leaving the Royal column marching in the cool prime of the bright June morning over the hills towards Naseby, eager and anxious to meet the enemy, whose movements they have been dodging and watching so many weary days, we must take a glimpse at the Parliamentary army, now a compact, well-disciplined, and numerous force, taking up the strong position which they held so stubbornly during the day; and from the selection of which, and his consequent victory, he who led their right wing found himself ere another lustre had elapsed, the occupant of a throne.

Cromwell had effected his junction with Fairfax the evening before, bringing to that commander the efficient aid of his own cool resolution and his formidable well-trained Ironsides, by this time the best cavalry in Europe. When Ireton's advanced guard had driven in the Cavalier outpost on the previous evening, they had discovered that the plain in front of Naseby village was still unoccupied. With grim satisfaction and practised skill, the Parliamentary General took up the strongest position that the ground admitted of—Fairfax throwing forward his left, and lining the thick boundary hedge which divides the manors of Sulby and Naseby with dismounted dragoons, thus doubly protecting his baggage (drawn up in battle order behind his left), his communications and line of retreat if necessary and his rear, occupied the centre in person, where he had placed the bulk of his heavy guns on a commanding slope to the north of the village, whence they could play upon any attacking column advancing up the hill, and open an enfilading fire on any flank movement of the enemy, should he show himself above the crest of the opposite eminence. Cromwell, as Lieutenant-General of the Parliamentary Horse, commanded the right wing, composed chiefly of his own invincible Ironsides, supported, as was the practice in those days, by a stout and trusty *tertia** or two of foot. His extreme right, again, rested on an abrupt declivity and a succession of broken ground, which must effectually discomfit any attempt at turning his flank, whilst the downward slope in front of him, and the open nature of the plain, offered a tempting opportunity for one of those irresistible charges with which, when once *the pace is in them*, cavalry sweep all before them. Skill and experience had done their utmost to make the best of that position on the celebrated arena where the decisive struggle was fought out between the King and his Parliament.

To return to the humble actors in our drama. Effingham, commanding his trusty regiment of Pikes, was placed in support of Ireton's Horse on the left wing—a duty which his previous experience rendered peculiarly suitable to the old officer of Royalist cavalry. With a critical eye he reconnoitred the ground upon his flanks and front, taking advantage of a few wet ditches and a marshy surface to render his position less assailable by cavalry, and retiring somewhat to afford greater protection to Bartlett's waggon-train in his rear. He had scarcely made his arrangements, and was in the act of emptying his havresack of his frugal breakfast, when a horseman rode rapidly up, and grasping him warmly by the hand, pointed to the dark columns of the Parliamentarians deploying slowly into line along the crest of the acclivity on his right, and preparing to pour

---

* Equivalent to a battalion.

their masses with every advantage of ground into the plain.

' Brother,' exclaimed the horseman, ' the armies are gathering to the slaughter. Lo! the eagles are already hovering over the plain of Armageddon. Verily it is the day of the Lord.'

Effingham looked up astonished. The voice was that of Simeon, but the armed figure in buff and breastplate, and morion, sitting so soldierlike upon his horse, was a strange contrast to the preacher in his black gown and Geneva band, to whose exhortations he had himself listened patiently on the eve of battle the day before.

The divine marked his surprise with a grim smile. ' The harvest indeed is ripe,' said he, ' but the reapers are few, therefore have I, Simeon the persecuted, entreated permission of the man of destiny, even Cromwell, that I might this day cast in my lot with his men of war, and charge, brother, through and through the Amalekites in the front rank of his Ironsides ! Horse and armour have been provided for me even as the ravens provided Elijah with food, yet lack I still a sword. I put not my trust in the arm of the flesh ; but methinks, with a long straight basket-hilted blade of keen temper I could do somewhat to further the good work. Hast thou such an one by thee, to lend for an hour or so ?'

Effingham could not help smiling as he sent a sergeant to the rear, where, amongst his baggage, such a weapon was indeed to be found. Pending its arrival the soldier-divine and the commandant of pikes, sharing their frugal meal, watched the movements of the enemy with an increasing interest.

Already the King's baggage and rear guard had taken up their position, just beyond the opposite eminence of Broad-moor, whence, though not a mile distant, the gradual rise of the ground prevented their discerning more than an occasional standard or the fluttering pennon of a lance. The plain between was still unoccupied; but gradually troop after troop of horse wound slowly into sight, extending themselves towards their proper right, where those green impervious hedges concealed the deadly musketeers, and supported by dark masses of infantry, above whose serried forest of shafts the steel pike-heads flashed dazzling in the morning sun.

'I can make out no guns,' observed Effingham, straining his eyes till they watered. 'And by the standard, I judge Charles himself occupies the centre. What a force of cavalry he must have : I can see them swarming by the young plantation on his far left. This will be a heavy day for England, Simeon !'

'Rather say a day of wrath and retribution for the ungodly,' replied the fanatic, poising and examining with a critical eye the heavy blade which had just been put in his hands. ' "For this day shall the wine-press be trodden out, and blood shall come out of the wine-press, even to the horse bridles." Fare thee well, my brother ! Lo ! I gird my sword upon my thigh, and go my ways even into the forefront of the battle !'

As he spoke he set spurs to his charger, and galloping along the rear made the best of his way to where

Cromwell was marshalling his cavalry on the extreme right. Effingham, gazing after his retreating figure, marvelled to note the warlike air and consummate horsemanship of the formidable divine.

He had little leisure to observe him, though, for a dropping fire flashing from the masking blackthorn hedge announced that the Royalist right was advancing, whilst the heavy ' boom' of Fairfax's ordnance proclaimed that ere long the action would be general along the whole line.

A few detached skirmishers dotting the plain, and reckless of the withering fire they sustained, dashed boldly out to clear the boundary hedge of its dangerous occupants, and succeeded so far as to drive the dismounted musketeers back upon their supports. Ireton, fearing a panic which might endanger his whole left, ordered a brigade of cavalry to their assistance; and Rupert's eagle eye spying the flank movement at a glance, the Prince seized the opportunity, and advancing his whole wing at a gallop, gave the word to ' Charge !'

The Royalist trumpets ring out merrily as the best blood of man and horse in England comes sweeping down the slope. There is Rupert, with his short red cloak floating on the breeze, three horses' lengths in front of Britain's proudest chivalry, waving his sword above his head, and shouting ' God and Queen Mary;' ' For the King ! for the King !' There is his brother Maurice, with calm, indomitable energy and stern knitted brows ; ever and anon glancing warily behind him at the line of which, even at the moment of contact, he hopes to preserve the even regularity. There is gentle Northampton, like a Paladin of romance, with a hero's arm, a lion's heart, and a woman's smile upon his face. There is fierce Sir William Vaughan, grim and unmoved in the onset of battle as in the manœuvres of parade; and old Sir Giles, swaying so easily to the long regular stride of that good sorrel horse, the property of one who would fain have been on him now—his eyes sparkling with delight and a cheerful smile curling his moustaches as he thinks of his pet brigade behind him, and chuckles to reflect how he will have the knaves through a stand of pikes yet; for he sees the grim steel-headed forest dark and lowering between the squadrons of the enemy. Every man has his favourite theory, and Sir Giles holds that cavalry properly led ought to break any infantry in the world. He is spurring to its demonstration even now.

Ireton is too good an officer not to rectify his mistake. He forms line like lightning, and advances to meet them; but the Royalists are irresistible, and although the hill is somewhat against them, those gallant horses fail not in their pace, and they ride down the wavering Roundheads with the very impetus of their charge.

In vain Ireton shouts and gesticulates and curses, Puritan though he be, both loud and deep. A pistol shot disables his bridle arm, and a sabre-cut slashes his brave stern face. 'God with us!' gasps the General—for the rebels, too, have their battle-word—and he cleaves the last assailant to the brisket: but he is faint and exhausted, and his share of the battle is well nigh lost. Through and through the Roundhead horse ride the maddened Cavaliers, shouting, striking, spurring wildly on, every heart afire to follow to the death where the short red cloak flashes like a tongue of flame through the dust and smoke of the encounter.

But the torrent is checked—the tide is turned at last. Sir Giles Allonby, catching sight of Effingham's regiment, calm and immovable like a rock amongst the breakers, shouts to his men to follow him, and makes a furious dash at the enemy. Another voice, clear and full as a trumpet-blast, rings above the confusion of the *mélée*.

'Steady, men!—form four deep! Advance your pikes!—stand to your pikes!' are the Colonel's confident orders; and the resolute veterans he commands know only too well that, if once broken, they have nothing to hope for. They have met Prince Rupert before: so they set their teeth and stand shoulder to shoulder, fierce and grim, like the old 'Die-hards' they are. The wet ditches and yielding nature of the ground, sapped by springs of running water, destroy the impetus of Sir Giles's charge, and the fiery old soldier can but reach his enemy at a trot. Nevertheless, so good is the sorrel, so resolute his rider, and so well backed up by a few of his gallant followers, that the old knight, striking madly right and left, forces his way completely through the front rank of the pikemen, and only finds himself unhorsed and bleeding in the very midst of the enemy, when it is too late to do aught but meet the death he has so long tempted, fearless and unshrinking, like a man.

A dozen pike-heads are flashing round the prostrate

Cavalier; a dozen faces with the awful expression, not of anger, but of stern, pitiless hatred, are bending their brows and setting their teeth for the death-thrust, when Effingham's arm strikes up the weapons, and Effingham's voice interposes to the rescue.

'Quarter, my lads,' exclaims the Colonel. 'For shame, men!—spare his grey head. He is my father!'

If ever falsehood counted to the credit side of man's account, surely this one did; and it speaks well for Effingham's control over his men and their affection to his person, that even at such an appeal they could spare a foe red-handed.

'Sir Giles,' whispered the Colonel, 'with me you are safe. Your wounds shall be looked to. You are my prisoner, but I will answer for your life with my own. We shall stand our ground here, I *think*;' then added in a louder tone to a sergeant, 'Catch that sorrel horse! 'Tis the best charger in England, and I would not aught should befal him for Humphrey's dear old sake!'

Sir Giles sat ruefully on the ground, and uttered not a word, for he was pondering deeply. He was wounded in two places, and the blood streamed down his white locks and beard, but of this he seemed utterly unconscious. At last he spoke, in the thoughtful tone of a man who balances the *pros* and *cons* of some knotty argument:—

'It was those wet ditches that did it,' quoth the old Cavalier, with a sigh. 'They broke our stride and so disordered us; otherwise, if we'd come in at a gallop, I still maintain we should have gone through!'

The check sustained by Sir Giles's brigade had meantime somewhat damped the success of the Royalist wing. Half the horses were blown, and from the very nature of cavalry it is impossible to sustain the efficiency of a charge for any lengthened period. Some horses tire sooner than others; men get excited and maddened; some go too far—others have had enough;—all separate. And that which, half a mile back, was an irresistible and well-ordered onset, becomes a mere aimless and undisciplined rush, like a scatter of beads when the string breaks.

Ere Rupert had reached the baggage under Naseby village, he found himself accompanied by scarce half his force. The baggage guard, entrenched behind their waggons, met him with a dropping fire. They presented a resolute and formidable front; the example of their comrades encouraged them to resistance, and their defences and position rendered them a dangerous enemy for blown and disordered cavalry to attack. The Prince summoned them to surrender.

From the centre of his fortress rose the grim reply, in Bartlett's loud fearless tones—

'God with us! Make ready, men, and fire a volley!'

A few Cavalier saddles were emptied. The Prince knew well that he had gone too far. With voice and gesture he strove to rally his followers, who had now got completely 'out of his hand;' and wheeling the small body that he could retain in his command rapidly along the eminence, he turned to see how fared the battle in the plain below.

Rupert was a thorough soldier. It needed no

second glance to satisfy him that the day was indeed
lost; and that all he could do now was to hasten back
with his division on the centre, where the King himself commanded in person, and endeavour to cover
that retreat which was fast degenerating into a rout.

The same courage, the same dash and mettle of
man and horse, that had demoralized Prince Rupert's
division, had, when tempered by discipline, crowned
the Ironsides with victory. The future Protector,
advancing his cavalry by alternate brigades, and
retaining a strong reserve to turn the tide in the
event of any unforeseen catastrophe, moved steadily
upon the left wing of the enemy almost at the same
moment that the corresponding onset of the Royalists
sustained its first check from the grim resistance of
Effingham's pikemen. Cromwell's thorough familiarity with cavalry manœuvres enabled him to take
every advantage of the ground, and his leading
squadrons came down upon Sir Marmaduke Langdale's division with the force and velocity of a torrent.
Regardless of a withering volley from Carey's musketeers, placed in support of the Royalist cavalry, he
drove the latter from their position, and their further
movements being impeded and disorded by the nature
of the ground into which he had forced them—a
treacherous rabbit warren and a young plantation—
they fell back in confusion upon their supports, consisting of two regiments of North-country horse,
whom they carried with them to the rear, despite of
the efforts and entreaties of the gallant Sir Marmaduke and the Yorkshire officers. Cromwell saw his
advantage, but was not to be led away by the bril-

liancy of his success into a departure from those tactics which he had studied so long and so effectually. Despatching a less formidable brigade in pursuit, he kept the Ironsides well in hand; and perceiving an advance of the King's centre, already checked and disordered by the heavy fire of Fairfax's ordnance, let them loose upon the flank of the Royalists at the happy moment when their cavalry were wavering and their infantry deploying into line.

Now came the fiercest of the carnage. The famous 'Blue Regiments,' forming with Lord Bernard Stuart's Life Guards the flower of the King's cavalry, sustained the charge of the rebels with their usual devoted courage and gallantry. Half the noblest names in England were striking for their lives—ay, and more than that, their honour and their order, and their King! The gentle Norman blood was flowing free and fast, as it has ever flowed when deeds of chivalry and daring have been required; but the stubborn Saxon element was boiling too in the veins of many a stalwart freeman; and those iron-clad warriors, in their faith and their enthusiasm, and the flush of their success, were *not* to be denied. Hand to hand and steel to steel, it was the death-grapple of the war; and he who played his bold stake to win a kingdom on that ghastly board spared not his own person in the encounter. Wherever blows were going thickest, there was Cromwell's square form and waving arm; there was the eagle eye, the loud confident voice, the cool head, unmoved and resolute on the field as in the Council; while not a lance's length behind him, smiting like a blacksmith on the anvil, and pouring with every blow a prophet's malediction on the enemy he struck to earth, Simeon the persecuted took ample vengeance on the Royalists for the inhumanity of their Star Chamber and his own cruel mutilation.

Like all non-combatants, when his blood was really up he fought as madly as a Berserkar; and many a goodly warrior, many a practised swordsman, went down to rise no more before the sweeping arm and the deadly thrust of him who represented a teacher of that religion which has longsuffering for its foundation, and mercy for its crown.

And now the Ironsides are almost upon the King's centre, where, pale, yet firm, the monarch rides in person, longing, for all his stately demeanour and enforced reserve, to strike in amongst the fray. With the one exception of his father, not a Stuart of the line ever shrank from personal danger; and had Charles's moral courage been equal to his physical, the grazier's son had not been now within a hundred paces, stretching with bloody grasp at his crown.

A desperate rally is made by the Cavaliers, and Colonel St. George, recognising Cromwell, deals him such a sabre stroke on the helmet as knocks the morion from his head and leaves him bare and defenceless, but cool and courageous as ever. The effect upon his Ironsides is encouraging rather than the reverse; they believe him to be under the especial protection of Heaven, as they believe themselves to be the veritable saints that shall inherit the earth. A reversion they seem well content to fight for to the death; the enthusiastic Simeon perceives his plight, and bringing his horse alongside of him, unfastens his own helmet and forces it on his chief. In the hurry Cromwell places it reversed on his head, and thus armed, fights on more fiercely than before. Does no secret sympathy tell him he is battling over his very grave?—not to-day, bold unswerving man; not till thou hast fulfilled thy destiny, and, to use thine own language, hast 'purged the threshing-floor and trodden out the wine-press,' shalt thou lie down on Naseby Field to take thy rest!

In the dead of night, in secresy and apprehension, shall he be brought here again who was once more than a king; and the man who ruled for years the destinies of England shall be buried in shame and sorrow, like some obscure malefactor, on the spot where the grass grows thick and tangled, because of the crimson rain that fell so heavily on the field of his greatest victory.

And Simeon, bare-headed and maddened, fights fiercely on. His devotion costs him dear. The goodly headpiece would have saved him from that swinging sabre-stroke that lays open cheek and temple, and deluges neck and shoulder with the hot red stream. His arm flies aimlessly up, and the sword drops from his grasp. The battle swims before his eyes ere they seem to darken and fill with blood; he reels in his saddle; he is down amongst the wounded and the dying, and his horse gallops masterless out of the *melée*.

And now Charles sees with his own eyes that all is lost. His right is scattered and disordered. Rupert is returning with but the shattered remnants of his

glorious force.   His left is swept from the field and
flying in hopeless confusion nearly to Leicester.   His
centre is broken and dismayed; his very baggage
unprotected and at the mercy of the enemy.   The
blood of a king rises for the effort; he will put
himself at the head of his reserve and make one
desperate struggle for his crown, or die like a Stuart
in his harness.   He has drawn his royal sword, and
waves his last devoted remnant on.

'Od's heart, sire!' exclaims the Scottish Earl of
Carnewath; 'will ye go upon your death in an instant?' and turns the King's bridle out of the press.
Degenerate earl! it was not thus thy steel-clad ances-
tor backed his father's great-grandsire at Flodden!
But the deed is done! the King turns round;
the rout becomes a flight, and, save the wounded
and the dead, the helpless women and the
dogged prisoners, not a Royalist is left upon the
field.

Effingham's regiment of Pikes has ere this moved
to the very centre of the plain.   When Fairfax saw
and seized the opportunity to advance his whole line,
the Colonel moved with the rest of the infantry in
support of a large cavalry reserve, and thus reached
the spot the King had so recently quitted, where the
fight had been deadliest and the carnage most severe.
Marching in close column, and still keeping Sir Giles
and the sorrel in the centre of his Pikes, Effingham
took up a position where the dead lay thick in heaps,
and at the spot from whence the track of the distant
flight might be marked by the rising dust and the
occasional shots fired by the pursuers, he placed Sir

Giles once more upon his horse, and bade him escape in the confusion.

The old Cavalier grasped him heartily by the hand. 'I wouldn't have believed it of thee, lad,' said Sir Giles. 'I never thought much of thee after thou changed sides; but faith! thou'rt a good lad still, I see, though thou be'st on the winning side, and a murrain to it! Well, well, I've lived long enough when I've seen the coil of to-day. I wouldn't care to be there with many an honest fellow,' pointing to a heap of corpses, 'were't not for Grace's sake.'

'It is for Grace's sake,' answered Ellingham, and squeezing him by the hand, bade him ride for his life.

Sir Giles turned his horse's head, but checked him for one last word. 'I think I could have broken in, too, lad, if I'd come up at a gallop,' said he, argumentatively.

In another minute he was striding away amongst pursuers and pursued over the plain.

A deep groan caused Ellingham to start as he looked down. Simeon lay dying at his feet. 'Too late, my brother,' gasped the enthusiast, as the Colonel propped him on his knee, and strove to stanch the gaping death-wounds. 'Fare thee well, my brother: we meet no more on earth.' Then faintly pushing away the flask George pressed to his lips, and pointing to a dying Cavalier, murmured, 'If thine enemy thirst give him drink;' and so, his features setting and darkening, his lips muttering faint words and texts of Scripture, in which George caught the accents of self-reproach and regret, and the awful emphasis of fear on the words, 'Whoso smiteth with the sword shall perish by the sword;' and 'Blessed are the merciful, for they shall obtain mercy,' the soul of the enthusiast passed to its account. George stood and gazed upon the ghastly harvest gathered in on Naseby Field, and not for the first time a shudder of horror seemed to chill his very soul as the thought swept across it, 'Can this be true religion, after all?—the religion of peace on earth and good-will amongst men?'

CHAPTER IV.

'THE WHEEL GOES ROUND.'

THE cultivated enclosures round Naseby village have been reaped and sown once and again. The grass on the wide expanse of Naseby-field, so poached and trodden down scarce two short years ago, has yielded one heavy crop, and promises again to enrich the peasant with its luxurious produce. In certain spots the sheep refuse to feed, so rank and coarse grows the herbage where the earth has been fattened with the blood of her children. The shepherd tending his flocks, or the herd watching his drowsy cattle, scarce stoops to notice sword or helmet, pike-head or musket-barrel, stained with rust, and protruding from the surface of the moor, so thickly are they strewn, these implements of slaughter that flashed bravely in the summer sun when he shone on the great battle only the year before last. Nay, there are ghastlier tokens than these of man's goodly handiwork and the devil's high festival. Bones of horse and rider still lie bleaching on the slopes, and skulls of the half-buried combatants grin at the labourer as he passes, whistling cheerfully, to his work. He heeds them not. Why should he? What though yon mouldering sphere of bone, with its broad white teeth and vacant sockets, was once the type of manly beauty and divine intellect, was once so fair and gallant, with its love-locks flaunting under its burnished head-piece, was once tended so carefully, and prized so highly, and kissed so fondly by lips that are even now perhaps writhing in their misery at the thought of the loved one lying where he fell on Naseby-field—why should the labourer care? He has his daily toil to urge, his daily pittance to receive, his daily wants to provide for. He turns the skull over with coarse raillery and a kick from his heavy boot. A peasant's jest is the epitaph of him who died with his blood a-flame for victory and renown, his heart beating high with the noblest impulses of chivalry and romance. What matter? Were he any better lapped in lead, under a marble monument, side by side with his knightly ancestors in the old church at home, than lying here under the wide changing sky, to rot, a nameless skeleton on Naseby-field?

Time takes no note of human life and worldly changes. The old mower works steadily on, stroke by stroke, and furrow by furrow; when he reaches the end of the ridge he pauses not to wipe the toil-drops from his brow, but turns and applies him to his task unchecked and unwearied, sparing the shrinking wild flower no more than the tall rank weed, and sweeping down all indiscriminately, level with the short close sward.

And yet, Destroyer though he be, he is the great Restorer too—at least in the natural world. Where the storm of civil war has passed over merry England, sullying many a fair scene and blighting many a happy homestead, the lull of even one short twelve-month has done much to bring back fertility to the meadow and comfort to the hearth. Spring has thrown her fair green mantle over the horrors of many a battle-field; and the daily recurring hopes and fears of Life have choked the pangs of sorrow, and dried the tears of many a weeping mourner. All but the few desolate ones that refuse to be comforted by Time, trusting, not unwisely, in the sure consolation of Eternity. The months that have passed over since the battle of Naseby have indeed been pregnant with great events; but ever since that fatal struggle the Royal Cause has been hastening step by step to its final downfall. The flame has flickered up in the north and west with a fitful and delusive flash, but in middle England a sombre and melancholy apathy seems to brood over the land. It is peace where there is no peace—a fusion of opposite interests into a hollow truce, a stifling under the strong hand of discontent that rankles now, and will burst into hatred hereafter.

Still the Northamptonshire peasant goes to his work unstartled by the tramp of squadrons or the clash of steel—undisturbed by the apprehension that his best team-horse may be taken from him to drag a gun, or himself snatched rudely away from wife and supper to act as a trembling guide, strapped behind some godless trooper, and stimulated to the better exercise of his local faculties by the cold circle of a pistol-barrel pressed ominously against his temple. The traders of Northampton's goodly town can ride abroad in security with their comely dames mounted on pillions or reclining in litters, without fear of exposure to scurrilous jests or rude insolence from Rupert's troopers and Goring's 'hell-babes.' Although the knaves mourn the decrease of the unnatural stimulus given to trade by the war, and the consequent waning of their own profits, they cannot but congratulate themselves on the combination of advantages offered to their town by the protection of a strong Parliamentary government, and the return of their own lawful Sovereign to their neighbourhood at his Royal Palace of Holmby.

Yes, the old oak at Holmby spreads its gaunt arms again over the plumed heads and rich dresses of courtly gallants, and puts forth its fresh green leaves to rest the aching eyes of a weary monarch who will see but one more earthly spring.

Charles is holding mimic state in his own fair palace; and, although he is to all intents and purposes a prisoner, the outward semblances of royalty are faithfully preserved, and the pleasant fiction still adhered to, that even in acts of coercion and opposition on the part of the Commons, it is his Majesty's Parliament which, under the authority of his Majesty, makes arrangements for the security of his Majesty's person; nay, actually denounces under pains of treason those who should harbour or conceal that sacred property, and, in truth, sets a price on his Majesty's head.

The game is indeed lost now. After the flight from Naseby, when camp-followers and baggage and all fell into the hands of the conquerors, even Charles's private cabinet did not escape. His letters were made public by the Parliament, and the sacred motives of a bigoted though conscientious nature, warped

by the influence of an injudicious wife, and constantly
acted on by the opinions of selfish and intriguing
statesmen, were submitted to the judgment of the
English people—perhaps of all people in the world
the least disposed to make allowances for motives, and
the most prone to decide entirely from results. It
may be questioned whether such a defeat, even as that
of Naseby, inflicted so deadly a blow on the Royal
Cause as the publication of these papers. It never
again held up its head till the atonement had been
made in a king's blood. Meantime, disaster after
disaster marked its decline and fall. Bridgewater
surrendered to Fairfax without a blow. Even Rupert
counselled peace; and, as though the very counsel had
unmanned him, lost Bristol at the first assault. At
Rowten Heath, the King narrowly escaped with his
life, and saw his favourite cousin, the gallant Earl of
Lichfield, struck down by his very side. Then came
misunderstandings and heartburnings; even faithful
Rupert made terms for himself to abandon the sinking
ship, though he returned in compunction to throw
himself at the royal feet and demand forgiveness for
his dereliction. Monmouth and Hereford, Wales and
all the north-country, were lost; Chester, Newark,
and Belvoir besieged; Glamorgan's treaty with the
Irish Catholics discovered, and that faithful scapegoat
bearing his imprisonment and attainder on the charge
of high treason with loyal resignation. Gallant old
Astley, the last remaining prop, was beaten and taken
prisoner at Stow-in-the-Wold, and Charles was compelled to make preparations to deliver himself up to
the victorious Parliament.

Then came the negotiations with the Scottish people, conducted through the intervention of the French agent, Montreuil; the consequent escape of the King and Lord Ashburnham from Oxford, and their arrival at the quarters of the Scottish army—an army that, to their eternal disgrace, fairly and literally sold the person of their Sovereign for the amount of arrears of pay due to them. Four hundred thousand pounds was thus established to be the market value of an English monarch's head. Some of the grim old northern Covenanters hugged themselves over their bargain, whilst the Independent party south of the Border doubtless esteemed Charles Stuart very dear at the money. Nevertheless the sale was concluded, and the King, accompanied by certain Parliamentary Commissioners, journeyed in royal state, though *de facto* a prisoner, to take up his temporary residence in Holmby House.

With politic clemency the Parliament had granted the most liberal terms of amnesty and forgiveness to the vanquished Royalists. Lives were spared, estates rarely sequestered, and but few fines imposed on the ' Malignants,' who indeed had by this time little ready money left. The adherents of Charles Edward suffered far more severely from the tender mercies of the House of Hanover than did the Cavaliers of the most unfortunate of his unfortunate line at the hands of the stern Parliamentarians whom they had encountered on so many battle-fields. The adviser of the ruling-party was as subtle a politician as he was a skilful soldier, and Cromwell possessed not only the daring intellect that can seize a Crown, but the consistent wisdom which keeps it firm on the head.

Far and near the inhabitants of Northamptonshire flocked to Holmby to pay their respects to their Sovereign. Peasants cheered him as he walked or rode in the neighbourhood of his Palace. Honest yeomen and sturdy farmers, who had ridden not so long ago in 'buff and bandeliers' to the sound of his trumpets, sent in their humble offerings of rural produce to his household; and the gentry, flaunting in as much state as their reduced circumstances would allow, crowded in their coaches and on horseback to pay their last tribute of loyalty to a monarch in whose cause many of them had sacrificed all they loved best on earth.

What was the charm about these Stuarts that men would thus pour out before them their treasure as readily as their blood, would offer up to them their liberties as ungrudgingly as their lives? Is it a peculiarity in their race that has thus served them? or is it simply the fact of their misfortunes? simply that they have been the only family who have found it necessary to draw upon the loyalty of the English people, whose drafts that people have never suffered to be dishonoured? Let the materialist scoff as he will, this same loyalty, like many another abstract sentiment, is a glorious quality, and has originated some of the noblest deeds which human nature can boast.

'I never thought to see him again,' soliloquized Sir Giles Allonby, as he reined in the well-broke sorrel, and looked back at a huge swinging vehicle, splashing and lumbering through Brampton ford. 'Never again! at least in courtly state like this. How pleased those foolish wenches will be too. Oh, if it be only not too good to last!'

Sir Giles sits in the saddle gallantly enough still, but the defeat on Naseby-field, to say nothing of the accompanying hard knocks and subsequent reverses, has aged the bold Cavalier sadly. The blue eye is dim now, the furrows deep and numerous on his sunken face, and the hand on which Diamond is still encouraged to perch trembles till her bells and jesses ring and jingle again. Nevertheless he loves a hawk, a hound, and a horse as dearly as of old ;—nor was Humphrey's sorrel ever better taken care of than in the stable at Boughton, where he is fed and littered by his former attendant, Hugh Dymocke, and regaled with many a choice morsel by two indulgent ladies, each of whom pays her visit to his stable at an hour when her friend is otherwise engaged.

They have not forgotten his master, though they rarely speak of him now. He has been long absent in France and elsewhere; no tidings have reached them for many a weary month. He has done his duty nobly by the Queen, that is all they know, and that is surely enough. Grace is satisfied, and so ought the loyal Mary to be, and so she affirms with unnecessary energy she is; yet her cheek looks a shade paler, her manner is a thought less stately and more restless than her wont.

The two ladies are decked out in the utmost splendour of Court dress, and roomy as is the interior of the old coach, they occupy the whole of it. Notwithstanding its four horses driven in hand, with a postilion and pair in front of these, they make but a slow five miles an hour, for the roads even in summer are rough and treacherous; while divers sturdy serving-men, armed to the teeth—of whom our friend Hugh is not the least prominent—cling to the outside of the vehicle. They are about to pay a visit of state to their sovereign, and should be overloaded accordingly.

Two handsomer specimens of English beauty were hard to be met with than the fair inmates of the coach. Grace, rejoicing in the elasticity of youth, has recovered her health and spirits. She has got her father safe back from the wars, and this is a wonderful cordial to poor Gracey. Moreover, she is at that period of life when every year adds fresh charms to the development of womanhood; and the long months that with their attendant anxieties have tarnished ever so little the freshness of her companion's beauty, have but rounded the lines of Grace's bewitching form, deepened the colour on her cheek, and brightened the lustre of her eye.

The dress she wears, much like the Court costume of the present day, is peculiarly adapted to her charms. For a description of this voluminous fabric of lace, brocade, tulle, transparency, and other dangerous materials, we must refer our reader to the columns of that daily organ of fashionable life which describes in glowing colours and accurate detail the costly armour decorating our enslavers at any of her Gracious Majesty's drawing-rooms. If a gentleman, let him peruse the inventory therein set forth of the articles of clothing worn on such high festival by the prettiest woman of his acquaintance; if a lady, by the rival for whom she entertains the most cordial aversion (probably it may be the same individual in both cases), and let each profit accordingly.

Mary contemplates her friend, and wonders in her own heart how any man can resist the attractions of that beautiful young face. To do her justice, the element of jealousy lies deep below the surface in Mistress Cave's character. Like many a woman of strong intellect, high courage, and a somewhat masculine turn of thought and ideas (an organization that is apt to be accompanied by the utmost womanly gentleness of bearing and refinement of manner), she is above the petty feelings and little weaknesses that disfigure the generality of her sex. She can and does admire beauty in another without envy or detraction. She does not at first sight set down to the worst of motives every word and action of an attractive sister; nay, she can even pardon that sister freely for winning the admiration of the opposite sex. Conscious of her own worth, and proud it may be in her secret heart to know of a certain shrine or so where that worth is worshipped as it deserves, she can afford to see another win her share of incense without grudging or discontent. In the abstract she is not of a jealous disposition. Individually, as she is never likely to have cause, God forbid she should ever become so! Such a passion in such a nature would work a wreck over which devils might smile in triumph, and angels weep for very shame.

Despite the jolting of the coach, it would be un-natural to suppose that an unbroken silence is pre-served between the two. Far from it. They talk incessantly, and laugh merrily enough at intervals. Whatever may be the subject lying deepest at their hearts, whatever hopes or fears, secrets or intrigues, private or political, may be nestling in those sanc-tuaries, we are bound to confess that their dialogue is frivolous as the veriest woman-hating philosopher could imagine. It turns upon dress, ribbons, courtly forms, and such trivial topics. Even now, as they jingle down into the ford, though each is thinking of a certain return from hawking that took place at this very spot some few years ago, and the consequent introduction of a young Cavalier officer, who has since occupied a large share of each lady's thoughts, neither reverts by word or sign to the reminiscence; and to judge by their conversation and demeanour, it would be supposed that neither of those fair heads contained an anxiety or an idea beyond the preserva-tion of their curls and dresses from that untidy state which is termed 'rumpled' in the expressive language of the female vocabulary.

'I wish they would mend the bridge,' observed Grace, as a tremendous jolt over a stone under water brought a ludicrous expression of dismay to her pretty features; 'father says it's not safe for a coach since the parapet tumbled down; but they will surely repair it now the King's come.'

'I wish they would, indeed!' assented Mary; 'it's hardly fit for horse-folk now, and Bayard and I have many a quarrel about going so near the edge. It's

wide enough for a coach too,' she added, ' and I dread
the water coming in every time we go through this
treacherous ford. Of all days in my life, I wouldn't
have a fold out of place to-day, Grace. I should like
to make my courtesy to him in his reverses with more
ceremony than I ever did at White '——

The word was never finished. Another jolt, accompanied by much splashing, struggling, and a
volley of expletives from Sir Giles, who had turned
his horse back into the water, and was swearing
lustily by the carriage window, interrupted the
speaker, and announced that some catastrophe had
taken place.

It was even so. A spring had given way in the
ford, and on arriving at the further bank it was
moreover discovered that an axle was injured so much
as to necessitate a halt for the repair of damages.
Sir Giles dismounted, the ladies alighted; and Dymocke, who was provided with the necessary tools—
without which indeed none ever dreamed of travelling
—commenced his operations; the party, congratu-
lating themselves on the fine summer's day which,
notwithstanding their Court dresses, made half an
hour's lounge in the pleasant meadows not even an
inconvenience. In the seventeenth century such
trifling mishaps were the daily concomitants of a
morning's drive.

' Woa, my man !' said Sir Giles, who was holding
the sorrel by the bridle, whilst Mary patted and
smoothed his glossy neck, and Grace gathered a posy
of wildflowers by the river's brim. The horse erected
his ears, snorted and neighed loudly, fidgeting, more-

over, despite of Mary's caresses and Sir Giles's impatient jerks, and describing circles round the pair, as if he would fain break from his restraint and gallop off.

'The devil's in the beast!' quoth Sir Giles, testily, as a shabbily-dressed man with a rod and line, apparently intent upon his angling, moved slowly down the river bank to where they stood, and the horse whinnied and pawed, and became more uneasy every moment.

The fisherman was clad in a worn-out suit of coarse brown stuff, his hat was slouched completely over his eyes; the upper part of his face—all that could be seen, however—was deadly pale; and the unsteadiness of his hand imparted a tremulous motion to his angle, which seemed either the result of inward agitation or the triumph of manual art.

Sir Giles was a brother of the craft—as indeed in what department of field-sports had the old Cavalier not taken his degree? Of course he entered into conversation with the angler despite the restlessness of his charge.

'What sport, master?' quoth Sir Giles in his cheery, boisterous tones; 'methinks the sun is somewhat too bright for your fishing to-day, and indeed the weight of your basket will scarce trouble you much if you have not better luck after your morning's draught. Zounds, man! have you caught never a fish since daybreak?'

The basket, as Sir Giles could see, was indeed open and—empty!

Thus adjured the fisherman halted within ten paces

of the knight, but apparently he was so intent on his occupation that he could not spare breath for a reply. He spoke never a word, and the sorrel was more troublesome than ever.

Sir Giles's wrath began to rise.

'The insolent Roundhead knave!' muttered the old Cavalier; 'shall he not answer when a gentleman accosts him thus civilly? Let me alone, Mistress Mary; I will cudgel the soul out of him, and fling him into the river afterwards, sweetheart, as sure as he stands there!'

Mary suggested that the poor man might perhaps be really deaf, and succeeded in pacifying her companion; whilst the angler, slouching his hat more than ever over his face, fished on, apparently quite unconscious of their presence.

Sir Giles and the sorrel—the latter most unwillingly—strolled off towards the coach, and Mary remained watching the fisherman's movements with a sort of dreamy satisfaction; she had become subject to these idle absent fits of late, and something about this man's coarsely-clad figure seemed to embark her thoughts upon a tide of pleasing associations that carried her far, far back into the past.

Psha! this dreaming is a pernicious habit, and must be broken through. She would accost the fisherman and ascertain if he remained as deaf to a lady's voice as he had been to that of old Sir Giles. Just then, however, Grace called to her to say the carriage was ready, and Mary with a heavy sigh turned slowly to depart.

The fisherman's line trembled as though a hundred

perches were tugging at it from the depths of the sluggish *Nene*. He watched her retreating figure, but never moved from his position. She reached her party, and they mounted once more into the coach, compressing as much as possible their spreading dresses to make room for Sir Giles, who was easily fatigued now, and who handed over the still refractory sorrel to the care of Dymocke, and proceeded to perform the rest of the journey on wheels.

As the coach lumbered heavily away, it passed the very spot where the angler still stood intent on his fishing. Both ladies glanced at his ill-dressed form as they drove by, and watched long afterwards from opposite windows the unusual proceedings of the sorrel, who, instead of suffering Dymocke to mount him quietly as was his wont, broke completely away from that attendant, and after a frolic round the meadow trotted quietly up to the stranger, and proceeded to rub his head against the brown jerkin with a violence that threatened to push its wearer bodily into the water.

The last the ladies saw as they ascended the hill towards the small hamlet of Chapel-Brampton was their serving-man in close conversation with the angler whom they had erroneously inferred to be deaf. Though it must have struck each of them as a strange circumstance, it is remarkable that neither expressed an opinion on the subject, and a silence broken only by the snores of Sir Giles, who always went to sleep in a carriage, reigned between them for at least two miles. At the termination of that distance, however, Grace, rousing herself from a fit of abstraction, addressed her no less absent companion : 'Did you notice that fisherman's dress, Mary?' was her innocent and appropriate observation. 'Shabby as it was, he had got a knot of faded pink ribbon under his doublet. I saw it quite plain when he lifted his arm to throw his line. Wasn't it strange?'

Mary grew as white as the laced handkerchief in her hand, and in proportion as the blood forsook her cheeks her companion flushed to the very temples. Each turned to her own window and her own thoughts once more. Despite the jolting, Sir Giles slept on. Dymocke, too, overtook the carriage; but it would have been indeed hopeless to question that functionary, whose gravity and reserve became deeper day by day, and who, since his interview with the King the night before Naseby, was never known to unbend even under the influence of the strongest potations.

Sir Giles snored comfortably on, and thus, without another word being exchanged, the Royalists arrived to pay their respects to their unhappy sovereign under the sheltering roof of Holmby House.

CHAPTER V.

HOLMBY HOUSE.

ON the fairest site perhaps in the whole fair county of Northampton stand to this day the outward walls, the lofty gates, and an inconsiderable remnant of what was once the goodly edifice of Holmby House. The slope of the ground which declines from it on all sides, offers a succession of the richest and most pastoral views which this rich and pastoral country can afford. Like the rolling prairie of the Far West, valley after valley of sunny meadows, dotted with oak and elm and other noble trees, undulates in ceaseless variety far as the eye can reach; but unlike the boundless prairie, deep dark copses and thick luxuriant hedgerows, bright and fragrant with wildflowers and astir with the glad song of birds, diversify the foreground and blend the distance into a mass of woodland beauty that gladdens alike the fastidious eye of the artist and the stolid gaze of the clown. In June it is a dream of Fairyland to wander along that crested eminence, and turn from the ruins of those tall old gateways cutting their segments of blue out of the deep summer sky, or from the flickering masses of still tender leaves upon the lofty oaks, yellowing in the floods of golden light that stream through the network of their tangled branches, every tree to the up-gazing eye a study of

forest scenery in itself, and so to glance earthward at
the fair expanse of homely beauty stretching away
from one's very feet. Down in the nearest valley,
massed like a solid square of Titan warriors, and
scattered like advanced champions from the gigantic
array profusely up the opposite slope, the huge old
oaks of Althorpe quiver in the summer haze, backed
by the thickly wooded hills that melt in softened
outlines into the southern sky. The fresh light green
of the distant larches blooming on far Harlestone
Heath, is relieved by the dark belt of firs that draws
a thin black line against the horizon. A light cloud
of smoke floats above the spot where lies fair Northampton town, but the intervening trees and hedgerows are so clothed in foliage that scarce a building
can be discerned, though the tall sharp spire of
Kingsthorpe pierces upward into the sky. To the
west, a confusion of wooded knolls and distant copses
are bathed in the vapoury haze of the declining sun,
and you rest your dazzled eyes, swimming with so
much beauty, and stoop to gather the wildflower at
your feet. Ah, 'tis a pleasant season, that same
merry month of June! Then in December—who
doth not know and appreciate the merits of December
at such a spot as Holmby? Of all climates upon
earth, it is well known that none can produce the
equal of a soft mild English winter's day, and such a
day at Holmby is worth living for through the gales
of blustering October and the fogs of sad November,
with its depressing atmosphere and continuous drizzle.
Ay, these are rare pastures to breathe a goodly steed,
and there are fences too hereabouts that will prove his

courage and your own! But enough of this. Is not Northamptonshire the very homestead of horse and hound, and Pytchley but a synonym of Paradise for all who delight therein?

Lord Chancellor Hatton—he whose skilful performances in the dance so charmed our Royal Elizabeth, and whose 'shoestrings green,' 'whose bushy beard and satin doublet'

> Moved the stout heart of England's Queen,
> Though Pope and Spaniard could not trouble it—

seems to have been a nobleman of undoubted taste in architecture as well as a thorough master of the Terpsichorean art. At a sufficiently mature age he built the fair palace which was destined hereafter for the residence of a king, to be, as he coxcombically expressed it, 'the last and greatest monument of his youth.' Its exterior was accordingly decorated with all the quaint ins and outs, mullioned windows, superfluity of chimneys, and elaborate ornaments which distinguish the 'earlier and lesser monuments' of the agile Lord Keeper. A huge stone gateway, with the Hatton arms carved on a shield above their heads, admitted our coach and its occupants into a large court-yard, around two sides of which extended the state and reception-rooms of the palace. This court itself was now filled with officers of the King's household and other personal retainers of a peaceful character; there were even a few goodly beef-eaters, but no clash of swords nor waving of standards; none of the gallant troop of Life Guards that seemed so appropriate to the vicinity of a sovereign. Alas, how many of them were sleeping where they fell, a

couple of leagues away yonder, where the flat skyline
of Naseby-field bounds the horizon to the north. Not
even a blast of trumpets or a roll of kettledrums
aroused Sir Giles from his slumbers, and Grace was
forced to wake him with a merry jest anent his drow-
siness as they lumbered in beneath the archway, and
sent their names on from one official to another, waiting patiently for their turn to alight, inasmuch as the
forms and ceremonies of a court were the more scrupulously observed the more the fortunes of the monarch
were on the wane, and an old family coach of another
country grandee was immediately before them. The
disembarkation of these honest courtiers was a matter
of time and trouble.   Loyalty and valour had deprived
them of their coach-horses, six of which had failed to
save one of the King's guns in the flight from
Naseby, and four huge unwieldy animals from the
plough had been substituted for the team of Flanders
mares with their long plaited tails and their slow but
showy action. One of these agricultural animals, a
colt, who seemed to feel that neither by birth nor
appearance was he entitled to the position he now
occupied, could in no wise be induced to face the
glories of the royal serving-men who crowded round
the door of reception. In vain the coachman flogged,
the grooms and running-footmen kicked and jerked at
the bridle, the ladies inside screamed, and the Cavalier
in charge of them swore a volley of the deepest Royalist
oaths, the colt was very refractory, and pending his
reduction, Sir Giles had ample time to look around him
at the walls he knew so well, and reflect how unaltered
they were when everything else was so changed.

Many a cup had he emptied here with gentle King Jamie, who to his natural inefficiency and stupidity added the disgusting tendencies of a sot. Many a jest had he exchanged with Archie Armstrong, the King's fool—like others of his profession, not half such a fool as his master. Many a rousing night had he passed in yonder turret, where was the little round chamber termed the King's Closet, and many a fair morn had he ridden out through this very gateway to hunt the stag on the moorlands by Haddon, or the wild hills of Ashby, far away with hound and horn to Fawsley's sheltering coverts, or the deep woodland of distant Castle-Dykes. Ay, 'twas the very morrow of the day when Grace's mother had made him a certain confession and a certain promise, that he saw the finest run it was ever his lot to enjoy with an outlying deer that had escaped from this very park, and though he killed his best horse in the chase, it was the happiest day in his life. He looked at Gracey, and the old man's eyes filled with tears. Sir Giles was getting a good deal broke now, so his neighbours said.

The country grandees are disembarked at last. The succeeding coach lumbers heavily up to the palace-door, and as their names are passed from official to official, Sir Giles and his two ladies stand once more under the roof of their sovereign, who despite all his reverses, still holds royal state and semblance in his own court. They like to think so, and to deceive themselves and him, if only for an hour.

As far as actual luxury or pleasure was concerned, Charles's daily habits, wherever he was, partook of a sufficiently self-denying and ascetic character to make his enforced residence at Holmby no more secluded than had been his life in the full flush of his early prosperity at Whitehall. The King was always, even in his youthful days, of a remarkably studious turn of mind, regular in his habits, and punctilious of all such small observances on the part of his household as preserved that regularity in its most unbroken course. The hours of devotion, of study, of state, of exercise, and of eating, were strictly portioned out to the very minute, and this arrangement of his time enabled the monarch, even in the midst of his busiest and most pressing avocations, to devote his leisure to those classical studies of which he was so fond. From his warlike ancestors—who indeed had been used to keep their crown with the strong hand, and who, thanks to Armstrongs and Elliotts on the border, not to mention a refractory Douglas or two nearer home, never left off their mail and plate, or forgot to close steel gauntlet on ashen spear for many months together—he had inherited a certain muscular energy of body and vigour of constitution which he strove to retain by the regular observance of daily exercise. 'It is well worth our observation,' says his faithful chronicler, worthy Sir Thomas Herbert, 'that in all the time of his Majesty's restraint and solitude he was never sick, nor took anything to prevent sickness, nor had need of a physician, which, under God, is attributed to his quiet disposition and unparalleled patience, to his exercise (when at home walking in the gallery and privy garden, and other recreations when abroad), to his abstemiousness at meat, eating but of few dishes, and, as he used to say, agreeable to his exercise, drinking but twice every dinner and supper, once of beer, and once of wine and water mixed, only after fish a glass of *French* wine; the beverage he himself mixed at the cupboard, so he would have it. He very seldom ate and drank before dinner, nor between meals.'

Thus did the captive monarch keep himself, so to speak, in training, both of body and mind, for whatever exercises either of effort or endurance might be required of him; and thus perhaps rendered more tolerable that period of restraint and *surveillance* which is so calculated to enervate the physical as well as the intellectual powers, and to resist the effects of which requires perhaps a combination of nobler qualities than to conquer armies and subjugate empires with the strong hand.

But the Stuart, though in reality worsted, conquered, and in ward, was permitted to enjoy all the outward semblance of royalty; was served with all the strict observances and ceremonious etiquette due to a sovereign. He had a household, too, and a Court, though neither were of his own choosing; and Court and household vied with each other in respectful deference to their charge. The Parliamentary Commission, stated, in the document which gave them their authority, to be his Majesty's *loyal* subjects, was composed, partially at least, of noblemen and gentlemen who were not personally obnoxious to their Sovereign, and who had for long supported him in his claims, till their better judgment convinced them those claims were unconstitutional and subversive of real liberty. The Earls of Pembroke, of Denbigh, and Lord Montague, were no violent Roundheads ; whilst of the inferior members who represented the Lower House, Major-General Browne was an especial favourite with the King; and Sir James Harrington came of a family on whose loyalty the slightest imputation had never hitherto been cast.

It rested with the discretion of this Committee to nominate the principal officers of his Majesty's household; and the list of their selection, including as it does the name of Herbert, afterwards Sir Thomas, who filled the post of Groom of the Chambers to the King, and attended him, an attached and faithful servant to the last, betrays at least a respect for Charles's prejudices, and a consideration for his comfort. Dr. Wilson was retained as the Royal physician; and the accustomed staff of cup-bearers, carvers, cooks, and barbers, were continued in their offices, with the single proviso, that such alone should be dismissed as had borne arms against the Parliament. The duties of roasting, boiling, filling, serving, and shaving, being of no warlike tendency, it is not to be supposed that this exception would weed the household of more than a very few familiar faces; and Charles found himself at Holmby surrounded by much the same number and class of domestics that would have been eating his Royal substance at Whitehall.

With a liberality that does credit to the rebellious Parliament, we find in their records a sumptuous provision for the maintenance of the King's table, and the payment of his attendance here. The roll of officials indispensable to a Court, comprises a variety of subordinates charitably presumed to be necessary to the daily wants of royalty ; and the 'clerks of green cloth, clerks of the assignment, of the bakehouse, pantrie, cellar, butterie, spicerie, confectionary, chaundrie, ewrie, landrie, and kitchen,' must have had but little to do, and plenty of time to do it, in the rural retirement of this Northamptonshire residence. Cooks —head and subordinate—' turn-brouches, porters and scowrers, with knaves of the boiling-house, larder, poultrie, scaulding-house, accaterie, pastrie, woodyard, and scullerie,' help to swell the hungry phalanx ; nor must the 'gate-ward' be forgotten, and another functionary termed the 'harbinger,' who, like the 'odd man' of modern times in large establishments, was probably the deliverer of messages, and did more work than all the rest put together.

'It is conceived that there be a number of the guard proposed to carry upp the King's meat,' quoth the record ; and for this purpose was daily told off a goodly detachment, consisting of two yeomen-ushers, two yeomen-hangers, and twenty yeomen of the guard ; when to this numerous force was added the swarm of ' pages of the bedchamber and back-stairs, gentlemen-ushers, gentlemen of the privy-chamber, cup-bearer, carver, server, and esquire of the body, grooms of the robes and privy-chamber, daily wayters, and quarter wayters, pages of the presence, and the removing wardrobe, grooms of the chamber, messengers of the chamber, physician, apothecary, barber, chirurgeon, and laundresse,' the King's household in his captivity will, we submit, bear comparison with

that of any of his Royal brethren in the full enjoyment of their power.

Thirty pounds sterling a day for his Majesty's 'diet
of twenty-eight dishes,' was the very handsome allow-
ance accorded by the Parliament; and the amount
of expenses incurred by the Royal household at
Holmby for the twenty days commencing on the 13th
February, and ending on the 4th of March, reaches
the large sum of £2990, between £50,000 and £60,000
a year.

There being a deficiency, too, of plate for the Royal
table, that article of festive state having been long
ago converted into steel, horseflesh, gunpowder, and
such munitions of war, it was suggested by the in-
ventive genius of the Committee, that the commu-
nion-plate formerly set on the altar of his Majesty's
chapel of Whitehall—consisting of ' one gilt shyppe,
two gilt vases, two gilt cuyres, a square bason and
fountain, and a silver rod'—should be melted down
to make plate for the King's use at Holmby, there
being none remaining in the jewel-office fit for service;
and this somewhat startling, not to say sacrilegious,
proposal seems to have been entertained, and acted on
accordingly.

For the bodily wants of the Sovereign no demand
seems to have been considered too exorbitant, but for
his spiritual needs the Parliament would not hear of
any but their own nominees, and instead of the Bishops
of London, Salisbury, or Peterborough, or such other
divines as his Majesty desired to consult, they substituted the bigoted Marshall and the enthusiastic
Carryl to be the keepers of the King's conscience, and

trustees for the welfare of his soul. Perhaps this arrangement was of all the most galling to Charles's feelings, and the most distasteful to the very strong tendency which he had always shown for casuistry and controversial religion. Though these chaplains preached alternately, in the chapel attached to the palace, every Sunday morning and afternoon to the Commissioners and the Royal household, the King, while he permitted such of his retinue to attend as were so disposed, preferred to perform his own devotions in private, rather than sanction with his presence the Presbyterian form of worship to which he was so opposed; and even at his meals the conscientious Monarch invariably said 'grace' himself rather than accept the services of either chaplain, both of whom were nevertheless always in close attendance upon his Majesty.

The King's daily life at Holmby seems to have been studious and regular to a degree. An early riser, he devoted the first hours of the morning to his religious exercises, praying with great fervour in his closet, and there studying and reading such works of controversial divinity as most delighted his somewhat narrow intellect and formal turn of mind. At the same hour every morning a poached egg was brought him, and a glass of fair water; after which, accompanied either by the Earl of Pembroke or General Browne, he took his regular exercise by walking to and fro for an allotted time, in fair weather, up and down the green terraces which lay smooth and level to the south of the palace, and in wet, through the long corridors and spacious chambers which adorned its eastern wing. At the expiration of the exact period, the King again retired to his own private apartments, where such public business as he still conceived himself empowered to undertake, the study of the classics, and the prosecution of a correspondence which indeed seldom reached its destination, occupied him till the hour of dinner, in those days punctually at noon. This meal, we need hardly say, was served with great state and ceremony. Ewer-bearers with napkin and golden bason, ushers with their white wands, preceded the entrance and presided over the conclusion of the banquet. No form was omitted which could enhance the stately nature of the ceremony; and the King dined on a raised dais six inches above the level floor of the dining-hall. After dinner a quarter of an hour exactly was devoted to conversation of a light and frivolous character, the only period in the day, be it observed, that such conversation was encouraged, or even tolerated, by the grave Charles; but anything approaching to levity, not to say indecency, was severely rebuked by that decorous Monarch, who could not endure that a high officer of his household should once boast in his presence of his proficiency in hard drinking, but inflicted on him a caustic and admonitory reprimand for his indiscretion. What a contrast to his successor!

A game at chess, played with the due attention and silence which befit that pastime, succeeded to this short space of relaxation; and we can imagine the reflections that must have obtruded themselves on the Monarch's mind when the ivory king was reduced to his last straits, cooped up to the three or four squares which formed his only battle-ground—his queen gone, his bishops, knights, and castles all in the hands of the adversary—now checking him at every turn, and the issue of the contest too painfully like that catastrophe in real life, which he *must* have seen advancing to meet him with giant strides.

At the conclusion of this suggestive pursuit, it was his Majesty's custom, when the weather permitted, to ride out on horseback, accompanied by one or more of the Commissioners, and attended by an armed escort, which might more properly be termed a guard. The King's rides usually took the direction of the Earl of Sunderland's house at Althorpe, or that of Lord Vaux at Boughton, at either of which places he could enjoy his favourite diversion of 'bowls;' for the green at Holmby, though level and spacious enough, did not run sufficiently true to please the critical eye and hand of so eminent a performer at this game as was Charles I.

The evening passed off in the like formal and somewhat tedious routine. An hour of meditation succeeded the ride, and supper was served with the same observances as the noonday meal. Grave discourse, turning chiefly upon the Latin classical authors, and studiously avoiding all allusion to those political topics which probably formed the staple of conversation in every other household in the kingdom, furbished up the schoolboy lore of the Commissioners, and gave the Royal pedant an opportunity of exhibiting his superiority to his keepers in this department of literature. The King's devotions then occupied him for a considerable period in his closet, and he retired to rest at an early hour, with a degree of languid composure surprising to witness in one so circumstanced, and which never seems to have deserted him even in the last extremity.

Such was the daily life of the vanquished King, varied only by such a public reception as the present, when his earlier glories seemed to flicker up once more in an illusive flash ere they were quenched in darkness for ever.

We have left Sir Giles and his fair charges in an inner-hall, which led directly to the presence of Royalty.

This chamber, lined with beautifully carved oak, and adorned with escutcheons and other heraldic devices, presented a quaint and pleasing appearance, not out of keeping with the rustling dames and plumed gallants that crowded its polished floor. In its centre stood three carved pyramids, of which the middle overtopped its two supporters by several feet; and around this shrine of heraldry were emblazoned the different coats of arms of the nobility and gentry of the surrounding districts.

At the further extremity of the hall stood a high wooden screen, such as in cathedrals portions off the altar from the nave, wrought into elaborate and fantastic ornaments, in which the grotesque nature of the imagery was only equalled by the excellence of the carving; and as the recess behind this framework communicated directly with the Presence-chamber, Maxwell, the Usher of the Black Rod, was here stationed to announce the names of those loyal gentlefolks who came to pay their respects to his Majesty.

'It reminds one of Whitehall,' whispered Mary to Sir Giles, as the latter delivered their names in the subdued and reverential whisper becoming the atmosphere of a Court, 'only there are some ludicrous figures amongst the ladies' dresses,' she added, womanlike, with a downward glance of satisfaction at her own well-chosen costume, and another of admiration at her companion's beautiful figure.

Sir Giles did not answer. He was thinking of the many Royal receptions he had attended during the troubles, and how each after each seemed thinner of the old familiar faces, the hearty friends and good blades that had hedged their Sovereign round with the wall of steel in vain; whose bones were strewed far and wide over the surface of merry England; whose estates were gone, their families scattered, their hearths desolate. How few were left now! and those few, like himself, rusty, worn-out, disused, yet retaining the keen temper of the true steel to the last.

'Welcome, Sir Giles,' whispered Maxwell, a courtier of forty years' standing, who had spent many a merry hour with the old knight under this very roof in days of yore, and who, albeit a man of peace from his youth upward, showed the marks of Time as plainly on his wrinkled face and snowy locks as did his more adventurous comrade, without however attaining the dignified and stately bearing of the veteran warrior. 'Welcome! The King spoke of you but yesterday. His Majesty will be indeed glad to see you. Fair ladies, you may enter at once. The dragon that watched over the gardens of the Hesperides neglected his post under the dazzling rays of beauty, whilst he was but Jupiter's Usher of the Black Rod!'

Maxwell esteemed himself only second to his royal master in classical lore, and piqued himself on two things in the world—the whiteness of his laced ruffles and the laborious pedantry of his compliments.

Grace smiled. 'What a formidable dragon!' she whispered, with an arch glance at the ancient courtier, that penetrated through brocade and embroidery —ay, and a flannel bulwark against rheumatism— to his susceptible old heart. Such shafts were never aimed at him in vain, but invariably reached their mark. Need we add that Maxwell was a confirmed bachelor of many years' standing?

Grace pursed up her pretty mouth into an expression of the gravest decorum, for she had now entered the magic circle, of which the centre was the King.

It was indeed a sad contrast to the assembly she remembered so well at Merton College. Where were the Newcastles, the Winchesters, and the Worcesters? —the brilliant aristocracy that had once formed the brightest jewels of the Crown? Where was Ormond's sagacious courage and Rupert's ready gallantry? Lichfield's goodly person and Sir Jacob Astley's fine old war-worn face? Where were the nobility and the chivalry of England? Alas! not here in Holmby, rallying round their king; and therefore dead, scattered, and swept away from the face of the earth.

Constrained and gloomy countenances surround him now, instead of those frank haughty fronts that quailed not before a Sovereign's eye, but ever greeted him with manly looks of loyalty and friendship—faces in which he could confide, and before which it was no shame even for a monarch to unbend. His manner, always stately, has now become gloomy and reserved to the extreme of coldness. He cannot but be aware that every word of his lips, every glance of his eye, is watched with the utmost vigilance, noted down, and in all probability reported for the behoof of his bitterest enemies; yet must he never betray his consciousness of *surveillance*—must never for an instant lose his judgment and self-command.

'Twas but this very morning that, taking his accustomed exercise abroad, accompanied by Major-General Browne and the devout Caryl, whose zeal to convert his Sovereign never suffered him to be absent a moment from his side, a poor squalid woman, carrying a child in her arms, marked and scarred with that scrofulous disease which, though its superstitious remedy has been long ago discarded, bears to this day the name of 'king's evil,' approached the person of her Sovereign, and begged him, in tones of piteous appeal, only to touch her child, that it might be healed. Poor woman! she had watched, and waited, and dodged the park-keepers, and stilled her own panting heart many a weary hour, ere she could penetrate to the King's presence; and she pleaded earnestly now, for she had implicit faith in the remedy.

Charles, ever merciful, ever kindly, and, like all his family, ever *good-natured*, listened patiently to the poor woman's tale; and whilst he bestowed on her a broad piece or two, borrowed from the General for the occasion, stretched forth his own royal hand to heal the whining infant of its malady.

'Hold, woman!' exclaimed Caryl, indignantly interposing his person between the royal physician and the little sufferer. 'Wouldst thou blaspheme before the very face of a minister of the Word? Who can heal save He alone, whose servants we are? And thou, sire!' he added, turning roughly upon the King, 'what art thou that thou shouldest arrogate to thyself the issues of life and death? Thou—a man! a worm!—a mere insect crawling on the face of the earth! Away with thee, Charles Stuart! in shame and penitence, lest a worse thing befal thee! Have we not read the Scriptures?—do they not enjoin us to "fear God?"'

'And "honour the king,"' added Charles, very quietly, and passing his hand gently over the child's forehead. Caryl sank back abashed, and the Major-General gave vent to his indignation in a volley of stifled oaths, which, Parliamentarian though he was, his military education called up at this instance of what he was pleased to term in his mutterings, 'a conceited parson's insubordination, worthy of the strappado!'

The King's gloomy countenance, however, broke into a melancholy smile when he recognised the honest face of Sir Giles Allonby advancing into the presence. He made a step forward, and extending both hands as the old Cavalier sank upon his knee, raised him to his feet, and led him a little aside from the surrounding throng, as though anxious to distinguish him by some especial mark of his royal favour. The devoted Royalist's whole face brightened at this instance of his Sovereign's condescension, and Sir Giles looked ten years younger for the moment as he basked in the rays of this declining sun of royalty.

'Express to good Lord Vaux our sympathy and sorrow for his malady, which confines him thus to his chamber. He must indeed be ill at ease when he fails to attend our Court, as well we know. Tell him that we will ourselves visit him ere long at his own good house at Boughton. Hark ye, Sir Giles! I have heard much of the excellence of your bowling-green yonder; we will play a set once more for a broad piece, as we did long ago, in days that were somewhat merrier than these are now.'

He sighed as he spoke; and Sir Giles professed himself, as indeed he was, overpowered at the condescension of his Sovereign.

The King warmed to the subject. He could interest himself in trifles still.

'The green below these windows,' said he, 'is so badly levelled that the bowl runs constantly against the bias. Even my Lord Pembroke can make nothing of it, and you and I can remember him, Sir Giles, many a point better than either of us. 'Tis a game I love well,' added Charles, abstractedly; 'and yet methinks 'tis but a type of the life of men—and kings. How many are started fair upon their object

with the surest aim and the best intentions; how few
ever reach the goal.   How the bias turns this one
aside, and the want of force lets another die out in mid
career, and an inch more would make a third the
winner, but that it fails at the last hair's-breadth.
That is the truest bowl that can best sustain the
rubs of the green.   'Tis the noblest heart that scorns
to escape from its crosses, but can *endure* as well as
face the ills of life—

Rebus in adversis facile est contemnere vitam,
Fortiter ille facit qui miser esse potest.

'Very true, your Majesty—quite correct,' observed
the delighted Sir Giles, whose Latin had been long
effaced by far more important pursuits.   'Everything
shall be ready for your Majesty and in order.   We
cannot thank your Majesty enough.'

The old Cavalier was quite overcome by his
emotion.

'And this is your daughter,' pursued Charles,
gravely and courteously saluting the young lady, who
followed close upon her father's steps; 'a fair flower
from a stanch old stem; and Mistress Mary Cave
too, whom I rejoice once more to welcome to my
Court.'   But a cloud passed across the King's brow
as he spoke, and the deep melancholy expression
darkened his large eyes as Mary's face recalled to him
the light of happier days and the image of his absent
Queen.   He turned from them with a sigh, and they
passed on, whilst a fresh arrival and a fresh presenta-
tion took their place.   His great-grandfather or his
son would have detained somewhat longer in conversation the two fairest ladies that adorned the Court;

but Charles I. was as insensible to female beauty as James V. and Charles II. were too dangerously susceptible of its attractions.

The party from Boughton sauntered through the lofty apartments of the palace, and entered into conversation with such of their friends and acquaintance as had passed through the Presence Chamber. Then the heavy coach once more lumbered through the courtyard, and they returned the way they came.

Sir Giles was in high spirits at the anticipation of his Majesty's visit, and talked of nothing else the whole way home. Mary, contrary to her wont, looked pale and tired, whilst Grace seemed somewhat abstracted and occupied with her own thoughts.

As they traversed Brampton-ford they both looked for the strange fisherman, but he was nowhere to be seen. The river stole on quiet and undisturbed, its surface burnished into gold by the hot afternoon sun, and rippled only by the kiss of the stooping swallow, or the light track of the passing water-fly.

CHAPTER VI.

KEEPING SECRETS.

HARD held in the sinewy grasp of honest Dymocke, whose features expanded into grim smiles with the excitement of a rousing gallop, the sorrel's regular stride swept round the park at Boughton, despite the heat of the afternoon sun and the hardness of the ground. Such a proceeding was indeed a flagrant departure from the rules of stable discipline, which would have enjoined the serving-man to bring his charge quietly home, and bed him up incontinently for the night. To judge, however, by Hugh's countenance, he had good reasons for this unusual measure, and after half-an-hour's walk through the cool shade of the avenues, he jumped from the saddle in the stable-yard, and contemplated the still reeking sides of his favourite with an expression of grave and critical approval.

'Ay,' said he, as the sorrel, after snorting once or twice, raised his excited head, as if ready and willing for another gallop, 'you could make some of them look pretty foolish even now. Regular work and good food has not done you any harm since you left off your soldierin'; and after this bit of a breather to-night, if you *should* be wanted to-morrow, why—whew!'

The prolonged whistle which concluded this soliloquy denoted an idea of such rapidity as words were totally inadequate to convey; and Dymocke proceeded to wash his charge's feet, and rub down his bright glossy sides in the cool air of the spacious stable-yard, with a demeanour of mysterious importance which argued the most alarming results.

Now by a curious coincidence it so happened that Faith, despising the allurements of the buttery, in which the other servants were partaking of one of their many repasts, tripped softly through the yard on her way to the laundry, one of those domestic offices the vicinity of which to the stables offers the men and maids of an establishment many opportunities of innocent gaiety and improving conversation. It was not surprising that Faith should loiter for a few minutes to enjoy the society of an individual with whom she avowedly 'kept company,' or that hereditary curiosity should prompt her to demand the cause of the horse's heated appearance, and the unusual care bestowed on him by his rider.

'You do frighten one so, Sergeant,' said Faith, addressing her swain by his title of brevet rank, with a coy look and one of her sweetest smiles—such a look and smile as argued ulterior intentions. 'It gave me quite a turn to see you as I did from Mistress Grace's window coming round the Cedars at such a break-neck rate. Is anything the matter, Hugh?' she added, anxiously. 'You're not going to leave us again for sure?'

Dymocke was splashing and hissing for hard life. He paused, winked ominously in his questioner's face, and shifting the bucket of water to the off side, set to work again more vigorously than before.

She had not 'kept company' with him all these months without knowing exactly how to manage him. She pulled a bunch of green leaves for the sorrel, caressed him admiringly, and looking askance at Dymocke's stooping figure, addressed her conversation to the horse.

'Poor fellow!' she said, smoothing his glossy neck, 'how you must miss your master. He wouldn't have rode you so unmercifully such a baking day as this. I wonder where he is now, poor young man. Far enough away, I'll be bound, or *you* wouldn't be put upon as you've been this blessed afternoon.'

The taunt rankled. Hugh looked up from his operations.

'There's reason for it, Mistress Faith; take my word, there's reason for it, though you can't expect to be told the whys and the wherefores every time as one of our horses gets a gallop.'

There *was* a mystery, then. To a woman such an admission was in itself a challenge. Faith vowed to know all about it ere she slept that night.

A sprig of green remained in her hand. She pulled it asunder pensively, leaf by leaf, and heaved one or two deep sighs. She knew her man thoroughly; despite his vinegar face his heart was as soft as butter to the sex.

'Ah, Hugh,' she said, 'it's an anxious time for us poor women, that sits and cries our eyes out, when you men you've nothing to brood over. I was in hopes the troubles was all done now. Whatever should I do to lose you again, dear? Tell me, Hugh, leastways, it's nothing up about yourself, is it?'

Faith's eyes were very soft and pretty, and she used them at this juncture with considerable skill.

Dymocke looked up, undoubtedly mollified.

'Well, it's nothing about myself—there!' he grunted out, in a rough voice.

A step was gained; he had made an admission. She would wheedle it all out of him now before the supper-bell rang.

'Nor yet the Captain,' exclaimed Faith, clasping her hands in an agony of affected alarm. 'Say it's not the Captain, Hugh, for any sake. Oh, my poor young mistress! Say it's not the Captain, or Major, or whatever he be; only say the word, Hugh, that he's safe.'

'Well, he's safe enough as yet, for the matter of that,' answered Hugh, saying the word, however, with considerable unwillingness. In such a 'pumping' process as the present the struggles of the victim are the more painful from his total inability to escape.

'As yet, Hugh?' repeated the operator: '*as yet?* Then you know something about him? you know where he is? you've heard of him? he's alive and well? He's come back from abroad? he's in England? perhaps he's in Northamptonshire even now?'

Dymocke's whole attention seemed bent on his currycomb and accompanying sibilations.

Faith set her lips tight.

'Sergeant Dymocke,' she said, with an air of solemn warning, 'you and me has kept company now for many a long day, and none can say as I've so

much as looked over my shoulder at ever a young
man but yourself. There's Master Snood, the mercer
in Northampton, and long Will Bucksfoot, the wild
forester at Rockingham, as has been down scores and
scores of times on their bended knees to me to say the
word, and I never said the word, and I never wouldn't.
I wont say what I've thought, and I wont say what
I've hoped; but if things is to end as they've begun
between you and me, I wouldn't answer for the consequences!'

With this mysterious and comprehensive threat,
Faith burst into a passion of tears, and burying
her face in her apron, wept aloud, refusing to be
comforted.

Another point gained. She had dextrously shifted
her ground, and put him in the position of the suppliant.

He was forced to abandon his horse and console
her to the best of his abilities, with awkward caresses
and blunt assurances of affection. By degrees the
sobs became less frequent; certain vague hints,
tending to hymeneal results, produced, as usual, a
sedative effect. Peace was established, and Faith
returned to the attack much invigorated by the tears
that had so relieved her feelings.

'Of course you'd trust a *wife* with everything you
knew,' observed Faith, in answer to an observation
of Dymocke's, which we are bound to admit was not
marked by his usual caution. 'And the Major *is*
come back?' she added, in her most coaxing accents
and with her sunniest smile.

'Yes, he's back,' said Hugh, laconically.

‘And you've seen him?’ added Faith, who felt she was winning easy.

Hugh nodded.

‘This afternoon?’

Another nod, implying a cautious affirmative.

‘Where?’

‘Close by, at Brampton. The horse knowed him at once, for all his disguise. It was beautiful to see the dumb creature's affection,’ urged Hugh, emphatically.

‘Disguised was he?’ echoed Faith, delighted with the result of her perseverance. ‘Where had he come from? where was he going to? what was he doing You may as well tell me all about it now, Hugh. Come, out with it; there's a dear.’

Out it all came, indeed, as a secret generally does, much to the relief of the proprietor and the satisfaction of the curious. Like a goat-skin of Spanish wine in which the point of a mountaineer's knife has been dextrously inserted, there is a little frothing and bubbling at first, then a few precious drops ooze through the orifice, and anon a fine generous stream comes flowing out continuously till the skin is emptied.

So Faith learned that the shabby fisherman at Brampton-ford was none other than Major Bosville; that he was waiting there with a political object, which it would be more than his life's worth to disclose; that he had been fishing there for two whole days, and had not achieved the object for which he had come; that the ladies and Sir Giles had been within ten yards of him, and never recognised him; and lastly, that the sorrel's attachment to his master was not to be obliterated by time, nor to be deceived by appearances.

'It *was* a sight to do your eyes good, my dear,' said Hugh, stroking the horse's nose, 'to see him break away from me and gallop all round the miller's close, as if he'd never be caught nor tamed again, and then trotting up to Major Humphrey as if he'd been a dog, and neighing for joy, and rubbing his head against his master, and the Major looking a'most as pleased as the horse. They've more sense and more affection too than many human beings,' added Hugh, impressively ; 'and now you needn't to be told, my dear, why I gave him this bit of a turn to keep his pipes clear in case of accidents. He might be wanted to-morrow, or he might *not* ; but if so be that he were, it shall never be said that he came out of *this* stable and wasn't fit to save a man's life. They're like the female sex, my dear, in many particulars, but in none so much as this. It's ruling them well and working of them easy that makes them *good* ; but it's ruling them strict and working of them hard that makes them *better*.'

With this philosophical axiom, the result, doubtless, of much attentive observation, Dymocke clothed up the sorrel, and led him into the stable, whilst Faith, with an expression of deeper anxiety than often troubled her pretty face, tripped away to her mistress's room, and to the best of our belief never visited the laundry after all.

Grace had to be dressed for supper. In those simple days people supped by daylight in the summer, and revised their toilets carefully for the meal, much as they dress for dinner now; and in those days, as in the present, a lady's 'back hair' was a source of much manual labour to her maid, and much mental anxiety to herself.

Though Faith worked away at the ebon masses with an unmerciful number of jerks and twitches and an unusually hard brush, she did not succeed in exciting the attention of the sufferer, who sat patient and motionless in her hands—not even looking at herself in the glass.

Faith heaved one or two surprisingly deep sighs, and even ventured upon a catching of the breath, such as with ladies of her profession is the usual precursor to a flood of tears, but without the slightest effect. Grace never lifted her eyes from the point of her foot, which peeped out beneath her robe.

At length the waiting-maid pressed her hand against her side, with an audible expression of pain.

'What's the matter, Faith?' said her mistress, turning round, with a wondering abstracted gaze, which brightened into one of curiosity, as she marked the excited expression of her attendant's countenance.

'Nothing, ma'am,' replied Faith, with another catching of the breath, real enough this time; 'leastways nothing's the matter at present, though what's to come of it, goodness only knows. Oh, Mistress Grace! Mistress Grace!' she added, letting all the 'back hair' down *en masse*, and clasping her two hands upon her bosom, 'who d'ye think's come back again? who d'ye think's within a mile of this house at this blessed minute? who d'ye think's been disguised and fishing by Brampton mill this very day? and the sorrel knew him though nobody else didn't, and all the troubles that was clean gone and over is to begin again; and who d'ye think it is, Mistress Grace, that might be walking up the stairs and into this very room even now?'

Startling as was the possibility, Grace seemed to contemplate it with wondrous calmness. Though she was blushing deeply, she exhibited no signs of surprise or alarm as she asked very quietly, 'Who?'

'Why, who but Major Humphrey?' replied Faith, triumphantly. 'Now, don't ye take on, Mistress Grace, my sweet young lady, don't you go for to frighten yourself, there's a dear! It's Dymocke that saw him; and the sergeant's a discreet man, you know, and as true as steel. And he says, the Major looked so worn and thin, and as pale as a ghost. But the horse he knew him, bless his sorrel skin; and the sergeant says he wouldn't have discovered the Major himself, if it hadn't been for the dumb animal. It's as much as his life's worth to be here, Mistress Grace, so the sergeant says; and the Roundheads—that's the rebels, as we was used to call them—the Parliamentarians (wise and godly men, too, some of them) would shoot him to death as soon as ever they set eyes on him; but don't you worrit and fret yourself, Mistress Grace, don't ye now!'

Grace received the intelligence with surprising composure. 'He *was* looking dreadfully altered,' she muttered to herself; but she only told Faith that if this very improbable story were really true, it was incumbent on the possessor of so deadly a secret to bridle her tongue, and not allow the slightest hint to escape that might be the means of throwing Bosville into the hands of his enemies; and she went down to supper with an unfaltering step and an air of outward composure that astonished and even somewhat displeased her susceptible handmaiden.

'She can't care for him one morsel,' said Faith, as she folded up her lady's things, and put them carefully away. The girl had no idea of the power possessed by some natures to 'suffer and be still.' In a parallel case she would have cried her own eyes out, she thought, and it would have done her good. She did not know, and would not have appreciated, the 'enduring faculty' that seems most fully developed in the two extreme races of the patrician and the savage, and esteemed herself doubtless happier without the pride that dries our tears, 'tis true, but dries them much in the same way that the red-hot searing-iron scorches up and stanches the stream from a gaping wound. Grace possessed her share of this well-born quality, for all her gentle manner and her quiet voice; nor did she ever draw more largely upon her stores of self-command than while she sat opposite Sir Giles at supper that evening, and filled out his 'dish of claret' again and again with her own pretty hands. She thought the meal never would be over. This stanch old Cavalier was in unusual spirits with the prospect of his Majesty's visit, and laughed and joked with his thoughtful 'Gracey,' so perseveringly as almost to drive her wild. She absolutely *thirsted* for solitude, and the enjoyment, if such it could be called, of her own thoughts. But supper was over at last. Sir Giles, leaning back in his high carved chair, sank to his usual slumber, and Grace was free to come and go unnoticed, for Lord Vaux was still on a sick bed, and Mary Cave, pleading fatigue and indisposition, had remained in her own chamber.

Now, it is a singular fact, that although neither of the ladies who occupied Lord Vaux's roomy old coach had immediately recognised the disguised fisherman at Brampton mill, a certain instinctive consciousness of his identity had come upon each of them at the same instant; and it is no less singular that neither of them should have offered the slightest hint of her suspicions to her companion; and that although the manner of each was more affectionate than usual, by a sort of tacit understanding they should have avoided one another's society for the rest of the day.

Thus it came to pass that Mary, who never used to be tired, went to her own room immediately she returned from Holmby, and begged she might not be disturbed even by the 'burnt posset,' which was our ancestors' jolly substitute for a ' cup of tea.'

It may seem strange that Mistress Cave should have been so ignorant of Bosville's movements, and that she of all women should have been so startled by his unexpected appearance in Northamptonshire; but truth to tell, Mary had long ceased to know his intentions, or to be consulted as of old about his every action. Though he had written to her frequently, all correspondence from the Queen's Court was so carefully watched, that his letters never reached their destination; and the same cause had intercepted an epistle which after a long interval of suspense, proud

Mary Cave had brought herself to write to the man whose absence she was astonished to find she bore so impatiently. It was galling, doubtless, but it was none the less true. When she parted from him at Exeter, there was indeed every probability that in those troublous times they might never meet again on earth ; and this separation she could not but feel was a most unpleasant contingency. Nay, it was actually painful, and many a secret tear it cost her. This it was which had made her so cold and haughty till he actually bid her farewell ; and how often since had she wished, till her heart ached, that she could live those few days over again ! As month after month passed on without further tidings, she seemed to feel her loss more and more. Self-reproach, curiosity, and pique combined to make her think and ponder on the absent one, whose merits, both of mind and body, seemed to come out so vividly now that it was possible they belonged to *her* no longer. Mary was no dull observer of human nature, and she knew well that if she really cared to retain his affections, she had been playing a somewhat dangerous game. Had he been employed in the alarms and excitement of warfare, subjected day by day to the ennobling influence of danger, his higher and better feelings kept awake by the inspiring stimulus of military glory, and the deepest, truest affections of his heart, enhanced as they always are by the daily habit of looking death in the face, she felt she would have reigned in that heart more imperiously than ever ; but the case was quite different now. He was living in the atmosphere of a pleasure-loving and profligate

Court. He was subjected to just so much excitement and dissipation as would serve to distract his thoughts, just so much interesting employment as would forbid his mind from dwelling continuously upon any single topic. From his position he was sure to be courted by the great, and with his person to be welcomed by the fair. To do him justice, he had ever shown himself sufficiently callous to the latter temptation, and yet—— Mary remembered the wit and the attractions of those French ladies amongst whom she had spent her youth; she even caught herself recalling his admiration of one or two of her own accomplishments derived from that source. He might find others fairer than she was now—kinder than she had ever been—some gentle heart would be sure to love him dearly, and the very intensity of its affection would win his in return; and then indeed he would be lost to her altogether: *she would rather he was lying dead and buried yonder on Naseby-field!* And yet, no! no!—anything were better than that. Mary was startled at the bitterness and the strength of her own passions. It was frightful! it was humiliating! it was unwomanly! to feel like this. Was she weaker as she grew older, that she could thus confess to herself so deep an interest in one who might perhaps already have forgotten her? She had not loved Falkland so—that was a pure, lofty, and ennobling sentiment—there was much more of the earthly element in this strange wild fascination. Perhaps it was none the less dear, none the less dangerous on that account.

So she resolved that whatever cause had brought

him back at last (for too surely she felt the disguised fisherman was no other than Bosville), *she* at least would appear to be ignorant and careless of his movements. Till his long silence was explained, of course he could be nothing to her; and even then, if people could forget for two whole years, *other* people could forget altogether. Yes, it would be far better so. He must be changed indeed not to have spoken to her that very day by the water side. Then she remembered what Grace had said about the knot of pink ribbon; and womanlike, after judging him so harshly, her heart smote her for her unkindness, and she wept.

The sun was sinking below the horizon when Grace stepped out upon the terrace at Boughton, and wrapping a scarf around her shoulders, paced slowly away for a stroll in the cool atmosphere and refreshing breezes of the park. It was delicious to get into the pure evening air after the hot drive and the crowded court, and Sir Giles's interminable supper; to be alone once more under God's heaven, and able to think undisturbed. The deer were already couching for the night amongst the fern, the rooks had gone home hours ago, but a solitary and belated heron, high up in the calm sky, was winging his soft, silent way towards the flush of sunset which crimsoned all the west. It was the hour of peace and repose, when nature subsides to a dreamy stillness ere she sinks to her majestic sleep, when the ox lies down in his pasture, and the wild bird is hushed on the bough, when all is at rest on earth save only the restless human heart, which will never know peace but in the grave.

Grace threaded the stems of the tall old trees, her foot falling lightly upon the mossy sward, her white figure glancing ghost-like in and out the dusky avenues, her fair brow, from which she put back the masses of hair with both hands, cooling in the evening breeze.

What did she here? She scarce knew herself why she had sought this woodland solitude—why she had been so restless, so impatient, so dissatisfied with everything and everybody, so longing to be alone. Deeply she pondered on Faith's narrative, though indeed she had guessed the truth long before her handmaiden's confidences. Much she wondered what *he* was doing here—whence had he come?—when was he going away?—what was this political mystery in which foolish Faith believed so implicitly? Why was he in Northamptonshire at all? Was there a chance of his wandering here to-night to visit his old haunts?—and if he should, what was that to her? The girl's cheek flushed, though she was alone, with mingled pain and pride as she reflected that she had given her heart unasked. No! not *quite* given it, but suffered it to wander sadly out of her own control; and that though she was better now, there *had* been a time when she cared for him a great deal more than was good for her. Well, it was over, and yet she *should* like to see him once again, she confessed, if it were only to wish him 'good-bye.' Were there fairies still on earth? Could it be possible her wish was granted? There he was!

Grace's heart beat violently, and her breath came and went very quick as the dark figure of a man emerged from the shade of an old oak under which he had been standing, not ten paces from her. She almost repented of her wish, that seemed to have been accorded so readily. Poor Grace! there was no occasion for penitence; ere he had made three strides towards her she had recognised him; and it was with a voice in which disappointment struggled with unfeigned surprise, that she exclaimed, 'Captain Effingham!'

He doffed his hat, and begged her, with the old manly courtesy she remembered so well, not to be alarmed. 'His duty,' he said, 'had brought him into the neighbourhood, and he could not resist the temptation of visiting the haunts of those who had once been so kind to him before these unhappy troubles had turned his best friends to strangers, if not to enemies.' His voice shook as he spoke, and Grace could not forbear extending her hand to him; as she touched his it was like ice, and he trembled, that iron soldier, as if he was cold.

Darkness was coming on apace, yet even in the fading light Grace could not but see how hardly Time had dealt with her old admirer—an admirer of whom, although undeclared, her womanly instinct had been long ago conscious as a very devoted and a very worthy one.

George's whole countenance had deepened into the marked lines and grave expression of middle age. The hair and beard, once so raven black, were now grizzled; and although the tall strong form was square and erect as ever, its gestures had lost the buoyant elasticity of youth, and had acquired the slow

and somewhat listless air of those who have outlived
their prime.

He seemed to have got something to communicate,
yet he walked by her side without uttering another
syllable. Grace looked down at the ground, and
could not mark the sidelong gaze of deep, melancholy
tenderness with which he regarded her beautiful
profile and shapely form. The silence became very
embarrassing; after the second turn she began to get
quite frightened.

He spoke at last as it seemed with a mighty effort,
and in a low, choking voice.

'You are surprised to see me, Mistress Grace, and
with reason; perhaps I am guilty of presumption in
even entering your kinsman's domain. Well, it is
for the last time. Forgive me if I have startled you,
or intruded on your solitude. May I speak to you
for five minutes? I will not detain you long.
Believe me, I never expected to see *you* here to-
night.'

'Then why on earth did you come?' was Grace's
very natural reflection, but she only bowed and faltered out a few words expressive of her willingness to
hear all he had got to say.

'I only arrived to-day at Northampton,' he proceeded, calming as he went on; 'I have been appointed to the command of a division of the army, to
watch this district, and preserve the peace of his
Majesty and his Parliament. We have reason to
believe that a conspiracy is being organized to plunge
this country once more in civil war. Suspicious persons are about.'

Grace glanced sharply at him.

'My troopers are even now scouring the country to arrest a messenger from France, of whom I have received information. It is sad work, my duty will compel me to hang him to the nearest tree.'

It was fortunate that the failing light prevented his seeing how pale she had turned.

'Believe me, Mistress Grace, it is hopeless for the "Malignants" to stir up civil war again. His Majesty's Parliament will act for the safety of his Majesty's person, and it will be my duty, with the large force I command, to escort him in security to the neighbourhood of London."

Grace listened attentively—the little Royalist was half frightened, and half indignant at the calm tone of conscious power in which the successful soldier of the Parliament announced his intentions.

Effingham paused, as if to gather courage, then proceeded, speaking very rapidly, and looking studiously away from the person he addressed.

'You have never known, Mistress Grace—God forbid you ever should know—such suffering and such anxiety as I have experienced now for many long months. I did not come here to-night to tell you this. I did not come here expecting to see you at all. It was weak, I grant you, and unmanly; but I could not resist the temptation of wandering near your home once again, of watching the house in which you were, and perhaps looking on the light that shone from your window. I am no love-sick swain, Mistress Grace,' he added, smiling bitterly, 'with my rough soldier's manners and my gray hair; but I plead guilty to this one infatuation, and you may despise me for it if you will. Well! as I have met you to-night, I will tell you all—listen. Ever since I have known you, I have loved you—God help me!—better than my own soul. You will never know, Grace, you *shall* never know, how truly, how dearly, how worse than madly—I feel it is hopeless—I feel it is no use—that I can never be more to you than the successful Rebel, the enemy that is only *not* hated because you are too gentle and kind to hate any human being. Many a weary day have I longed to tell you this, and so to bid you farewell, and see you never more. It is over now, and I am happier for the confession. God bless you, Grace! If you *could* have cared for me I should have been worthy of you —it cannot be—I shall never forget you—farewell!'

He raised her hand, pressed it once to his lips, and ere she had recovered from her astonishment he was gone.

Grace looked wildly around her, as one who wakes from a dream. It seemed like a dream indeed, but she still heard the tramp of his step as he walked away in the calm night, and listening for a few minutes after he was gone, distinguished the clatter of a horse's hoofs on the hard road leading to North-ampton. Grace was utterly bewildered and con-fused. There was something not unpleasant in the sensation too. Long ago, though she was a good deal afraid of it, she had hugely admired that stern enthusiastic nature, but the image of another had prevented the impression ripening into any feeling deeper than interest and esteem. And now to discover for a certainty that she had subjugated that strong, brave heart, that the rebel warrior had been worshipping her in secret all those long months, in the midst of his dangers and his victories, that her influence had softened his rigour to many a Royalist, and that he had saved her own dear old father at Naseby for *her* sake,—all this was anything but disagreeable to that innate love of dominion which exists in the gentlest of her sex, and such a conquest as that of the famous Parliamentary general (for to that rank George had speedily risen) was one that any woman might be proud of, and was indeed a soothing salve to her heart, wounded and mortified by the neglect of another. But then the danger to that other smote her with a chill and sickening apprehension. It could be none but Bosville that had been seen and suspected by the keen-eyed Parliamentarians. He might be a prisoner even now, and she shuddered as she reflected on that ghastly observation of Effingham's about the nearest tree. Word by word she recalled his conversation, and the design upon the King's liberty, which she had somewhat overlooked in the contemplation of more personal topics, assumed a frightful importance as she remembered that she was the depositary of this important intelligence. What ought she to do? Though Effingham had trusted her, he had extorted no promise of secresy, and as she had always been taught besides that her first duty was towards her Sovereign, there was no time for consideration. What was to be done? The King was in danger—Bosville was in danger—and she alone had the knowledge, though without the power of prevention. What was she to do? What *could* she do? She was completely at her wit's end!

In this predicament Grace's proceedings were characteristic, if not conclusive; she first of all began to cry, and then resolved upon consulting Mary, and making a ' clean breast of it,' which she felt would be an inexpressible relief. With this object, she returned at once to the house, and hurried without delay to her friend's chamber.

That lady's indisposition had apparently not been severe enough to cause her to go to bed. On the contrary, she was sitting up, still completely dressed, and with a wakeful, not to say harassed, expression on her countenance, which precluded all idea of sleep for many hours to come. She welcomed Grace with some little astonishment, ' her headache was better, and it was kind of dear Gracey to come and inquire after her—she was just going to bed—she had been sitting up writing,' she said.

There was a sheet of paper on the table, only it was blank.

Grace flung herself into her arms, and had ' the cry' fairly out, which had been checked whilst she ran into the house.

' And the thing must be told,' sobbed the agitated girl, when she had detailed her unexpected meeting with Effingham, and its startling results ; ' and father mustn't know it, or it will all be worse than ever ; he'll be arming the servants and the few tenants that have got a horse left, and all the horrors will have to begin again, and he'll be killed some day, Mary, I know he will. What shall I do? What *shall* I do?'

Mary's courage always rose in a difficulty; her brow cleared now, and her head went up.

'He must not be told a word, and the King must! Leave that to me, Gracey.'

Grace looked unspeakably comforted for a moment, but the tide of her troubles surged in again irresistibly, as she thought of the suspected fisherman and the noose at the nearest tree.

'But Bosville, Mary—Bosville—think of him, close by here, and those savages hunting for him and thirsting for his blood. Oh! Mary, I *must* save him, and I *will*. What can be done? advise me, Mary—advise me. If a hair of his head is hurt, I shall never sleep in peace again.'

'I wish we had stopped and spoken to him to-day,' observed Mary, abstractedly; 'and yet it might only have compromised him, and done no good.'

Grace looked up sharply through her tears. 'Did you know it was Bosville, Mary, in that disguise? So did I!'

Notwithstanding Mistress Cave's self-command, a shadow as of great pain passed over her countenance. It faded, nevertheless, as quickly as it came. She took Grace's hand in her own, and looked quietly and sadly in the girl's weeping face.

'Do you love him, Gracey?' she said, very gently, and with a sickly sort of smile.

Grace's only answer was to hide her face between her hands and sob as if her heart would break.

Till she had sobbed herself to sleep in her chamber, her friend never left her. It was midnight ere she returned to her own room, and dotted the blank sheet of paper with a few short words in cipher. When this was done, Mary leaned her head upon her hand, and pondered long and earnestly.

We have all read of the pearl of great price in the holy parable, and how, when the seeker had found it, he went and sold all that he had, and bought it and made it his own. Lightly he thought of friends, and fame, and fortune, compared to the treasure of his heart. We have often imagined the weary look of utter desolation which would have overspread his features, could he have seen that pearl shivered into fragments, the one essential object of his life existent no more—the treasure destroyed, and with it the heart also. Such a look was on Mary's pale face as she sat by her bedside watching for the first flush of the summer dawn.

CHAPTER VII.

'THE FALCON GENTLE.'

THE sun shone bright on the level terraces of Holmby House—huge stone vases grotesquely carved and loaded with garden-flowers studded the shaven lawns and green slopes that adorned the southern front of the palace—here and there a close-clipped yew or stunted juniper threw its black shadow across the sward, and broke in some measure the uniformity of those long formal alleys in which our forefathers took such pleasure. Half-way down the hill, through the interstices of their quivering screen of leaves, the fishponds gleamed like burnished gold in the morning light; and far below the sunny vale, broken by clumps of forest timber, and dotted with sheep and oxen, stretched away till it lost itself in the dense woodlands of Althorpe-park.

Two figures paced the long terrace that immediately fronted the mansion. To and fro they walked with rapid strides, nor paused to contemplate the beauties of the distant landscape, nor the stately magnificence of the royal palace—shafted, mullioned, and pinnacled like a stronghold of romance. It was Charles and his attendant, the Earl of Pembroke, taking their morning exercise, which the methodical King considered indispensable to his health, and which was sufficiently harassing to the old and enfeebled

frame of the noble commissioner. Charles, like his
son, was a rapid and vigorous pedestrian. His bodily
powers were wonderfully unsusceptible to fatigue;
and perhaps the concentrated irritation awakened by
a life of continuous surveillance and restraint may
have found vent in thus fiercely pacing like some wild
animal the area of his cage. Poor old Lord Pembroke,
on whom the duty of a state-gaoler to his Sovereign
had been thrust, sorely against his will, and for whom
‘a good white pillow for that good white head’ had
been more appropriate than either steel headpiece or
gilded coronet, had no such incentive to exertion, and
halted breathlessly after the King, with a ludicrous
mixture of deference and dismay, looking wistfully at
the stone dial which stood midway in their course
every time they passed it, and ardently longing for
the time of his dismissal from this the most fatiguing
of all his unwelcome duties.

The King, whose lungs, like his limbs, were little
affected by his accustomed exercise, strode manfully
on, talking, as was his wont, upon grave and weighty
subjects, and anon waiting with gentle patience for
the answers of the lagging courtier. His Majesty
was this morning in a more than usually moralizing
mood.

‘ Look yonder, my Lord Earl,’ said he, pointing to
the beauteous scene around him—the smiling valley,
the trim pleasure-grounds, the sparkling waters, with
the lazy pike splashing at intervals to the surface, and
the blossoms showering pink and white in the soft
summer breeze. ‘ Look yonder, and see how the sun
penetrates every nook and· cranny of the copsewood,

even as it floods the open meadows in its golden glory. That sunlight is everywhere, my lord, in the lowest depths of the castle-vaults, as on yon bright pinnacle, around which the noisy daws are wheeling and chattering even now. 'Tis that sunlight which offers day, dim, though it be, to the captive in the dungeon, even as it bathes in its lustre the eagle on the cliff. Is there no moral in this, my lord? Is there no connexion, think you, between the rays which give warmth to the body, and the inner light which gives life to the soul?'

Lord Pembroke was out of breath, and a little deaf into the bargain. 'Very true, your Majesty,' he assented, having caught just enough of the King's discourse to be aware that it related in some measure to the weather. 'Very true, as your Majesty says, we shall have rain anon!' And the old Earl looked up at the skies, over which a light cloud or two were passing, with a sidelong glance, like some weatherwise old raven, devoutly hoping that a shower might put an end at once to the promenade and the conversation.

'Ay! it is even so,' proceeded the King, apparently answering his own thoughts rather than the inconsequent remark of his attendant. 'There is indeed a cloud athwart the sun, and yet he is shining as brightly behind it upon the rest of the universe, as though there were no veil interposed between our petty selves and his majestic light. And shall we murmur because the dark hour cometh and we must grope in our blindness awhile, and mayhap wander from the path, and stumble and bruise our feet, till

the day breaks in its glory once more? Oh man!
man! though thou art shrinking and shivering in the
storm, the sun shines still the same in its warmth and
dazzling light; though thou art cowering in adversity, God is everywhere alike in wisdom, power, and
goodness.'

As the King spoke, he turned and paced the length
of the terrace once more. The clouds passed on, and
the day was bright as ever. It seemed a good omen;
and as the unhappy are prone to be superstitious, it
was accepted as such by the meditative Monarch. In
silence he walked on, deeply engrossed with many a
sad and solemn subject. His absent Queen, from
whom he had been long expecting tidings, whom he
still loved with the undemonstrative warmth of his
deep and tender nature—his ruined party and proscribed adherents—his lost Crown, for he could scarce
now consider himself a Sovereign—his imperilled life,
for already had he suspected the intentions of the
Parliament, and resolved to oppose them if necessary,
even to the death—lastly, his trust in God, which,
weak, imprudent, injudicious as he may have been,
never deserted Charles Stuart even in the last extremity—which never yet failed any man who relied
upon it in his need, from the King on the throne to
the convict in the dungeon.

But the Monarch's walk was doomed to be interrupted, and Lord Pembroke's penance brought to an
earlier close than usual, by a circumstance the origin
of which we must take leave to retrograde a few hours
to explain, affecting as it does the proceedings of a
fair lady, who, in all matters of difficulty or danger,

was accustomed to depend on no energies and consult no will but her own.

We left Mary Cave in her chamber at Boughton, watching wearily for the dawn, which came at length, as it comes alike to the bride, blushing welcome to her wedding-morn, and to the pale criminal, shrinking from the sunlight that he will never see more—which will come alike over and over again to our children and to our children's children, when we are dead and forgotten, but which shall at last be extinguished too, or rather swallowed up in the Eternal Day, when Darkness, Sin, and Sorrow shall be destroyed for evermore.

Pale and resolute, Mary made a careful toilet with the first streaks of day. Elaborately she arranged every fold of her riding-gear, and with far more pains than common pinned up and secured the long tresses of her rich brown hair. Usually they were accustomed to escape from their fastenings, and wave and float about her when disordered by a gallop in provokingly attractive profusion; but on this occasion they were so disposed that nothing but intentional violence was likely to disturb their shining masses. Stealthily she left her apartment, and without rousing the household sought the servants' offices—no difficult task, as bolts and bars in those simple times were usually left unfastened, except in the actual presence of some recognised danger; and although such an old-fashioned manor-house as that of Boughton might be fortified securely against an armed force, it was by no means so impregnable to a single thief who should simply use the precaution of taking off his shoes. Not a single domestic did Mary meet as she took her well-known way towards the stables; and even Bayard's loud neigh of recognition, echoed as it was by the delighted sorrel, failed to disturb the slumbers of Dymocke and his satellites. With her own fair hands Mary saddled and bridled her favourite, hurting her delicate fingers against the straps and buckles of his appointments. With her own fair hands she jessed and hooded 'Dewdrop,' and took her from her perch in the falconer's mews, without leave asked of that still unconscious functionary; and thus dressed and mounted, with foot in stirrup and hawk on hand, Mary emerged through Boughton-park like some female knight-errant, and took her well-known way to Brampton-ford.

We are all more or less self-deceivers, and this lady was no exception to the rule of humanity. Secresy was no doubt judicious on such an expedition as that which she had now resolved to take in hand; yet it is probable that Dymocke at least might have been trusted so far as to saddle her horse and hood her falcon; but something in Mary's heart bid her feel shame that any one, even a servant, should know whither she was bound; and although other and unacknowledged motives besides the obvious duty of warning Charles of his danger prompted her to take so decided a step, she easily persuaded herself that zeal for the King's safety, and regard for his person, made it imperative on her to keep religiously secret the interview she proposed extorting from his Majesty; and that in so delicate and dangerous a business she ought to confide in no one but herself.

So she rode gently on towards Brampton-ford,
Bayard stepping lightly and proudly over the spangled
sward, and 'Dewdrop' shaking her bells merrily
under the inspiriting influence of the morning air.
A few short years ago she would have urged her
horse into a gallop in the sheer exuberance of her
spirits; nay, till within the last twenty-four hours,
she would have paced along at least with head erect,
and eye kindling to the beauties of the scene; but a
change had come over her bearing, and her brow wore
a look of depression and sadness, her figure stooped
listlessly on her saddle; her whole exterior denoted
that weary state of dejection which overcomes the
player in the great game of life, who has thrown the
last stake—and lost !

As she neared the river, she looked anxiously and
furtively around, peering behind every tree and haw-
thorn that studded the level surface of the meadow.
In vain: no fisherman disturbed the quiet waters of
the Nene—no solitary figure trampled the long grass,
wet with the dews of morning. There was no chance
of a recognition—an explanation. Perhaps he avoided
it on purpose—perhaps he felt aggrieved and wounded
at her long silence—perhaps he had forgotten her
altogether. Two years was a long time. Men were
proverbially inconstant. Besides, had she not resolved
in her own heart that this folly should be terminated
at once and for ever? Yes, it was providential he
was not there. It was far better—their meeting
would have been painful and awkward for both.
She could not be sufficiently thankful that she had
been spared the trial. All the time she would

have given her right arm to see him just once again.

With a deep sigh she roused Bayard into a gallop, and the good steed, nothing loth, stretched away up the hill with the long, regular stride that is indeed the true 'poetry of motion.' A form couching low behind a clump of alders watched her till she was out of sight, and a shabbily-dressed fisherman, with sad brow and heavy heart, then resumed his occupation of angling in the Nene with the same studious pertinacity that he had displayed in that pursuit for the last two days.

It would have required indeed all the instincts of a loving heart, such as the sorrel, in common with his generous equine brethren, undoubtedly possessed, to recognise in the wan, travel-stained angler the comely exterior of Humphrey Bosville. The drooping moustaches had been closely shaved, the long lovelocks shorn off by the temples to admit of the short flaxen wig which replaced the young Cavalier's dark, silky hair. His worn-out beaver too, slouched down over his eyes, and his rusty jerkin, with its high collar devoid of linen, completed the metamorphosis, while the small feet were encased in huge, shapeless wading boots, and the hands, usually so white and well kept, were now embrowned and stained by the influence of exposure and hard usage. His disguise, he flattered himself, was perfect, and he was not a little proud of the skill by which he had escaped suspicion in the port at which he landed, and deceived even the wary soldiers of the Parliament as to his real character, at several military posts which they occupied, and where he had been examined. Humphrey Bosville, as we know, had passed his parole never again to bear arms against the Parliament, but his word of honour, he conceived, did not prohibit him from being the prime agent in every hazardous scheme organized by the Royal Party at that intriguing time. True to his faith, he missed no opportunity of risking life in the service of his Sovereign, and he was even now waiting in the heart of an enemy's country to deliver an important letter from the Queen to her wretched and imprisoned husband.

For this cause he prowled stealthily about the river Nene, waiting for the chance of Charles's crossing the bridge in some of his riding expeditions, and the sport of fishing in which he seemed to be engaged enabled him to remain in the same spot for several hours, unsuspected of aught save a characteristic devotion to that most patience-wearing of amusements.

Though he saw his ladye-love ride by alone in the early morning, a feeling of duty, still paramount in his soldier nature, prevented his discovering himself even to her. So he thought and persuaded himself there was no leaven of pique, no sense of irritation at long and unmerited neglect, embittering the kindly impulses of his honest heart. He watched her receding form with aching eyes. 'Ay,' thought poor Humphrey, all his long-cherished love welling up in that deep tide of 'bitter waters' which is so near akin to hate, 'ride on as you used to do in your beauty and your heartlessness, as you *would* do without drawing rein or turning aside, though my body were beneath your horse's feet. What care you that you have taken from me all that makes life hopeful and happy, and left me instead darkness where there should be light, and listless despair where there should be courage, and energy, and trust? I gave you all, proud, heartless Mary, little enough it may be, and valueless to you, but still *my all*, and what have I reaped in exchange? A fevered worn-out frame, that can only rest when prostrated by fatigue, a tortured spirit that never knows a respite save in the pressure of immediate and imminent danger. Well, it will soon be over now. This last stroke will probably finish my career, and there will be repose at any rate in the grave. I will be true to the last. *Loyally before all.* You shall hear of him when it is too late, but of his own free will, proud, heartless woman, he will never look upon your face again!'

Our friend was very much hurt, and quite capable of acting as he imagined. These lovers' quarrels, you see, though the wise rate them at their proper value, are sufficiently painful to the poor fools immediately concerned, and Major Bosville resumed his sport, not the least in the frame of mind recommended by old Izaak Walton to the disciple who goes a-fishing.

Meanwhile Mary Cave stretched on at Bayard's long easy gallop till she came in view of the spires and chimneys of Holmby House towering into the summer sky, when, with a gleam of satisfaction such as she had not yet displayed kindling on her beautiful face, she drew rein, and prepared for certain active operations, which she had been meditating as she came along.

Taking a circuit of the Palace, and entering the park at its westernmost gate, she loosed Dewdrop's jesses, and without unhooding her, flung the falcon aloft into the air. A soft west wind was blowing at the time, and the bird, according to the nature of its kind, finding itself free from restraint, but at the same time deprived of sight, opened its broad wings to the breeze, and soared away towards the pleasure-grounds of the Palace, in which Charles and the Earl of Pembroke were taking their accustomed exercise.

Mary was no bad judge of falconry, and the very catastrophe she anticipated happened exactly as she intended. The hawk, sailing gallantly down the wind, struck heavily against the branches of a tall elm that intervened, and fell lifeless on the sward almost at the King's feet. Mary at the same time urging Bayard to his speed, came scouring rapidly down the park as though in search of her lost fa-vourite, and apparently unconscious of the presence of royalty or the proximity of a palace, put her horse's head straight for the sunken fence which divided the lawns from the park. Bayard pointed his small ears and cleared it at a bound, his mistress reining short up after performing this feat, and dismounting to bend over the body of her dead falcon with every ap-pearance of acute and pre-occupied distress.

The King and Lord Pembroke looked at each other in mute astonishment. Such an apparition was indeed an unusual variety in those tame morning walks, and the drooping figure of the lady, the dead bird, and the roused, excited horse, would have made a fit group for the sculptor or the painter.

'Gallantly ridden, fair dame!' said the King, at length breaking the silence, and discovering himself to the confused equestrian. 'Although this is a somewhat sudden and unceremonious intrusion on our privacy, we are constrained to forgive it, in consideration of the boldness of the feat, and the heavy nature of your loss. Your falcon, I fear, is quite dead. Ha!' added the monarch, with a start of recognition; 'by my faith it is Mistress Mary Cave! You are not here for nothing,' he proceeded, becoming visibly pale, and speaking in an agitated tone; 'are there tidings of the Queen?'

Mary was no contemptible actress; acting is, indeed, an accomplishment that seems to come naturally to most women. She now counterfeited such violent confusion and alarm at the breach of *etiquette* into which her thoughtlessness had hurried her, that the old Earl of Pembroke began to make excuses for her impetuosity, and whilst Mary, affecting extreme faintness, only murmured 'water, water,' the old courtier kept urging upon the King that 'the lady was probably ignorant of court forms—that she did not know she was so near the palace—that her horse was running away with her,' and such other incongruous excuses as his breathless state admitted of his enumerating.

The King lost patience at last.

'Don't stand prating there, man,' said he, pointing to Mary, who seemed indeed to be at the last gasp;

'go and fetch the lady some water—can you not see she will faint in two minutes?'

And while the old Earl hobbled off in quest of the reviving element, Charles raised Mary from her knees, and repeated, in a voice trembling with alarm, his previous question, 'Are there tidings from the Queen?'

'No, my liege,' replied Mary, whose faintness quitted her with extraordinary rapidity as soon as the Earl was out of ear-shot. 'This business concerns yourself. There is a plot to carry off your Majesty's person, there is a plot to lead you to London a prisoner, this very day. I only discovered it at midnight. I had no means of communicating unwatched with my Sovereign, and I took this unceremonious method of intruding on his privacy. Forgive me, my liege, I did not even know that I should be so fortunate as to see you for an instant alone; had you been accompanied by more than one attendant, I must have taken some other means of placing this packet in your hands.'

As Mary spoke she unbound the masses of her shining hair, and taking a paper from its folds, presented it to the King, falling once more upon her knees, and kissing the royal hand extended to her with devoted loyalty. 'I have here communicated to your Majesty in cipher all I have learned about the plot. I might have been searched had I been compelled to demand an interview, and I knew no better method of concealing my packet than this. Oh, my liege! my liege! confide in me, the most devoted of your subjects. It is never too late to play a bold stroke; resist this measure with the sword—say but the word, lift but your royal hand, and I will engage to raise the country in sufficient force to bring your Majesty safe off, if I, Mary Cave, have to ride at their head!'

The King looked down at the beautiful figure kneeling there before him, her cheek flushed, her eyes bright with enthusiasm, her long soft hair showering over her neck and shoulders, her horse's bridle clasped in one small gloved hand, whilst the other held his own, which she had just pressed fervently to her lips; an impersonation of loyalty, self-abandonment, and unavailing heroism, of all the nobler and purer qualities which had been wasted so fruitlessly in the Royal cause; and a sad smile stole over his countenance, whilst the tears stood in his deep, melancholy eyes, as he looked from the animated living figure, to the dead falcon that completed the group.

'Enough blood has been shed,' said he; 'enough losses sustained by the Cavaliers of England in my quarrel. Charles Stuart will never again kindle the torch of war—no, not to save his crown—not to save his head! Nevertheless, kind Mistress Mary, fore-warned is forearmed, and your Sovereign offers you his heartfelt thanks, 'tis all he has now to give, for your prompt resolution and your unswerving loyalty. Would that it had cost you no more than your falcon —would that I could replace your favourite with a bird from my own royal mews. Alas! I am a King now only in name—I believe I have but one faithful subject left, and that is Mistress Mary Cave!'

As the King spoke, Lord Pembroke returned with the water, and Mary, with many acknowledgments of his Majesty's condescension, and many apologies and excuses, mingled with regrets for the loss of her falcon, remounted her horse, and leaving the pleasure-grounds by a private gate or postern of which the Earl had the key, returned to Boughton by the way she had come, pondering in her own mind on the success of her enterprise and the impending calamities that seemed gathering in to crush the unhappy King.

Much to the relief of the aged nobleman, this adventure closed the royal promenade for that morning, and Charles, giving orders for his attendants to be in readiness after dinner, as it was his intention to ride on horseback and indulge himself in a game of bowls at Lord Vaux's house at Boughton—an intention which may perhaps have accounted for his abrupt dismissal of Mary Cave—retired to the privacy of his closet, there to deliberate, not on the stormy elements of his political future, not on the warning he had just received, and the best means of averting an imprisonment which now indeed threatened to be no longer merely a matter of form; not on the increasing power of his sagacious enemy, who was even then taking his wary, uncompromising measures for his downfall, and whose mighty will was to that of the feeble Charles as his long cut-and-thrust broadsword to the walking rapier of a courtier; not of Cromwell's ambition and his own incompetency; not of his empty throne and his imperilled head—but of an

abstruse dispute on casuistical divinity and the un-
finished tag of a Latin verse!

Truly in weaker natures constant adversity seems
to have the effect of blunting the faculties and lowering the whole mental organization of the man. The
metal must be iron in the first instance, or the blast
of the furnace will never temper it into steel.

CHAPTER VIII.

'A RIDE ACROSS A COUNTRY.'

ON the day during which the events recorded in our last chapter were taking place, the good sorrel horse, with the instinctive sagacity peculiar to his kind, must have been aware that some trial of his mettle was imminently impending. Never before in the whole course of his experience had the same care been bestowed on his feeding, watering, and other preparations for an appointed task; never before had Dymocke so minutely examined the soundness of every strap and buckle of his appointments, inspected so rigidly the state of his shoes, or fitted the bit in his mouth, and the links of his curb-chain with such judicious delicacy. Horses are keenly alive to all premonitory symptoms of activity, and the sorrel's kindling eye and dilated nostril showed that he was prepared to sustain his part, whatever it might be, in the impending catastrophe. Dymocke, too, had discarded the warlike air and pompous bearing which he usually affected; he had considerably shortened his customary morning draught, and as he was well known to be a man of few words and an austere demeanour, none of his fellow-servants dared take upon themselves to question him when he left the stable-yard in a groom's ordinary undress, and rode the sorrel carefully out as it were for an airing.

'Patrolling!' quoth Dymocke to himself, as he emerged from the park-gates, and espied at no great distance two well-mounted dragoons pacing along the crest of a rising ground, and apparently keeping vigilant watch over the valley of the Nene below. 'A picket!' he added with a grim leer, and a pat on his horse's neck, as the sun glinted back from a dozen of carbines and the same number of steel breastplates drawn up near a clump of trees, where the officer in command flattered himself he was completely hidden from observation. 'Well, they've no call to say nothing to me,' was his concluding remark as he jogged quietly down towards the river-side, affecting as much as possible the air and manner of a groom training a horse about to run for some valuable stake—a process sure to meet with the sympathies of Englishmen, whatever might be their class and creed, and one which even the most rigid Presbyterian would be unwilling to embarrass or interrupt.

It was a good stake, too, that the sorrel was about to run for—a stake of Life and Death, a match against Time, with the course marked out by Chance, and the winning-post placed by Destiny. The steed was sound and trim, his condition excellent, his blood irreproachable; to use the language of Newmarket, would he *stay the distance and get home?*

There was a marshy meadow by the river's brink, which even at this dry season of the year was moist and cool, grateful to the sensations of horse and rider. As the sorrel approached it, he snorted once or twice, erected his ears, and neighed long and loudly. The neigh was answered in more directions than one, for dragoons were patrolling the road in pairs, and no less than two outposts of cavalry were distinctly visible. It seemed as though the war had broken out afresh. Dymocke rode quietly round and round the meadow, apparently attending solely to his horse, and an indefatigable angler, who ought ere this to have caught every fish in the Nene, looked up in a startled manner for an instant, and resumed his sport with redoubled energy and perseverance.

Meanwhile a goodly cavalcade was approaching the half-ruined bridge of Brampton, which here spanned the Nene, and which, although impassable to carriages, admitted of the safe transit of equestrians riding in single file. Bit and bridle rang merrily as the troop wound downwards to the river side; feathers waved, scarfs and cloaks floated gaudily in the breeze, and gay apparel glistened bright in the summer sun. It was the King and his courtiers bound for their afternoon's amusement at Boughton, discoursing as they rode along on every topic save the one that lay deepest in each man's heart, with that mixture of gay sarcasm and profound reflection which was so pleasing to the sovereign's taste, and hazarding opinions with that happy audacity stopping short of freedom which always met with encouragement from the kindly dispositions of the Stuarts.

It seemed to be no captive monarch surrounded by his gaolers that reined his good horse so gallantly in front of the trampling throng; not one of his royal ancestors in the plenitude of his power could have been treated with greater outward show of respect than was Charles by the attendants who spied his

most secret actions, and the commissioners who were
employed by the Parliament to deprive him of his
personal liberty. Old Lord Pembroke, riding on his
right hand a little in rear of the King, bowed his
venerable head to his horse's mane at every observation of his sovereign. The Lords Denbigh and Montague, with the ceremonious grace which they had
acquired years before at Whitehall, remained at the
precise distance prescribed by etiquette from the person of royalty, and conversed when spoken to with
the ready wit of courtiers and the frank bearing of
English noblemen. Doctor Wilson as physician, and
Mr. Thomas Herbert as groom of the bedchamber in
waiting, made up the tale of the King's personal
attendants, whilst servants with led horses, and
one or two yeomen of the guard, completed the
cavalcade.

No armed escort surrounded the King, no outward
display of physical force seemed to coerce his will or
fetter his actions; yet the Parliament had chosen
their emissaries so well that for all their decorous observances and simulation of respect, with the exception of Herbert, not an inhabitant of Holmby House,
from the earl in the presence to the scullion in the
kitchen, but was more or less a traitor to his sovereign.

Charles beckoned his groom of the bedchamber
to ride up alongside, and old Lord Pembroke fell
respectfully to the rear. It might have been remarked, however, that Montague immediately spurred
on and remained within earshot. Herbert was a
favourite with the monarch. His affectionate dispo-

sition was not proof against that fascination which Charles undoubtedly exercised over those with whom he came in daily contact, and a similarity of tastes and habits, a congeniality of disposition between master and servant, each being of a speculative temperament deeply imbued with melancholy, laid the foundation of a friendship which seems to have been a consolation to the one in the darkest hours of adversity, the pride and glory of the other to the latest day of his life.

'What sayest thou, Master Herbert?' said Charles, laying his hand familiarly on the neck of his servant's horse as he paced slowly down towards the bridge. 'Did not the Stoics aver that the wise man is alone a king? and was not their ideal of wisdom the *nil admirari* of the satirist? Did they not hold that it was a quality which made its possessor insensible to pain or pleasure, pity or anger; alike impervious to the sunshine of prosperity as immovable by the storms of adversity; that the wise man knew neither hope nor fear, neither tears nor laughter; that he was essentially all-in-all to himself, and from his very nature equally a prophet, a priest, a cobbler, and a king?'

'Even so, your Majesty,' answered Herbert; 'and it has always appeared to me that the ox browsing contentedly in his pasture, satisfied to eat and drink, and ruminate and die, approaches more nearly to the philosopher's ideal of wisdom, than Socrates with his convictions of the future, and Plato, with his speculations on the soul.'

'Right, Master Herbert,' answered the King, readily losing himself as was his wont in the labyrinth of abstract discussion which he delighted to provoke. 'The two schools of ancient philosophy arrived, but by different paths, at the same destination. "Eat and drink," urges the Epicurean, "for to-morrow you die." "Rest and ponder," quoth the Stoic, "for there is no reality even in life." Either maxim is directly opposed to the whole apparent scheme of the natural world. The one would impress you with the uselessness of sowing your grain; the other convince you of the absurdity of reaping your harvest. Did either really prevail among men, the world could scarce go on a year.

'Doth it not show us that without the light of revelation, our own intrinsic blindness leads us but farther and farther into error? That man, with all his self-sufficient pride, is but a child in leading-strings at his best; that he must have his hopes and fears, his tears and smiles, like a child; and that though he wince from the chastening Hand, it deals its stripes in mercy, after all. Yet, Herbert, have I often found it in my heart to envy these callous natures, too. Would that I could either place complete reliance on Heaven, or steel myself entirely against the anxieties and affections of earth. Would that I could keep down the turbulent heart that rises in wrath against the treatment it feels it has not deserved; that longs so wearily for the absent, that aches so painfully for the dead, that cannot stifle its repinings for the past, nor cease to hope in a future, which becomes every day darker and more threatening. No tidings, and yet no tidings,' proceeded the King, in a lower voice, and musing as it were aloud, whilst his large eyes gazed far ahead into the horizon; 'and yet letters may have been sent, may have been intercepted. I am so watched, so surrounded. Still there might be means. There are loyal hearts left in England, though many are lying cold. Alas, it is a weary, weary world! Yonder is a happy man, Herbert, if you will,' added Charles, brightening up, and once more addressing his conversation to his companion. 'He has not a care for aught but the business in hand. He is a Stoic, a king, a cobbler —what you will. Good faith! he should be a successful fisherman at the worst: I have watched him for the last ten minutes as we rode along. Doth he see kings and courts every day that he hath not once lifted his head from his angle to observe us, or is he indeed the sage of whom we have been talking—the " *sutor bonus et solus formosus, et est rex?*" '

As the King spoke he pointed to an angler who, having taken up a position on Brampton-bridge, had been leaning there immovable, undisturbed by the noise of the approaching cavalcade, and apparently totally devoid of the two sentiments of admiration and curiosity which the neighbourhood of a sovereign is accustomed to provoke.

The man seemed deaf or stupid. He remained leaning against the broken parapet, apparently unconscious of everything but his rod and line, which he watched vigilantly, with his hat drawn over his brows, and his cloak muffling his face to the eyes.

Lord Montague pressed forward to bid the angler stand out of the way, and leave room for Royalty to pass; but the King, who was an admirable horseman, edged his lordship so near the undefended brink of the half-ruined bridge, that Montague was fain to fall back with a bow and an inward thanksgiving that he was not overhead in the river. Etiquette forbade any one else to ride in front of the Sovereign, and Charles was consequently at the head of the party, who now defiled singly across the bridge.

The angler's back was turned, and he fished on without looking round.

'By your leave, good man,' quoth Charles, who, though somewhat haughty, particularly since his reverses, with his nobility, was ever courteous and good-humoured to those of humbler birth : ' there is scant room for us both, and the weakest, well we know, must go to the wall.' While the King spoke, his knee, as he sat in the saddle, touched the back of the preoccupied fisherman.

The latter started and turned round; quick as thought he thrust a small packet into his Majesty's hand, and almost with the same movement flung himself upon his knees at the royal stirrup in a paroxysm of pretended agitation and diffidence as unreal as the negligence for which it affected to atone.

Rapid as was the movement, it sufficed for Charles to recognise his trusty adherent. He crumpled the paper hurriedly into his glove.

' Faithful and true !' he whispered, ' save thyself !' and added aloud, for the edification of his attendants, ' Nay, good man ! we excuse thy rudeness on account of thy bodily infirmity. Look that thou be not trodden down by less skilful riders and less manageable steeds.'

As he spoke the King passed on to the other side,

followed by all his attendants save only the Lord Montague, who had turned back to give directions to a patrol of the Parliamentary cavalry which had arrived at the bridge at the same moment as the Royal cavalcade, and had drawn up to pay the military compliments due to a sovereign.

The patrol, consisting of two efficient-looking dragoons, were remarkably well-mounted, and armed, in addition to sword and pistols, with long deadly carbines. They listened attentively to Lord Montague's directions; and while his lordship rode off in pursuit of the King and his party, scanning the fisherman as he passed him with a strange look of malicious triumph, each soldier unslung his carbine, and shook the powder carefully up into its pan.

The King looked back repeatedly, as he rose the hill, in the direction of Boughton. Once he beckoned Lord Montague to ride alongside of him.

'We thought we had lost your good company, my lord,' quoth his Majesty; 'what made you turn back down yonder by Brampton Mill?'

'I dropped my glove, your Majesty,' replied the nobleman, scarcely concealing a smile.

'Whoever picks it up, my lord, will find a bitter enemy!' answered Charles; and he spoke not another word till he reached the great gates of Lord Vaux's hospitable hall.

Meanwhile the angler, resuming his occupation, fished steadily on, glancing ever and anon at the retreating troop of horsemen who accompanied the King. When the last plumed hat had disappeared over the verge of the acclivity, he took his rod to pieces with a deep sigh of relief; and exchanging his slow listless demeanour for one of resolution and activity, strode briskly away, with the air of a man who has performed a good day's work, and is about to receive for the same a good day's wages.

He thought, now that he had accomplished his task, he would linger about her residence and see Mary Cave once more—just once more—ere he went into exile again. He trusted none, but the King had recognised him; and he had delivered his packet with such secresy and rapidity that he could not conceive it possible for any other eye to have perceived the movement. He little knew Montague's eagle glance. He little knew that, in spite of his disguise, he had been suspected for more than four-and-twenty hours, and that measures had already been taken for his capture. He would know it all time enough. Let him rest for a moment on the thought of his anticipated meeting with his ladye-love. The wished-for two minutes that were to repay the longings and misgivings of as many years, that he must live upon perhaps for another twelvemonth, and be grateful that he has had even such a crumb of comfort for the sustenance of his soul. Strange hunger of the heart, that so little can alleviate, so much fails to satisfy! He walked swiftly on through the fragrant meadows, waving with their long herbage, and bright with buttercups and field-flowers; his head erect, his eye gazing far into the horizon as is ever the glance of those who look forward and not back. Bosville had still a future; he had not yet thoroughly learned the bitterest of all life's lessons—to live only in the past.

No; he was a man still, with a man's trust and hope, a man's courage and self-reliance, a man's energy and endurance. He would want them all before the sun went down. Suddenly a shout smote upon his ear; a voice behind him called on him to stop and surrender. Halting, and turning suddenly round, he beheld a mounted trooper, the tramp of whose horse had been smothered in the long grass, close upon him; another was nearing him from the river side. Both had their carbines unslung, and even in the confusion of the moment he had time to perceive an expression of calm confidence on each man's countenance, as though he was sure of his prey. For an instant his very heart seemed to tighten with a thrill of surprise and keen disappointment; but it was not the first time by a good many that Humphrey had looked a catastrophe in the face, and in that instant he had time to think what he should do. Twenty yards in front of him grew a high luxuriant hedge; in that hedge was a gap fortified by a strong oaken rail. The foremost horseman's hand was almost on his shoulder when he dashed forward and cleared it at a bound. Accustomed to make up his mind in a moment, his first idea was to run under shelter of the fence down to the river, and place the stream between himself and his pursuers, trusting that neither heavily-armed trooper would choose to risk man and horse in deep water. Alas, on the opposite bank he spied another patrol gesticulating to his comrades, and watching for him should he attempt to land. In the mean time his first pursuers, both remarkably well mounted, had ridden their horses boldly over the fence, and were once more close upon his tracks. In another stride he must be struck down and made a prisoner! But, as is often the case, at the supreme moment succour was at hand. Not twenty yards in front of the fugitive stood Hugh Dymocke, holding the sorrel by the bridle. The wily old soldier had anticipated this catastrophe the whole morning, and was not to be taken unawares at the crisis. He had been watching the movements of the fisherman and the patrol, nor, except for a chance shot, had he much fear of the result. With a rush and a bound, like that of some stricken wild deer, Humphrey reached the sorrel and vaulted into the saddle. As he turned the horse's head for the open meadow with a thrill of exultation and delight, Dymocke let go the bridle and hurriedly whispered in his ear, 'God speed ye, master! Never spare him for pace; he had a gallop yesterday, and he's fit to run for a man's life!'

Ere the sentence was finished they were a hundred yards off, and the good horse, flinging his head into the air and snatching wildly at his bridle, indulged in a few bounds and plunges in his gallop ere he settled down into the long sweeping stride his rider remembered so well.

With a bitter curse and a shrewd blow from the butt of his carbine, which Dymocke avoided like a practised tactician, the foremost trooper swept by the old soldier, calling to his comrade in the rear to secure him and take him to head quarters. Both were, however, so intent on the pursuit that Dymocke, greatly to his surprise, found himself totally unnoticed, and walked quietly home with his usual air of staid gravity, reflecting, much to his own satisfaction, on the speed and mettle of his favourite and the probable safety of his young master.

And now the chase began in serious earnest. It was a race for life and death, and the competitors were well aware of the value of the stakes dependent on their own skill and the speed of the horses they bestrode.

Each trooper knew that a large sum of money and speedy promotion would reward his capture of the Royalist, whom they had now succeeded in identifying. Each was mounted on a thoroughly good horse whose powers he had often tested to the utmost, and each was moreover armed to the teeth, whilst the fugitive possessed no more deadly weapon than the butt of his fishing-rod, which he had retained unconsciously in his hand. Being two to one they had also the great advantage of being able to assist each other in the pursuit, and like greyhounds coursing a hare, could turn the quarry wherever opportunity offered into each other's jaws. Despite of broken ground, of blind ditches choked with grass, and high leafy hedges rich in Midsummer luxuriance, through which they crashed, bruising a thousand fragrant blossoms in their transit, they sped fiercely and recklessly on. All along the low grounds by Brampton, where the rich meadows were divided by strong thorn fences, the constantly recurring obstacles compelled Humphrey, bold rider as he was, to diverge occasionally from a straight course, and this was an incalculable advantage to his two pursuers, who, by playing as it were into each other's hands, were enabled to keep within sight and even within shot of the pursued, though the pace at which they were all going forbade any appeal to fire-arms, or indeed to any weapons except the spurs.

But on emerging from the low grounds into a comparatively open country and rising the hill towards Brixworth the greater stride and speed of the sorrel began to tell. His condition, moreover, was far superior to that of the troopers, and it was with a glow of exultation not far removed from mirth, that Humphrey, finding at last a hand to spare with which to caress his favourite, looked back at his toiling pursuers, whose horses were now beginning to show undoubted symptoms of having had enough.

Even in mid-winter, when the leaves are off those formidable blackthorns, and the ditches, cleared of weeds and grass, yawn in all their naked avidity for the reception and ultimate sepulture of the horse and his rider, it is no child's play to cross one of these strongly-fenced Northamptonshire valleys. Ay, with all the fictitious excitement produced by the emulation of hunting, and the insatiable desire to be nearer and nearer still to that fleeting vision which, like happiness, is always just another stride beyond our reach ; though the hounds are streaming silently away a field in front of us; though the good horse between our legs is fresh, ardent, and experienced ; though we have already disposed of our dearest friend on his best hunter at that last ' double,' and are sanguine in our hopes of getting well over yonder strong rail, for which we are even now ' hardening

our heart' and shortening our stride; though we hope
and trust we shall go triumphantly on, from fence to
fence, rejoicing, and at last see the good fox run into
in the middle of a fifty-acre grass field,—yet for all
this we cannot but feel that when we have traversed
two or three miles of this style of country, without
prostration or mishap, we have effected no contemptible
feat of equitation, we have earned for the nonce a consciousness of thorough self-satisfaction intensely gratifying to the vanity of the human heart.   And so perhaps it was one of the pleasantest moment's of Humphrey's life when he pulled the sorrel into a trot and
looked back upon the vale below.   The horse snorted
and shook his head.   He was only breathed by the
gallop that had so distressed the steeds of the two
Parliamentarians.   His master patted him fondly and
exultingly once again.   What a ride he had enjoyed!
how the blood coursed through his veins with the
anxiety, and the excitement, and the exercise.   For
two years he had not mounted what could be called a
horse   certainly not one that could be compared
with the sorrel.   How delightful it was to feel his
favourite bound under him as he used to do, once
more!   What a sensation to speed along those rich
meadows, scanning fence after fence as he approached
it, and flying over the places he had marked out, like
a bird on the wing, to the unspeakable discomfiture of
the dragoons toiling in his track.   How gallantly he
had cleared the rivulet that the two soldiers had been
forced to flounder through.   Well for them that it
had shrunk to its summer limits, or they would have
been there still.   And now in another mile or so he

would be safe. His pursuers' horses were too much exhausted even to continue on his track. They would soon lose all traces of him. Near Brixworth village was a cottage in which he had already passed two or three nights whilst waiting to fulfil his mission. Its owner was a veteran who had fought in his own troop at Edge-hill and Newbury, who would think little of imperilling his life for his old officer and King Charles. Arrived at the cottage, he would disguise himself again, and sending the sorrel out of the way, would lie hid till the search was past; he might then venture a few miles from his hiding-place, and at last reach the seashore and embark scatheless for the Continent. In this manner, too, he would have a chance of seeing Mary once more before he departed.

Trotting gently along, he was thus busily weaving the thread of his schemes and fancies, his hopes and fears, when, alas! the web was suddenly dispelled by a shot! The crafty Parliamentarians finding themselves completely outstripped by the sorrel, and aware of a picket of their comrades stationed close under the village of Brixworth, had turned their attention to driving their quarry as much as possible towards the hill. In this they had been successful, and Humphrey's line of flight had already brought him within a few hundred yards of the enemy's post. As is often the case, however, their strict anxiety to preserve themselves unseen, had somewhat abated the vigilance of their look-out, and Bosville, accidentally changing his direction, narrowly escaped passing the negligent picket without observation or interruption.

But the veterans who pursued him were skilled in all the various practices of war; the leading horseman, quietly dismounting from his jaded steed, slowly levelled his carbine, and took a long roving shot at the fast diminishing figure of the fugitive. The bullet whistled harmlessly over Humphrey's head, but the report roused the inattentive sentry in advance of the picket, and the well-known sound of a trumpet rang out within musket range, whilst a dozen horsemen emerging from a clump of trees not two hundred yards to his right, dashed forward at a gallop, with the obvious intention of intercepting or riding him down.

Unarmed as he was, and notwithstanding the number of his foes, Humphrey never lost heart for a moment.

' Not trapped yet, my lads !' he ground out between his teeth, as with a grim smile he caught the sorrel fast by the head, and urged him once more to his speed, reflecting with fierce exultation on the mettle and endurance of his favourite, still going fresh and strong beneath him, and on the ' neck-or-nothing' nature of the chase, in which his only safety lay in placing some insurmountable obstacle between himself and his pursuers.

They, for their part, seemed determined to make every effort for his capture, dividing into parties so as to cover as large an extent of country as possible, and so prevent any attempt at turning or dodging on the part of the quarry, and forcing him by this means into a line of difficult and broken ground, such as must at last tell even on the power and stride of the indefatigable sorrel. The two original pursuers, moreover, whose horses had by this time recovered their wind, laboured on at a reduced pace along the low grounds, so that a diversion in that direction was impossible.

There was nothing for it but to go straight ahead, and straight ahead he went, laughing a strange wicked laugh to himself, as he thought of the Northern Water, no mean tributary to the Nene, which was even now gleaming in the distance a mile or so in front of him, and reflecting that if he were once well over such a ' yawner' as that, he might trot on and seek safety at his leisure, for not a dozen horses in England could clear it from bank to bank !

He trusted, nevertheless, that the sorrel was one of them. So he spared and nursed him as much as possible, choosing his ground with the practised eye of a sportsman, and bringing into use every one of the many methods which experience alone teaches, and by which the perfect horseman can assist and ease his steed. At the pace he led his pursuers, he cared but little to be out of musket-shot, and he reserved all the energies both of himself and his horse for a dash at the Northern Water.*

Down the hill they come at headlong pace : the troopers, espying Bosville's object, now tax all their

---

* A fair leap in the present day, when, under its later appellation of the ' Brixworth Brook,' it spoils many a silk jacket, as the flower of the British army can testify, who, in their modern substitute for Tilt and Tournament, yclept ' The Grand Military Steeple-Chase,' plunge into its profound with a reckless haste truly edifying to the less adventurous civilian.

energies to catch him ere he can reach the brook, and spurs are plied and bridles shaken with all the mad recklessness of a neck-and-neck race.

Humphrey's spirits rise with the situation. He longs to give vent to his excitement in a wild 'hurrah!' as a man does in a charge, but he is restrained from the fear of maddening his horse, already roused by the shouts and clatter behind him, and pulling harder than his wont. Were he to get the least out of his hand now it would be fatal.

He steadies him gradually till within a hundred yards of the brink, and regardless of his followers' close vicinity, pulls him back almost into a canter—then tightening his grasp on the bridle, and urging him with all the collective energies of knee, and thigh, and loins, he sets him going once more, the horse pointing his small resolute ears, the rider marking with his eye a sedgy patch of the soundest ground from which he intends their effort shall be made.

Straining on his bridle, the sorrel bounds high into the air, the waters flash beneath them, and they are landed safe on the far side with half a foot to spare! Humphrey gives a cheer now, and a hearty cheer it is, in answer to the yell of rage and disappointment that rises from the baffled Parliamentarians.

Was there ever man yet that could 'leave well alone?' Alas! that we should here have to record the only instance of bravado on the part of our hero during the whole of his perilous and adventurous career. What demon prompted him to waste the precious moments in jeering at a defeated foe? Humphrey could not resist the temptation of pulling up to wave an ironical 'farewell' to his pursuers. The movement was fatal; in making it, he turned his broadside to the enemy, and half a dozen carbines were discharged at him on the instant. One bullet truer than the rest found its home in the honest heart of the good sorrel. The horse plunged wildly forward, fell upon his head, recovered himself—fell once more, and rolling over his rider, lay quivering in the last convulsions of death.

When Humphrey had extricated himself from the saddle and risen to his feet, he had no heart to make any further effort for his escape. He might perhaps have still had time to elude his enemies even on foot, but the strongest nature can only resist a given amount of difficulty and disappointment. 'Tis the last drop that bids the cup brim over, the last ounce that sinks the labouring camel in the sand.

He was weak, too, from mental anxiety as from bodily privation, from the conflict of his feelings as from the harassing nature of his task. Brave, generous, hopeful as he was, something seemed to give way within him at this last stroke of fortune, and when his captors, after making a long circuit to cross over by a ford, arrived to take him prisoner, they found him sitting on the ground, with the sorrel's head upon his knees, weeping like a woman or a child over the dead horse he had loved so well.

CHAPTER IX.

'FOR THE KING!'

WE left our honest friend Dymocke, with the sweep of the trooper's carbine still whistling in his ears, sauntering quietly homewards, his grim visage bespeaking more than usual satisfaction, his mental reflections sometimes rising into soliloquy, and taking much such a form as the following.

'Ah! Hugh! Hugh!' quoth the old soldier, apostrophizing the individual whom of all in the world he should have known best, 'there's few of them can hold a candle to thee, old lad! when the tackle's got fairly in a coil. Brave!—there's plenty of 'em brave enough—leastways there's plenty of 'em afraid not to seem so—but it's discretion, lad, it's discretion that's wanting; and thankful ought thou to be, that thou'st gotten enough for thyself and the whole household. There's not a man of 'em, now, could have managed this business, and not made a botch of it! Take the old lord to begin with. He'd have gone threatening and petitioning, and offering money and what not, till the Major was blown just the same as if he'd had him cried in the market. That's the way with your quality; they can't abide to see a thing stand simmering; they must needs go shaking the frying-pan, and then they wonder that all the fat's in the fire! The women! I'll not deny but the women are keen hands at plotting and planning, and many's the good scheme they hit upon, no doubt, but where *they* fail is in the doing of it. It's "not now," or "I'm so frightened!" or a fit of crying just in the nick of time; and then the clock strikes or the bell rings, and it's too late. For the women must either wait too long, or else they'll not wait long enough, so it's as well they wasn't trusted to have anything to do with it. As for the steward, it's my opinion he's a rogue! and a rogue was never good for anything yet that wanted a bit of 'heart' to set it straight; and the rest of 'em's fools one bigger than another, there's no gainsaying *that*.

'No! there was just one man that *could* do it, and he's gone and *done* it. To think of the sense of the dumb animal, too! Never but once did he neigh the whole blessed morning, though there was his master fishing within a pistol-shot of him; and every time he came by the turn of the meadow, he laid his ears back, as much as to say "I see you! I am ready for you when you want me." Ready! I believe he *was* ready. I should know a good horse when I'm on him; but the way he came round the park with me yesterday afternoon—— Oh! it's no use talking. A hawk's one thing, and a round shot's another; but he's the fastest horse in Northamptonshire at this blessed moment, and well he need to be. St. George! to see the example he made of those two! and the Major sitting down upon him so quiet, the way I always told him I liked to see him ride, popping here and popping there, with the horse as steady as a psalm-singer, and every yard they went the soldiers getting farther and farther behind. Well, the ladies will be best pleased to hear the Major's safe off, no doubt of that; and my pretty Faith, she wont cry her eyes out to see *me* come back in a whole skin— poor little woman! she hasn't the nerves of a hen. It was a precious coil, surely, and precious well I've got 'em all out of it. There's few things that can't be done by a man of discretion, 'specially when he's got the care of such a horse as *that!*'

Dymocke had arrived at home by the time he reached this conclusion. His self-satisfaction was unbounded. His triumph complete. It was well for him that his powers of vision were limited by distance—that he possessed no intuitive knowledge of the events of the day. It would have broken honest Hugh down altogether to know that the good sorrel was lying within four miles of him, down there by the Northern Water, with a bullet through his heart.

But the news he brought was right gladly received by every one of the anxious inhabitants of the old house at Boughton.

'Safe!' shouted Sir Giles with a loud 'hurrah!' that shook the very rafters of the hall. 'Ay! safe enough, no doubt, with that good horse beneath him, if he did but get a fair start! We'll drink the sorrel's health, my lord, this very night, after the King's.'

'Safe!' echoed Lord Vaux: 'delivered out of the jaws of death. Blood has been shed more than enough in these disastrous times, and I thank a merciful Providence that his young life has been spared.'

'Safe!' repeated Grace Allonby, with a sparkling glance at her father, and the old smile dimpling her triumphant face. 'Far out of danger by this time, and perhaps not recognised, after all.'

'Safe!' whispered Mary Cave, keeping out of observation as much as possible, her hands clasped tight upon her bosom, and her eyes looking up to heaven, filled with tears.

When the intelligence thus reached them, the party were assembled in the great hall immediately subsequent to the King's departure. Whilst honoured by the presence of Royalty, Dymocke had no opportunity of communicating with any of the family, and being, as he himself opined, a particularly discreet individual, he wisely abstained from dropping the slightest hint of his errand that might in any way compromise his employers, or afford a clue to his connexion with the fugitive fisherman.

Even Faith was not esteemed worthy of his confidence till he had made his report to her superiors; and to do her justice, that deserving damsel was so much taken up by the presence of Royalty, and her own multifarious duties of assisting to provide refreshments for the attendants who waited on the King, that the only notice she vouchsafed her admirer was a saucy inquiry as to whether 'he had been courting all the morning?' to which Hugh replied with a grim leer, 'It was like enough, since he confidently expected to be married next month;' whereat she blushed, and bade him 'go about his business,' returning with much composure to the prosecution of a demure flirtation, on which she had even now entered, with a solid and sedate yeoman of the guard.

The King's visit was short and ceremonious enough. His manner to Lord Vaux and Sir Giles Allonby was as gracious as usual, the few words he addressed to the young ladies kindly and paternal as his wont; but his Majesty was evidently pre-occupied and ill at ease! The intelligence he had that morning received from Mary harassed and disturbed him, though indeed, somewhat to her surprise, he had made no further allusion to it, and indeed addressed but a few commonplace remarks to that lady.

It was evident to her that he was brooding over the threatened violation of his personal liberty, which was in effect about to take place that same night, and that this apprehension united with other causes to make him very anxious and unhappy. The letter from the Queen, which Humphrey had delivered at such risk, was also unsatisfactory and distressing. He had looked for this epistle for weeks, and when it came at last, behold! he had been happier not to have received it.

It is often thus with subjects as well as kings.

Under these circumstances, Charles was unable, according to his custom, to forget all other considerations in the trifles on which he was immediately employed—could not as usual throw himself heart and soul into the fluctuations of the game, as though life offered no other interests than a bowl and bias— did not, even for the short half-hour of his relaxation, succeed in stilling the bitter consciousness that he was a prisoner, though a king.

With his usual grave demeanour and mild dignified bearing, he played one set with the old Earl of Pembroke and a few others of his *suite*, Lord Vaux and Sir Giles Allonby standing by to hand his Majesty the implements of the game, and then taking his leave with sad and gentle courtesy, the Monarch called for his horses to depart, resisting his host's humble entreaties that he would re-enter the house and partake of a collation ere he rode.

Walking down the terrace to the gate at which his horses awaited him, accompanied by Lord Vaux and the two ladies, and followed at the prescribed distance by his personal attendants, a damask rose-tree, ou which Mary had expended much time and care, caught the King's attention, and elicited his admiration, tinged as usual with the prophetic melancholy that imbued his temperament.

'"Tis a fair tree and a fragrant,' observed Charles, stopping in his progress; 'grateful to those who, like myself, love the simple beauties of a garden better than the pomps and splendours of a Court. In faith, the husbandman's is a happier lot than the king's. Yet hath he, too, his anxieties and his disappointments. Frosts nip the hopes of his earliest blossoms; and the pride even of successful maturity is but the commencement of decay.'

As the King spoke, Mary, from an impulse she could not resist, plucked the handsomest flower from its stem, and presented it to her Sovereign. He accepted it with the grave courtesy peculiar to him.

'If we ever meet at Whitehall, Mistress Mary,'

said Charles, with his melancholy smile, 'neither you nor I will forget the blood-red rose presented to me this day by the most loyal of all my loyal subjects. Had other hearts been true as yours,' he added, in a low solemn voice, 'I had not been a mimic king, soon to lose even the shade and semblance of royalty.'

As he spoke, with a courtly obeisance he mounted his horse and departed, riding slowly and dejectedly, as though loth to return to his Palace, where he already anticipated the insults and humiliations to which he was about to be subjected.

She coloured deeply with gratified pride, and a sense of duty strenuously and consistently fulfilled. Poor Mary! it was the last act of homage she was destined ever to pay the Sovereign in whose cause she would cheerfully have laid down her life. The damask-rose was fresh, and bright, and fragrant—the very type of beauty and prosperity, and a worm was eating it away, silently and surely, at the core.

After the King's departure, however, Dymocke's intelligence was imparted to rejoice the hearts of the somewhat dejected Royalists. When people are thoroughly 'broken in,' so to speak, and accustomed to misfortune, it is wonderful how small a gleam of comfort serves to shed a light upon their track, and dissipate the gloom to which they have become habituated. Everything goes by comparison, and a scrap of broken meat is a rich feast to a starving man; nevertheless, the process of training to this enviable state is painful in the extreme.

So the ladies sauntered out into the park, and enjoyed the balmy summer afternoon, and the luxuriant summer fragrance of leaf and blossom, and the hum of the summer insects all astir in the warmth of June. Grace laughed out merrily, as she used to do years ago; and Mary's step was lighter, her cheek rosier than it had been of late as they discoursed. The King's visit, and the peculiarities of the courtiers, formed their natural topics of conversation; but each lady felt a weight taken from her heart, and a sensation of inexpressible relief which had nothing to do with kings or courtiers, save in as far as the actions of those important personages affected the fortunes of one Major Humphrey Bosville.

We must now return to that adventurous gentleman, gradually awakening to a sense of his situation as he sat on a raw-boned troop-horse between two stern-visaged Roundhead dragoons, his elbows strapped tight to his sides, his feet secured beneath his horse's belly; and notwithstanding such impediments to activity, his attempts to escape, if indeed any were practicable, threatened with instant death by his rigorous custodians.

The Major accepted it as a compliment that not less than eight men and a sergeant were esteemed a sufficient force to secure the person of the unarmed fisherman. This formidable escort was commanded by his old acquaintance, 'Ebenezer the Gideonite,' who still slung his carbine across his back in the manner that had once saved his life; and who, to do him justice, bore his old antagonist not the slightest malice for his own discomfiture on that occasion. It was composed, moreover, of picked men and horses from the very flower of the Parliamentary cavalry.

Humphrey rode in the midst of them, and tried to recal his scattered senses, and realize the emergency of his present position.

Weak and worn-out, we have already said that after his horse was shot he had fallen an easy prey to his pursuers. When brought before the officer in command of the party that had captured him, he was neither in a mood nor a condition to answer any questions that might be put. The subaltern's orders, however, seemed sufficiently peremptory to absolve him from the vain task of cross-examining a fainting and unwilling prisoner. In the event of capturing a certain mysterious agent described, he was strictly enjoined to forward him at once to the Parliament, with as much secresy and dispatch as was consistent with the security of the captive. So after providing Humphrey with the food and drink of which he stood so much in need, and suffering him to take a short interval of repose, whilst men were mustered and horses fed, the officer started prisoner and escort without delay on the road to London.

Thus it came to pass that while Grace Allonby and Mary Cave were taking their afternoon stroll through the park at Boughton, Humphrey Bosville and his escort were winding slowly down the hill on the high road to the metropolis.

The Major's eye brightened as he caught sight of their white dresses, and recognised the form of the woman he had loved so long and so dearly. He started with an involuntary gesture that brought the hands of his guardians to trigger and sword-hilt. Although at a distance, it was something to see her just once again.

The ladies were turning homewards when, startled by the tramp of horses, both were aware of an armed party advancing in their immediate vicinity. An unconsicous presentiment prompted each at the same moment to stop and see the troop pass by. The captive's heart leapt within him as he rode near enough to scan every lineament of the dear face he might never hope to look upon again.

'They have a prisoner!' exclaimed Mary, turning as white as her dress. 'God's mercy! it is Humphrey.'

Not another word did either speak. They looked blankly in each other's faces, and Grace burst into a flood of tears.

CHAPTER X.

'THE BEGINNING OF THE END.'

THE soft June night sank peacefully upon Holmby Palace, with all its conflicting interests, all its complications of intrigue and treachery, as it sank upon the yeoman's adjoining homestead, and the shepherd's humble cottage in the vale below. The thrush had finished the last sweet tones of her protracted even-song, and not a sound disturbed the surrounding stillness, save an occasional note from the nightingale in the copse, and the murmur of a fountain playing drowsily on in the garden. Calmly the stars shone out in mellow lustre, looking down, as it seemed, mild and reproachful on the earth-worms here below. What are all the chances and changes, all the sorrows and struggles, of poor grovelling mortality in the sight of those spirit eyes? Age after age have they glimmered on, careless as now of man's engrossing troubles and man's predestined end. They shone on Naseby-field, whitening in their faint light, here a grinning skull, there a bleached and fleshless bone turned up by the hind's careless ploughshare, or the labourer's busy spade, as they shone on Holmby Palace, stately in its regal magnificence, sheltering under its roof a circle of plotting courtiers, with a doomed King; and their beams fell the same on both, cold, pitiless, and unvarying. What are they, these

myriads of flaming spheres? Are they worlds? are
they inhabited? are they places of probation, of
reward, of punishment? are they solid anthracite, or
but luminous vapour? material masses, or only an
agglomeration of particles? Can their nature be
grasped by the human intellect, or defined in the
jargon of science? Oh for the child's sweet simple
faith once more, that they are but chinks in the floor
of Heaven, from which the light of eternal day shines
through!

The King was preparing to retire for the night.
Notwithstanding all the anxieties and apprehensions
that had arisen from the warning he had that morning received, notwithstanding the reception of his
Queen's letter—a document by no means calculated
to soothe his feelings or alleviate his distress—the
force of habit was so strong that the numerous preparations for his Majesty's 'coucher' were made with as
scrupulous an attention to the most trifling minutiæ
as when he was indued with all the pomp of real
royalty and conscious of actual power long ago at
Whitehall.

After 'the word for the night' had been given, a
word which it seemed a mockery to ask the prisoner
himself to select, and the other attendants had been
dismissed, after Doctor Wilson had paid his customary
visit and received to his respectful inquiries the customary answer that nothing was amiss with the royal
health, preserved as it was by rigid and undeviating
temperance, Mr. Herbert, as groom-in-waiting, presented the King with an ewer and cloth, making at
the same time the prescribed obeisance, and setting a

night-lamp, consisting of a round cake of wax in a silver basin on a chair, proceeded himself to retire to the couch prepared for him in a small ante-room opening into the apartment occupied by his Majesty, so that the King might not, even in the watches of the night, be left entirely alone.

We have often thought that this habit of being constantly, to a certain extent, before the public, may account in a great measure for the fortitude and dignity so often displayed in critical moments by sovereigns who have never before been suspected of possessing these Spartan virtues. Never, like a humbler individual, in his most unguarded hours of privacy entirely throwing off the character which it is his duty to sustain, a sovereign, even a weak-minded one, acquires a habit of reticence and self-command which becomes at last second nature; and he who is every day of his life obliged to appear a hero to his *valet de chambre*, finds little difficulty in sustaining the part to which he is so well accustomed under the gaze of a multitude, even in a moment of general confusion and dismay.

As Herbert backed respectfully from the room, the King recalled him, as though for a few minutes' confidential conversation.

'Herbert,' said he, taking up at the same time his jewelled George and Garter, which, with his customary attention to trifles, he insisted should be placed near his bed-head, 'Herbert, you are becoming negligent; you have omitted to lay these gauds—empty vanities that they are!—in their accustomed place.　Also this morning you neglected to observe the command I gave last night.'

His Majesty spoke with a grave and somewhat haughty air, which concealed a covert smile.

The attendant, in some confusion and no little surprise at the unusual displeasure of the King's tone, admitted that he had aroused his Majesty five minutes too late, and pleaded in extenuation the usual excuse of a discrepancy amongst the clocks.　The King preserved an ominous frown.

'You are aware,' said he, 'that I never pardon a fault, nor overlook even the most trifling mistake. Have you not often heard me called harsh, vindictive, and exacting?　I have prepared your punishment; I trust it will admonish you for the future. Here is a gold watch,' he added, his assumed displeasure vanishing at once in a hearty burst of laughter at the scared expression of his attendant's countenance, 'a gold alarm-watch, which as there may be cause shall awake you.　Wear it for Charles Stuart's sake; and years hence, perhaps when he is no more, may it remind you of the stern, unkindly sovereign, who, albeit he valued to the utmost the affection and fidelity of his servant, could not pass over the slightest omission without some such token of his displeasure as this.'

So speaking, and good-humouredly pushing Herbert from the room, he bade him a cordial ' goodnight,' leaving his groom of the bedchamber more devoted to his person, if possible, than before.

Such was one among many instances of Charles's benevolent disposition; such little acts of kindness as this endeared him to all with whom he came in daily contact, and the charm of such a temperament accounts at once for the blind devotion on the part of his followers, commanded by one who was the most amiable and accomplished of private gentlemen, as he was the most injudicious and inefficient of kings.

Musing upon the fortunes of his master, and regretting in his affectionate nature his own powerlessness to aid the sinking monarch, Herbert fell into a broken and disturbed slumber, from which, however, he soon awoke, and observed, somewhat to his dismay, that the King's chamber was in perfect darkness. The door of communication being left open, in case his services should be required during the night, the attendant's first impulse was to rise and re-light the lamp, which he concluded had been accidentally extinguished. He was loth, however, to disturb the King's rest, and whilst debating the point in his own mind, fell off to sleep. After a short slumber, he was again aroused by the King's voice calling to him, and was surprised to see that the lamp had been rekindled.

'Herbert,' said his master, 'I am restless, and cannot sleep. Thou wilt find a volume on yonder table; read to me, I prithee, for a space. It may be the good bishop's discourses will lull me to repose. Thou, too, art wakeful and watchful. I thank thee for thy vigilance in so readily rekindling my light, which had gone out.'

Herbert expressed his surprise.

'I have not entered your Majesty's chamber,' said

he. 'I have never left my couch since I lay down; but being restless, I observed your Majesty's room was dark, and when I woke even now reproached myself that your Majesty must have risen to perform a duty that should have devolved upon your servant.'

'I also awoke in the night,' replied the King, 'and took notice that all was dark. To be fully satisfied, I put by the curtain to look at the lamp. Some time after I found it light, and concluded then that thou hadst risen and set it upon the basin lighted again.'

Herbert assured his Majesty it was not so.

Charles smiled, and his countenance assumed that mystical and rapt expression it so often wore.

'I consider this,' said he, 'as a prognostic of God's future favour and mercy towards me and mine—that although I am at this time so eclipsed, yet either I or they may shine out bright again!'

Even as he spoke a loud knocking was heard at the outer door, communicating as it did with a back staircase that led to a private entrance into the court. Sounds of hurry and confusion at the same time pervaded the palace, and the tramp of horses mingled with the clash of steel, was distinctly audible outside the walls. Major-General Browne's voice was heard, too, above the confusion, calling on the few yeomen of the guard and other officials who formed the garrison to 'stand to their arms,' exhorting them at the same time to preserve the King's person from injury, and the majesty of the Parliament, as represented by the Commissioners, from insult. Meantime, Mawl,

Maxwell, and Harrington, all personal attendants of the Sovereign, rushed to his bedchamber, scared, pale, and half-dressed, but ready, if need were, to sacrifice their lives in defence of the King.

Charles alone preserved his usual composure. The knocking at the door of his private apartments being violently repeated, he desired Maxwell to hold converse with this unmannerly disturber of his repose. Reconnoitring the assailant through a panelling in the door, the old courtier was horrified to observe a Cornet of the Parliamentary dragoons standing at the head of the stairs in complete armour, with a cocked pistol in his hand, and clamouring for admittance.

The dialogue was carried on with a military sternness and brevity shocking to the prejudices of the Gentleman-Usher, more accustomed to the circumlocutions of diplomacy and the compliments of a Court.

'What would you?' inquired Maxwell, through the panelling. 'Who are you, and by whose orders do you come here?'

The Cornet was a stout, resolute-looking man, with all the appearance of having risen from the ranks. His voice was deep and harsh, his countenance of that dogged nature which sets argument and persuasion alike at defiance. His answers were short and categorical.

'I would see Charles Stuart,' he replied. 'My name is Joyce, Cornet in the service of the Parliament. I am here on my own responsibility.'

'Have you the authority of the Commissioners for

your intrusion?' gasped out Maxwell, totally aghast at the unheard-of breach of etiquette, in which he felt himself aiding and abetting.

'No!' thundered the Cornet; 'I have placed a sentry at the door of every man of them. Keep quiet, old gentleman—I take my orders from them that fear neither Commissioners nor Parliament.'

In effect, the Cornet's entrance into Holmby House, and his rapid occupation of every post in its vicinity, as of the palace itself, had been achieved in a masterly manner that showed him to be no inexperienced practitioner in war.

With a numerous body of cavalry at his disposal, he had been all day occupied in concentrating them silently and stealthily around the beleaguered palace. His main body had that afternoon bivouacked on Harleston Heath, strong pickets had been placed in every secluded spot which admitted of concealment within a circuit of a few miles, and constant patrols had been watching every road by which an escape from Holmby was practicable. As darkness fell he had pushed forward his several posts to one common centre, and by the hour of midnight a summer moon shone down on the court-yard of Holmby Palace, filled with a mass of iron-clad cavalry, whose numbers rendered resistance hopeless and impossible.

Colonel Graves and General Browne, however, two old Parliamentary officers, seemed to have had some inkling that an attack was meditated: for without any apparent reason they had doubled the guards around the King's person, and contrary to their wont had remained astir till midnight. When the first files of the approaching cavalry marched into the court, they had called upon the handful of soldiers and yeomen that formed the garrison to resist to the death, and had themselves held a parley with the redoubtable Cornet. When asked his name and business, he had replied, with the same bluntness that so discomfited Maxwell, that 'his name was Joyce, Cornet in Colonel Whalley's regiment of horse, and his business was to speak with the King.'

'From whom?' said Browne, with rising indignation.

From myself!' replied the Cornet, with provoking coolness.

The two old soldiers burst into a derisive laugh.

'It's no laughing matter,' said the unabashed intruder; 'I came not hither to be advised by you, nor have I any business with the Commissioners. My errand is to the King, and speak with him I must and will.'

'Stand to your arms,' exclaimed Browne, to the handful of soldiers inside the palace : but these had in the meantime held some conference with the intruders, and finding that they all belonged to the same party, and that several were old comrades who had charged together many a day under the same banner, they refused to act against their friends, and drawing bolts and bars, admitted them without further parley, bidding them welcome, and shaking them cordially by the hand.

Thus it was that the Cornet obtained admittance even to the very door of his Majesty's bedchamber. A certain sense of propriety, however, which almost always accompanies the responsibility of a command, forbade him from offering any further violence, and with a most ungracious acquiescence he consented to leave the King undisturbed till morning, stipulating, however, that he should himself take up a position for the night on the staircase, which in effect he did, being with difficulty persuaded to lay down his fire-arms and return his sword to its sheath.

Charles sought his couch once more in that frame of placid helplessness which seems usually to have taken possession of him when in the crisis of a difficulty. He slept soundly, and awoke with characteristic regularity, little before his ordinary hour. His toilet was performed with elaborate care, his devotions not curtailed of a single interjection, his poached egg and glass of fair water leisurely discussed, and then, but not till then, his Majesty expressed his readiness to hold an interview with the personage who seemed to have power of life and death over his Sovereign.

The King's simplicity of manner, and quiet dignified bearing overawed even the rough and low-born officer of the Parliament. Half ashamed of his insolence, half bullying himself into his naturally offensive demeanour, Cornet Joyce was ushered into the presence with a far different aspect from that which he had assumed the night before. Such is the innate dignity afforded by true nobility of soul, that Charles and his captor seemed to have changed places. The King appearing to be the offended though placable judge, the Cornet wearing the sullen, apprehensive, and abashed look of a guilty prisoner.

Charles's good-nature, however, soon restored the official to his self-possession, and by an easy transition, to a large portion of his original insolence. In reply to the monarch's gentle interrogative as to the cause of the last night's outrage, he answered boldly, 'My orders are to remove your Majesty at once, without further delay.'

This frank avowal created no small dismay in the little circle then assembled in his Majesty's outer apartment. Herbert turned pale, and trembled. Maxwell, as red as fire, seemed to doubt the evidence of his senses; whilst General Browne, stepping aside into the recess of a window, swore fearfully for five consecutive minutes in tones not loud but deep.

The King remained totally unmoved.

'Let the Commissioners be sent for,' said he, with a dignified air, 'and let these orders be communicated to them.'

The Cornet was fast recovering his former audacity. 'I have taken measures with them already,' said he; 'they are in watch and ward even now, and must return, will they, nill they, to the Parliament.'

'By whose authority?' demanded the King, sternly, but with visible uneasiness.

The Cornet shook his head, laughed rudely, and pointed with his forefinger to his own coarse person.

'I would ask you, sir, as a favour,' said the King, 'to set them at liberty; and I demand, as a right,' he added, drawing himself up, and flushing with a sense of impotent anger and outraged dignity, 'to be permitted a sight of your instructions.'

'That is easily done,' answered Joyce, 'if your Majesty will take the trouble to step as far as this window.'

And opening the casement, he pointed into the court-yard below, where indeed was drawn up as goodly a squadron of cavalry as the whole Parliamentary army could boast, well armed, well mounted, bold and bronzed, with stalwart frames and stern, unflinching faces, possessed, moreover, of the self-confidence and disciplined valour inspired by a career of hard-won victories. They were the same material, some of them the same men, that confronted Charles at Edge Hill, routed him at Marston Moor, and finally vanquished him at Naseby. The finest cavalry in the world, and, bitterest thought of all, his own subjects. The King's heart was sore as he looked down into the court, but he had played the part of royalty too long not to know how to dissemble his feelings, and he turned to the Cornet with a smile as he said,

'Your instructions, sir, are in fair characters, and legible without spelling. The language, though somewhat forcible, is sufficiently intelligible, and admits of no further argument. I am ready to attend your good pleasure, with this proviso, that I stir not unless accompanied by the Commissioners. You have had your audience, sir; you may withdraw.'

The Cornet, somewhat to his own surprise, found himself making a respectful obeisance and retiring forthwith; but the King's coach was ordered to be got in readiness without delay, and that very day Charles

Stuart, accompanied, as he had stipulated, by the Commissioners, commenced the journey which led him, stage by stage, to his final resting-place—the fatal window at Whitehall—the scaffold and the block.

CHAPTER XI.

'THE BEACON AFAR.'

'EBENEZER the Gideonite' was no bad specimen of the class he represented—the sour-visaged, stern, and desperate fanatic, who allowed no consideration of fear or mercy to turn him from the path of duty; whose sense of personal danger as of personal responsibility was completely swallowed up in his religious enthusiasm; who would follow such an officer as George Ellingham into the very jaws of death; and of whom such a man as Cromwell knew how to make a rare and efficient instrument. Ebenezer's orders were to hold no communication with his prisoner, to neglect no precaution for his security; and having reported his capture to the general in command at Northampton, to proceed at least one stage further on his road to London ere he halted for the night.

Humphrey's very name was consequently unknown to the party who had him in charge. As he had no papers whatever upon his person when captured, the subaltern in command of the picket at Brixworth had considered it useless to ask a question to which it was so easy to give a fictitious answer; and Ebenezer, although recognising him personally as an old acquaintance, had neglected to ascertain his name even after their first introduction by means of the flat of the Cavalier's sabre. Though his back had tingled for weeks from the effects of a blow so shrewdly administered; though he had every opportunity of learning the style and title of the prisoner whom he had helped to bring before Cromwell at his head-quarters; yet, with an idiosyncrasy peculiar to the British soldier, and a degree of Saxon indifference amounting to stupidity, he had never once thought of making inquiry as to who or what was this hard-hitting Malignant that had so nearly knocked him off his horse in the Gloucestershire lane.

Erect and vigilant, he rode conscientiously close to his prisoner, eyeing him from time to time with looks of curiosity and interest, and scanning his figure from head to heel with obvious satisfaction. Not a word, however, did he address to the captive; his conversation, such as it was, being limited to a few brief sentences interchanged with his men, in which Scriptural phraseology was strangely intermingled with the language of the stable and the parade-ground. Strict as was the discipline insisted on amongst the Parliamentary troops by Cromwell and his officers, the escort, as may be supposed, followed the example of their superior with stern faces and silent tongues; they rode at 'attention,' their horses well in hand, their weapons held in readiness, and their eyes never for an instant taken off the horseman they surrounded.

Humphrey, we may easily imagine, was in no mood to enter into conversation. He had indeed enough food for sad forebodings and bitter reflections. Wild and adventurous as had been his life for many weeks

past—always in disguise, always apparently on the
eve of discovery, and dependent for his safety on the
fidelity of utter strangers, often of the meanest class
—not a day had elapsed without some imminent
hazard, some thrilling alternation of hope and fear.
But the events of the last few hours had outdone
them all. To have succeeded in his mission!—to
have escaped when escape seemed impossible, and
then to fail at the last moment, when safety had been
actually gained!—it seemed more like some wild and
feverish dream than a dark hopeless reality. And
the poor sorrel! How sincerely he mourned for the
good horse; how well he had always carried him;
how gentle and gallant and obedient he was; how he
turned to his master's hand and sprang to his master's
voice. How fond he was of him; and to think of
him lying dead yonder by the water-side! It was
hard to bear.

Strange how a dumb animal can wind itself round
the human heart! What associations may be connected with a horse's arching crest or the intelligent
glance of a dog's eye. How they can bring back to
us the happy 'long, long ago;' the magic time that
seems brighter and brighter as we contemplate it from
a greater and greater distance; how they can recal
the soft tones and kindly glances that are hushed,
perhaps, and dim for evermore : perhaps, the bitterest
stroke of all, estranged and altered now. 'Love me,
love my dog!'—there never was a truer proverb.
Ay! love my dog, love my horse, love all that came
about me; the dress I wore, the words I have spoken,

the very ground I trod upon,—but do not be surprised that horse and dog, and dress and belongings, all are still the same, and I alone am changed.

So Humphrey loved the sorrel, and grieved for him sincerely. The rough Puritan soldiers could understand his dejection. Many a charger's neck was caressed by a rough hand on the march, as the scene by the Northern Water presented itself vividly to the dragoons' untutored minds; and though the vigilance of his guardians was unimpeachable, their bearing towards Humphrey was all the softer and more deferential that these veteran soldiers could appreciate his feelings and sympathize with his loss.

He had but one drop of comfort, one gleam of sunshine now, and even that was dashed with bitter feelings of pique and a consciousness of unmerited neglect. He had seen Mary once again. He liked to think, too, that she must have recognised him; must have been aware of his critical position; must have known that he was being led off to die.

'Perhaps even her hard heart will ache,' thought the prisoner, 'when she thinks of her handiwork. Was it not for her sake that I undertook this fatal duty—for her sake that I have spent years of my life in exile, risked that life ungrudgingly a thousand times, and shall now forfeit it most unquestionably to the vengeance of the Parliament? Surely, surely, if she is a woman, she must be anxious and unhappy now.'

It was a strange morbid sensation, half of anger, half of triumph; yet through it all a tear stole to his eye from the fond heart that could not bear to think the woman he loved should suffer a moment's uneasiness even for his sake.

Silently they rode on till they reached Northampton town. The good citizens were too much inured to scenes of violence, too well accustomed to the presence of the Parliamentary troops, to throw away much attention on so simple an event as the arrival of an escort with a prisoner. Party-feeling, too, had become considerably weakened since the continued successes of the Parliament. Virtually the war was over, and the Commons now represented the governing power throughout the country. The honest townsmen of Northampton were only too thankful to obtain a short interval of peace and quiet for the prosecution of 'business'—that magic word, which speaks so eloquently to the feelings of the middle class in England—and as their majority had from the very commencement of the disturbances taken the popular side in the great civil contest, they could afford to treat their fallen foes with mercy and consideration.

Unlike his entry on a previous occasion into the good city of Gloucester, Humphrey found his present plight the object neither of ridicule nor remark. The passers-by scarce glanced at him as he rode along, and the escort closed round him so vigilantly that a careless observer would hardly have remarked that the troop encircled a prisoner.

In consequence of their meditated movement against the King's liberty, the Parliament had concentrated a large force of all arms at Northampton, and the usually smiling and peaceful town presented the ap-

pearance of enormous barracks. Granaries, manufac-
tories, and other large buildings were taken up for
the use of soldiers; troop-horses were picketed in the
streets, and a park of artillery occupied the market-
place; whilst the best houses of the citizens, somewhat
to the dissatisfaction of their owners, were appropri-
ated by the superior officers of the division. In one
of the largest of these George Ellingham had established himself. An air of military simplicity and
discipline pervaded the general's quarters: sentries,
steady and immovable as statues, guarded the
entrance; a strong escort of cavalry occupied an adjoining building, once a flour-store, now converted
into a guard-house. Grave upright personages, distinguished by their orange scarfs as officers of the
Parliament, stalked to and fro, intent on military
affairs, here bringing in their reports, there issuing
forth charged with orders; but one and all affecting
an austerity of demeanour which yet somehow sat
unnaturally upon buff coat and steel head-piece. The
general himself seemed immersed in business. Seated
at a table covered with papers, he wrote with unflinching energy, looking up, it is true, ever and anon
with a weary abstracted air, but returning to his work
with renewed vigour after every interruption, as
though determined by sheer force of will to keep his
mind from wandering off its task.

An orderly-sergeant entered the room, and, standing at 'attention,' announced the arrival of an escort
with a prisoner.

The general looked up for a moment from his papers,

'Send in the officer in command to make his report,' said he, and resumed his occupation.

Ebenezer stalked solemnly into the apartment: gaunt and grim, he stood bolt upright and commenced his narrative:

'I may not tarry by the way, General,' he began, 'for verily the time is short and the night cometh in which no man can work; even as the day of grace, which passeth like the shadow on the sun-dial ere a a man can say, Lo! here it cometh, or lo! there.'

Effingham cut him short with considerable impatience. 'Speak out, man,' he exclaimed, 'and say what thou'st got to say, with a murrain to thee! Dost think I have nought to do but sit here and listen to the prating of thy fool's tongue?'

Ebenezer was one of those preaching men of war who never let slip an opportunity of what they termed 'improving the occasion;' but our friend George's temper, which the unhappiness and uncertainty of the last few years had not tended to sweeten, was by no means proof against such an infliction. The subordinate perceived this, and endeavoured to condense his communication within the bounds of military brevity, but the habit was too strong for him: after a few sentences he broke out again—

'I was ordered by Lieutenant Allgood to select an escort of eight picked men and horses, and proceed in charge of a prisoner to London. My instructions were to pass through Northampton, reporting myself to General Effingham by the way, and to push on a stage further without delay ere I halted my party for the night. With regard to the prisoner, the captive, as indeed I may say, of our bow and spear, who fell a prey to us under Brixworth, even as a bird falleth a prey to the fowler, and who trusted in the speed of his horse to save him in the day of wrath, as these Malignants have ever trusted in their snortings and their prancings, forgetting that it hath been said—'

'Go to the devil, sir!' exclaimed George Ellingham, with an energy of impatience that completely dissipated the thread of the worthy sergeant's discourse; 'are you to take up my time standing preaching there, instead of attending to your duty? You have your orders, sir; be off, and comply with them. Your horses are fresh, your journey before you, and the sun going down. I shall take care that the time of your arrival in London is reported to me, and woe be to you if you " tarry by the way," as you call it in your ridiculous hypocritical jargon. To the right— face!'

It was a broad hint that in an orderly-room admitted of but one interpretation. Ebenezer's instincts as a soldier predominated over his temptations as an orator, and in less than five minutes he was once more in the saddle, wary and vigilant, closing his files carefully round the captured Royalist as they wound down the stony street in the direction of the London road.

George Ellingham returned to his writing, and with a simple memorandum of the fact that a prisoner had been reported to him as under escort for London, dismissed the whole subject at once from his mind.

Thus it came to pass that the two friends, as still they may be called, never knew that they were within

a hundred paces of each other, though in how strange
a relative position; never knew that a chance word,
an incident however trifling, that had betrayed the
name of either, would have brought them together,
and perhaps altered the whole subsequent destinies of
each.   George never suspected that the nameless
prisoner, reported to him as a mere matter of form,
under the charge of Ebenezer, was his old friend
Humphrey Bosville; nor could the Cavalier Major
guess that the General of Division holding so important a command as that of Northampton, was none
other than his former comrade and captain, dark
George Effingham.

The latter worked hard till nightfall. It was his
custom now. He seemed never so uneasy as when in
repose. He acted like a traveller who esteems all time
wasted but that which tends to the accomplishment of
his journey. Enjoying the confidence of Cromwell
and the respect of the whole army, won, in despite of
his antecedents, by a career of cool and determined
bravery, he seemed to be building up for himself a
high and influential station, stone by stone as it were,
and grudging no amount of sacrifice, no exertion to
raise it, if only by an inch. The enthusiasm of
George's temperament was counterbalanced by sound
judgment and a highly perspicuous intellect, and consequently the tendency to fanaticism which had
first impelled him to join the Revolutionary party,
had become considerably modified by all he saw and
heard, when admitted to the councils of the Parliament, and better acquainted with their motives and
opinions. He no longer deemed that such men as

Fairfax, Ireton, even Cromwell, were directly inspired by Heaven, but he could not conceal from himself that their energies and abilities were calculated to win for them the high places of the earth. He knew, moreover, none better, the strength and the weaknesses of either side, and he could not doubt for a moment which must become the dominant party. If not a better, the *ci-devant* Cavalier had become unquestionably a wiser man, and having determined in his own mind which of the contending factions was capable of saving the country, and which was obviously on the high road to power, he never now regretted for an instant that he had joined its ranks, nor looked back as Bosville would have done under similar circumstances, with a wistful longing to all the illusions of romance and chivalry which shed a glare over the downfall of the dashing Cavaliers. Effingham's, we need hardly say, was a temperament of extraordinary perseverance and unconquerable resolution. He had now proposed to himself a certain aim and end in life. From the direction which led to its attainment he never swerved one inch, as he never halted for an instant by the way. He had determined to win a high and influential station. Such a station as should at once silence all malicious remarks on his Royalist antecedents, as should raise him, if not to wealth, at least to honour, and above all, such as should enable him to throw the shield of his protection over all and any whom he should think it worth his while thus to shelter and defend. Far in the distance, like some strong swimmer battling successfully against wind and tide, he discerned the beacon which he had resolved to reach, and though he husbanded his strength and neglected no advantage of eddy or back-water, he never relaxed for an instant from his efforts, convinced that in the moral as in the physical conflict, he who is not advancing is necessarily losing way. Such tenacity of purpose *will* be served at last, as indeed it fully merits to be, and this Saxon quality Effingham possessed for good or evil in its most exaggerated form.

The weaknesses of a strong nature, like the flaws in a marble column, are, however, a fit subject for ridicule and remark. The general, despite his grave appearance and his powerful intellect, was as childish in some matters as his neighbours. Ever since the concentration of a large Parliamentary force around Northampton, and the investment, so to speak, of Holmby House by the redoubtable Cornet Joyce, it had been judged advisable by the authorities to station a strong detachment of cavalry at the village of Brixworth, a lonely hamlet within six miles of head-quarters, occupying a commanding position, and with strong capabilities for defence. This detachment seemed to be the general's peculiar care; and who should gainsay such a high military opinion as that of George Effingham? Whatever might be the press of business during the day, however numerous the calls upon his time, activity, and resources, he could always find a spare hour or two before sundown, in which to visit this important outpost. Accompanied by a solitary dragoon as an escort, or even at times entirely alone, the general would gallop over to beat up Lieutenant Allgood's quarters, and returning leisurely in the dark, would drop the rein on his horse's neck, and suffer him to walk quietly through the outskirts of the park at Boughton, whilst his master looked long and wistfully at the casket containing the jewel which he had sternly resolved to win. On the day of Humphrey's capture, the very eagerness on the part of Effingham to fulfil his daily duty, or rather, we should say, to enjoy the only relaxation he permitted himself, served to render him somewhat impatient of Ebenezer's long-winded communications; and by cutting short the narrative of that verbose official, perhaps prevented an interview with his old friend, which, had he believed in its possibility, he would have been sorry to miss.

A bright moon shone upon the waving fern and fine old trees of Boughton Park as George returned from his customary visit to the outpost. He was later than usual, and the soft southern breeze wafted on his ear the iron tones that were tolling midnight from Kingsthorpe Church. All was still, and balmy, and beautiful, the universe seemed to breathe of peace, and love, and repose. The influence of the hour seemed to soothe and soften the ambitious soldier, seemed to saturate his whole being with kindly, gentle feelings, far different from those which habitually held sway in that weary, careworn heart; seemed to whisper to him of higher, holier joys than worldly fame and gratified pride, even than successful love—to urge upon him the beauty of humility, and self-sacrifice, and hopeful, child-like trust—the triumph of that resignation which far outshines all the splendours of conquest, which wrests a victory even out of the jaws of defeat.

Alas that these momentary impressions should be transient in proportion to their strength! What *is* this flaw in the human organization that thus makes man the very puppet of a passing thought? Is there but one rudder that can guide the bark upon her voyage, veering as she does with every changing breeze? but one course that shall bring her in safety to the desired haven, when all the false pilots she is so prone to take on board do but run her upon shoals and quicksands, or let her drift aimlessly out seaward through the night? We know where the charts are to be found—we know where the rudder can be fitted. Whose fault is it that we cannot bring our cargo safe home to port?

The roused deer, alarmed at the tramp of George's charger, sprang hastily from their lair under the stems of the spreading beeches, blanched in the moonlight to a ghastly white. As they coursed along in single file under the horse's nose, he bounded lightly into the air, and with a snort of pleasure rather than alarm broke voluntarily into a canter on the yielding moss-grown sward. The motion scattered the train of thought in which his rider was plunged, dispelled the charm, and brought him back from his visions to his own practical, resolute self. He glanced once, and once only, at the turrets of the hall, from which a light was still shining, dimly visible at a gap in the fine old avenue; and then with clenched hand and stern, com-pressed smile, turned his horse's head homeward, and galloped steadily on towards his own quarters in Northampton town.

CHAPTER XII.

'PAST AND GONE.'

PERHAPS had Effingham known in whose room was twinkling that light which shone out at so late an hour from the towers of the old manor-house; could any instinctive faculty have made him aware of the council to which it was a silent witness; could he have guessed at the solemn conclave held by two individuals in that apartment, from which only a closed casement and a quarter of a mile of avenue separated him, even his strong heart would have beat quicker, and a sensation of sickening anxiety would have prevented him from proceeding so resolutely homewards, would have kept him lingering and hankering there the livelong night.

The solitary light was shining from Grace Allonby's apartment. In that luxurious room were the two ladies, still in full evening costume. One was in a sitting posture, the other, with a pale, stony face, her hair pushed back from her temples, and her lips, usually so red and ripe, of an ashy white, walked irregularly to and fro, clasping her hands together, and twisting the fingers in and out with the unconscious contortions of acute suffering. It was Mary Cave who seemed thus driven to the extremity of apprehension and dismay. All her dignity, all her self-possession had deserted her for the nonce, and left her a trembling, weeping, harassed, and afflicted woman.

Grace Allonby, on the other hand, sate in her chair erect and motionless as marble. Save for the action of the little foot beneath her dress, which tapped the floor at regular intervals, she might, indeed, have been a statue, with her fixed eye, her curved, defiant lip and dilated nostril expressive of mingled wrath and scorn.

Brought up as sisters, loving each other with the undemonstrative affection which dependence on one side and protection on the other surely engenders between generous minds, never before had the demon of discord been able to sow the slightest dissension between these two. Now, however, they seemed to have changed natures. Mary was writhing and pleading as for dear life. Grace sat stern and pitiless, her dark eyes flashing fiercely, and her fair brow, usually so smooth and open, lowering with an ominous scowl.

For five minutes neither had spoken a syllable, though Mary continued her troubled walk up and down the room. At last Grace, turning her head haughtily towards her companion, stiffly observed,

' You can suggest, then, no other method than this unwomanly and humiliating course?'

' Dear Grace,' replied Mary, in accents of imploring eagerness, ' it is our last resource. I entreat you— think of the interest at stake. Think of him even now, a prisoner on his way to execution. To execution! Great Heaven! they will never spare him now. I can see it all before me—the gallant form walking erect between those stern, triumphant Puritans, the kindly face blindfolded, that he may not look upon his death. I can see him standing out from those levelled muskets. I can hear his voice firm and manly as he defies them all, and shouts his old battle-cry—"God and the King!" I can see the wreaths of white smoke floating away before the breeze, and down upon the greensward, Humphrey Bosville—dead!—do you understand me, girl? *dead*—stone dead! and we shall never, *never* see him more!'

Mary's voice rose to a shriek as she concluded, towering above her companion in all the majesty of her despair; but she could not sustain the horror of the picture she had conjured up, and sinking into a chair, she covered her face with her hands, and shook all over like an aspen leaf.

Grace, too, shuddered visibly. It was in a softened tone that she said, 'He *must* be saved, Mary. I am willing to do all that lies in my power. He shall not die for his loyalty, if he can be rescued by any one that bears the name of Allonby.'

'Bless you, darling, a thousand, thousand times!' exclaimed Mary, seizing her friend's hand and covering it with kisses; 'I knew your good, kind heart would triumph at the last. I knew you would never leave him to die without stretching an arm to help him. Listen, Gracey. There is but one person that can interpose with any chance of success on his behalf—I need not tell you again who that person is, Gracey; you used to praise and admire my knowledge of the world; you used to place the utmost faith in my clear-sightedness and quickness of perception. I am not easily deceived, and I tell you George Effingham

loves the very ground beneath your feet.   Not as men
usually love, Grace, with a divided interest, that
makes a hawk or a hound, a place at court, or a brigade of cavalry, too dangerous and successful a rival,
but with all the energy of his whole enthusiastic
nature, with the reckless devotion that would fling the
world, if he had it, at your feet.   He is your slave,
dear, and I cannot wonder at it.   For your lightest
whim he would do more, a thousand times more, than
this.   He has influence with our rulers (it is a bitter
drop in the cup, that we must term the Roundhead
knaves *our* rulers at last); above all, he has Cromwell's confidence, and Cromwell governs England
now.   If he can be prevailed on to exert himself, he
can save Bosville's life.   It is much to ask him, I
grant you.   It may compromise him with his party,
it may give his enemies the means of depriving him
of his command, it may ruin the whole future on
which his great ambitious mind is set.   I know him,
you see, dear, though he has never thought it worth
his while to open his heart to *me;* it might even endanger his safety at a future period, but it *must* be
done, Grace, and you are the person that must tell
him to do it.'

'It is not right,' answered Grace, her feminine
pride rousing itself once more.   'It is not just or fair.
What can I give him in exchange for such a favour?
How can I, of all the women upon earth, ask him to
do this for *me?*'

'And yet, Grace, if you refuse, Humphrey must
die!' said Mary, in the quiet tones of despair, but with
a writhing lip that could hardly utter the fatal word.

Grace was driven from her defences now. Conflicting feelings, reserve, pride, pity, and affection, all were at war in that soft heart, which so few years ago had scarcely known a pang. Like a true woman, she adopted the last unfailing resource, she put herself into a passion, and burst into tears.

'Why am I to do all this?' sobbed Grace. 'Why are my father, and Lord Vaux, and you yourself, Mary, to do nothing, and I alone to interfere? What especial claim has Humphrey on me? What right have I, more than others, over the person of Major Bosville?'

'Because you love him, Grace,' answered Mary, and her eye never wavered, her voice never faltered, when she said it. The stony look had stolen over her face once more, and the rigidity of the full white arm that peeped through her sleeve showed how tight her hand was clenched, but the woman herself was as steady as a rock. The other turned her eyes away from the quiet searching glance that was reading her heart.

'And if I did,' said poor Grace, in the petulance of her distress, 'I should not be the only person. You like him yourself, Mary, you know you do— am I to save him for your sake?'

The girl laughed in bitter scorn while she spoke, but tears of shame and contrition rose to her eyes a moment afterwards, as she reflected on the ungenerous words she had spoken.

Mary had long nerved herself for the task, she was not going to fail now. She had resolved to *give him up*. Three little simple words; very easy to say, and comprising after all—what? a mere nothing! *only* a heart's happiness lost for a life-time—*only* a cloud over the sun for evermore—*only* the destruction of hope, and energy, and all that makes life worth having, and distinguishes the intellectual being from the brute. *Only* the exchange of a future to pray for, and dream of, for a listless despair, torpid and benumbed,—fearing nothing, caring for nothing, and welcoming nothing but the stroke that shall end life and sufferings together. This was all. She would not flinch—she was resolved—she could do it easily.

'Listen to me, Grace,' she said, speaking every word quite slowly and distinctly, though her very eye-brows quivered with the violence she did her feelings, and she was obliged to grasp the arm of a chair to keep the cold, trembling fingers still. 'You are mistaken if you think I have any sentiment of regard for Major Bosville deeper than friendship and esteem. I have long known him, and appreciated his good qualities. You yourself must acknowledge how intimately allied we have all been in the war, and how staunch and faithful he has ever proved himself to the King. Therefore I honour and regard him, therefore I shall always look back to him as a friend, though I should never meet him again. Therefore I would make any exertion, submit to any sacrifice to save his life. But, Grace, *I do not love him.*' She spoke faster and louder now. 'And, moreover, if you believe he entertains any such feelings on my behalf, you are wrong—I am sure of it—look at the case yourself, candidly and impartially. For nearly two years I have never exchanged words with him, either by speech or writing—never seen him but twice, and you yourself were present each time. He may have admired me once. I tell you honestly, dear, I think he did, but he does not care two straws for me now.'

Poor Mary! it was the hardest gulp of all to keep back the tears at this; not that she quite thought it herself, but it was so cruel to be obliged to *say* it. After all, she was a woman, and though she tried to have a heart of stone, it quivered and bled like a heart of flesh all the while, but she went on resolutely with a tighter hold of the chair.

' I think you and he are admirably suited to each other. I think you would be very happy together. I think, Grace, you like him very much—you cannot deceive me, dear. You have already excited his interest and admiration. Look in your glass, my pretty Grace, and you need not be surprised. Think what will be his feelings when he owes you his life. It requires no prophet to foretell how this must end. He will love you, and you shall marry him. Yes, Grace, you can surely trust *me*. I swear to you from henceforth, I will never so much as speak to him again. You shall not be made uneasy by me of all people—only save his life, Grace, only use every effort, make every sacrifice to save him, and I, Mary Cave, that was never foiled or beaten yet, promise you that he shall be yours.'

It is peculiar to the idiosyncrasy of women that they seem to think that they have a perfect right to dispose of a heart that belongs to them, and say to it,

' you shall be enslaved here, or enraptured there, at our good pleasure.' Would they be more surprised or angry to find themselves taken at their word?

Grace listened with a pleased expression of countenance! She believed every syllable her friend told her. It is very easy to believe what we wish. And it was gratifying to think that she had made an impression on the handsome young Cavalier, for whom she could not but own she had once entertained a warm feeling of attachment. Like many another quiet and retiring woman, this consciousness of conquest possessed for Grace a charm dangerous and attractive in proportion to its rarity. The timid are sometimes more aggressive than the bold; and Grace was sufficiently feminine to receive considerable gratification from that species of admiration which Mary, who was surfeited with it, thoroughly despised. It was the old story between these two: the one was courteously accepting as a trifling gift, that which constituted the whole worldly possessions of the other. It is hard to offer up our diamonds, and see them valued but as paste.

' There is no time to be lost, Mary,' observed Grace, after a few moments' reflection. 'I will make it my business to see General Effingham before twenty-four hours have elapsed. If, as you say, he entertains this—this infatuation about me, it will perhaps make him still more anxious on behalf of his old friend, to provide for whose safety I should think he would strain every nerve, even if there were no such person as Grace Allonby in the world. We will save Major Bosville, Mary, whatever happens, if I have to go down on my bended knees to George Effingham. Not that I think such a measure will be needful,' added Grace, with a smile; ' he is very courteous and considerate, notwithstanding his stern brows and haughty manner. Very chivalrous, too, for a Puritan. My father even avows he is a good soldier; and I am sure he is a thorough gentleman. Do you not think so, Mary?'

But Mary did not answer. She had gained her point at last. Of course it was a great comfort to know that she had succeeded in her object. Had the purchase not been worth the price, she would not surely have offered it; and now the price had been accepted, and the ransom was actually paid, there was nothing more to be done. The excitement was over, and the reaction had already commenced.

' Bless you, Grace, for your kindness,' was all she said. ' I am tired now, and will go to bed. To-morrow we will settle everything. Thank you, dear, again and again.' With these words she pressed her cold lips upon her friend's hand; and hiding her face as much as possible from observation, walked quietly and sadly to her room. It was an unspeakable relief to be alone, face to face with her great sorrow, but yet *alone*. To moan aloud in her agony, and speak to herself as though she were some one else, and fling herself down on her knees by the bed-side, burying her head in those white arms, and weep her heart out while she poured forth the despairing prayer that she might die, the only prayer of the afflicted that falls short of the throne of mercy. Once before in this very room had Mary wrestled gallantly with suffering, and been victorious. Was she weaker now that she was older? Shame! shame! that the woman should give way to a trial which the girl had found strength enough to overcome. Alas! she felt too keenly that she had then lost an ideal, whereas this time she had voluntarily surrendered a reality. She had never known before all she had dared, if not to hope, at least to dream, of the future with *him* that was still *possible* yesterday—and now—

Lost, too, by her own deed, of her own free will. Oh! it was hard, *very* hard to bear!

But she slept, a heavy, sound, and exhausted sleep. So it ever is with great and positive affliction. Happiness will keep us broad awake for hours, to rise with the lark; gladsome, notwithstanding our vigils, as the bird itself, refreshed and invigorated by the sunshine of the soul. 'Tis an unwilling bride that is late astir on her wedding-morn. Anxiety, with all its harassing effects, admits of but feverish and fitful slumbers. The dreaded crisis is never absent from our thoughts; and though the body may be prostrated by weariness, the mind refuses to be lulled to rest. We do not envy the merchant prince his bed of down, especially when he has neglected to insure his argosies; but when the blow has actually fallen, when happiness has spread her wings and flown away, as it seems, for evermore, when there is no room for anxiety, because the worst has come at last, and hope is but a mockery and a myth, then doth a heavy sleep descend upon us, like a pall upon a coffin, and mercy bids us take our rest for a time, senseless and forgetful like the dead.

But there was a bitter drop still to be tasted in the full cup of Mary's sorrows. Even as she laid her down, she dreaded the moment of waking on the morrow; she wished—how wearily!—that she might never wake again, though she knew not then that she would dream that night a golden dream, such as should make the morning's misery almost too heavy to endure.

She dreamed that she was once again at Falmouth, as of old. She walked by the seashore, and watched the narrow line of calm blue water and the ripple of the shallow wave that stole gently to her feet along the noiseless sand. The sea-bird's wing shone white against the summer sky as he turned in his silent flight; and the hushed breeze scarce lifted the folds of her own white dress as she paced thoughtfully along. It was the dress *he* liked so much; she had worn it because he was gone, far away beyond those blue waters, with the Queen, loyal and true as he had ever been. Oh that he were here now, to walk hand-in-hand with her along those yellow sands! Even as she wished he stood by her, his breath was on her cheek, his eyes were looking into hers, his arm stole round her waist. She knew not how, nor why, but she was his, his very own, and for always now. 'At last,' she said, putting the hair back from his forehead, and printing on the smooth brow one long, clinging kiss, 'at last! dear. You will never leave me, now?' and the dream answered 'Never, nevermore!'

Yet when she woke, she did not waver in her resolution. Though Mary Cave looked ten years older than she had done but twenty-four hours before, she said to her own heart, 'I have decided: it *shall* be done!'

CHAPTER XIII.

' THE LANDING-NET.'

FAITH had excited Dymocke's jealousy. This was a great point gained; perhaps with the intuitive knowledge of man's weaknesses, possessed by the shallowest and most superficial of her sex, she had perceived that some decisive measure was required to land her fish at last. Though he had gorged the bait greedily enough, though the hook was fairly fixed in a vital spot, and nothing remained—to continue our metaphor—but to brandish the landing-net, and subsequent frying-pan, the prize lurked stolidly in deep waters. This state of apathy in the finny tribe is termed 'sulking' by the disciples of Izaak Walton; and the great authorities who have succeeded that colloquial philosopher, in treating of the gentle art, recommend that stones should be thrown, and other offensive measures practised, in order to bring the fish once more to the surface.

Let us see to what description of stone-throwing Faith resorted to secure the prey, for which, to do her justice, she had long been angling with much craft, skill, and untiring patience.

Dymocke, we need hardly now observe, was an individual who entertained no mean and derogatory opinion of his own merits or his own charms. An essential article of his belief had always been that

there was at least one bachelor left, who was an
extraordinarily eligible investment for any of the
weaker sex below the rank of a lady; and that
bachelor bore the name 'Hugh Dymocke.' With
such a creed, it was no easy matter to bring to book
our far-sighted philosopher. His good opinion of
himself made it useless to practise on him the usual
arts of coldness, contempt, and what is vulgarly
termed 'snubbing.' Even jealousy, that last and
usually efficacious remedy, was not easily aroused in
so self-satisfied a mind; and as for hysterics, scenes,
reproaches, and appeals to the passions, all such re-
coiled from his experienced nature, like hailstones
from an armour of proof. He was a difficult subject,
this wary old trooper. Crafty, callous, opinionated,
above all, steeped in practical as well as theoretical
wisdom. Yet, when it came to a trial of wits, the
veriest chit of a silly waiting-maid could turn him
round her finger at will.

We have heard it asserted by sundry idolaters, that
even 'the *worst* woman is better than the best man.'
On the truth of this axiom we would not venture to
pronounce. Flattering as is our opinion of the gentle
sex, we should be sorry to calculate the amount of
evil which it would require to constitute *the worst* of
those fascinating natures which are so prone to run
into extremes; but of this we *are* sure, that the *silliest*
woman in all matters of *finesse* and subtlety is a
match, and more than a match, for the wisest of mankind. Here was Faith, for instance, who, with the
exception of her journey to Oxford, had never been
a dozen miles from her own home, outwitting and

outmanœuvring a veteran toughened by ever so many campaigns, and sharpened by five-and-twenty years' practice in all the stratagems of love and war.

After revolving in her own mind the different methods by which it would be advisable to hasten a catastrophe that should terminate in her own espousals to her victim, the little woman resolved on jealousy as the most prompt, the most efficacious, and perhaps the most merciful in the end. Now, a man always goes to work in the most blundering manner possible when he so far forgets his own honest doglike nature as to play such tricks as these. He invariably selects some one who is diametrically the opposite of the real object of attack, and proceeds to open the war with such haste and energy as are perfectly unnatural in themselves, and utterly transparent to the laughing bystanders. When he thinks he is getting on most swimmingly, the world sneers; the fictitious object, who has, indeed, no cause to be flattered, despises; and the real one, firmer in the saddle than ever, laughs at him. It serves him right, for dabbling with a science of which he does not know the simplest rudiments. This was not Faith's method. We think we have already mentioned that in attendance upon the King at Holmby was a certain yeoman of the guard on whom that damsel had deigned to shed the sunshine of her smiles, in which the honest functionary basked with a stolid satisfaction edifying to witness. He was a steady, sedate, and goodly personage; and, save for his bulk, the result of little thought combined with much feeding, and his comeliness, which he inherited from a Yorkshire mother, was the very counterpart of Dymocke himself. He was nearly of the same age, had served in the wars on the King's side with some little distinction, was equally a man of few words, wise saws, and an outward demeanour of profound sagacity, but lacked, it must be confessed, that prompt wit and energy of action which made amends for much of the absurdity of our friend Hugh's pretensions.

He was, in short, such a personage as it seemed natural for a woman to admire who had been capable of appreciating the good qualities of the sergeant; and in this Faith showed a tact and discernment essentially feminine. Neither did she go to work 'hammer-and-tongs,' as if there were not a moment to be lost; on the contrary, she rather suffered than encouraged the yeoman's unwieldy attentions; and taxed her energies, not so much to captivate him, as to watch the effect of her behaviour on the real object of attack. She had but little time, it is true, for her operations, which were limited to the period of the King's short visit at Boughton; but she had no reason to be dissatisfied with the success of her efforts, even long before the departure of his Majesty and the unconscious rival.

Dymocke, elated with his last exploit, and full of the secret intelligence he had to communicate, at first took little notice of his sweetheart, or indeed of any of the domestics; and Faith, wisely letting him alone, played on her own game with persevering steadiness. After a time, she succeeded in arousing his attention, then his anxiety, and lastly his wrath. At first he seemed simply surprised, then contemptuous, afterwards anxious, and lastly undoubtedly and unreasonably angry, with himself, with her, with her new acquaintance, with the whole world; and she looked so confoundedly pretty all the time! When the yeoman went away, Faith gazed after the departing cavalcade from the buttery-window with a deep sigh. She remarked to one of the other maids 'that she felt as if she could die for the King; and what a becoming uniform was worn by the yeomen of the guard.' Dymocke, who had approached her with some idea of an armistice, if not a treaty of peace, turned away with a smothered curse and a bitter scowl. All that night he never came near her, all the next morning he never spoke to her, yet she met him somehow at every turn. He was malleable now, and it was time to forge him into a tool.

It was but yesterday we watched two of our grandchildren at play in the corridor. The little girl, with a spirit of unjust acquisitiveness, laid violent hands upon her brother's toys, taking from him successively the whole of his marbles, a discordant tin trumpet, and a stale morsel of plum-cake. The boy, a sturdy, curly-headed, open-eyed urchin, rising five, resented this wholesale spoliation with considerable energy; and a grand quarrel, not without violence, was the result. The usual declaration of hostility, '*then I wont play,*' was followed by a retreat to different corners of the gallery; and a fit of 'the sulks,' lasting nearly twenty minutes, afforded a short interval of peace and quiet to the household.

A child's resentment, however, is not of long duration; and we are bound to admit that in this instance

the aggressor made the first advances to a reconcilia-
tion. 'You began it, dear,' lisped the little vixen, a
thorough woman already, though she can hardly speak
plain. 'Kiss and make up, brother: *you began it!*'
And we are persuaded that the honest little fellow,
with his masculine softness of head and heart, believed
himself to have been from the commencement wholly
and solely in the wrong.

So Faith, lying in wait for Dymocke at a certain
angle of the back-yard, where there was not much
likelihood of interruption, stood to her arms boldly,
and commenced the attack.

'Are you never going to speak to me again, sergeant?' said Faith, with a half-mournful, half-resent-
ful expression on her pretty face. 'I know what new
acquaintances are—the miller's daughter's a good girl,
and a comely ; but it's not so far from here to Brampton Mill that you need to be in such a hurry as not to
spare a word to an old friend, Hugh !'

The last monosyllable was only whispered, but
accompanied by a soft stolen glance from under a pair
of long eyelashes, it did not fail to produce a certain
effect.

'The miller's daughter ! Brampton Mill !' exclaimed Hugh, aghast and open-mouthed, dumb-
foundered, as well he might be, at an accusation so
devoid of the slightest shadow of justice.

'Oh ! I know what I know,' proceeded Faith, with
increased agitation and alarming volubility. 'I know
where you were spending the day yesterday, and the
day before, and the day before that ! I know why
you leave your work in the morning, and the dinner

stands till it's cold, and the horse is kept out all day, and comes home in a muck of sweat; and it's "where's the sergeant?" and "has anybody seen Hugh?" and "Mistress Faith, can you tell what's become of Dymocke?" all over the house. But I answer them, "I've nothing to do with Dymocke; Dymocke don't belong to me. Doubtless he's gone to see his friends in the neighbourhood; and he knows his own ways best." Oh! *I* don't want to pry upon you, sergeant; it's nothing to *me* when you come and go: and no doubt, as I said before, she's a good girl, and a comely; and got a bit of money too; for her sister that married Will Jenkins she's gone and quarrelled with her father; and the brother, you know, he's in hiding; and they're a bad lot altogether, all but *her;* and I hope you'll be happy, Sergeant Dymocke; and you've my best wishes; and (sob) prayers (sob), for all that's come and gone yet (sob), *Hugh!'*

To say that Dymocke was astonished, stupefied, at his wit's end, is but a weak mode of expressing his utter discomfiture; the old soldier was completely routed, front, flanks, and rear, disarmed and taken prisoner, he was utterly at the mercy of his conqueror.

'It's not much to ask,' pursued Faith, her cheeks flushing, and her bosom heaving as she wept out her plaint; 'it's not much to ask, and I *should* like to have back the broken sixpence, and the silver buckles, and the—the—bit of sweet marjoram I gave you yesterday was a fortnight, if it's only for a keepsake and a remembrance when you're married, Hugh, and you and me are separated for ever!'

With these desponding words, the disconsolate damsel buried her face in her apron and moaned aloud.

What a brute he felt himself! how completely she had put him in the wrong—how his conscience smote him, innocent as he was concerning the miller's daughter, for many little instances of inattention and neglect towards his affianced bride, who was now so unselfishly giving him up, with such evident distress. How his heart yearned towards her now, weeping there in her rustic beauty, and he pitied her, *pitied* her, whilst all the time, with his boasted sagacity and experience, he was as helpless as a baby in the little witch's hands.

'Don't ye take on so, Faith,' he said, attempting an awkward caress, from which she snatched herself indignantly away, ' don't ye take on so. I never went *near* the miller's daughter, Faith—I tell ye I didn't, as I'm a living man !'

'Oh ! it's nothing to me, sergeant, whether you did or whether you didn't, returned the lady, looking up for an instant, and incontinently hiding her face in her apron for a fresh burst of grief. 'It's all over between you and me now, Hugh, for evermore !'

'Never say such a word, my dear,' returned Dymocke, waxing considerably alarmed, as the possibility of her being in earnest occurred to him, and the horrid suspicion dawned on his mind that this might be a *ruse* to get rid of him in favour of the comely yeoman, after all ; 'and if you come to that, lass, you weren't so true to your colours yourself yesterday, that you need to turn the tables this way upon me.'

She had led him to the point now. Then he *was* jealous, as she intended he should be, and she had got him safe.

'I'm sure I don't know what you mean, Sergeant Dymocke,' answered Mistress Faith, demurely, sobbing at longer intervals, and drying her eyes while she spoke. 'If you allude to my conversation with one of his blessed Majesty's servants yesterday, I answer you that it was in presence of yourself and all my lord's servants; and if it hadn't been, I'm accountable to no one. A poor lone woman like me can't be too careful, I know; a poor lone woman that's got nobody to defend her character, speak up for her, or take care of her, and that's lost her best friend, that quarrels with her whether she will or no. Oh! what shall I do?—what shall I do?'

The action was very nearly over now. Another flood of tears, brought up like a skilful general's reserve, in the nick of time, turned the tide of affairs, and nothing was left for the sergeant but to surrender at discretion.

'It's your own fault if it be so,' whispered Hugh, with that peculiarly sheepish expression which pervades the male biped's countenance when he so far humiliates himself as to make a *bonâ fide* proposal. 'If you'll say the word, Faith, say it now, for indeed I love you, and I'll never be easy till you're my wife, and that's the truth!'

But Faith wouldn't say the word at once, nor indeed could she be brought to put a period to her admirer's sufferings, in which, like a very woman, she found a morbid and inexplicable gratification, until she had

well-nigh worried him into a withdrawal of his offer,
when she said it in a great hurry, and sealed her sub-
mission with a kiss.

On the subsequent festivities held both in the par-
lour and the hall—for Sir Giles drank the bride's
health in a bumper, and the ladies of the family
thought nothing too good to present to their favourite
on the happy occasion of her marriage—it is not our
province to enlarge. In compliance with the maxim
that 'happy's the wooing that's not long in doing,'
the nuptials took place as soon as the necessary preparations could be made, and a prettier or a happier-
looking bride than Faith never knelt before the
altar.

The sergeant, however, betrayed a scared and somewhat startled appearance, as that of one who is not
completely convinced of his own identity, bearing his
part nevertheless as a bridegroom bravely and jauntily
enough.

At his own private opinion of the catastrophe we
can but guess by a remark which he was overheard to
address to himself immediately after his acceptance by
the pretty waiting-maid, and her consequent departure
to acquaint her mistress.

'You've done it now, old lad,' observed the sergeant, shaking his head, and speaking in a deliberate,
reflective, and somewhat sarcastic tone. 'What is to
be must be, I suppose, and all things turn out for the
best. But there's no question about it—*you've*—*done*
—*it*—*now!*'

CHAPTER XIV.

'YES OR NO.'

OLD Sir Giles never refused his daughter anything now. He had always been an indulgent parent, but it seemed that of late years Grace had more than ever wound herself round his heart. The old Cavalier was getting sadly broken and altered of late. Day by day his frame became more bent and more attenuated; the eye that used to gleam so bright, was waxing dim and uncertain; the voice that had rung out so clear and cheerful above the tramp of squadrons and the din of battle, now shook and quivered with the slightest exertion, and the once muscular hand that used to close so vigorously upon sword and bridle-rein, had wasted down, thin, white, and fragile like a girl's. The spirit alone was unaltered—bold, resolute, and unyielding as of old, the stanch Cavalier drank the King's health as unshrinkingly every night as was his wont; and lacked opportunity only to lead the King's troops into action as undauntedly as ever. Ay, although too feeble to sit upright in a saddle, he had waved them on to certain death from a sick man's litter. It is glorious to think how the spirit outlives the clay. But with Grace it seemed as if he could not be tender and gentle enough. Whether it was an instinctive feeling that his child was not happy, or an inward presentiment that they must soon take leave of each other in this world, something seemed to prompt him to lavish all the affection of his warm old heart on his darling, and bade him grant her all she asked, and anticipate her lightest wish while it was yet in his power. Thus it befel that to Grace's unexpected proposal, 'Father, may I write in your name to bid General Effingham to the Hall?' he answered feebly in the affirmative, and the young lady found herself in consequence sitting down for the first time in her life to pen a formal letter to the Parliamentary General.

Now this invitation, albeit unnatural and unexpected enough, scarcely did as much violence to Sir Giles's feelings as might have been supposed. Years before, at Oxford, he had imbibed a strong personal liking for George Effingham, and although the latter's desertion of his colours had been a grievous offence to the loyal old Cavalier, he could not but respect the successful and distinguished soldier, who had won such laurels on the side he had espoused too late; he could not forget that he owed his life to Effingham on the fatal field of Naseby, nor could he be insensible to the many kindnesses conferred upon him and his by the General since he had entered upon his high command at Northampton. It was bitter, truly, thus to be beholden to a renegade, and a Roundhead to boot; but then the rebel, though a political enemy, was a personal friend, and it was doubtless pleasant to be exempt from the fines, penalties, domiciliary visits, and other inconveniences to which those Cavaliers were liable who were not so fortunate as to possess a protector on the winning side. So Sir Giles answered in the affirmative, though a little testily, considering it was Grace to whom he spoke.

'As thou wilt, wench, as thou wilt. Let him come and see the two poor old cripples, an' he choose. Vaux is a-bed, and I'm little better, but the time has been that he's ridden alongside of us in buff and steel, the renegade. 'Slife, he's seen us front, and flanks, and rear, and all,' laughed the old knight, grimly, reverting to the defeats at Marston-moor and Naseby. 'Let him come and have a look at us, now we're laid upon the shelf and he's got the sun his own side o' the hedge, with a murrain to it! But write him a civil cartel, Gracey, too, for we're beholden to the black-muzzled varlet, Roundhead though he be.'

And thus it came to pass that Grace sat alone in the great hall at Boughton, with her colour coming and going, and her heart beating a very quick march the while George Effingham's orderly led his horse from the door, and the General himself walked into her presence, trembling in every limb, and in a state of nervous alarm sufficiently contemptible for a man who could face a battery without wincing. The usual ceremonious observances were gone through. Grace presented a cold cheek to her visitor's salute as she bade him welcome. And the latter dropped the hand extended to him as if it were some poisonous reptile, instead of the very treasure on earth for which he would have given every drop of blood in his body. They did not speak much of the weather, but according to the custom of the time, the gentleman made the most minute and circumstantial inquiries as to

the state of health enjoyed by each separate member
of her family, and the lady answered categorically,
and by rule. Then there was a dead silence, very
awkward, very painful, apparently interminable.
Grace began almost to wish he hadn't come.

She broke it at last with an effort.

'I have to thank you, General Effingham, for so
promptly attending to my request. Were you not
surprised to receive my letter?' she added, with an
attempt to lapse into a more playful vein.

George muttered something unintelligible in reply.
He was no carpet knight, our honest friend, and the
last man on earth to help a lady either out of, or into,
a difficulty.

She was obliged to go on unassisted. It was not
so formidable as she fancied, now that the ice was
broken, and she had recovered the alarm of hearing
her own voice.

'I can count upon you as a friend, General,' she
said, one of her frank, cordial smiles lighting up the
whole of her pretty face; 'and I am about to put
your friendship to the test. You can do me a kindness that will make me the happiest girl in the world
—can I depend upon you? If you promise me, I
know I can.'

He coloured with a swarthy glow of pleasure. This
frank dealing accorded well with his honest earnest
nature.

'I am a plain soldier, Mistress Grace,' he replied; 'I would give my life to serve you, and you
know it.'

Grace's head began to turn. Now for it—she must

plead with her lover to save one whom he could not
but consider his rival, and perhaps the effort would
cost the mediator all that makes life most valuable.
Well, she was in deep water now, and must sink or
swim. She struck out boldly at once.

'Do you know that your old comrade, Humphrey
Bosville, is a prisoner in London, on a charge of high
treason?'

He had not heard a word of it. He was grieved
beyond measure. Bosville was so devoted, so persevering, had been so stanch to the Royal cause, had
been concerned in every plot and every scheme, had
been pardoned once by the Parliament. It would go
hard with him this time—he was very, very sorry to
hear of it.

'And that is exactly what I ask you to prevent,'
she broke in. 'I have sent for you that I might
implore you to save him. George Effingham, you are
the only man alive that I would ask to do so much.
Grant me my desire as freely and frankly as I entreat
it of you.'

It was exactly the way to take him. Had she beat
about the bush and *finessed* and coquetted with him,
he would probably have refused her sternly, although
such a refusal would have forbidden him ever to see
her again. He would have set up some objection of
duty or principle, and hardened himself to resistance,
even against *her*, but he was not proof against this
open-hearted, confiding, sisterly kind of treatment,
and had she asked him to ride to London incontinently,
and beard Cromwell to his face, he must have yielded
on the spot. Where had Grace acquired her know-

ledge of human nature? Surely it is by intuition
that women thus readily detect and take advantage
of our most assailable points. They need no Vauban
to tell them that 'a fortress is no stronger than its
weakest part,' but direct their attack unhesitatingly
where the wall is lowest, and carry everything before
them by a *coup de main*.

George saw all the difficulties in his path plainly
enough. He knew that to ask for his old comrade's
life would subject him to much suspicion and mis-
representation on the part of his colleagues. Like all
successful men, he had no lack of rivals, and now that
the fighting was over it had already begun to be
whispered that the converted Cavalier was but a luke-
warm partisan after all, nay, the fanatics averred that
he was, alas, but 'a whited sepulchre,' and little better
than a 'Malignant' in his heart. Cromwell indeed,
whose religious enthusiasm was strongly dashed with
political far-sightedness, knew his valour, and to Cromwell he trusted; but he could not conceal from himself that he was about to stake on one throw the whole
of that influence and position he had so ardently
coveted, and which it had cost him such strenuous and
unceasing efforts to attain.

But George's was a generous nature, and the instant he had determined to make this sacrifice for
the woman he loved, he had resolved that she should
be the last person to learn its value and importance.

'Is it to save my old friend's life, Mistress Grace,'
he said, 'that you think it necessary thus to entreat
me? I should indeed be grateful to *you* for informing
me of his danger. I will lose no time in making

every exertion on his behalf, ay, even should I have to give my life for his. I only wish you had proposed to me some more unwelcome task, that I might have shown you how ready I am to comply with your every wish.'

He spoke with a playful, for him, even with a courtly air. He marked the glistening eye and the flush of pleasure with which she listened, nor did he wince for a moment, and though his lip trembled a little, the brave face was as firm as marble.

Did he think he could blind her? Could he believe she did not calculate his danger, and appreciate his unselfishness? Did he not feel how her woman-nature must respond to a generosity so akin to its own? If ever you would win her, George Effingham, open your arms now, and take her to your heart!

The tears were coming to his eyes, but he drove them back with a strong effort, as, seeing she was too much moved to speak, he proceeded—

'I will bring him back to you without a hair of his head being harmed, Mistress Grace. Perhaps in happier days you will both think kindly of the renegade Cavalier.'

She put her hand in his, smiling sweetly through her tears.

'Do this,' she murmured, 'and ask me what you will in recompense.'

He was too proud to understand her.

'There is not a moment to be lost,' he said; 'make my excuses to Sir Giles and good Lord Vaux, that I must take my leave without waiting on them. Farewell, Mistress Grace; fear not. Farewell!'

Without another word, without even touching her hand, he made a profound obeisance and left the room.

Grace's knees were knocking together, and she shook in every limb. She sank into Sir Giles's huge arm-chair, and there she sat and pondered the momentous question that some day or another presents itself to every woman's heart. 'How noble,' thought Grace, 'how generous, how chivalrous, and how good ! Never to show that he was conferring a kindness, never to place me under the sense of an obligation ; and all the time he is willing to give up his fame and his command and his position ; nay, a dearer, fonder future still, and for my sake.' Grace blushed up to her temples though she was alone. 'This is indeed true affection—the affection I have heard of and dreamt of; that I never thought any one would be found to feel for me. For me !—what am I that that brave, determined, goodly man should thus be at the disposal of my lightest word ?' Grace went to the end of the hall, peeped in the glass, and sat down again, apparently a little more satisfied and composed. 'If their positions were reversed, would Humphrey have acted so? I trow not. Has he the firmness and the energy and the strength of mind of this one ? Oh ! why did I not love George Effingham instead ? Stay ! do I not love him now ? Shame, shame !— and I almost told him so. And perhaps he sees how wavering and unworthy I am, and despises me after all.' Grace sat back in her chair, in a most unenviable frame of mind—provoked with the past, impatient of the present, and undecided as to the future

George stepped calmly along the terrace, with the sad composure of a man who has nothing more to fear on earth. He had long known it must come to this at last; had long anticipated the moment when the frail cobwebs of self-deception which weave themselves insensibly around the human heart must be swept away in a breath; when the vain imitation of Hope that had beguiled its loneliness must be surrendered once for all; and he accepted his lot with a proud, quiet resignation. At least he would make her happy, ay, though it cost him every treasure he had in the world; and when he could bear it he would see her again, and in her welfare should be his reward.

The rustle of a lady's dress behind him caused him to start and stop. Could she have followed him for one more last word? Could his self-sacrifice have touched and softened her? No; as he turned his head it was Mary Cave that hurried up to him with trembling steps, and accosted him in the faltering accents of extreme anxiety and distress.

She was so altered he hardly knew her. She, whose manner used to be so composed and queenly, dashed it may be with a little too much self-confidence and assumption, was now nervous and pre-occupied; apparently humbled in her own estimation, and abrupt, almost incoherent, in her address. She had lost her rich colour, too, and there were lines on the brow he remembered so smooth and fair; while the soft blue eyes that formerly laughed and sparkled, and softened all at once, had grown fixed and dilated, even fierce in their expression of defiance and endurance.

'One word with you, General Effingham,' she said,
without waiting to go through any of the common
forms of salutation; 'have you seen Mistress Allonby?'

He answered in the affirmative with a bow. She
seemed to know it, for she scarcely waited for a reply.

'You have heard it all,' she hurried on, speaking
very fast and energetically, with a certain action of
the hand and wrist that was habitual to her, but
never (and this was so unlike her), never looking her
companion in the face. 'Grace has made no sub-
terfuge, no concealment; she has told you everything
—everything? And you are going to London immediately?—this very day? You will not lose an
instant? He will be saved, Effingham—don't you
think he will?'

'I shall be on the road before the sun goes down,'
he replied courteously, affecting to ignore her agitation; 'I have already promised Mistress Allonby that
I will leave no stone unturned to save Humphrey
Bosville. I think I can answer for his life being
spared.'

She could not help it; she burst into tears. Alas!
they came easier every time, and she had so often
cause to weep now! But it relieved her, and after
this display of weakness she relapsed into something
of her old air of composure and superiority.

'He is a very dear friend,' she said, the colour gradually stealing over her pale face; 'a very dear friend
to us all. You will command Grace's eternal gratitude, and Sir Giles's and Lord Vaux's—and mine.'

He was only too happy to serve them, he said;
and he, too, valued Humphrey as much as any of

them—so brave, so kindly; above all, so gentle and true-hearted.

'Hush!' she stopped him, quite eagerly, the while she laid her hand in his with a frank cordial pressure, but her face worked as though she would fain burst out crying once more. 'There is not a moment to lose; I must detain you no longer. There is one thing more I had to say. You will see him; you will tell him how anxious we have all been for him, and you will give him this packet yourself,' she drew it from her bosom as she spoke, 'and you will entrust it to no hand but his own. It is only a matter of—of—business,' she faltered out, 'but I wish it to arrive safe at its destination. Thank you—God bless you.'

She would not have been a woman had she not reserved this one little bit of concealment. Effingham must not know, no one must ever know, how she had loved Humphrey Bosville. The packet was but a matter of *business*—business, forsooth!—exchange and barter, and dead loss and utter bankruptcy; but none must fathom it. They are all alike; reeling from a death-blow they can find a moment to dispose their draperies decently, nay, even tastefully, around them. And whilst on the subject of drapery we may remark, that even in the deepest affliction they preserve no slight regard to the amenities of dress. Though Mary's heart was breaking, her robe was not disordered, neither was her hair out of curl.

As Effingham ordered out his horses and betook himself to the saddle, he little thought how he had created so deep an interest in the two gentle hearts he left behind him. Grace was already studiously comparing him with a previous idol, a comparison which generally argues the dethronement of the prior image from its pedestal in the female breast; and Mary, of all people, could most thoroughly enter into his feelings, pity his loneliness, and appreciate his self-sacrifice.

Humphrey's case was indeed one of extreme peril. Heavily manacled, and committed to New-gate like a common malefactor, his only prospect of release was when he should be brought before the Parliament and placed on trial for his life. Scant mercy, too, could he expect from that conscientious assemblage. A confirmed Malignant, a brave and zealous officer, an adherent of the Queen; lastly—setting at nought his previous pardon—an emissary from the French Court to the imprisoned King, nothing was wanting to prove him guilty of high trea-son against the majesty of the Commons House of Parliament by law assembled,—nothing but an extra-ordinary reversal of the usual sentence could prevent his paying the extreme penalty attached to that heinous offence.

In vain he pleaded the innocence of the letters with which he was charged; in vain he urged that they contained a simple application to his Majesty from the Prince, his son, for permission to accompany the Duke of Orleans to the wars. In vain he pleaded his own position as a mere domestic functionary attached to the person of the Queen. His well-known cha-racter for loyalty and reckless daring, accompanied by his steady refusal to sign his name to a written state-ment embodying the above explanations, utterly nullified all that could be said in his defence, and left him nothing to anticipate but an adverse verdict, a short shrift, and a speedy end.

It was evident, however, that some strong influence was at work below the surface in favour of the Royalist prisoner. Powerful debaters in the House of Commons itself urged the policy of clemency, and the antecedents of the culprit, as arguments for a mitigated sentence, if not a free acquittal. Shrewd lawyers reserved points of law in his behalf. One eminent patriot boldly expressed his admiration of such devoted constancy even in an enemy; and although the case was too clear to admit of doubt, and Lenthall (the Mr. Speaker of his day) was compelled to do his duty and commit the prisoner for trial on the capital charge, he was not even then abandoned by friends, who must indeed have felt *themselves* secure to make such exertions in his behalf.

On his return to Newgate from Westminster, the coach in which he sat was curiously enough upset. Two of his guards appeared strangely stupefied, a third was drunk, and the fourth, slipping a note into his hand, bade him run for his life the while he extricated the horses and rated the driver soundly for their misfortune. Perhaps Humphrey was not so surprised as he might have been, had he not previously held an interview with Effingham in his prison, whose writing he recognised in the slip of paper in his hand. Its contents were short and pithy:

'Keep quiet and in hiding,' it said, 'for a few months. You will be purposely overlooked, but remain where you are not known, and above all—keep still.'

There was no signature, but Humphrey wisely tore it into shreds as he made his escape through the increasing darkness.

And now Ellingham was anticipating his reward. As he journeyed rapidly back to Northampton, riding post, and urging the good horses beneath him to their swiftest pace, he was thinking of Grace's grateful smile when he should assure her that her lover had been saved by his exertions; and his own gratification, in which indeed there was no inconsiderable leaven of pain, at her delight.

He was to see her just *once* again—that once which, contrary to all the rules of arithmetic, is multiplied by itself into so many, many times—to witness her happiness with his own eyes, and feel that henceforth he was never so much as to think of her again. For this he had worked and fawned, cajoled and promised, intrigued and threatened; done constant violence to his stern, true nature, and lost that position with his party which it had cost him so much to attain. And for this he would have done as much and twice as much again, because, you see, he was going to have his Reward.

How even this consolation was denied him, we must detail in another chapter.

CHAPTER XV.

'WELCOME HOME.'

THERE was hurrying to and fro in the old house at Boughton; a hushed confusion seemed to pervade the establishment, and though the servants rushed here and there in aimless anxiety, everything was done as noiselessly as possible, and they did not even venture to express in words that which their scared faces and white lips told only too well.

Horses had been saddled hastily, and ridden off at speed in search of medical assistance. With the strange piteous earnestness to do *something* which pervades us helpless mortals when we feel that *nothing* can avail, mounted messengers had been dispatched in needless repetition. There was little to be done but to wait for the leech and summon fortitude to endure his confirmation of their worst fears. The sick man said himself there was no hope. He seemed less affected than any in the household by the recent catastrophe.

Sir Giles was down under a mortal stroke. He preserved his senses and his speech; the rest of the man was a mere helpless shell; but his mind was as vigorous as ever, and the old knight's courage had not given way even now—no, not an inch.

He had often looked on Death before, and fronted him in the field, spurring his good horse against him, with a jest on his lips, and told him that he feared him not, to his face. He had seen all he loved best on earth fast in the skeleton's embrace, and he had not quailed even then. Would he shrink from him now? Pshaw! let him do his worst.

We have said it before, and we say it again, that the mind which has never prepared itself for the great change, is usually incapable of doing so when that change is actually present. Far be it from us to aver that it is ever too late whilst there is life; we only remark that it seems ill-advised to make no preparation for a long, what if it be an endless, journey? till the foot is actually in the stirrup.

Grace was weeping by his bedside, her hand in his, her face turned from him to hide the big drops that coursed each other down her cheeks. Poor Gracey! Many a true friend loves you well, many a heart leaps to the glance of your kind eyes, and warms to your gentle voice; but where will you find an affection so constant, so unwavering, so regardless of self, so patient of ingratitude, as his who lies gasping there on his death-bed? Where will you find another love that shall be always willing to give everything and receive nothing? that shall pour on you its unceasing stores of care and tenderness, nor ask even for a word of thanks in return?

'I've been a kind old father to thee, lass,' said the dying man, 'and thou'st been a rare daughter to me; but I must leave thee now.'

What could Grace do but bow her head down upon

the poor thin hand she held, and weep as if her heart would break?

He folded the pretty head to his bosom as he used to do when she was a little child, stroking the hair down, and fondling and consoling her.

'Don't ye cry so, my darling,' said the old warrior. 'What! Gracey, little woman, cheer up! 'tis not for long, lass, not for long.'

She seemed to be the dying one of the two. She lay motionless, her head buried in his breast. She was praying for him to *his* Father and hers.

He was still for a time. Conscious of his failing powers, he was gathering himself, as it were, for an effort. When he spoke again she looked up astonished at his strength of voice.

'Is Mary here,' he asked—'Mary Cave? bid her come round here. God bless thee, Mistress Mary.'

She had been sitting afar off at the window, quietly waiting, as was her custom, till she could be of use. She came to the bedside now, and put her arm round Grace, and looked down upon the helpless knight with a calm, sad face. The greater grief absorbs the less, and constant pain will make callous the most sensitive nature. Poor Mary! two short years ago she would hardly have stood so composed and statue-like at good Sir Giles's death-bed.

'Care for her, sweet Mistress Mary,' he resumed, with something of his old energy of voice and manner; 'take charge of my pretty one when I am gone. I thought sometimes to see her married to yon good lad, him that rode the sorrel horse so fairly—my

memory fails me now, I think—how call you him?
Ay, I thought to have seen her married and all; but
she's young, very young yet.   I am failing fast,
Mistress Mary; don't ye speak to Gracey about it;
she loves her old father, and it might disturb the
child; but I'm not for long here.   I know not if
my senses may be spared me.   I must speak out
whilst I can.   Gracey, are you there?'   Where is
Gracey?'

She was close to him still, pressing her wet cheek
to his.

'Here, father,' she whispered, '*dear* father;' and
her voice seemed to revive him for the time.

'Mary will take care of thee, my little lass,' he
said, feebly stretching his hand to hers, and trying to
place it in that of her friend.   'Thou wilt not leave
her, Mary; never leave her till she's married to some
good man—not a rebel, Gracey, never a rebel, for the
old father's sake.   I loved that bold lad well; why
doth he never come to see us now?   Kiss me, Gracey.
I shall see thee again, my child.   God forgive my sins!
I have never sinned by thee.   I shall see thee again,
and thy mother too.   God bless thee, Gracey!'

He sank into a stupor.   The leech had not arrived
yet.   Something told their hearts that all the leech-
craft on earth would be of no avail, and the two
women sat noiselessly weeping in the silence of the
death-chamber.

He spoke again after awhile; but his eyes shone
with a strange brightness, and the indescribable
change was on him—the change which we cannot
but instinctively acknowledge, and which pervades

the dying, like a gleam of pale light from the land beyond the grave.

He spoke of the old times now. Anon he was charging once more at the head of his brigade on Naseby field; the tramp of squadrons and the rattle of small arms were in his ears, and Effingham's steel-headed pikes lowered grimly in his front. Alas! the battle shout was but a hoarse labouring whisper, yet the two pale listeners could recognise the tactics of an action and the stirring old war-cry, 'God and Queen Mary! For the King! for the King!'

Then he prayed for his Sovereign, fervently, loyally, prayed that he might recover his power and his throne, intermingling short pithy phrases from the ritual of his Church, and expressing himself proud, happy, privileged, that he might die for his king.

Yet a thread of consciousness seemed to run through these fitful wanderings of departing reason. It was pitiful to hear him urge on his fancied retainers to ease his saddle and curb his good horse tighter, as he flew his hawk once more in the green meadows under the summer sky.

'He was getting infirm,' he said, 'and the days were long at this time of year; but it was evening at last, and he was glad, for he was tired, very tired. It would be dark before they got home. It was very dark even now.'

There was a dead silence. The startled women thought he was gone; but he breathed yet, though very faintly, and with parted lips. His eyes were closed, but he was wandering still. He called to his hawk, his horse, and his hounds. He must see Gracey, too, he said, 'before he took his boots off.'—'She was very little, surely, *very* little to run alone;' and he spoke fondly and tenderly to another Grace—a Grace that had been treasured up many a long year in the depths of his stout old heart, a Grace that would almost weary expecting him, even in heaven—that was surely waiting for him now on the other side.

He opened his eyes once more, but they rolled aimlessly around, fixing themselves at last feebly upon his daughter. Grace felt to her heart's core that his last look was one of consciousness upon *her*—that he knew *her* even while that look was glazing into death—that the 'God bless thee, Gracey!' which he gasped out with his last breath, was the same old fond familiar farewell with which he was always used to depart upon a journey.

So he went upon his way, and surely when he reached the promised land he found a fond face there, waiting to welcome him home.

Ere the surgeon arrived in hot haste there was nothing left on earth of the stout old Cavalier but a goodly war-worn frame, a fixed marble face, smooth and placid, renovated, as it were, to the sculptured beauty of its prime. He shook his head as he acknowledged himself to be too late, and left the mourners to the sacred indulgence of their grief. Grace Allonby wept in her friend's arms, clinging to her in her distress with the helpless abandonment of a child, and Mary, roused from her own sorrows by the necessity for exertion, soothed her gently and pitifully like a mother. Lord Vaux was by this time a helpless invalid, and both women felt they had at last lost their only protector, as well as their best and kindest friend.

' You must never leave me, Mary,' sobbed out Grace again and again, as a fresh burst of grief broke wildly forth, ' never leave me now, for I have but you in the world.'

It was a goodly funeral with which they did honour to the brave old Cavalier. Many a stout yeoman came from far and near to see him laid in his last resting-place, and told, not without pride, as he quaffed the ale which ever flowed freely on such occasions, how he had charged to the old knight's battle-cry at Naseby, or followed him through serried columns and levelled pikes at Edgehill or Roundway-down. Not a brave heart within three counties but when he heard of Sir Giles's death said, ' God rest him ! he *was* a bold one.' The King himself, the harassed, careworn Charles, wrote a letter of condolence with his own royal hand to the daughter of his faithful servant; and Prince Rupert, pining in exile, vowed that ' the last of the real old Cavaliers was buried with Sir Giles.'

But better than troopers' admiration, prince's approval, and king's autograph, there was more than one poor friendless widow that came with her orphans in her hand, whilst the turf was fresh and ere the stone was up, to weep over the grave of her kind friend and benefactor. Epitaphs may lie, monuments may crumble, deeds of arms and mortal fame may pass away, but the tears of the widow and the fatherless are treasured up as a lasting memorial in a certain stronghold, where ' neither moth nor rust doth corrupt, and where thieves do not break through nor steal.'

CHAPTER XVI.

'WESTMINSTER HALL.'

'WRAP thy cloak well round thee, Gracey; the wind strikes chill to the very marrow.' It was Mary Cave who spoke, and suiting the action to the word, drew with a tender hand the folds of a large dark mantle round the form of her companion.

Grace shivered from head to foot, her teeth chattered, and she tottered as she walked, supported by her friend, who, faithful to the trust he left her, seemed to take a maternal charge of Sir Giles's orphan daughter.

'I never thought they would have dared to do it,' observed Mary, pursuing the train of her own reflections, 'but it has come at last. He was brought from Windsor last night. I saw him myself by torchlight as he descended from the coach—so altered, Grace, so altered, in a short eighteen months!'

The expression of Grace's countenance was as that of one who sees some horrible deed of sacrilege committed, which the witness is powerless to prevent. She hurried on nervously, and without answering a word.

More than a year had elapsed since the events recorded in the preceding chapter—a year of trouble and anxiety to the nation—a year of sorrow and seclusion to these two hapless mourners. Lord Vaux, whose failing health had long been a subject for alarm, seemed utterly unable to recover the shock occasioned by his old friend's death.   His kinswomen had brought him to the capital in search of the best medical assistance, and the two Royalist ladies were naturally anxious to be near the centre of those desperate measures which agitated the politics of the day. A powerful hand, too, seemed to protect this Malignant family. They came and went unquestioned where they would, and were free from the annoyances to which so many of their friends were subjected.   It is possible that Grace may have been able to guess the shield which thus guarded her; but if so, gratitude did but add another painful ingredient to the total of her sufferings.   Her father's kind old face was ever before her eyes as she saw it last, and the dying whisper, 'not a rebel, Gracey, never a rebel, for the old father's sake!' seemed to ring in her ears day and night.

She shivered again as she drew the dark heavy folds tight around her : it was so cold—so bitter cold.

A keen black frost, very different from his gladsome brother who comes sparkling down upon us, his stiff crisp raiment glittering with diamonds in the sunshine, bound the shrinking earth in a churlish embrace.   A cutting north-easter, sweeping over her surface in fitful gusts, whirled up clouds of dust that stung and irritated the unprotected face like pinpoints, and a dull leaden sky, against which the leafless trees of the Mall seemed to wave their skeleton branches as it were in mockery, lowered over all.

London wore her blackest, her most forbidding look, and the pinnacles and spires of proud old Westminster frowned hard and threatening in the dense cold atmosphere.

Yet people were standing about in groups, some talking in whispers with suppressed though eager gestures; others waiting patiently, as if for some show or pageant. As is usual in a crowd, the women slightly predominated, yet was there but little sarcastic questioning and shrill reply, while the gambols of the London urchin—a race never on any public occasion to be sought in vain—failed to excite more than a transient smile in the grave and preoccupied multitude.

As Mary and Grace passed rapidly on they heard many an ominous whisper and broken phrase respecting the great event which was thus collecting the agitated citizens. Strange improbable rumours flew from lip to lip; hints of impossible combinations and contradictory circumstances obtained implicit credence. Here a sedate-looking personage assured his auditors that 'his Majesty was never firmer on the throne; that he was coming in state to Westminster to open his faithful Parliament in person; that the Lords at Windsor, the greatest personages in the kingdom, served him daily on their knees; and that he knew this to be a fact, he who now spoke to them at the present time, for his sister's son, a gardener by trade, had the King's own commands for the sowing of certain Spanish melons at Wimbledon. And is it likely,' added the orator, looking up to the gloomy sky, 'that his Majesty would be sowing melons, especially Spanish ones, and in this weather too, unless he felt confident of seeing them ripen?' 'God bless him!' he would have added, but he caught the scowl of a wild fanatical-looking personage glaring so fiercely at him that the words died upon his lips.

Then a little dirty man, a cobbler by trade, something of a demagogue by profession, and a drunkard by choice, gave it as his own opinion, with much unnecessary circumlocution, that 'Charles,' as he called him, was about to place himself unreservedly in the hands of his Parliament. 'Do we not know,' said the little man, brandishing aloft a pair of much-begrimed hands, and steadying his whole person by fixing his lack-lustre eye on a quiet individual in the crowd, who thus found himself, much to his annoyance, an object of considerable interest—'do we not know that the people, under God, are the original of all just power; that the Commons, chosen by and representing *us*' (the little man smote his shabby breast violently with his dirty hands), 'are the fountain of all power and authority, so that what the Commons declared law *is* law and nothing *but* law? and all the people of this nation are concluded thereby, although the consent and concurrence of the King and the House of Peers be not had thereunto!'

The little man had got the last clause of the Parliament's proclamation carefully by rote, and used the same for his peroration with considerable skill, much to the delight of his auditors, who very generally expressed themselves satisfied with the soundness of his reasoning and the correctness of his principles.

But still, amongst all the conflicting reports alluded to, all the different opinions expressed by this motley assemblage, not a whisper was breathed as to the dreadful event which was really impending, not a suspicion seemed to exist even amongst the strongest partisans of the Parliament, that the people of England would exact the penalty of a king's blood.

It was only the well-educated and the far-seeing—those, in fact, who might be said to be behind the scenes—that could anticipate the worst; those who knew that the Commons had declared themselves independent of the Lords, that a commission had already been nominated for the trial of Charles Stuart on the charge of high treason, and that out of the hundred and thirty-five members appointed, scarce eighty consented to act, might indeed acknowledge the signs of the coming storm—the blast that was so soon to level the loftiest head in England with the dust.

As the hour of noon approached the crowd thickened considerably, and as it drew into its vortex more and more of the lowest rabble, the feeling against the King seemed to gain greater strength. Coach after coach rolled by, bearing the magnates of the country to the important scene in Westminster Hall, and as these were mostly well known to the populace, it might be remarked that such as were suspected even of a leaning towards royalty were assailed with groans and execrations, sometimes even with missiles of a more injurious nature, whilst those whose levelling principles were beyond doubt received a perfect ovation of cheers and congratulations, sometimes ridiculously personal, but always intended to be complimentary in the highest degree.

Amongst the rest one equipage in particular aroused a perfect tumult of applause : it was the coach of General Fairfax, containing his lady, seated alone in all the pomp of her native dignity and her robes of state. Like every successful man for the moment, Fairfax was at that period an immense favourite with the mob, and they clustered round the carriage that conveyed his wife with coarse and boisterous expressions of goodwill. The face inside was a study of strong suppressed feeling. Sitting there in the majesty of her beauty, she could scarce restrain the overpowering sentiments of hatred and contempt with which she regarded those who now surrounded her with such demonstrations of affection. The blood of the Veres boiled within her as she thought of her husband's forfeited loyalty, and the scene from which she had persuaded him to be absent, but to which she was herself hurrying. Her face turned red and white by turns, she bit her lip and clenched her hand as she bid her coachman lash his horses recklessly and drive on. Like the proud Tarquin's prouder wife, she would scarce have stopped had a human form been down beneath her feet.

Jostled by the crowd, notwithstanding her haughty step and imperious gestures, Mary could scarce make her way, and Grace's visible agitation increasing more and more, rendered her position one of peculiar annoyance and discomfort.

They narrowly escaped being run over by the rapidly approaching carriage, but as it passed so close that its wheels brushed Mary's garments, a well-known face appeared at the window, a familiar voice she had not heard for many a year called to the coachman to stop, and Lady Fairfax bade them enter and come with her, in her usual accents of command.

'Mary Cave! I thought it was you,' she exclaimed. 'What are you doing amongst this *canaille?* Jump in, and your friend too. Let us see the end of this shameful business in Westminster Hall.'

The unconscious *canaille* gave her ladyship and friends three hearty cheers as they drove off.

Under such protection as that of Lady Fairfax, with whom Mary had been intimate in girlhood's brighter days, the two ladies found no difficulty in obtaining access to the Hall.

Seats had been apportioned, and what were even then termed 'boxes,' partitioned off for the wives and families of the chief actors to witness the proceedings, and one of the principal of these had been reserved for the lady of the powerful Parliamentary General.

It was an awful and a solemn scene which burst upon the sight of our two devoted Loyalists as they entered. The King's trial was about to commence, and already had the Commissioners taken their seats, with more than the usual pomp of form and ceremony. The stern and able Bradshaw, he whose sense of duty has earned him an unenviable immortality under the title of 'The Regicide,' stood erect as President, supported by his assessors, Lisle and Say, skilful lawyers both, and bold, uncompromising men.

All heads were turned, all eyes directed towards the bar, at which was set a velvet chair of state. This inanimate object seemed to excite universal interest. It was to receive the royal prisoner, but it was still empty.

Anon the vague murmur that pervades all large assemblies increased audibly, and a certain stir was apparent at the far end of the Hall; then succeeded the deep hush of intense expectation, and many a heart heard nothing but its own thick beating, as it strained for a forward glimpse of but a few hours.

A sedan-chair was carried slowly up the Hall; many uncovered as it passed them; one or two voices were even heard to murmur a blessing. But that chair contained Charles Stuart, and his judges sat doggedly with their hats on, neither rising nor showing the slightest mark of respect to their unfortunate Sovereign.

When the King reached the bar he alighted, and without removing his hat, seated himself at once in the chair appointed for him; but presently rising again, looked sternly about him, at the president, at the court, at the people in the galleries; his nerve was as unshaken as it had ever been in the presence of *physical* danger. He was at bay now, and he was every inch a king.

But he was altered, sadly altered too. Mary's heart sank within her as she traced the furrows that suffering and anxiety had ploughed in those royal lineaments, for which she had all her life been taught to cherish an affectionate veneration. His well-knit figure was firm and upright as ever; nor were his locks, though slightly tinged with grey, much thinner than of old; but his features were sharpened, and his eyes hollowed, as if he had been suffering acute physical pain; while the *doomed* expression that had always been the chief characteristic of his face, had deepened to an intensity of melancholy that it was piteous to look upon.

When Bradshaw spoke, however, his features hardened into defiance once more.

Silence was proclaimed, and a whisper might have been heard from one end to the other of that vast hall. Then the clerk, in a sonorous and business-like voice, read over the ordinance for the King's trial, a formal document, couched in terms of legal obscurity. When this ceremony was concluded, the list of commissioners was called over by the same functionary, those present answering to their names.

' John Bradshaw !'

' Here,' replied the President, in a loud undaunted voice, looking sternly at the King, who returned his glance with a haughty and contemptuous frown.

' Thomas Fairfax !'

There was no response. A stir pervaded the hall as men turned and stared, and whispered their neighbours with eager, anxious faces.

Again the clerk called in a loud voice, ' Thomas Fairfax !'

' He has more wit than to be here,' was answered, in distinct confident tones; but though Bradshaw bent his brows in anger, and the commissioners made hasty inquiries, and gave peremptory orders to their officials to secure the offender, it was not easy, in the increasing confusion, to ascertain whence the bold reply had come.

It originated, however, a murmur and a disturbance which it took some minutes to quell. Signs of disapprobation were swamped by a strong inclination to applaud; and it was evident that a powerful feeling in favour of the royal prisoner existed even in the very court in which he was to be tried.

The impeachment was then read over, accusing the monarch of 'designs to erect to himself an illimited and tyrannical power, to overthrow the rights and liberties of the people; of high treason in respect of the levying war against the present Parliament, and the people therein represented;' as denoted by his appearance at York and Beverley with a guard; by the setting up of the standard at Nottingham; by the battle of Edgehill; and so on in order enumerating the different battles at which the King had been present. The document then went on to say, that he had caused the death of thousands of free-born people; that after his forces had been defeated, and himself made prisoner, he had stirred up insurrection in the country, and given a commission to the Prince, his son, to raise a new war against the Parliament; and that, 'as he was the author and contriver of these unnatural, cruel, and bloody wars, so was he therein guilty of all the treasons, murders, rapines, burnings, spoils, desolation, damage, and mischief to the nation which had been committed in the said wars, or been occasioned thereby; and that he was therefore impeached for the said treasons and crimes, as a tyrant, traitor, and murderer, and a public implacable enemy to the Commonwealth, on behalf of the good people of England.'

The King had sat perfectly silent and composed during the reading of the above strangely-worded impeachment, save that at the terms 'tyrant and traitor' as applied to himself, he had smiled contemptuously in the faces of the court. He raised his head, however, as the clerk paused to take breath after enunciating the last paragraph, and seemed about to make some objection or remark, but was arrested in the act, for the same female voice that had already interrupted the proceedings of the court, now rose once more, distinct and forcible through the hush of the attentive audience.

'The good people of England!' it exclaimed, in clear mocking tones. 'No! nor one hundredth part of them!'

Great was the disturbance that ensued; several members rose hurriedly from their seats, and a tumultuous rush in the body of the hall added to the general confusion. Some even thought a rescue was impending; and a few of the more timorous were already glancing about for a speedy egress. Colonel Hacker, who commanded the guard of musketeers, and to whom was confided the custody of the King's person, gave orders to fire into the box whence these sounds of disapproval had arisen; and the stern soldiers had already levelled their muskets to obey this unmilitary command. Lady Fairfax rose undauntedly and faced their muzzles with a bold imperious brow. Mary, too, rushed to the front to share the danger of her friend. Grace, trembling and weeping, shrank behind them, half paralyzed with fear. For a few moments all was breathless confusion; but a voice,

that even in her terror the frightened girl recognised
only too plainly, was heard to exclaim, in loud re-
proving tones, ' Shame ! shame ! Recover your arms !
Cowards ! would you fire upon your countrywomen ?'
and George Effingham, in his uniform as a general
of the Parliament, struck up the barrels of the muskets, and threatened to put Hacker under immediate
arrest.

An usher of the court, however, came round to the
box occupied by Lady Fairfax, and endeavoured to
prevail upon her to withdraw. It was only under a
promise that she would remain tranquil, extorted from
her by the entreaties of her companions, that she was
permitted to remain. With clenched hands and angry
brow she sat out the remainder of the proceedings.

When order was once more restored, Mr. Cook, the
Attorney-General, being about to speak, the King
laid the long amber-headed cane which he usually
carried, upon his shoulder, and bade him ' hold ;' but
the Lord President requiring him to proceed, his
Majesty folded his arms, and bending his brows fixedly
upon him, listened attentively to a summary of the
charges against him, which was now repeated.

His Majesty then required to know by what authority he was brought hither.

' I have,' said Charles, ' a Trust committed to me
by God by old and lawful descent ; I will not betray
it to answer to a new unlawful authority ; therefore,
resolve me that, and you shall hear more of me.'

' Sir,' replied the President, ' you are required to
answer these charges in the name of the people of
England, of whom you are the elected king.'

'I deny that,' interrupted the indignant monarch. 'England has been no elective kingdom, but a hereditary monarchy for near a thousand years. I dispute your authority. I do stand more for the liberty of my people than any here that come to be my pretended judges.'

Bradshaw in an insolent tone bade him interrogate the court with becoming deference and humility.

His pride aroused, his royal dignity insulted, Charles lost his assumed calmness and that presence of mind for which he was not always too conspicuous. With intemperate voice and gesture, he inveighed against the injustice of the proceedings, calling on Divine Providence, in no measured language, to avenge him of his enemies, and right him in the face of the whole world. Whilst thus declaiming, the amber-head of his staff fell off, and this little incident, ominous as it might have appeared to a superstitious mind, served to change the current of his ideas, and to moderate the violence of his deportment.

Mary's loyal heart swelled with indignation as, sitting unobserved behind Lady Fairfax, she could not but remark how no obedient courtiers pressed to pick it up—how the King, with a gesture of patient surprise, was fain to stoop for it himself, and as though reminded by the very act of the friendlessness of his position, and the necessity for resignation, rose once more with the calm brow and the air of quiet long-suffering that had become habitual to that careworn face.

But Mary, too, with all her Cavalier enthusiasm and exaggerated sentiments of the devotion due to her

Sovereign, had other matters to occupy her wandering thoughts, other causes for agitation and excitement, apart from the great political tragedy of which she was then and there witnessing the first act. Each one of us lives an inner as well as an outer existence. How curious would it have been to have analysed the thoughts of the different individuals who thronged that spacious hall! Met there for a common object, and that an object of vital importance, not only to the destinies of their country, but to the personal safety of the lieges, how many minds amongst them were bent, to the exclusion of all other images, solely on the affair in hand! How many even of the judges but had a large share of their attention preoccupied by matters solely personal and interesting to themselves—by a farm far off in Lincolnshire, a wife sickening at Bath, a child unhappily married in Scotland; nay, even by such trifling annoyance as domestic difficulties with a servant, or the lameness of a favourite horse! How many but had some overpowering interest at heart, to which the justice of the trial and the guilt or innocence of the royal prisoner was a mere gossamer, and who could scarce withdraw their minds for a few minutes at a time from the one engrossing object, to bend them on the paramount duty they had sworn to fulfil! What was Charles's condemnation or acquittal, to the idol each had privately raised up and worshipped, as men worship false idols alone—the schemes of selfish aggrandizement, the acquisition of wealth, the fascinating temptations of intrigue, or the thrilling satisfaction of revenge? Even Lady Fairfax, wrathful and defiant as she was, pitying with a woman's pity the innocent victim, and chafing with a woman's indignation at the palpable injustice, could not forbear a glance into the possible future, when that royal prisoner should be no longer the first personage in England, could not keep back a swell of pride as she bethought her of one who had no slight prospect of assuming the reins of power, who *might* rise from a Parliamentary General (as his comrade really did) to be a Parliamentary Dictator; and how for such an one she was herself no unworthy mate.

And Mary, too, no longer bent her whole attention on that velvet chair and its hapless occupant. In glancing wearily round the hall, searching, as it were, for a friendly face on which to rest, her eye had caught a glimpse of a countenance that reminded her—oh! so painfully—of one which even now to think of brought the blood to her cheek, and left it paler than before. Yes, though lost again instantaneously in the crowd, there was a face somewhere, she was sure of it, that resembled *his*. That it was himself, of course, was impossible. He was in strict hiding, no doubt, and probably had taken refuge on the Continent; at all events, the last place in the world to which even *his* recklessness would bring him, was the very stronghold of his enemies in Westminster Hall. But weak, childish, humiliating as it was, there would be something gratifying, something of a strange indefinable pleasure, mixed with pain, in looking once more on lineaments which could recall those that all the schooling in the world had not taught her to forget; so her eyes wandered over the Hall, and refused to rest until they had found that which they desired.

A momentary stir amongst the group immediately surrounding the Sovereign exposed the object of her search once more. It was but one of the musketeers who formed the escort, after all, that had so reminded her for an instant of one now lost to her for ever, and on regarding him attentively, though there was something in the air and figure that resembled Humphrey Bosville, the colour and complexion were so totally different from those of the proscribed Cavalier, that the resemblance became every moment more indistinct, and Mary smiled to herself, a faint, heart-sick smile, as she thought how harmless in its utter hopelessness was folly such as hers.

But it beguiled her mind from the afflicting present, it led her fancy wandering away through the enamelled meadows and by the golden streams of that fairy land in which it is so dangerous to linger, and it was with a start of returning consciousness and the confused sensations of one awaking from a deep slumber, that she was aware of the general stir created by the departure of the prisoner from the Hall.

The proceedings had terminated for the day. Charles, after vainly protesting against the authority of his judges, had relapsed into the quiet dignified bearing of one who, while he feels the injustice to which he is subjected, resolves bravely and patiently to sustain his fate. As he was conducted down the hall, loud expressions of loyalty greeted him from many an unknown and unsuspected partisan even amongst those therein assembled, although a strong majority of his enemies strove to drown these ebullitions by violent cries for 'justice.'

When the King passed the sword of state, placed conspicuously in the sight of the whole assemblage, he manned himself with an air of dignity, and facing the court, pointed to the emblem of death, while he exclaimed in a loud, firm tone, ' I do not fear *that !*'

It was no empty boast. How little Charles Stuart feared the extreme moment from which poor human nature instinctively recoils, he proved nobly and resignedly on the scaffold.

CHAPTER XVII.

'THE MUSKETEER.'

THE Guard was strengthened more than common at St. James's. Sentries were doubled in all the principal avenues to the Palace, not only for the increase of vigilance, but for the nullifying of any attempt at tampering with those unmoved functionaries. Stringent orders were given as to the exclusion of strangers, and a watchful expression pervaded the countenance of sergeants and corporals as they visited their respective posts with unusual frequency and circumspection. Nevertheless, within the guard-room the men off duty for the time lounged and laughed and smoked as soldiers will whether they have a crowned head in ward or an enemy at the gates. Small respect did these rude men of war pay to the former consideration. Their commander, Colonel Hacker, was a stern and coarse-minded person: a leveller in politics and a fanatic in religion, he was not likely to insist on any inordinate reverence for his illustrious captive; and the private soldiers, taking their cue from their chief, lighted their pipes and laughed out their ribald jokes in the presence of patient and outraged Royalty itself.

It was the first day of the King's trial. The escort

which had conducted him back to St. James's were off
duty for the nonce, and the guard-room was thronged
with the usual complement of idle, talking, preaching,
and smoking champions who constituted the flower of
Hacker's redoubtable musketeers. Here a stalwart
warrior, lying at his lazy length along the coarse
oaken form, and puffing forth volumes of tobacco-
smoke, expressed his own opinions as to the proceedings of the day with a degree of irreverence for all
concerned—judges, prisoner, and spectators—such as
nothing but a guard-room could produce. There a
grim war-worn corporal, with an open Bible in his
hand and a stern, dogmatic frown upon his brow,
waited impatiently for a moment's silence to commence what he termed 'an exercise,' and to vilify
and vituperate in every possible manner 'the man
Charles Stuart,' 'for the improvement of the occasion.' Some were rubbing up their belts, inspecting
the pans of their firelocks, or exploring the contents
of their havresacks previous to going again on duty;
whilst others, fatigued with watch and ward, and
regardless alike of King and Commons, right and
wrong, accusers and accused, were stretched supine in
sound and snoring sleep.

One soldier, however, stood at the grated window
of the guard-room, apart from the rest, seemingly immersed in thought. His eyes, fixed on vacancy, were
looking back far into the Past; his dark face, strangely
at variance with the light flaxen curls that stole from
under his iron head-piece, wore an expression of acute
pain, borne with resolute endurance—such an expression as betrays the existence of a fatal malady,

bodily or mental, to which the sufferer scorns to give way.

His spare and muscular figure was cast in a more graceful mould than generally pertains to those of humble birth; and the hand, in which he crumpled a much-creased letter, though strong and sinewy, was shapely as a woman's. He seemed struggling with some powerful influence or temptation : ever and anon a soft, tender expression swept across his swarthy features, but a glance at the paper in his hand hardened them into bronze once more.

This soldier had but lately joined the corps of Hacker's musketeers. He was no raw recruit, as was soon apparent by his thorough knowledge of military details; and more than one scar on his neck and arms argued the presumption that he had been a brave front-rank man in his time. His own account was that he had served for a while in the Netherlands, and afterwards sailed as a buccaneer on the Spanish Main; and this story tallied well with his soldierlike habits and the unnaturally dark colour of his skin where it had been exposed to the sun. He won the good opinion of the sergeant who enlisted him by one or two feats of strength and agility; and in those days of tumult few questions were asked as to the antecedents of a soldier who brought into the ranks an iron frame and a thorough familiarity with his profession. But his comrades scarcely knew what to make of their new acquisition. With a peculiar frankness and kindliness of manner, he was more prompt than is the custom of that boisterous class to check a liberty or resent an insult. And his personal strength, added to the self-evident daring of his character, made them chary of rousing him by any of those rude aggressions or disagreeable jests which the rough musketeers loved to practise on one another. Of the soundness of his religious views there were grave suspicions. The preaching corporal opined that he was one of those predestined backsliders who fall into utter and hopeless reprobation; but this uncharitable opinion, biassed as it seemed to be by the impatience he had frequently manifested of that worthy's long-winded discourses, was scarcely shared by his comrades in so unmodified a form. That he was a stanch anti-Monarchy man was apparent less from his words, for he seldom enlarged much upon that or any other topic, than from the anxiety he displayed to lose no opportunity of witnessing the humiliations to which Charles was subjected. For all duties of guard or escort about the person of the monarch, Henry Brampton, as he called himself, was an eager volunteer. His comrades liked him, too; there was a nameless fascination in his pleasant manner that told on those rude, good-humoured natures; and then—he treated one and all to liquor whenever there was an opportunity.

Undisturbed by the noise and confusion in the guard-room, Brampton stood gazing long and fixedly into the narrow paved yard which bounded his view from that grated window. Once only a large tear gathered in his eyelashes, and dropped heavily on the back of his hand. Startled, as it seemed, and bitterly shamed by the incident, he fell to one more perusal of the letter he had been crushing in his grasp—a letter that had reposed inside his buff-coat for months; that had been read and re-read day by day, again and again; that had opened the old wound afresh at each repetition; and yet a letter that now constituted all his wealth on earth. It was cold, cruel, bitterly ungrateful and unfeeling. Why did he treasure it so? We will peep over the musketeer's shoulder, and read with him the words he knew so well by heart:—

'General Effingham will bear you this paper; you will easily recognise the hand of one who has always looked upon you, who always *will* look upon you, as an esteemed and valued friend.

'The General will spare no exertions to save you from the consequences of that last rash act of yours, to which I of all people cannot but offer my tribute of admiration and approval. It is right you should know that to Grace's influence with him, and to Grace alone, you owe your life. It is right you should be made aware of her great regard and esteem for you—of the effort she has made for your sake; of the claim she must always have upon your gratitude— nay, upon a warmer, holier feeling still. As a man of honour I entrust you with her secret; as a man of honour you must feel that you owe everything to her, and that she has a right to your affection and devotion such as *no other* ever has had, or ever could have. You will do as you have always done—follow the path of duty and gratitude and loyalty; and you will be very, *very* happy together, for you know what she is, and you have proved her regard for you. Indeed, I hope and pray you have a long and happy life before you. You are still young, though old enough for the follies and illusions of youth to have passed away for evermore; and with such a companion as dear Grace, you have every cause to anticipate a bright unclouded lot. I shall perhaps not see you again—I will not pretend that it is without regret I wish you farewell; but surely friends may be parted by the force of circumstances, and yet remain true and faithful friends. My own prospects are very uncertain; you will, however, hear *of* me, though it is better that you should not hear *from* me again. You have my earnest prayers for your welfare. You will like to know that I am well, and shall be quite happy when I hear of your safety, about which we are all so anxious—quite happy. Farewell!'

It was indeed a cruel letter. Had she been a surgeon, and the recipient an insensible patient under the knife, she could scarce have laid her cuts straighter, cleaner, deeper, than she did. How his honest heart bled when he received it; how it ached afterwards in the daily self-inflicted penance of its perusal. Could she give him up so calmly, so coldly, without an effort and without a pang? Could she thus transfer to another the wealth of an affection which she could surely not calculate, not appreciate? Was *he* nothing in the compact—he whose destiny she had been, who had built the whole fabric of his life on that faithless, heartless woman? and now what was all this glorious superstructure, with the noble elevation of its hope, and the golden embellishments of its romance? A wreck—and oh, what a wreck!

Poor Humphrey!—for we need scarcely say that Henry Brampton, with his dyed skin and his flaxen curls, was none other than the disguised Cavalier—poor Humphrey! it was the first real well-delivered thrust that had ever reached his heart; he might be excused for wincing when it pierced home to the core. He was a boy in his affections still, and he felt it very keenly, like a boy. He did not know—how should he?— what it had cost the writer. He could not fathom the inscrutable depths of the female character, or comprehend the morbid satisfaction with which it can inflict suffering on those it loves, if only feeling that it is undergoing pangs tenfold more unendurable itself. He only knew that he had lost the light of his life, and he felt sorely inclined to sit him down in the darkness without an effort for evermore.

And now it was well for Humphrey that he had long proposed to himself one great object on which to direct all his energies and all his thoughts. A heart thus driven back upon itself, whether it belong to man or woman, is a fatal possession; and the better it was originally, the worse is likely to be its eventual fate. Deprive a human being of hope, and you drive that being into physical or moral suicide. What is the cause of nine-tenths of the vice and immorality in the world? The absence of a glimpse of something brighter in the future than adorns the present. The material becomes all-in-all to him for whom the ideal is a blank; and the desperate man is nearly always a sensualist. When disappointment is keen enough to upset the foundations of a reason not originally very strong, the fool who was so weak as to hang all his hopes on an earthly thread, who built, in fact, 'his house upon the sand,' slips quietly out at a side door of the tenement, with an ounce of lead to the brain, or an edge of steel to the throat; but is he much less to be pitied who drowns the whole mansion that he loathes to live in, though he dare not quit it, in floods of wine and revelry, content to wallow in the swine's filth, so as he may but purchase the swine's insensibility?

It is the salvation of a noble nature to have some task of self-denial, some motive for self-sacrifice left, when all that made the daily burden of life endurable has passed away. Happy he who has habituated himself to look upon his whole earthly career but as a task of which the reward, though not given *here*, is as priceless as it is certain.

Our Cavalier, however, had long considered that, next to his God, he owed his whole service to his Sovereign. Whilst Charles was a dethroned monarch, and indeed a helpless prisoner, there was no room in Humphrey's mind for despair. 'Loyalty before all!' was still the motto of his shield, though the blazoning that adorned it was defaced, and the flowers that had graced and charmed it with their sweetness were withered away. After the first stunning effects of the blow which prostrated him had passed off, he summoned his whole energies to return once more to the task he had set himself in happier times. That he should feel utterly lonely and miserable was to be expected. His was a disposition on which a disappointment of the affections tells most severely. Naturally confiding, where he trusted at all he trusted entirely, ignoring, as most sincere men do, the existence of deceit. Constant and sensitive himself, he could not conceive the possibility of change or unkindness in another; nor although the last to overrate his own value, could he be blind to the merit of his unswerving truth and fidelity. Above all, inexperienced as he was in the ways of women, his straightforward honesty of purpose could not understand how they delight in the generous duplicity which, for the beloved one's welfare, feigns to yield of its own free will all that it best delights to keep, and veils its sufferings with a smile, the sweeter in proportion to the pain it affects to hide.

Well, come what might, as long as Charles Stuart was in adversity, so long was Humphrey Bosville his reckless and devoted servant. Cautiously walking in the most crowded parts of London, which then even more than now afforded the securest hiding-place for a fugitive, he had passed a few weeks subsequent to his interview with Effingham and release from Newgate in the enforced inactivity which he loathed. This was the period at which he felt most keenly the disappointment he had undergone. It was during these long leaden weeks that Vice stretched her ghastly arms to enfold him, not in her most alluring, but in her most dangerous form. When she offers her treacherous goblet, sparkling with nectar and wreathed with flowers, though thirsty nature may quaff greedily at the poison, there is yet an instinctive antipathy to the draught, a speedy reaction when its intoxicating effects have passed away. All happiness is heaven-born, and even its spurious copy, mere enjoyment, cannot entirely divest itself of the reflected light shed by that which it strives to imitate; so he who in the exuberance of youth, and health, and animal spirits, laughs the merriest laugh, and drains the fullest cup of riot and revelry, feels inwardly conscious the while that he is meant for better things. But it is when she assumes the garb, not of the garlanded Goddess, but of the dark and shrouded Fate, when she says to her votary, 'My child, here is the deadly opiate; drink, and feel no more! Mine is the dull trance of oblivion; come to my arms, poor wretch, to slumber and forget!' that she offers her most fatal temptation, that she drags the devoted sufferer headlong into her whirlpool, to wheel a few giddy turns in vain around its edges, and then sink into its vortex without hope for evermore.

But Humphrey was saved by his devotion to his King. While something womanly in his nature caused him to shrink from grosser vices, the noble ambition to serve the Stuart to the last bade him preserve to the utmost his mental and bodily powers for that sacred purpose ; and so the while he waited his opportunity, he led a weary life of solitude and self-denial. It was a long time to be immured in an obscure lodging, uncheered by comrades, forgotten by friends, with nothing but that cruel letter for a solace and a study —a long time, but it came to an end at last.

After much consideration, it appeared to Humphrey that the only method by which he could have a chance of assisting his royal master was to obtain some appointment, if possible, about his person, and then trust to accident for an opportunity either of effecting his escape or communicating between him and his friends. For one so well known, however, as the young Cavalier officer, whose daring attempts had already marked him out as the most dangerous 'Malignant' of them all, this was no such easy matter; and he resolved at length to disguise his person and enlist in one of the Parliamentary regiments quartered in the metropolis, by which means he hoped at one time or another to be in immediate attendance on Charles himself.

Fortune favoured him, as she often does those who trust in her guidance while they make light of her favours; and it was not long before the name of Henry Brampton was added to the roll-call of Hacker's musketeers, that worthy commander remarking when the recruit was brought up for inspection, that 'The Spanish Main was no bad school for a soldier of the Parliament; and he would scarce boggle at anything demanded of him to further the good cause here, who had stuck at nothing in the service of the devil yonder.'

So Brampton mounted his buff and bandeliers, shouldered his shining musket, took his round of fatigue duty, and tramped up and down his post on sentry, as though he had not been a few short years ago one of the most promising officers in Prince Rupert's cavalry division.

It was seldom, though, that he had an opportunity of being near the person of the monarch. It was not till the first day of the royal prisoner's trial that he was permitted to come actually into his presence. He could not but think, however, that Charles had recognised him. Like the rest of his line, the latter possessed an extraordinary memory for faces, and a wonderful facility in identifying those which he had once seen; it was not therefore surprising that he should have penetrated the disguise of one whom, indeed, he would scarce have been justified in forgetting, and whose features he had once before detected under the fisherman's slouched hat at Brampton Mill.

Yes, he felt sure the King must have known him again, but it was during a moment of great confusion, and even Humphrey's coolness had not kept his head as clear as it should have been at that trying period. It was after the keen bitter tones of Lady Fairfax had for a second time disturbed the judicial proceedings in Westminster Hall. Hacker had just delivered his brutal command to fire into the box occupied by that lady, and the musketeers were preparing to obey. Like the rest, Brampton was compelled to step to the front, and bring his firelock to the ' Present;' not that he dreamed for an instant of fulfilling so barbarous an order, but that any appearance of hesitation or unwillingness might have invited detection. It was at this moment that he caught Charles's eye fixed upon him with a peculiar and impressive glance. It seemed at once to instil caution, patience, and forbearance; but all was lost in the mist that came before his eyes and the whirl that stupified his brain, occasioned by the face that met his own as he levelled his musket in the direction of Lady Fairfax.

Standing forward in the old attitude he knew so well, looking just as she used to do, only graver and paler, but still, as his heart told him, even in that moment of surprise and confusion, as dear, as beautiful as ever, appeared the woman he had vowed he would love no longer, he had resolved he would never see again. There she was, ready to confront danger, ready to die if need be, rather than show the slightest symptom of cowardice; and hurt, angry, maddened as he had been, he felt *proud* of her even then.

As he stood at the guard-room window it required many a perusal of the fatal letter to harden him into indifference once more; and it was with a feeling of no small relief and satisfaction that he heard his name read out by the sergeant on duty as one of the permanent escort told off to guard the person of the imprisoned Sovereign.

CHAPTER XVIII.

'THE PROTEST.'

AS a venturous swimmer striking out fearlessly from the bank finds himself carried downward by the current far lower than he intended, and discovers that all his energies, all his powers, will be severely taxed to make good his landing on the opposite shore, so doth he who embarks on the stream of political life learn to his cost that the river runs swifter still as it gets deeper, and that if he would keep his head above the surface, rather than sink into oblivion, he must consent to be borne onwards, in defiance of his own better judgment, at the mercy of the flood.

George Effingham had long ago cast in his lot with the Parliament; of what avail was his single arm to arrest the desperate measures which had now become necessary to the existence of that body, clinging as it did to the shadow of power whereof the substance was already in the iron grasp of the Dictator.

Effingham had won a position such as would have satisfied the ambition of any ordinary man, such as any ordinary man would have made considerable sacrifices of conscience and feelings to retain, but George was not an ordinary man, and his character was altered, his heart softened by the ordeal he had undergone. Long ago he had dreamt of religious freedom, of personal and political liberty, of a mo-

narchy based on those utopian principles which form
the foundations of all theoretical governments, which
men will see carried out when the golden age comes
back once more; and for the realization of these
visions he had been content to give up friends, party,
military honour, all the hopes that make life
dearest and sweetest, and to wade knee-deep in blood
and guilt for the establishment of peace and holiness
on earth. It was sad to find the conviction growing
stronger on him day by day that he had been mistaken—that the party he had joined was no whit less
ambitious, less selfish, less intolerant, and less tyrannical, than that which he had left; to see the leaven
of ambition, the restless thirst for self-aggrandizement,
as strong in the formal Puritan as in the dissolute
Cavalier, to be forced to acknowledge that the son of
the Lincolnshire grazier could be no less regardless of
principles and defiant of consequences than the scion
of the Stuarts, and to watch with horrified gaze the
inevitable approach of that tragedy in which it was
never his intention to participate.

He had been a stern pitiless man once, a man who
would have hesitated at nothing in the execution of a
purpose which he had determined it was his duty to
fulfil, but many influences had combined to temper
the strength and harshness of his original character;
the habits of high command had accustomed him to
a broader and consequently a more tolerant view of
men and things; the practice of that true religion of
which the very essence is the 'Charity that thinketh
no evil,' had brought out, as it never fails to do, the
kindlier impulses of his nature, and the chastening

hand of sorrow had taught even proud George Effingham that he must bow resignedly to a stronger will than his own. There was little left of the haughty unbending soldier, save the gallant spirit that still could not be brought to acknowledge fear of any man that ever stepped the earth.

He had been present during the King's trial in Westminster Hall. He had loudly remonstrated against the disrespect with which his Majesty was treated during the ceremony. He had rebuked Hacker sufficiently sharply for his intemperate and unofficer-like conduct, and he had even recognised the well-known form of Grace Allonby shrinking behind the two Cavalier ladies who stood forward so proudly to vindicate their loyalty even in that moment of danger. It was painful to see her again, but George was accustomed to pain now—what did it matter? She was married to his old comrade by this time, of course, his old comrade whom he had himself saved to give her, his old comrade who was within three paces of him all the time, but whom he did not detect under the disguise of a Parliamentary musketeer. From feelings of delicacy he had kept aloof from all communication with the family of her whom he felt he had lost; it was enough that he had done all in *his* power to make her happy, and he hoped she *was* happy, and had forgotten him altogether, at least so he told himself; and yet perhaps it would not have affected him inconsolably to have known that she was pining and solitary, and that Humphrey Bosville had neither seen her nor heard from her since his release.

Each day Effingham attended the trial, and when it was concluded, contrary to his wont, he made no comment or remark upon a topic which engaged all voices and occupied all thoughts; but next morning he issued from his lodging dressed in full uniform as a Parliamentary General, and with a darker brow and more compressed lip than usual took his way, silent and preoccupied, towards the residence of the most powerful man at that moment in England, Oliver Cromwell.

It was perhaps, with one exception, the saddest day of his life. Each by each his visions had all departed from him, each by each he had given up, first his enjoyments, then his hopes, lastly his consolations. When he had resigned his command, and repudiated all further connexion with those whom he had deserted his colours to join, what would be left to him on earth? He could see before him the weary useless life, the long leaden days, wanting even the distraction of professional occupation and the stimulus of professional exertion. He would have no position, no station in the world—he who was at that very moment one of the most important men in the kingdom; but he never wavered: it was right, and he would do it. God would find him some task to fulfil, if it was good that he should have an appointed task, and if not, he would accept a humble lot without repining. Once only he thought how different things might have been, thought of a happy quiet home, with domestic duties and domestic pleasures, and a smile that could make a sanded floor brighter and fairer than a palace; but he drove these visions from him with an effort, and resolved to carry his burden, heavy as it might be, without shrinking from the labour. He had gone through the crucible at last, and had learned, bold, powerful, and successful as he was, the most difficult task of all, *to bear* humbly, resignedly, and without a murmur.

As he strode resolutely along he overtook a female figure that he seemed instinctively to recognise, although, preoccupied as he was, he had scarcely noticed its movements or appearance. It stopped as he approached, and putting back its hood, disclosed an extremely comely face, blushing to the very edge of its cap at its recognition in the open street by so distinguished a personage as General Effingham.

'No offence, General,' exclaimed Faith, curtseying, for indeed it was no other than Grace Allonby's waiting-maid, grown into a sedate and matronly personage. 'No offence, I hope, but when I looked back and saw it was you and none other, I couldn't help stopping, just for old times' sake. Ah! great changes have taken place, General, since you've seen me and my young lady; but, dear me, it's a world of change, and who'd ever have thought of my taking up at last with Hugh Dymocke! but no offence, General, I humbly hope.'

Faith dropped another curtsey, and looked very demure and pretty as she did so.

George muttered a few unintelligible words of greeting. The distinguished officer was far more agitated at this chance meeting than the humble waiting-maid. He stammered out at last a confused inquiry as to the well-being of 'Mistress Cave, and—

and—Mistress Grace,' he could not trust himself to add her maiden surname now, lest she should have changed it for another.

'Alack! General,' answered Faith, 'truly they are ill at ease. Indeed, the world never seems to have gone rightly with us since poor Sir Giles Allonby went to his account; and there's my Lord lying sick in his lodging down here by Whitehall, and my good-man, that's Dymocke—Hugh Dymocke—asking your pardon, General, you remember him,' quoth Faith, with another blush and another curtsey; 'he's an altered man since they took the poor young Major, and Mistress Grace, she takes on sadly to get no news of him, for dead or alive he might be, and none of us one whit the wiser; and as for Mistress Cave, it's never a word, good nor bad, she says to any one, but walks about pale and silent like a ghost; and I'm scarcely half so merry as I used to be, though that's not to be expected, of course; and indeed I never thought to see such days as these, though I'm sure when I took Hugh Dymocke, I humbly hoped it was all for the best.'

She stopped to take breath, and George, who had by this time recovered his composure, observed with considerable simplicity,

'I thought your young lady had by this time followed your good example, Mistress Dymocke, and was married.'

'Married!' echoed Faith, with a laugh of derision; 'not she—and never likely to be; she's a sweet young lady, Mistress Grace, and a winsome, but she's been looking too long for the straight stick in the wood, and after rejecting this one and that one, here and there, she'll come out into the fields again and never find what she seeks. It was but yesterday I said to her as I was doing her hair—for leave her I never will till I see the colour in her cheeks once more— "Out of such a number," says I, "Mistress Grace, it ought not to be so hard to choose." "Never speak of it, Faith," says she, taking me up mighty short, and turning so pale, poor thing. "And why not?" says I, for I can be bold enough when I like, and I was determined once for all I'd know how and about it. "Isn't there gallants here and gallants there, all ready to fling themselves at your feet? Wasn't there Major Bosville, and many another of the Cavaliers, that would have gone barefoot to Palestine and back again, only for a touch of your hand; and now that the Parliament's uppermost, and the land is purged, as they call it, from vanity, couldn't you pick and choose among the saints, God-fearing men though they be?" With that she fired up as red as scarlet. "How dare you, Faith!" says she; "leave me this instant!" but she turned quite white again, and was all of a tremble, and I heard her muttering-like "Never a Rebel, for the old father's sake," and though I was forced to do as she bid me, and go out of the room, I made bold to peep through the key-hole, and she had flung herself down on her knees by the bedside, and was weeping as if her heart would break. Oh! she'll never marry now, wont Mistress Grace. And as for the poor young Major, that they make such a talk about, it's my belief that Mistress Cave loves him a deal better than my young lady ever did, though I durstn't ask *her* such a question, not to save my life!'

Having arrived at her destination and the end of her disclosures at the same moment, Faith deemed it incumbent on her to point out the house now occupied by Lord Vaux and his relatives, which was indeed on the opposite side of the street, and to invite the General on her own account to step in and see his old friends once more. George was sorely tempted to break through all his good resolutions; but he had a duty to fulfil, and he determined until that task was accomplished he would suffer no human weaknesses, no earthly considerations, to turn him aside from the path of truth and honour. The waiting-maid's revelations had indeed made sad havoc of the dull mental equilibrium he had sworn to preserve. It was much to learn that Grace was still free; much to hear that her antipathy to a rebel could create such a turmoil in her feelings. He was no fool, George Effingham, and who shall blame him if he drew his own conclusions, and became conscious that hopes which he had stifled and eradicated with the strong hand only waited a favourable opportunity to germinate and blossom once more? Nevertheless, he would not permit himself to dwell for more than an instant on the dream that had so affected his outer life; but taking a courteous leave of Faith, and forcing on her at the same time a munificent wedding-present, he pursued his walk with even a firmer step and a more resolute brow than before.

If one short hour ago he was strung to a dogged, obstinate defiance of danger, he could have faced the deadliest peril now with positive exultation and delight.

It was the 29th of January, and Lieutenant-General Cromwell's leisure was not likely to be at the disposal of the first comer; nevertheless the sentry at his door made room for Effingham to pass with a military salute, and after a very brief interval of waiting in an ante-room, a pale and agitated secretary ushered George into the presence of the Lieutenant-General, with a grave apology that so distinguished a servant of the Parliament should be kept in attendance even for a few minutes.

Cromwell was standing in the middle of the room, attired with his usual plain simplicity, but somewhat more carefully than his wont. The pale secretary reseated himself after the entrance of Effingham, and continued his occupation of writing from the Lieutenant-General's dictation, but his hand was so unsteady that it shook even the massive table on which he leaned his arm. His master took a short turn or two up and down the room, and for some minutes did not appear to notice the new arrival. George had time to scan him minutely. He had been familiar with him for a long period, had watched him in many an emergency of difficulty and danger, yet had he never seen him quite like what he was now.

In the turmoil of battle, in the critical moments on which his own destiny and that of England depended, it was a part of the man to become cooler and cooler as the plot thickened. His cheek would glow and his eye would brighten when leading the

Ironsides to a successful charge; but should their advance be checked and the scales of victory hang doubtful in the balance, those plain heavy features seemed to settle into lineaments of iron. Now, though the orders he was enunciating were but trifling matters of military detail, a faint sallow flush came and went over his countenance, and the large lips twitched and trembled, while the broad jaw beneath them closed ever and anon with a convulsive clasp. He seemed to speak mechanically, and with his thoughts fixed on some topic far distant from the strategical movements he was directing, and he started—positively started—when in one of his short restless turns he encountered George Effingham.

There were but those three in the room—the pale secretary bowing his head over his writing; the parliamentary officer loftily confronting his chief; and the Dictator himself, hiding an air of remorse, irritation, and perplexity under an assumption of more than military brevity and decision.

'What would you,' demanded Cromwell, his brow darkening as, with the perspicuity of all great men, he read Effingham's face like a book—'what would you with us in this press of business? Be brief, for the time is short, and lo! even now the hour is at hand.'

'I come to resign my commission into your Excellency's hands,' answered Effingham in slow, steady tones, emphatic as they were sorrowful. 'I come to demand my dismissal from your Excellency's service. I come to protest against the murder of Charles Stuart.'

Cromwell's brow had grown darker and darker as the officer went on; but when he reached his climax, all the wrath he had so long repressed, all the accumulated feelings of self-reproach which had burdened him for days, broke forth in a burst of incontrollable fury. His face became purple, his features swelled, and his eyes glowed like coals as, with a shout that made the pale secretary start out of his chair, he thundered forth—

'Out upon you, George Effingham! vile traitor and doubly-dyed renegade—will you put your hand to the plough and dare now to look back? Will you come into the Lord's vineyard, and shrink like a coward from your share of the work? God do so to me and more also if I lay not your head as low before evensong as that of Charles Stuart will lie to-morrow, to spare whom I take heaven to witness I would give my right arm—yea, the very apple of mine eye!'

George had nerve as well as courage. He remained perfectly firm and erect during this outbreak, and at its conclusion repeated, in tones if possible more distinct and accusatory than before, 'I protest against the murder of Charles Stuart!'

We have already said that a stern daring akin to his own never failed to touch the keystone of Cromwell's character. His wrath abated as rapidly as it had risen. With the inevitable self-deception of all who would fain stretch conscience too far, he was willing to vindicate his actions to his subordinate, though he felt he could not justify them to himself. Perhaps something within told him that, had he been in Effingham's position, he would have acted in the same manner.

'Nay, I do wrong thus to chafe that thou art still in darkness,' said he, with a strong effort at composure, and a countenance paling rapidly now that his natural violence of temper had expended itself. 'Thou art a tried comrade, Effingham, and a fellow-labourer in the good work; yet it may be that thine eyes have not been opened, and thou canst not see the hand of the Lord in our dealings with this man of blood. I would not be hasty with thee, my trusty friend. Take back thy resignation, and forget that thou hast thus bearded one of the Lord's appointed servants in the execution of his work.'

Cromwell turned to his secretary as if to continue the previous employment which Effingham's presence had interrupted, and made as though the subject was now concluded between them; but George was not to be thus put off. Eyeing the Lieutenant-General gravely and sternly, he once more placed his written resignation in his hands.

'I will no longer serve,' said he, ' with those who set at nought the Divine ordinance, and dip their hands in blood for the security of their temporal power. How shall I answer at the Great Day when the life of Charles Stuart, king though he be, is required at my hands, and I stand convicted of aiding and abetting in his murder—ay, his murder, General Cromwell, of whom the Scripture itself hath said, "Touch not mine Anointed?" How wilt thou answer for it thyself *there*, who canst not give an account of it that shall satisfy mankind even *here?*"

Cromwell paced the room with rapid and irregular strides, his hands folded together, and the fingers entwining each other as of one in the extreme of perplexity. His features worked and trembled with the conflict of his emotions, and his breath came short and quick as he muttered out his vindication partly to himself and partly to the brave captain, whose defiance he could not but admire.

'It is not for me to answer it—surely not only for *me!* Do I stand alone amongst the people of England? Am I at once accuser, judge, and executioner in my own person? By the verdict of sixty just men; by the decree of a nation pronounced through its Parliament; by the laws of God and man—the head of the unrighteous hath been doomed to fall, and shall I alone be called to give account for it here and hereafter? And yet can you divide bloodguiltiness by figures, and mete out the portions of crime as one meteth out corn in a bushel? Nay, it is a just decree, and by its justice must we stand or fall—Council and Commons, Peers and Parliament, down to the meanest trooper of the army—and let none shrink from his share of the great work in which all are alike bound to take a part.'

'You can save him if you will,' said Effingham, fixing his eye calmly on the agitated countenance of his powerful superior, the pale secretary looking at the pleader the while as one who watches a man placing his head voluntarily in the lion's maw.

'None can save him now,' answered Cromwell in grave prophetic tones, ' but He in whose hands are the issues of life and death. What am I but a sword

in the grasp of the slayer—an instrument forged to
do the bidding of the saints, the despised and jeered
saints, that have yet triumphed in despite of their
enemies?　Albeit the lowest and the humblest in that
goodly communion, I will not flinch from the duty
that wiser and holier men than I have set me to perform.　"It is expedient for us that one man should
die for the people, and that the whole nation perish
not."　Enough of this, George Ellingham—thou in
whom I have trusted, who wert to me even as a
brother, go out from among us, if it must be so, lest
a worse thing befall thee.　He that is not with us is
against us.　Go out from among us, George Effingham, false and unprofitable servant!　Begone and see
my face no more!'

Cromwell turned from him angrily and abruptly.
He had lashed himself into wrath again, and the imploring looks of the secretary warned Ellingham to
withdraw.　He placed his resignation on the table,
and keeping his eye on Cromwell, whose averted face
and troubled gestures betrayed the storm within,
walked steadily from the room.　As he reached the
door the Lieutenant-General was heard to mutter,
'It is the Lord's doing!　It is the Atonement of
Blood!'

The Council were already assembled in the Painted
Chamber, and were waiting but for him who was indeed as their very right arm and the breath of their
nostrils.　While Effingham walked home afoot, a
ruined, and in the eyes of his own world a degraded
man, Lieutenant-General Cromwell stepped from his
coach amidst the clang of arms and the deferential

stare of the populace, the most powerful individual in England. Which of the two looked back on the 29th of January with the most tranquil heart?

But the future Lord Protector was by this time fully nerved for the stern measures he had undertaken to carry out. If his conscience told him that the life of Charles Stuart would be required at his hands, was not the iron will powerful enough to stifle the still small voice? Could not Ambition and Fanaticism, the ambition that had originated in Patriotism, the Fanaticism that had once been piety, march hand-in-hand to their triumph, calling themselves Duty and Necessity? Was Cromwell the first who ever forced himself to believe that honour and interest pointed to the same path, or the only man who has persuaded himself he was a tool in the hands of the Almighty whilst he was doing the devil's work? Saint or hypocrite, patriot or usurper—perhaps a mixture of all—can we judge of his temptations or realize to ourselves the extremity to which he found himself reduced? Sacrilege or justice, crime or duty, he went about it with a bold brow and a steady hand.

Small deliberation did they hold, those gloomy men who met in the Painted Chamber. Their nerves were strung, their minds made up, they had even leisure to trifle with their awful task; and the ink that was to witness the shedding of a king's blood was flirted from one to another in ghastly mockery of sport. The DEATH WARRANT lay before them, the merciless document that pronounced ' Charles Stuart, King of England, to stand convicted, attainted, and condemned of high treason, and other high crimes;' that sentenced him 'To be put to death by the severing of his head from his body, of which sentence execution yet remaineth to be done. These are therefore to will and require you to see the said sentence executed in the open street before Whitehall upon the morrow, being the thirtieth day of this instant month of January, between the hours of ten in the morning and five in the afternoon, with full effect. And for so doing this shall be your warrant.

'And these are to require all officers and soldiers and others the good people of this nation of England, to be assisting unto you in this service. Given under our hands and seals.'

And then they signed their names in full, thus:—

' JOHN BRADSHAW.

' THOMAS GREY, Lord GROBY.

' OLIVER CROMWELL.'

(And fifty-six others.)

And the third signature was written in the steadiest hand amongst them all.

CHAPTER XIX.

'A FORLORN HOPE.'

CHARLES STUART'S last day was come. He had undergone his trial with a dignity and calmness which many attributed to his conviction that even at the last the Parliament dare not proceed to extremities, that at least the *person* of a sovereign must always be respected in England. If such was the reed on which he leaned, he must have found it broken in his hand. If he had cherished any expectations of a reprieve or commutation of his sentence, had been deceived by any of those visions which are so apt to take the place of Hope when Hope herself is stricken to the earth, he must have seen them now completely cleared away; and yet his courage never failed him. The King was as composed, as gentle, as majestic, in his warded chamber at St. James's on that bitter 29th of January, as though he had been the most powerful monarch in Europe seated triumphantly on a throne.

In the ante-room of the prisoner's apartment was stationed a guard of Hacker's musketeers: rough, careless soldiers were they, opposed to royalty both from interest and inclination; and yet, now that the sentence was passed, now that the prisoner whom they guarded was no longer a monarch on his trial, but a human soul that would be in eternity to-morrow, their boisterous jests were checked, their rude voices hushed, and all appeared to feel alike the influence of that majesty with which the King of Terrors clothes him whom he is about to visit.

One amongst them, indeed, seemed more restless than his comrades. Henry Brampton, with his dark face and flaxen curls, had omitted no opportunity of approaching the prisoner; and yet even now the last hour was almost come, and his duty had not yet brought him in immediate contact with Charles's person. The suspense was getting absolutely maddening; and the disguised Cavalier's feelings, outraged and lacerated by the sufferings he saw his sovereign compelled to undergo, worked upon him to a degree that it cost him all the efforts of which he was capable to hide from the observation of his companions.

Brampton had laid his plans with the energy and decision of his character. For weeks he had been ingratiating himself with the more dissolute and desperate men in the company to which he belonged. He had prayed with them, preached with them, jested with them, and, above all, drank with them, till he could count some dozen or so of choice spirits with whom he felt his influence to be all-powerful. These he had sounded cautiously and by degrees. Like most men with nothing to lose, he had found them totally without fixed principles, and perfectly ready for any undertaking which promised to conduce to their own advantage. Without committing himself to any one of them, or letting them into his confidence, he had given them to understand that he meditated some bold stroke at a fitting opportunity, in which he counted upon their adhesion, and which, if successful, would render them independent of military service for life, and give them wherewith to drink to their heart's content for the rest of their days.

These myrmidons he had contrived with infinite pains to unite in one squad, or division, which generally went on guard together, and which formed in rotation the escort of his Majesty. Could he but depend upon them at the important moment, a plan for the King's escape was practicable. Relays of horses were ready at all hours to carry his Majesty to the coast; and if the fidelity of his guards could once be seduced, it would be no impossibility to hurry him out of St. James's, and away to a place of safety under cover of night. Two obstacles stood in the way of the dauntless Cavalier. The first was so to arrange as that this escort, and no other, should guard him during the hours of darkness, a difficulty which appeared at length to be overcome, as they had been told off for duty this very evening; the second, to apprise the King of his intentions, no easy matter, guarded as was the Royal prisoner, every word scrupulously noted, and every action rigidly watched.

The great stake must be played out to-day. To-morrow it would be too late; and Brampton's manifest restlessness and perturbation began to excite the remarks of his reckless companions.

'Thy conscience pricks thee, Henry,' said one rude musketeer. 'Overboard with it, man! as thou didst with the Dons yonder on the Spanish Main.'

'Nay,' quoth another, 'the time hath come at last; and Brampton's plot, whatever it be, is about hatching just now.'

'Well, I for one am tired of doing nothing,' observed a third. 'Have with thee, lad, be it to rob a church or to skin a bishop!'

'Or to put Fairfax in irons,' said a fourth.

'Or to take the New Jerusalem by escalade. Hurrah! for three hours' plunder of those streets, my boys, after the storm,' shouted a fifth. They were ripe for anything now, and the 'hurrah!' was re-echoed more than once through the guard-room, when the last speaker, the wildest reprobate amongst them all, raised his hand with a warning gesture, and a wistful look upon his dissipated war-worn face. 'Hush, lads!' he said, in a hoarse whisper! and whilst he spoke the guard-room became still as death. 'Hush, for pity's sake. His children are going into him even now. God help them, poor things! I've got young ones of my own!'

There was a tear on more than one shaggy eyelash, as the Princess Elizabeth and her little brother, the infant Duke of Gloucester, were led by faithful Herbert through the guard-room, to see their father for the last time on this side the grave.

Charles sat at a small table on which lay a Bible, a work of controversial divinity—for even at this extreme hour he could not take his religion pure from the fountain-head—and a casket containing a few small diamond ornaments and other jewels.

This casket had been sent to him the night before, in return for a signet-ring which he had forwarded to its guardian as a voucher, and had been religiously kept by that custodian, the Lady Wheeler, until such time as the King's necessities should force him to ask for it. Its contents were scarcely of Royal value, being but a few dilapidated 'Georges' and 'Garters;' but as they lay spread out upon the table before him, they constituted all the worldly possessions left to Charles Stuart.

He was looking at them wistfully, and with a sad pensive expression on his brow. Many a gorgeous scene did those glittering toys recal, many an hour of Royal state and courtly splendour when he who was now a prisoner waiting for his doom, needed but to lift his hand to bid the proudest heads in England bend lowly before him, when he was the centre of that charmed circle which numbered in its ranks the flower of the noblest aristocracy in the world, now, alas, scattered, exiled, ruined, and destroyed—when he was the first personage in its peerage, the first knight in its chivalry, the powerful sovereign, the happy husband, the law-giver, the benefactor, the fountain-head of honour, and wealth, and renown. Where had it all fled? Could those times have ever been real? or was it not some vision that had melted dreamily away? Alas! those broken ornaments typified too truly the broken fortunes of him who now gazed on them for the last time. It is said that on the near approach of death, especially a death of violence undergone while body and mind are still untouched by decay, the whole of a man's life passes before him like a pageant. What a strange eventful pageant must it have been that thus glided across the spiritual vision of the doomed

King! His careless boyhood, his indulgent father's
kindly smile and awkward ungainly form ; the romantic expedition to Madrid, the gorgeous feasts, the
tournaments and bull-fights of chivalrous old Spain ;
the face of Buckingham, beautiful exceedingly, and
the sparkling smile of his own young Bourbon bride ;
the assembled Parliaments, a royal figure standing out
in relief as that of one with whom he was not personally identified, calling them together and pro-
roguing them at will ; Laud's stately bearing, Hamp-
den's goodly presence, respectful even in defiance, and
scapegoat Strafford's pale reproachful smile ; then the
Scotch progress, and the magnificence of Newcastle's
princely hospitality, the unfurling of the standard, the
marches and counter-marches of civil warfare ; the
Court at Oxford, with its narrowing circle of the
loyal and true, stanch Ormond's noble brow, hot
Rupert's towering form, Goring's long love-locks, and
stout old Astley's honest war-worn face ; then the
midnight bivouac and the morning alarm, the sweeping charge, the thrilling war-cry, the shattered rout
of Naseby's fatal field ; a prisoner, still a king, at
Holmby House, Hampton Court, Carisbrooke Castle,
Windsor itself; the poor bird beating its wings more
and more hopelessly against the bars of each successive
cage ; to end in Bradshaw's pitiless frown and the
final sentence read out to consenting hundreds in
Westminster Hall. Ay, it *was* reality, after all, else
why this sombre apartment, with its barred doors and
lofty window-sills ? why the sad faces of his few personal attendants? why the rude oath and jest and
clang of arms in the adjoining guard-room? above all,

why the chill dull foreboding, creeping and curdling even round *his* brave heart, the stunned consciousness that *to-morrow* he must be in another world.

It is a splendid pageant, truly, that of a king's life; yet perhaps at the extreme hour its scenes appear no whit more important, no whit more satisfactory to look back upon, than those which flit through the brain of a beggar, laying him down to die homeless by the wayside.

It was pitiful to see the children as they came gently into their father's presence. On each little face there was a dim prescience of evil, a dread of something felt but not understood—fear for themselves, sorrow for him, although they knew not why, mingled with childish wonderment, not altogether painful, and interest, and awe.

Charles had need of all his fortitude now. He took the Princess lovingly on his knee, and the child looked up wistfully and fondly in his face. Something that crossed it caused her to burst out a-crying, and she hid her wet cheek on her father's shoulder in a passion of tears. Her little brother, frightened at her distress, wept plentifully for company. The rough soldiers in the guard-room had rather have fronted the King's culverins at point-blank distance, than entered that chamber sanctified by sorrow. They herded together as far as might be from the door, and if they exchanged words it was not above their breath.

The King took his few diamond ornaments from the table.

'My children,' said he, 'behold all the wealth I have it now in my power to give you.'

With that he placed the gauds in their little hands, reserving only a ' George,' cut in an onyx and set with diamonds, the which he wore on his breast like a true knight, as he walked steadfastly to death on the morrow.

Then he blessed them with a father's blessing. ' My children,' said Charles, ' I shall be with you no more: you will never again see your earthly father in this world. But you have a Father in Heaven of whom none can rob you. To Him I commend you —to Him I bid you commend yourselves. Observe your duty to the Queen your mother. Swerve never in your loyalty to the Prince your brother, who is, and who always must be, my rightful successor. Fear not the face of man ; fear only to do evil in the sight of Heaven. Farewell, my children ! Be comforted, and Farewell !'

Then lifting his little son upon his knee, a boy that could scarce speak plain, he bade him for the love of his father never to supplant either of his brothers ; never to believe that he could be a rightful Sovereign while they lived ; never to allow wicked designing men to tempt him to the Throne ; and the little one understood him, and kindled as he spoke, lisping out that he never would—

' I will be torn in pieces first !' said the sturdy child. So he dismissed them ; and calling them back once more folded them in one long parting embrace, and blessed them for the last time. Then he turned away to the window ; and when the door closed upon them it seemed to him that the bitterness of death was past.

Good Bishop Juxon was then admitted to the Royal presence, and Charles Stuart's last evening on earth was passed in penitence and trustful prayer.

Henry Brampton's suspense was becoming too painful to endure; but the welcome order came at last, and our Cavalier found himself once more on the eve of one of those desperate enterprises in which it was his destiny to be continually engaged; in which, indeed, only he seemed now to live. Personal danger had for long been a stimulant of which he could ill forego the use, and it had become his normal existence to work in a perpetual plot on the King's behalf.

With a brutality which was hardly characteristic even of that stern commandant, Hacker had issued an order that two musketeers should remain in the prisoner's chamber the whole night previous to his execution; and it was with a deep, thrilling sense of triumph that Brampton heard his assumed name read out by the corporal of the guard as selected for this otherwise unwelcome duty. As he ran over in his own mind the arrangements he had completed—the adherents on whom he could calculate as sufficiently numerous to overpower any refractory sentinel; the coach which was in waiting night after night, on some pretext or another, in the Mall; the relays of the best horses then in England, furnished from many a nobleman's and gentleman's stable, stationed at short intervals along a direct and unfrequented cross country road to the coast; the raking corvette, that stood off and on from an obscure seaport during the day, and coming into harbour at night, was kept ready at any hour to trip her anchor, shake out her topsail, and, fair wind or foul, beat out to sea; the disguise prepared for the well-known person of the King; nay, the very papers which should vouch for his assumed character in case he were stopped at any of the numerous armed posts pervading the country, and for which friends in high places had actually procured the impression of the new Parliamentary seal, with the English arms and the Irish harp, and the inscription, 'In the first year of freedom, by God's blessing restored;'—as he ran over all these well-assorted arrangements in his mind, he felt that the moment could no longer be delayed, and that now or never he must make proof of the inferior instruments with the assistance of which his plan must necessarily be carried out.

One by one he sounded them in different corners of the guard-room; one by one he found them, as he had anticipated, men ready to undertake any measure, however desperate, for an adequate consideration. All of them loved adventure for its own sake; none of them were inaccessible to a bribe.

There was something about Brampton, too, that made its way rapidly with *men*; a certain womanly kindliness which—joined to obvious daring and reckless contempt for consequences, has an unspeakable charm for the grosser sex—had invested him with a high degree of interest in those untutored minds; and the stories they told each other of his miraculous adventures and romantic crimes on the Spanish Main and elsewhere—stories which originated solely in their own imaginations—had surrounded him with a halo of renown and mystery by which they were com-

pletely dazzled. He was not slow to take advantage
of this spurious fascination. Singly and collectively
he bound them by an oath to do his bidding, whatever it might be, for that one night; and pledged
himself equally solemnly to endow them severally
with sums which, to private soldiers, represented unheard-of affluence on the morrow. His own patri-
mony was well nigh exhausted, it is true, but the
King's adherents had not yet been completely rooted
out of the land. Broken, dispersed, sequestered,
ruined as was the Cavalier party, he had no fear that
the money would not be forthcoming. When Brampton belted on his bandeliers and shouldered his musket
to take his post in the King's bed-room, his heart
bounded under his buff-coat to think that at last he
had saved his Sovereign.

Good Bishop Juxon had taken leave of his beloved
master for the night; faithful Herbert had prepared
the pallet on which, as an act of especial favour to the
prisoner, he was permitted to repose by the King's
bedside. Charles had completed his usual devotions,
and had busied himself in the observance of all the
accustomed *minutiæ* of his toilet, as though it were
but one of the many ordinary evenings which lead up
surely and successively to the last. When he was
ready to undress he seemed to indulge in a short interval of contemplative repose—calm, resigned, nay,
even hopeful, like a man who is about to undertake a
journey on which he has long speculated, and for
which, now that his departure is near at hand, he has
neither repugnance nor fear. Herbert busied himself
about divers matters in the chamber, to hide his

troubled countenance and overflowing eyes, which the King observing, spoke to him cheerfully and with a smile, bidding him rouse himself at an early hour on the following morning, 'for,' said Charles, 'I must be astir betimes; I have a great work to do to-morrow.'

The attached servant's fortitude here gave way completely, and clasping his master's hand to his bosom, he burst into a passion of grief.

'Nay,' said the King, 'be comforted; to-morrow is a day of rejoicing rather than of sorrow. Is it not my second marriage-day? To-morrow I would be as trim as may be, for before night I hope to be espoused to my blessed Jesus.'

For even now, on the verge of eternity, trifling matters wrested their share of attention from the grief of the one and the pre-occupation of the other. Herbert asked his master what clothes he would be pleased to wear on the morrow, and the warrior-spirit of the old English Kings flashed up for the last time, tempered, but not extinguished, by the resignation of the Christian—

'Let me have a shirt on more than ordinary,' said Charles, 'by reason the season is so sharp as may probably make me shake, which some observers will imagine proceeds from fear. I would have no such imputation. I fear not death; death is not terrible to me. I bless my God I am prepared!' These last words the King uttered in a low, devout, and solemn tone. He had done with everything now, on this side of eternity.

Yet is life passing sweet, even to him who has most

manned himself for its loss; and one more trial was
in store for the prisoner ere the gates of earthly hope
were closed upon him for ever. A loud knock was heard
at the door of his apartment, and without waiting for
permission to enter, a file of musketeers marched
steadily into the room, and stationed themselves one
on each side of the King's couch.

In vain Herbert stormed and expostulated; in vain
he threatened the vengeance of the Colonel, the General, the Council, and the Parliament: the soldiers
had their orders, they said; and the King, calming
his servant's indignation, gently bade him be still and
submit with patience, as he did himself, to this last
indignity.

One of the musketeers seemed stupified with drink,
as was indeed the case, and remained like a statue on
his post; but the door had scarcely closed upon the
stir and clang of the guard-room ere the other, flinging his musket on the floor, was prostrate at the
King's feet, covering his hand with kisses, and pouring forth expressions of loyalty and devotion such as
the Sovereign had not heard for many a long month.
Despite the flaxen curls and the dyed skin, the King
recognised him at once; and to the Cavalier's
hurried entreaties that he would save himself, as
he poured forth a torrent of explanations and ad-
jurations that not an instant was to be lost, did but
reply—

'It was like thee, Humphrey Bosville, bold, gallant
heart!—loyal to the last. It is no fault of thine that
Charles Stuart must wear no more an earthly crown.
But it is not to be. Listen, good Bosville; already

they are changing the guard in the ante-room. Thy plot hath failed thee even at the eleventh hour. God grant they may not have suspected thee and thy comrades. Surely, ere this time to-morrow enough blood will have been shed. Fare thee well for ever, my truest, bravest servant. It is the will of God—God's will be done!'

It was indeed too true. The last chance had failed, like all the rest. No sooner had Lieutenant-General Cromwell been informed of Hacker's directions that the prisoner's last hours should be subject to intrusion, than he rescinded the brutal order; but the practised warrior at the same time commanded that the guard in the ante-room should be relieved every four hours, and that the same men should not be warned twice for this duty until after the execution—thus nullifying any attempt at tampering with the soldiers' fidelity, unless the seducer was prepared to corrupt the whole regiment.

Humphrey had but time to resume his arms and his soldierlike attitude, when he was recalled to his comrades in the ante-room, and with them marched back to his regimental quarters. He carried off with him, however, one of the King's gloves, which Charles, with his accustomed kindliness in trifles, had taken from the table and slipped into his hand as he bade him farewell. That glove was treasured by Bosville's descendants as the most precious relic of their house.

At roll-call on the following morning some dozen or so of Hacker's musketeers were missing. Amongst the deserters was one Henry Brampton, of whom no further intelligence was ever obtained, though, unlike the rest, he had left his buff-coat, his arms and accoutrements, for the benefit of his successor in the ranks.

CHAPTER XX.

'THE WHITE KING.'

WITH grave and doubting looks the people in the streets asked each other if it would really be? In twos and threes, and small distinct groups, they conversed in low tones, glancing anxiously now towards St. James's, now in the direction of Whitehall. No crowd was collected, no circulation stopped. Ere a knot of persons, gathering like a snowball, could exceed a score, they found themselves insensibly dispersed and moving on. Compact bodies of soldiers, horse and foot, paraded to and fro in all directions, while St. James's Park was lined with a double row of musketeers, in review order, their drums beating, their colours flying, and their ranks opened. Officers and men wore a grave determined air; there was little of triumph, much of sorrow, in their honest English faces. The day had broken gloomily enough—not a ray of sunshine lighted the lowering sky. The wind swept up the streets and across the open Mall in moaning fitful gusts, and it was bitter cold. Masons had been knocking and scraping all night long at the wall of the banqueting-house in Whitehall, and carpenters in paper caps had concluded their work in front of the King's palace. The multitude looked up

at that solemn fabric with a dull stupified air.   It was
the scaffold.

One man amongst the crowd in St. James's Park,
habited in the dress of a plain country gentleman,
and muffled in a sombre-coloured cloak, was recognised
by several of the officers and men on duty.   They
would have accosted him, but he shunned all their
greetings, and exchanged not a word with any of
them.   His countenance bore the impress of a deep
sadness and contrition, his very gait was that of one
who is bowed down by sorrow and remorse.   Though
he had thrown up his part, George Effingham had
come to see the end of the tragedy played out.

The moments seemed to move like lead to the expectant thousands; perhaps to One they passed more
swiftly, perhaps even he could have wished the agony
of expectation were over at last.

Many a false alarm, many a stir about St. James's,
caused every head to turn in that direction; but the
drums beat up at last, the colours flew out once more,
the long line of soldiers brought their firelocks to the
'shoulder,' and in the open space between their ranks
a small group of persons moved slowly, solemnly,
steadily, towards the place of doom.

The good Bishop on his right hand trembled like a
leaf.   Herbert's face was blanched and swollen with
weeping; even the Parliamentary Colonel who attended him, drilled soldier though he was, marched
not with so firm a step as He.

Ay, look at him well, George Effingham; you have
not been so near him since he reviewed your squadron,
on the eve of Newbury; was his eye brighter, his

mien more stately when he sat his charger, in mail
and plate, before your drawn swords, than it is now?
Look at him well; would you ever have deserted his
service had you thought it would come to this?

As the King passed on, the musketeers on either
side wheeled up behind him, closing in their ranks
and forming an impassable barrier to the multitude
in their rear. By favour of a stalwart sergeant who
had served in his own stand of pikes at Naseby,
Effingham was permitted to advance with this unbroken column. An inexpressible fascination compelled him to see out the end of that which his very
soul abhorred.

On arriving at Whitehall, his Majesty passed along
the galleries to his bedchamber, where he halted for a
while to take a short interval of repose. Here he was
served with a morsel of bread and a goblet of claret
wine, upon a silver salver. Charles broke off a corner
of the manchet and drank from the cup. Herbert
meanwhile gave to the Bishop a white satin cap which
he had in readiness for his master; he could not endure to see him under the axe of the executioner.

It was now time. Colonel Hacker, who was in
attendance, and on whose stern nature the patience
and dignity of the Royal sufferer had made no slight
impression, knocked respectfully at the chamber door.
It was the signal of leave-taking. Herbert and the
Bishop sank on their knees before their Sovereign,
covering his hand with kisses. The latter, old and
infirm, bowed down moreover with excessive grief,
had scarcely strength to rise again. Gentle and
kindly to the last, Charles helped the prelate up with

his own hand. He bade the door be opened, and followed the Colonel out with the free step and the
majestic bearing of an English King.

The galleries and banqueting-house were lined with
soldiers. Firm and unwavering, they stood upon
their posts, but those warlike faces bore an expression
of unusual dejection : glances of pity, changing fast to
admiration and even reverence, were cast upon the
King from under their steel head-pieces, and the duty
was evidently little to the minds of those frank, bold
men. They had confronted him in battle, they had
fought him, and beaten him, and reviled him, but
they had never thought it was to end like this !

Men and women crowded in behind them, peering
and peeping under their elbows and between their
heads at the doomed monarch. Fervent expressions
of loyalty and goodwill greeted him from these bystanders, expressions not rebuked, nay, sometimes
even echoed, by the very guards who kept them back.

'God bless your Majesty!' exclaimed George Ellingham, in loud, fearless tones, baring his head at the
same time with studied reverence.

The blessing was caught up and repeated by many
a broken voice, and the King, returning his salutation, looked his old officer kindly and steadily in the
face. Whether he recognised him or not, George was
the happier for that glance during his lifetime.

He would fain have remained near him now, would
fain have done him homage and returned to his
allegiance even at the block, but the press became
more and more resistless, and he was swept away by
the crowd to a distance from which he could with

difficulty watch the last actions and catch the last words of the King against whom he had rebelled.

He saw him emerge upon the fatal platform with the same dignified bearing, the same firm step. He saw him expostulate for an instant with those around him as he asked for a higher block, that he might not stoop lower than became a Stuart even in his death. He could see, though he could not hear, that the King was speaking with animated gestures in vindication of his conduct throughout the war; but the royal voice rose audibly with the last sentence it ever spoke on earth, and every syllable struck loud and distinct as a trumpet-blast, while it declared in the face of earth and heaven—

' I have a good cause—I have a gracious God, and I will say no more !'

Had Effingham lived to a hundred, he could never have forgotten the picture that was then stamped indelibly on his brain. For many a year after he never shut his eyes that it did not present itself in all the firm strokes and glowing colours of reality. The sea of white faces upturned and horror bound, as the face of one man—the spars and props of the scaffold— the little groups that broke its level line—the sparrow that flitted across his vision and diverted his eye and his thoughts for an instant even then—the Bishop's white rochet and the Parliamentary Colonel's burnished helmet—the masked headsman's gigantic figure and the clean sharp outline of the axe—the satin doublet and the veiled head bowed down upon the block—the outstretched hand that gave the signal—

*   *   *   *   *

Effingham was a brave stout soldier, but he grew
sick and faint, and turned his eyes away. A hollow
groan, more terrible, more ominous in its stifled
earnestness, than the loudest shout that ever shook
the heavens, told how Charles the First had been
beheaded, and the reaction that placed Charles the
Second on the throne had already commenced. And
one more scene closed the eventful drama. The faithful servants who had attended him to the threshold of
eternity did not desert his mortal remains when he
had passed its portal. The parliament was memo-
rialized and petitioned till that body, already startled
at what it had done, gave permission for his burial.
The decency and respect that had too often been
refused the living monarch were not denied to his
senseless corpse. It was brought from St. James's to
Windsor in a hearse with six horses, like that of any
private gentleman, and attended by four mourning
coaches and the remnant of his Majesty's household.
The service for the burial of the dead appointed by the
Church of England was not permitted to be read;
but good Bishop Juxon, stanch to his post even when
all was lost, stood ready with the Prayer Book in his
hand to have used the prescribed ritual. In a vault
at Windsor Castle—his own old Windsor—amongst
his kingly ancestors, he was laid in his last resting-
place. A few high-born Cavaliers chose the spot for
his burial; a few devoted servants attended the obse-
quies of the master whom they loved. He lay, like a
true knight, in St. George's Hall, with the banners of
the noblest order of chivalry waving over him, and

winter sunbeams struggling through the emblazoned windows to gild his rest. When they carried him thence to the vault wherein he was to lie, the sky that had been bright and serene clouded over; a heavy storm of snow came on, and fell so fast that it covered coffin and hangings and pall with a pure and spotless robe—fit emblem of his innocence who slept so sound beneath.

The mourners looked significantly in each other's faces, and so they bore the White King reverently to his grave.

CHAPTER XXI.

A GRIM PENITENT.

IT is never too late to make reparation for evil, and George Effingham, although he had put it off till the eleventh hour, felt a stern satisfaction in remembering that he had thrown up his appointment on the King's condemnation, and that he at least was guiltless of Charles Stuart's death.

His case was not unlike that of other powerful champions of his party. Many a grim Puritan, though prepared to resist with the strong hand and to the death all assumption of irresponsible power, all aggressive interference on the part of the Crown, shrank with horror from so desperate a measure as the sentence of his sovereign to a criminal's death upon the scaffold, turned away with disgust from those who had completed the ghastly work when it was over. The very men who had fronted him so boldly in battle entertained a certain respect for the brave antagonist they had defeated, and the soldierlike feeling with which years of warfare had saturated their English hearts, especially revolted from the slaughter in cold blood of a vanquished foe. Fairfax himself—'*the General*,' as he was then termed *par excellence* by his party, and supposed at that juncture to be the most powerful man in England—

was not aware of the execution till it was over; but Fairfax could not have stopped it even had he known in time, for with all his *prestige* and all his popularity, the Man of Destiny was twice as powerful as he. The deed was now fairly done, and Effingham, shocked, repentant, and sick at heart, resolved to bear arms no more.

It is a serious matter for a man of middle age—by middle age we do not mean thirty or forty, or fifty, or any term of actual years, but simply that period at which the bloom is off the fruit once for all—it is a serious matter, we insist, for such an one to have lost his profession. A fortune kicked down can be built up again; like a child's house of cards, the same skill, the same labour, and the same patience, will not fail to erect a similar fabric, while those who have studied most deeply the enjoyment of wealth affirm that the pleasure of *making* money far exceeds that of spending it. Friends may fail or die, old and tried friends, but the gap they leave closes of itself far sooner than we could have supposed possible, and although we cannot quite

Go to the coffee-house and take another,

we resign ourselves to the inevitable with sufficient calmness, and go on much as we did before. Even a lost love may be replaced; or should the old wound be too deep to stanch, we cover it up and hide it away, ashamed, as well we may be, to own an incurable sore. But the profession, if *really* a profession, is a part of the man; other privations are but forbidding him wine, this is denying him water: it is an everyday want, a perpetual blank that irritates him at every turn. He would fain be in mischief rather than remain idle; be doing harm rather than doing nothing.

Ellingham was very restless, very unhappy. The dull despondency of resignation that had oppressed him for so many months, that he had soothed and blunted with constant duty and unremitting labour, was indeed gone, but in its place was a feverish irritation, a morbid desire for change, an intense thirst for happiness, which is of itself the most painful of longings, and a rebellious encouragement of that discontent which asks repiningly, 'Why are these things so?' He could not forget Grace Allonby, that was the truth; worse still, he felt that he would not if he could. To deceive another is often, as indeed it ought to be, a task of considerable difficulty; to deceive oneself the easiest thing in the world. One knows the dupe so well, his petty weaknesses, his contemptible pliancy, his many faults, which he cultivates and cherishes as virtues. It is a poor triumph truly over a disarmed and helpless adversary, so we do it every day.

Ellingham considered himself a proud man; it was the quality on which he most plumed himself. Never to bow his lofty head to human being, never to yield an inch of his self-sustaining dignity, this was his idea of manhood, this was the character he had trained himself to support. Perhaps it was for his pride that meek Grace Allonby loved him. Well she might. She had humbled it, and put her little foot upon it, and trod it into the dust.

After his last interview with her, this pride forbade him ever to see her more. Even after he heard she was still free, after gossiping Faith had poured such balm unconsciously into his heart, something told him that it was not for *him* to sue again, that he must leave everything now to *her;* and that as she did not seem anxious to communicate with him, and he was determined to remain stern and immovable towards her, the probability was that they would never meet again.

This point finally settled, it was no wonder that an irresistible longing came over him to visit Lord Vaux at the lodging wherein he lay on a sick bed; to request, nay, if necessary to demand, an interview with Mistress Cave, who inhabited the same house; not to shun—why should he?—the presence of any other lady who might happen to be with them at the time. That would indeed be ridiculous. It would look as though there *were* something between them, as though she could influence proud George Effingham in any one hair's-breadth of his conduct, as though he *cared* for her, which of course he did not now—not the least in the world—and this was the proof. Also a morbid desire came to possess him of justifying his conduct before these old Royalist friends, of disavowing his share in the King's death, a crime on which they must look with unmitigated horror, and of proving to them that though a strict Puritan and a determined adherent of the Parliament in its previous resistance, he was no regicide; nay, he was now no rebel. He had but fought for liberty, not revolution; he had opposed, not the King, but the King's dishonest advisers. Under proper restrictions, he would wish to see the monarchy restored, and in the person of the

late King's natural successor. Certainly he was no
rebel. Sincere, earnest George Ellingham was turning sophist.

He was turning coxcomb too, it seemed, else why
did he linger so long over his preparations to go
abroad that fine winter's morning? Why did he put
on his sad-coloured raiment with so much care, and
comb out those iron-grey locks and that grizzled
beard with such an unpleasant consciousness that he
was indeed turning *very* grey. He had not heeded
his appearance for years: it set him well now, a worn
and broken man, to be taking thought of his looks
like a girl. He turned from the mirror with a grim
sardonic smile, but he smothered a sigh too as he recalled a comely brown face that was not so bad to
look at less than twenty years ago, and he wished, he
knew not why, he had it back again just for to-day.
Pshaw! he was not going wooing *now*. He began to
think he was turning foolish. Why did his hand
shake so as he tied his points, and at that early hour
why so restless and eager to be off? Then, although
the day was fine for walking, keen and bracing as a
winter's day should be, Ellingham felt very hot as he
turned the corner of that street once so uninteresting
and so undistinguished from the thousand and one
adjacent streets, its fellows. There must have been
some peculiarity in the street, too, else why should he
have traversed it so often, examining its different
houses so minutely ere he stopped carelessly, and quite
by accident as it were, at the one he sought? It was
reassuring, however, to be admitted by Faith, with
her inspiriting glances and well-known smile; it was

not reassuring to be turned loose in an empty room, to await my Lord's leisure, on whom, by a pleasant fiction, this visit was supposed to be made, and who, as an invalid, could scarcely be expected to be astir at half-after nine in the morning, the early hour, even for those early times, at which George arrived.

How the room reminded him of that other room at Oxford, of which every detail was printed so indelibly on his memory. Photography, forsooth, is no invention of this or any other century. It came with mankind fresh and perfect upon earth. When Adam left the garden and knew he should see it no more, he took with him into the dreary waste of the outer world an impression of his Paradise that had not faded when his eyes were dim and his years had numbered nine hundred one score and ten. Eve, too, carried another in her aching bosom, though she could scarcely see it through her tears. Their children, one and all, possess the art and its appliances. Effingham's 'positive' was no less vivid than that of his fellow creatures.

Men inhabit a room as an Arab pitches his tent in the desert, careful only for immediate shelter and convenience, as a place that, when they have left it and done with it, shall know them no more. Women, on the contrary—at least *some* women, and these, we think, are not seldom the gentlest and most loveable of their sex—seem to pervade it, as it were, with their influence, though for the time they may be absent indeed in the body ; shedding, so to speak, an atmosphere of beauty and refinement about them which clings around the place when they are gone.

'Tis an old hackneyed quotation, though none the worse for that, about 'The vase in which roses have once been distilled;' but it describes as poetically and as adequately as language can, the charm we all know so well, the spell that a loved and loving woman casts upon the threshold of her home.

Mary Cave possessed this faculty in a high degree. Any one who knew Mary intimately could tell at a glance on entering a room whether she was in the habit of stationing herself there; and the something that George recognised here in the London lodging, which he had learned to appreciate in his Oxford experiences, was but one of the many attractions belonging to that lady of which he had never made any account. Lover like, he attributed it all to Grace, and looked round the apartment with a softening eye, believing that it was *here* she sat and worked and pondered, thinking perhaps sometimes, and not unkindly, of *him*.

Poor Grace! she was generally too restless now to sit still anywhere. When not occupied with the invalid, to whom both the women devoted themselves as only women can, she spent most of her time in wandering to and fro about the house, looking out of all the windows that commanded the street, and turning away from them as if she expected somebody who never came, varying this dreary amusement by long political discussions with her friend, in which she sought to prove the Parliament not so far in the wrong, shocking that Cavalier lady much by the disloyalty of her opinions, which seemed to incline daily more and more towards Puritanism, and as Mary told her, almost with indignation, 'flat rebellion.'

Had George Ellingham known all this, perhaps he would hardly have trembled so ridiculously as he stood bending his sheathed rapier about unconsciously in that sacred apartment. No; he was a bold man, George, and he loved her very honestly. It would have made him more nervous still.

In his stirring and eventful career he had faced as much danger as most men, not only the open dangers of the battle-field, which to one of his calibre were indeed no great trial of courage, but the more thrilling hazards of advanced outposts, night attacks, and such uncertain duties, when a moment's relaxation of vigilance, a moment's loss of coolness, might not only have destroyed himself, but imperilled the very existence of the army for whose safety he was answerable. Never in his whole life, however—as George once confessed, many a long day afterwards to a certain individual, who received the confession with happy smiles, melting into happier tears—never before, on picket, with Rupert hovering about his flanks at midnight, or detached with a handful of men to make his way in broad daylight between Goring's keen-sighted vigilance and Astley's unerring tactics, no, not even when he stood face to face with old Sir Giles at Naseby, and bore the brunt of that impetuous charge in which the stout knight fell wounded, had he felt his lips blanch and his heart leap to his mouth as they did on this eventful day simply to hear a light footfall coming along the passage, and a gentle hand lifting the latch of the door.

To him entered no more important a personage than his friend Faith, whose sense of the ludicrous, damped, yet not altogether smothered, by the grave realities of matrimony, was sorely tried by George's open-mouthed expression of countenance, denoting anything but coolness or self-command.

'My Lord prays the General will excuse his waiting on him in this apartment,' quoth Faith, demurely, 'and begs the favour of his company in the sick chamber to which his Lordship is still confined;' with that she bade him follow her guidance, and make as little noise as possible, in consideration of the invalid—an unnecessary injunction to a man who, though conscious of no evil intention, felt already like a convicted thief. George, however, was too experienced a soldier not to recognise the inspiriting influence of locomotion; his courage came gradually back as he advanced to the attack.

She was in the room. He knew it somehow without seeing her. He was conscious of a presence, and a grave, formal courtesy and the old stupifying sensation, that was yet so fascinating. He was conscious also of another lady, pale and faded, who greeted him with stately coldness, and of the suffering nobleman himself reclining languidly on his couch.

Poor George Ellingham! they were drawn up in battle order to receive him, horse, foot, and dragoons. For an instant he was coward enough to wish he hadn't come!

There is nothing like a plunge at once in *medias res* to brace the nerves for an encounter. To his Lordship's distant salutation, and somewhat haughty inquiry as to the cause which had obtained him the honour of the General's visit, though he could not forbear adding, courteously enough, 'that he trusted it was to give them some opportunity of returning the many favours they had received from the Parliamentary officer,'—George replied with manly frankness at once, 'that he had come to see his old friends, in order to do himself justice. He had but few now,' he said, 'and could not afford to lose one of them. He was no longer in a position either to ask or to confer a favour. He was neither a general now, nor an officer in the service of the Parliament.'

The party looked from one to the other in some perturbation. Grace turned very red and very white again in less than a second. Lord Vaux feebly signed to the ladies to withdraw. One of them could not, and the other would not, see the signal. An embarrassing silence succeeded: the three were at what is termed a 'dead lock.'

Mary was the first to break it. He quite started at her voice; it was so changed from the full, steady tones he remembered; he looked attentively in her face, and was sorry to see how time and grief had altered her. It was a beautiful face still, but it had lost for ever the rounded outlines and the bright comeliness of youth.

'We are glad to know that it is so,' said Mary, assuming for the nonce the old queenly air that sat so well upon her. 'You can understand our feelings. You see our loyalty is no whit shaken even now. Mourning for him as we do, ay, even in our outward garb'—she glanced as she spoke at her own dress, for all there were in the deepest black—'how is it possible for us to forgive his murderers? Had you come here with the King's blood on your hands, George Effingham, not one of us could have spoken a kind word to you again.'

Grace looked up at him with one rapid, speaking glance; the next instant her eyes were fixed intently on the floor. She at least would listen to his justification with no unfavourable ear.

In a few manly, simple words George told his tale. Addressing himself to the old Cavalier nobleman, he detailed his early experiences of the Royal army and the Royal party, his scruples of conscience, his change of faith, the moral obligation he felt to join the champions of liberty, and the contagious enthusiasm kindled in his mind by their religious zeal. Without dwelling on his own deeds or his own feelings, he confined himself to a simple narrative of facts, relating how he had served his country and his party at once; how he had mitigated the rigorous measures of the Parliament towards the Royalists, as indeed they themselves knew, to the utmost of his power; and how even at the very last he had gone to Cromwell with his commission in his hand, and protesting against the sacrilege which he was powerless to prevent, had thrown it at the Dictator's feet, and stripped off the uniform which he had resolved from henceforth he would never wear again. 'And now,' said George, kindling as he spoke, and fixing his eyes unconsciously on Grace, who sat blushing and trembling, drinking in every word, 'I see, too late, the error into which we have fallen. I see that we have trusted too little to the people, too much to the sword. I see that we have ourselves built up a power we are unable to control;

and that, setting aside every question of Right, we must return within those limits we ought never to have overstepped, resume the allegiance that we have never intentionally shaken off, and re-establish a Monarchy to save our country. I may have gone too far; but in these times there has been no middle course. I have borne arms not against my sovereign, but against those who would have persuaded him to be a tyrant. No! There is not a drop of Charles Stuart's blood on my hands, and I have never been a rebel, my Lord, never a rebel, as I am a living man!'

Grace thanked him with a look that made Effingham's heart leap for joy.

Poor Lord Vaux, sadly weakened and broken down, had listened courteously and with a well-pleased air to a man for whom in his heart he had always entertained a high respect, and to whose kind offices he had often of late owed his own welfare and security. He bowed his head feebly, and said, 'he was glad to hear it;' then looked wearily around as though to ask when his noonday draught would be ready, and when his visitor was going away. Mary alone remained obdurate and uncompromising.

'You have justified yourself,' she said, 'of the Blessed Martyr's blood, but you can never deny that you, and such as you, have been the unconscious instruments of this odious sacrilege. You are not *of* us, George Effingham, and you must not be *with* us. We are glad to have heard you in your defence; to have seen you once more; to thank you for the favours we have received at your hands; and to bid you farewell.

We wish you no evil, we bear you no malice; but between us and *you* stands the scaffold at Whitehall. It is a barrier that can never be removed. I speak for Sir Giles Allonby's daughter as well as myself. Come, Grace, you and I have no business here!'

How could she say such hard, such cruel words? What was this impulse that bade her do violence to her own better feelings, and trample so ruthlessly on those of her friend? Her tone, too, was unnaturally calm and constrained; and she pressed her hand upon her bosom, as if in physical pain.

He had bent his head down, down to his very sword-hilt while she was speaking, but he raised it more loftily than his wont when she had done, and Grace observed that he looked sterner than usual, and had turned very pale. Her woman's heart was rising rapidly; her woman-nature rebelled fiercely against this assumption of authority by her friend. She sat swelling with love, pride, anger, pity, a host of turbulent feelings. It wanted but little to create an outbreak.

He rose slowly, and bade Lord Vaux a courteous farewell. He bowed to the ground before Mary, who acknowledged his salutation with one of those miraculous courtesies which the dames of that period performed to such perfection. Then he turned to the door, and in doing so he must pass close by Grace's chair. How her heart beat. Once she thought he would pass without speaking. For more than a minute she had never taken her eyes off his face, and a sad, hopeless expression crossed it now that made her thrill with pain. He stopped before her chair, and took her by the hand. 'Farewell,' he said, 'a long farewell, *Grace!*' There was a world of quiet sorrow in the tone with which he spoke that last word; a world of hopeless love in the deep eyes that looked down so reproachfully, yet so fondly, into hers. The girl's heart was full to suffocation. She could bear it no longer; the room seemed to swim before her eyes. The next moment she was sobbing on his breast like a child.

Effingham walked out of that London lodging perhaps the happiest man that day in England. He was no accepted suitor, no affianced lover, it is true; but for the first time he knew now beyond a doubt that the blessing for which he had pined so long was his own; that even if she might never be his, Grace Allonby loved him dearly in her heart; and the light which the poet affirms 'never was on sea or shore,' but without which both sea and shore are but dull and dreary wastes, began to shed its golden gleams on a life that only too joyfully accepted this one boon in lieu of everything else which it had lost.

Trembling, weeping, agitated, horribly ashamed, yet by no means repentant of what she had done, Grace retired to her chamber, whither, from the sheer force of habit, she was followed by her friend; and where, in broken sentences and frequent sobs, not un-mingled with smiles, she told her how she had loved their enemy so long, ever so long, ay, even before she had entreated him to save Bosville's life, only she was not quite sure he cared for her; and how she had nevertheless always believed it was for her sake Effing-ham had been so kind to the Royalists; and how proud she always was, though she knew it was very wrong, of his prowess and his successes; lastly, how she had feared she must never see him nor speak to him again; and how to-day was the happiest day in her life; 'for, you see, Mary, he is not a rebel, after all—he says so himself—not a rebel at all; and even, if I never see him again, I shall always love him better than any one else in the world.'

And Mary listened, and soothed her, and remonstrated, like a confirmed hypocrite as she was. (All good women are, far, far more so than the bad ones.) And even urged the claim of another, with a pale smiling face too, and dissuaded her in every way she could think of from what she termed 'this wicked folly;' and Grace, cheering up rapidly, laughed at the latter argument, and said with a mocking voice, 'If ever he turns up, you will have to marry him yourself, Mary. You have taken charge of him ever since we have known him. It is very careless of you to have lost him now!'

They reached home, those unconscious friendly stabs, dealt so innocently by a loving hand—home to the very quick, every one of them. Grace could not guess why her friend bent down to kiss her so assiduously at this moment, and talked on so volubly immediately afterwards; but the conversation was resumed again and again; the argument against marriage, so resolutely urged by the elder lady, becoming weaker and weaker at every fresh attack.

The contest ended as such contests usually do when the one side is thoroughly in earnest, the other fighting against its own convictions. Lord Vaux, an easy good-tempered man, devotedly fond of Grace, and in the intervals of his malady only too glad to make every one happy about him, was soon brought to think that George Effingham would be an extremely fit person to take charge of his dear Grace, provided always they would both come and live with him in the old Hall at Boughton. With much reluctance— so much indeed as to seem more feigned than sincere— Mary withdrew her opposition, and the spring, gloomy and disastrous as it proved to the Royalist party, smiled on at least one happy heart amongst the despondent and ruined Cavaliers.

CHAPTER XXII.

' COMING HOME.'

MASTER DYMOCKE sat basking in the beams of an early summer's sun on the terrace at Boughton. He had been left in trustworthy charge of that establishment for several months, as was indeed well known to the inferior domestics of the household, on whom his military strictness and somewhat peevish disposition, by no means improved after matrimony, had produced an impression the reverse of agreeable. The males held him in considerable awe; the females, excepting one or two of the prettiest, to whom he relaxed considerably, opined, and, womanlike, freely expressed their opinion, that he was ' a thankless old curmudgeon.' Perhaps as he was now altogether out of the game, the single ladies may have regarded him with a peculiarly unfavourable eye.

He seemed, however, thoroughly satisfied with the current of his own reflections. The family were expected to return that very day, and although he was sufficiently habituated to his pretty wife's absence to bear it with conjugal composure, he had no objection on earth to see her smiling face again. Though firmly convinced in his own mind that he had paid too high a price for that treasure, Dymocke, we need scarcely repeat, was a philosopher, and the last man to be guilty of such an absurdity as that of under-valuing a purchase because it had cost him pretty dear.   No, Faith belonged to *him*, and that was of itself a very considerable merit.   It is only right to add that the little woman ruled him most thoroughly, and tyrannized over him as only such a little woman can.

The afternoon was rapidly verging towards evening, and the sun was already beginning to shed that golden haze athwart the distant valleys which makes our English scenery, dotted with timber, and clothed with copse and hedgerow, like a dream of fairyland, and yet they had not arrived.   Well !   It was three good days' journey from London to Northampton for a horse litter, and thankful they might be that my Lord was sufficiently recovered to come home at all, and a merry home-coming it would turn out, with Miss Grace's happy face, as pleased with her dark grim lover as if he had been a bran-new gallant from the French Court ; and Mistress Mary, whom the poor old folk for many a mile round had missed sadly during her absence, and his own little vixen's saucy smiles, and my Lord's calm weary approval of all that had been done whilst he was away.   Dymocke had imperceptibly usurped the authority of every other functionary in the establishment, and had constituted himself butler, gardener, groom, and steward, with a grave tenacity peculiarly his own.   It was now most gratifying to reflect that the house was clean, the garden trim, the stable in order, and the very pig-sties arranged with military method and precision ; also to be convinced that he, Hugh Dymocke, was the only man in England who could so completely have set everything to rights.

Thus absorbed in his self-satisfied meditations, honest Hugh rose from the bench over which Mary's roses were already putting forth a thousand tiny buds, and strolled into the park to catch the first glimpse of the expected cavalcade.

Dazzled with the slanting sunbeams, he shaded his eyes with his hand as he perceived the figure of a man in the park apparently threading the old trees so as to avoid observation.

'Something wrong,' thought Dymocke. 'Some one here for mischief, I'll be sworn. 'Tis too tall for old Robin the molecatcher, and "Forester Will" is away psalm-singing at Harborow, with a murrain to him! He'd better not come home drunk as he did the last time, a prick-eared knave! It must be some poaching scoundrel looking after the young fawns. I'll raddle his bones for him if I catch him, I'll warrant; and I can run a bit still for as old as I am, and wrestle too with here and there a one.'

Thus soliloquizing, our veteran, in whom the pugnacious propensity was still strongly developed, hastened towards the intruder with long swift strides, craftily careful, however, to keep every advantage of ground in case his new acquaintance should take fright and make a run for it.

This, however, seemed to be the last thing in the stranger's mind. He leaned his back against a tree, with his eyes fixed on the ground, as though the young fern springing up beneath his feet were a study of absorbing interest and importance. If he were really a botanist, he seemed a most attentive one, and took not the slightest notice, as indeed he was probably quite unconscious, of the sturdy sergeant's approach.

That worthy's conduct was, to say the least of it, remarkable. On perceiving that the stranger's dress and exterior denoted a gentleman, he had halted at a distance of about a hundred yards and reconnoitred. Then, without further preliminary, he sent an excellent new beaver spinning high into the air, bounded three feet from the ground as if he were shot, and with a howl of mingled triumph, affection, and astonishment, ran the intervening distance at the very top of his speed, and seizing the stranger's hand with famished eagerness, mouthed and kissed it much as a dog would do a bone, while down his brown cheek and on to that hand, stole the first and only tear the stout sergeant is ever recorded to have shed.

' He's alive and well! he's alive and well!' gasped the old soldier as if a giant's fingers were griping his throat. 'God bless thee, Master Humphrey—my dear young master!' and he burst out with a snatch of one of their jolly Cavalier songs in a hoarse hysterical voice that would have tempted a bystander to laugh had he not indeed been more inclined to weep.

It was sad to see how little Humphrey responded to the sergeant's affectionate welcome. He pressed his hand indeed kindly, for it was not in Bosville's nature to hurt the feelings of a single soul, but his countenance never for an instant lost the expression of deep melancholy that had become habitual to it, and he looked so sadly in his old servant's face that the latter's triumph soon turned to apprehension and dismay.

'What is it, Master Humphrey?' he asked eagerly, and using unconsciously the old familiar appellation of long ago; 'you are safe here—quite safe; surely the bloodhounds are not after you now? Oh, Master Humphrey, d'ye mind how we gave them the slip, and what an example the sorrel made of 'em that blessed day? We've got his half-brother now; goes in my Lord's coach; and I've kept one of his hoofs. I went and cut it off myself when he lay dead down yonder by the waterside, and it's stood ever since over the corn-bin against you should come home!'

Humphrey smiled a forced sad smile. 'Thanks, honest Hugh,' he answered; 'I have not many treasures left. I should like the sorrel's hoof, for your sake and that of the good old horse. Go and fetch it me now. I will wait here till you come back. I must be in the saddle again to-night, and in a few more hours I shall leave England for ever. Hugh, you're an old soldier; I can trust you. Do not let any of the family know you have seen me here to-day.'

'Why, bless you, there isn't a soul of them at home,' answered Dymocke, and his master's face fell visibly the while. 'They're all expected back to-night. I was out looking for them just now, when I saw you. My Lord's getting quite hearty again, Heaven be praised! and you've heard the news? Our young lady's going to be married, and to our old Captain, too. Ah, Major, there wasn't as smart a troop in the King's army as ours. D'ye mind what the Prince said at Newbury when he bid the whole brigade take up a fresh alignement upon *us?* "Dress," says he, "upon Captain Effingham's troop, and be d—d to ye!" He was a hearty free-spoken gentleman, was Prince Rupert; "for they stand," says he, "like a brick wall," says he; and so we did, and a pelting shower we got from Essex's culverins before they'd done with us; but we never broke our line! Well, well, it's a world of change; and I'm married, too, Major—married and settled and all. Oh, my dear Master Humphrey, don't ye be in too great a hurry. But that's neither here nor there; and you've heard doubtless of Mistress Mary's good luck, and the fortune that's fallen to her?'

He had, indeed. We must be more than estranged from those we love when we cease to hear *of* them if not *from* them, to make inquiries, needlessly disguised and indirect, about their welfare—to take an interest all the keener that we are ashamed to own it in the remotest trifles that can affect them. He had heard what was indeed true, that by the death of a relative Mary Cave had become possessed of broad lands away by the winding Avon, waving woods, and smiling farms and acres of goodly pasturage; nor, though he rejoiced in aught that was likely to benefit her, could he stifle a bitter and unworthy pang to feel that this succession was but another barrier raised between himself and the woman from whom he felt he was hopelessly separated. If he had been voluntarily discarded by her before, could he condescend to sue her now that she was a wealthy heiress? Not he. That at least was a folly he had done with for evermore, and when his softer nature got the better of him, and he felt too

keenly how sweet that folly was, he would fall to reading the letter once more that he still carried in his
bosom, thin and almost illegible now from frequent
perusals, yet perhaps scarcely so frayed and worn as
the heart against which it lay. Had he known—had
he only known! But such is life. Can we wonder
at the bumps and knocks we receive when we think
what a game at Blind-man's-buff the whole thing
is!

And Mary's pleasure in her succession to this heritage
was of a strangely sober nature. 'Too late—too late!'
was all that lady said when she heard of it. Too
late, indeed! The cause was irretrievably lost that
had been with one exception the thing nearest and
dearest to her heart, and he for whom alone she
feared she would have been capable of abandoning
that cause itself, was parted from her for ever! She
could not even gain tidings that he was alive now.
No wonder Mary had grown so pale and haggard!
No wonder she was so altered from the proud, careless, free-spoken Mary Cave who had asserted her in-
dependence so haughtily while she flew her hawk at
Holmby with stout Sir Giles not so many years ago.
The wheels of Old Time run smoothly enough, but
they leave their marks as surely dinted on the barren
sand as on the fresh green turf, alike impartial whether
they grind weed and thistle into their beaten track,
or bruise the wildflower to the earth never to lift its
gentle head again.

It was with no small difficulty that Humphrey
could impress upon his old servant the necessity of
his remaining *incog.*; could persuade him it was really

his wish that none of the family should be informed of his presence; or could make him believe that he was in sober earnest in the intention he had expressed of leaving England forthwith. Dymocke was even sorely tempted to throw up his own comfortable and lucrative situation in order to follow once more the fortunes of a master to whom he had been always attached, but the thought of his lately-married wife and his fresh ties stifled this new-born impulse even as it rose. Dymocke put it in this way—'If I should once get back to my bachelor habits, I should never be able to settle down again. Perhaps I'd best stay as I am. What's done can't be undone; and maybe it's easier to keep the barrow trundling, than to stop, once and again, for a fresh start!'

'Not a word more at present, Hugh,' said the Major, after a few further inquiries and observations about old times had been made; 'I have good reasons for wishing my visit here to remain a secret. See! they are arriving even now. Meet me to-night under the cedars when they are all gone to bed. Bring the old horse's hoof with you for a keepsake, and we will wish each other a last farewell.'

As he spoke he disappeared amongst the old trees; and Dymocke, vainly endeavouring to settle his countenance into its habitual calmness, hurried back to receive his master at the hall.

It was indeed a happy party. The old lord, benefited by the advice of his London physician, and no longer harassed by the share he had so long sustained in that unequal conflict, which for the present was terminated by unequivocal defeat, had regained somewhat of his former strength and spirits, was able to alight from his litter without assistance, and gladdened Master Dymocke's heart with an appropriate jest and a kindly smile as he trod once more the threshold of his home. Happy Grace, still young enough to possess that elasticity of temperament which makes light of past suffering as though it had never been, blushed and sparkled as she did at sixteen, pressing her lover's hand with shy affection as he assisted her from her horse, but already beginning to treat him with that playful tyranny which a young wife is apt to assume over a grave and superior husband in whom she has perfect confidence, and of whom in her heart of hearts she is immensely proud. George's dark face beamed with a light which had been a stranger to it for years. Happiness is a wonderful restorative, and already the lines were beginning to fade from his rugged brow, the harsh defiant expression was changing for one of deep grateful contentment; the dark eyes, no longer glittering with repressed feelings and feverish excitement, shone with the lustre of health and strength; while the swarthy glow upon his cheek accorded well with his bold, frank bearing, and square, well-built frame. It was a manly, vigorous beauty still, thought Grace, and none the worse for the grizzled hair and beard. He looked joyous and light-hearted, although in the false position of a man 'about to marry.' The practice of humiliating the lords of the creation, when thus disarmed and at the mercy of their natural enemies, is by no means peculiar to the present era. From time immemorial, ay, since Father Laban imposed so cruelly upon Jacob, the bridegroom expectant has ever been discomfited as much as possible by the bride and her auxiliaries. It may be that this disheartening process is considered a salutary purgatory, such as shall enhance the paradise of the subsequent honeymoon, or it may be simply intended as a judicious foretaste of conjugal discipline hereafter; but that it has existed among all civilized nations as a great social institution, we take every Benedick to witness who has found, like George Effingham, that bodice and pinners are a match, and more than a match, for doublet and hose.

Dymocke's face as he lifted his pretty wife from her horse was worth a mine of gold. There were tenderness, self-restraint, a comical consciousness of shame, and a sly glance of humour, all depicted at once on his rugged features.

'Welcome home, lass!' he whispered, winding his arm round her trim waist, 'welcome home! I can do well enough without thee; but it warms my heart like a tass of brandy to see thy bonny face again!'

This was a great deal from Hugh, and Faith stooped her pretty head and kissed him accordingly.

But 'some must work while others sleep;' and although the majority of the party were basking merrily in the sunshine, one was drooping visibly in the shade. Kindly, gentle, and forbearing—trying to forget her own grief in the joy of others—purified and softened by sorrow—there was yet on Mary Cave's brow a weight of care which it was sad to see in one still in the prime of life and the meridian of beauty. Her temperament, like that of many who possess abilities above the average, was impressionable enough on the surface, but hard as adamant beneath. In her younger days she was quite capable of enjoying and even reciprocating the empty and harmless gallantries which were the fashion of the Court; but though it was always easy enough to attract Mary Cave's attention, none save Falkland could boast that he had won her interest; and this attachment to an ideal, strong as it undoubtedly was, had in its very nature a false and morbid fascination which would too surely pass away. When it was gone it left her colder, haughtier, more inwardly reserved than ever. Then came the daily association with one possessed of many winning qualities; above all, of that which in the long run cannot fail to be appreciated—a faithful, loving heart; whom she had accustomed herself to consider as her own peculiar property; whose affection she regarded as neither obtaining nor expecting a return; whom she had taught herself to look upon as a devotee, a slave—always true, always unchanging, never to assume any other character. Little by little the unyielding disposition became saturated with an insidious and delightful sentiment. The wilful heart, so difficult to tame, found itself enclosed in meshes it had been weaving insensibly for its own subjection. In time it began to hint to her that she could ill afford to part with her secret treasure; at last it told her that it must break at once if she was to lose him altogether.

Then arose the fearful struggle out of which she came a victor indeed, but too surely conscious that *such* a victory was more crushing than any defeat.

For Grace's sake, for the sake of every one—nay, for his *own* sake—she voluntarily gave him up : and while she did so she knew and felt she gave up all her hopes this side of eternity. Subsequent events added but little to her despondency. The one great fact was ever before her—that of her own freewill she had discarded the man she loved ; and Mary's love, once won, was no light matter. She would look at her hand—the shapely hand he used to admire and praise with a lover's childish folly, and wish it had withered to the bone ere it had penned that fatal letter. For of course he could never forgive her now. Even his kindly nature would be estranged by heartlessness such as hers. He would avoid her and forget her—nay, he *had* avoided and forgotten her. It was all over at last— he was lost to her for ever, and she had done it herself !

It was a mockery to see George and Grace so happy; to feel how utterly she had sacrificed her own future in vain. It was a mockery to hear the joyous girl prattling of her future household and her wedding-dress, and to be asked for grave matronly advice, as though she herself were indeed without the pale of the loving and the hopeful. Above all, it was a bitter mockery to have inherited broad lands, and wealth that was valueless to her now, since she might not share it with the ruined Cavalier.

It was cruel work. What could she do? There was but one resource—there never has been but one resource for human sorrow since the world began. When the burden became too heavy to bear, she knelt beneath it, and she rose again, if not hopeful, yet resigned; humbled but consoled as those alone rise who ask for comfort meekly on their knees. She was often in that position now; had she never known sorrow, she had never sought Heaven. Providence leads us like children through the wilderness, by many a devious track towards our Home. Joy brightens the path for one, and he walks on thankfully and happily in its rosy light. Grief takes another by the hand, and clutching him in her stern gripe, points with wasted arm along the narrow way. What matter for so short a distance, how we reach the goal? Brother! help me with my knapsack the while I guide thy feebler steps, and share with thee the crumbs in my homely wallet. Let us assist rather than hinder one another. Yonder, where the lights are twinkling, is a welcome for us all. Dark is the night, and sore the weary feet, and rough the way. Cheer up!—toil on!—we shall get there at last.

CHAPTER XXIII.

'LOST AND FOUND.'

DYMOCKE was uneasy and full of care. 'There's something wrong,' muttered the old trooper in his beard, as he went fidgeting about the house and offices, putting everybody out under pretence of seeing things done correctly with his own eyes. A sumptuous supper was soon served in the great hall for the travellers, and Lord Vaux looked round him with an air of thorough comfort and enjoyment to be at home once more. The flush of sunset softening in the south to a pale transparent green, but edging the light clouds that roofed the meridian with flakes of fire, flooded the quaint old Hall in crimson light richer than the very hues of the stained glass above the casements, opened wide to the fragrant evening air. A solitary star twinkled already in the pure clear depths of the infinity above, while the highest twigs and branches of the old trees, not yet clothed in their summer garments to their very tops, cut clear and marked against the pale, calm sky. The rooks were drowsily cawing out their evensong, and a young moon peeping shyly above the horizon, afforded no more light to the outer world than did the needless lamp burning on the supper table to the domestic circle within. Lord Vaux was a quiet studious man of earnest temperament but of few words. He saw his fine old home preserved to him, his oaks uninjured, his fortune, though impaired, still amply sufficient for his wants; above all, his old retainers around him, and the two last of his kinsfolk left alive sitting at his board. He stretched his hand across the table to Effingham.

' God help the Cavaliers !' said he in a broken voice; 'George, I owe all this to you !'

It was the first time he had called him by his Christian name, and Grace thanked him with such a happy, grateful glance. Then she stole a look at her lover, proud, radiant, full of tenderness and trust. George blushed, stammered, looked down—and finally said nothing. It was all he had to say—would he not have given his heart's blood long ago for any one connected, however remotely, with the name of Allonby, and never asked for thanks? There was nothing to be grateful for, he did but follow his nature. The three talked quietly, but cheerily, not laughing much, nor jesting, but in the soft, low tones of those who have a deep store of happiness within. For two indeed the cup was brim full, and running over.

Mary, too, joined in the conversation, but Dymocke, bringing in a tapering flask of Hippocras, could not but observe her absent manner and pale dejected looks.

' There's something wrong,' muttered the old soldier once more, and he fell to reflecting on all the circumstances he could think of which bore in any way on that lady's case, for whom, like the rest of the household, he felt and professed a chivalrous devotion. He had obtained a few vague hints from Faith that

Mistress Mary was 'sadly changed—not herself, by
any means—took the King's death much to heart,'
and ' was over-anxious also about absent friends ;' but
Faith, besides holding the person of whom she spoke
in considerable awe, was one of those women who are
far more discreet in entrusting secrets to their hus-
bands than to their own sex, and Dymocke's con-
jectures, whatever they might be, were but little
assisted by the penetration of his wife. True to his
profession, however, his ideas naturally reverted to
the sorrel, as indeed they were apt to do whenever
the old trooper fell into a despondent mood. He
bethought him how, although the two ladies had both
been in the habit of petting and fondling so good and
handsome an animal, Mistress Mary's attention to
that chesnut favourite were paid much more secretly
than her friend's—how, going in and out of the
stable at odd times, he had come unexpectedly on the
latter lady making her accustomed visit when the servants were at meals or otherwise engaged, and how
upon one occasion, noiselessly descending a ladder
from the hay-loft during the important hour of
dinner, he had seen her with his own eyes lay her
soft cheek against the horse's neck, and he could have
sworn he heard her sob, though she walked away with
a statelier step than ever when she found herself disturbed, and as the stout soldier confessed to himself,
he dared not have looked in her face for a king's ransom. Then he remembered sundry little weaknesses of
the Major's, which, being his personal attendant and
valet, he had not failed to remark. How he had often
been surprised at the value that careless young officer

seemed to attach to the most insignificant trifles. What a fuss he made about a worn-out riding-glove, which had been unaccountably lost by one of the ladies on a journey to Oxford, and as unaccountably found with the thrust of a rapier right through the palm, a few hours after the duel with Goring; also how his master's usually sweet temper had been ruffled, and he had sworn great oaths totally unwarranted by the occasion, when Dymocke, in his regard for cleanliness and order, had emptied a vase of a few roses, which had been kept there in water till indeed by any other name they could scarcely have smelt less sweet. ' All these matters he revolved and pondered in his mind, till at last, having, as he termed it, 'put stock and barrel together,' he came to his own conclusions, and resolved to act, soldier-like, on his own decision. It required, however, a good deal of courage to carry out his undertaking. The affection with which Mary inspired her subordinates, and indeed her equals, was tempered with awe. There are some natures with which no one ever presumes to take a liberty, some persons, often the most amiable, and best-tempered of their kind, who, without the least effort or self-assertion, inspire general respect. It required no little courage and effrontery even for an old soldier to go up and tell Mary Cave, if not in so many words, at least in substance, that she was over head in love with a ruined Cavalier, and that if she didn't go out to-night and meet him under the cedars, she would probably never set eyes on him again!

Dymocke manned himself for his task. After supper,

Effingham and Grace, lover-like, strolled out upon the terrace to look at the young summer moon: much of her they saw—neither of them found out she rose the other side of the house! Lord Vaux, fatigued with his journey, hobbled quietly off to bed. Mary, with her head upon her hand, seemed lost in thought. She had no heart for her embroidery to-night, to-morrow she would begin new duties, new tasks; she must not sink, she thought, into a useless apathetic being, but this one night may surely be given to remembrance and repose. Dymocke made two efforts to speak to her, but each time his courage failed him. She thought the man lingered somewhat about the room, but she was in that mood which we have all of us known, when the spirit is so weary that any exertion, even that of observation, becomes a task; when we are too much *beat* even to be astonished or annoyed. She rose as if to go away, and Dymocke felt that now or never he must take his plunge. He coughed with such preposterous violence that she could not but lift her sad eyes to his face. She might reasonably have expected to see him in the last stage of suffocation.

'Mistress Mary,' said the sergeant, blank and gaping with agitation, and there he stopped.

She thought he was drunk, and eyeing him with a calm, sorrowful contempt, passed on to leave the room.

'Mistress Mary!' gasped the sergeant once more, 'good Mistress Mary—no offence—he's here—I've seen him!'

No need to tell her *who*. Her limbs trembled so that she was fain to sink into a chair, and she grasped its arms in each hand like an old palsied woman, as, true to her mettled heart, she turned her face to Dymocke, and tried to steady her voice to speak. Not a sound would come save a husky stifled murmur in her throat—not a sound, and the soldier in very pity hurried on with what he had got to say.

' He's to meet me to-night in the Park—under the cedars—he's there now—he's going away at once, for good and all—going over sea—we'll never see him more. Oh! Mistress Mary, for pity's sake!'

She smiled on the honest sergeant, such a wild, strange smile. Never a word she spoke, but she rose steadily to her feet, and walked away with her own proud step; only he noticed that her face was deadly white, and she kept one hand clasped tight about her throat.

Humphrey sat under the cedars in the misty moonlight, and mused dreamily and sadly enough on his past life, which indeed seemed to be gone from him for evermore. A man's strong heart is seldom so hopeful as a woman's; it is harder for his more practical nature to cling, like hers, to a shadow; perhaps he has not so studiously reconciled himself to suffering as his daily lot; perhaps his affections are less ideal, but his despondency is usually of a fiercer and less tractable kind than her meek sorrowing resignation. Humphrey had gone through the whole ordeal, the trial by fire, which scorches and destroys the baser metal, but from which the sterling gold comes out purified and refined. He had suffered bitterly; he sometimes wondered at himself that he could have endured so much; but his faith had not wavered: to use the language of that old chivalry which has never yet died out in England, though it might cover his death wound, his shield was bright and spotless still.

After the King's martyrdom, as the Royalists termed the fatal execution at Whitehall, Bosville, a deserter and a conspirator, was fain to hold himself concealed in one of the many hiding-places provided by the Cavaliers for their more conspicuous friends. It took time, and cosmetics too, for the dye to wear itself out of his natural skin. It took time for his comely locks and dark moustache to grow once more, and thus efface all resemblance to the flaxen-haired Brampton, whilome a private in Hacker's redoubtable musketeers. Although when he was at length able to go abroad again, it was a nice question whether the proscribed Cavalier major did not incur as much peril by being recognised in his own real character, as in that of the sentinel who had plotted for the King's rescue, and then absconded from the ranks of the Parliamentary army. Many long weeks he remained in hiding, and it was during this interval of inaction that he heard of Effingham's proposed marriage to Grace, and of Mary's succession to her goodly inheritance. It was bitter to think how little she must have ever cared for him, that she should have made not the slightest effort to discover his lurking-place. He judged her, and rightly, by his own heart, when he reflected that she ought to know he could not sue to her now—that if ever they were to become even *friends* again, the advances must come from *her*. His spirit sank within him when he thought that heartlessness such as this affected even the past, that she never could have loved him for five minutes to forget him so easily now, and that he had bartered his life's happiness for that which was more false and illusive than a dream. God help the heart that is sore enough to say of the loved one, 'I had rather he or she *had died* than used me thus!' and yet poor Bosville had thought so more than once.

As is often the case with blind mortality, much of this self-torture was wholly uncalled-for and unjust. While Humphrey was blaming her with such bitter emphasis, Mary busied herself day by day and hour by hour in endeavouring to find out what had become of him. Without compromising his safety, she was bringing into play all her abilities, all her experience of political intrigue, all her new wealth and old personal influence for this purpose, but in vain. The Cavalier party was so completely broken-up and disorganized, that it was almost impossible to obtain information concerning any one of the proscribed and scattered band. Mary was fain to give up her search in despair, concluding that he had either fled the country or was dead. The latter possibility she combated with a reasoning all her own. She was not superstitious, only very fond and very sorrowful.

'It was all my fault, I know,' she used to think, that humbled, contrite woman; 'and yet he loved me so once, he could not surely rest in his grave if he knew how anxious and unhappy I am.' She would rather have seen him thus than not at all.

After a time, his pride came to his assistance, and he resolved to seek in other lands, if not forgetfulness, at least distraction and employment. His fortunes were nearly ruined with the ruined cause he had espoused. He had little left save his brave empty heart and the sword that had never failed him yet. In the golden tropics there were spoils to be won and adventures to be found. Many a bold Cavalier who, like himself, had been more used to bit and bridle than bolt-sprit and mainstay, was already afloat for the Spanish Main, with a vague thirst for novelty and a dim hope of romantic enterprise. Fabulous accounts were rife of those enchanted seas, with their perfumed breezes and their coral shores, their palm trees and their spice islands, their eternal summers and their radiant skies. Nothing was too extravagant to be credited of the Spanish Main, and many an enthusiast, gazing at sunset on the flushing splendour of the Western heaven, was persuaded that he might realize on earth just so gorgeous a dream far away in yonder hemisphere to which his eyes were turned.

So the Cavaliers clubbed their diminished means together, and chartered goodly brigantines, and loaded them with merchandize, looking well to their store of arms and ammunition the while, and launched upon the deep with mingled hopes of trade and conquest, barter and rapine; the beads to tempt the dusky savage in the one hand, the sword to lay him on his golden sands in the other.

And Bosville had a share in one of these pirate-ships, lying, with her fore-topsail loosed, in the Thames. She was well found, well manned, well freighted, and ready to sail at a moment's notice. Before he left England for ever, he thought he would go and take one more look at the old haunts that had always been so dear, that had witnessed the one great turning-point of his life; and thus it came to pass that Humphrey had met his former servant that afternoon in the park at Boughton, and sat at nightfall under the cedar, musing dreamily in the misty moonlight.

He was not angry with her now. The bitterness had all passed away. He could no more have chid her than one can chide the dying or the dead. Already they were parted as if the past had never been. He could never again suffer as he had done. The worst was over now. Ay, there was the light glimmering in her chamber; he could see it through the trees. Well, well; he had loved her very dearly once. It was no shame to confess it, he loved her very dearly still. Large tears welled up in his eyes. He knelt upon the bare turf, with his forehead against the gnarled trunk of the old cedar, and prayed for her from his heart, God bless her! God in heaven bless her! He should never see her more!

A dark figure rushed swiftly across the park. She stood before him in that pale moonlight, white and ghastly like a corpse in those mourning garments she had worn ever since the King's murder. As he rose to his feet she grasped his hand. How long those two stood there without speaking, neither ever knew. It might have been a moment, it might have been an hour. Each heart beat thick and fast, yet neither spoke a syllable.

She broke the silence first.

'You would not go without bidding me good-bye?' she said, and he felt her grasp tighten; then the proud head sank lower, lower still, till it rested upon his hand, and the hot tears gushed over it as she pressed it to her eyes, and she could say never another word than 'Forgive me, forgive me, Humphrey!' again and again.

These scenes are all alike. Most of us have dreamt them; to some they have come true. None dare ignore them from their hearts. The moon rose higher and higher in the sky, and still they stood, those two, under the cedar, her wet face buried in his breast, his arm around her waist. They must have had much to tell each other, yet is it our own opinion that but little was said, and that little sufficiently unintelligible; but Humphrey Bosville never sailed for the Spanish Main, and that he had good reasons to forego his departure, we gather from the following reply to one of his whispered interrogatories under the cedar, murmured out in soft broken tones by weeping, blushing, happy Mary Cave—

'My own, you never knew it, but I loved you so fondly all the time.'

CHAPTER XXIV.

'THE FAIRY RING.'

ONCE more we gather the friends, from whom we are about to part, in a fairy ring under the old oak-tree at Holmby. More than two lustres have elapsed, with their changes, political and private, since we saw them last,—lustres that have stolen on insensibly over many a birth and many a burial, over much that has been brought gradually to perfection, much that has wasted silently to decay. The Man of Destiny has gone to his account. The Man of pleasure reigns, or rather revels, on his father's throne. All over England bells have rung, and barrels been broached, to celebrate the Restoration. A strong re-action, to which our countrymen are of all others in Europe the most subject, has set in against Puritanism, propriety, everything that infers moderation or re-straint. Wine and wassail, dancing and drinking, quaint, strange oaths, and outward recklessness of demeanour, are the vogue; and Decency, so long bound hand and foot in over-tight swaddling clothes, strips off her wrappers one by one, till there is no saying where she may stop, and seems inclined to strike hands and join in with the frantic orgy, nude and shameless as a Bacchanal. As with boys fresh out of school, there is a mad whirl of liberty all over the playground ere each can settle steadily to his peculiar pleasure or pursuit. And the old oak looks down on all, majestic and unchanged. There may be a little less verdure about his feet, a few more tender chaplets budding on his lofty brows, a few less drops of sap in the hardening fibres of his massive girth, but what are a couple of lustres to him? He stands like a Titan, rearing his head to heaven, and yet *his* time too will come at last.

He spreads his mighty arms over a happy party; not so noisy perhaps (with one exception), as most such parties are in these roaring times, but one and all bearing on their countenances the stamp, which there is no mistaking, of a destiny worked out, of worthy longings fulfilled, above all, of a heart at peace with itself. They are well mounted, and have had to all appearance an excellent afternoon's sport; a brace of herons lie stricken to death on the sward, and Diamond herself, that long-lived child of air, proud, beautiful, and cruel, like a *Venus Victrix*, perches on her mistress's wrist, unhooded, to gaze upon the spoils. Grace Effingham takes but little notice of Diamond beyond an unconscious caress to her father's old favourite; for her attention, like that of the others, is taken up by an addition to this familiar party, who seems indeed, as doubtless he esteems himself, the most important personage of the whole.

He is a bright laughing child, of frank and sturdy bearing, not without a certain air of defiance. He has his mother's soft blue eyes and rich clustering hair, with something of the wilful tones and playfully imperious gestures which sat so well on the loveliest lady that adorned Henrietta's court, but his father's kindly disposition is stamped on his open, gentle brow, and his bonnie, rosy mouth. He has his father's courage, too, and physical delight in danger, as Mary often thinks with a glow of pride and happiness, while she watches him riding his pony hither and thither over fortuitous leaps, and galloping that obstinate little animal to and fro with reckless and uncalled-for speed.

A tall old man, his visage puckered into a thousand wrinkles, his spare form somewhat bent, but active and sinewy still, bends over the boy with assiduous tenderness, adjusting for the twentieth time the pony's saddle, which is always slipping out of its place. Hugh Dymocke has no children of his own—an omission on the part of Faith which does not, however, disturb their married harmony—and of all people on earth he is most devoted to the urchin, who never allows him to have a moment's peace. The two are inseparable. The child knows the whole history of the Civil War, and the details of each of its battles, as furnished with considerable embellishments by his friend, far better than his A B C. He believes stoutly that his father and Hugh are the two greatest and bravest men that ever lived, inclining to award the superiority, if anything, to the latter, and that his own destiny must be necessarily to do precisely as they have done. Besides all this, Dymocke has taught him to ride, to fish, to play balloon, to use his plaything sword, and a host of bodily accomplishments; also he has promised to give him a crossbow on his seventh birthday. Wherever little

Master Humphrey is seen (and heard too, we may be sure), there is Dymocke not very far off. Faith, grown stout, easy, and slipshod, having moreover deteriorated in good looks as she has improved in amiability, gives her husband his own way on this single point and no other. 'Indeed, he's crazed about the child, and that's the truth,' says Faith; generally adding, 'I'm not surprised at it, for you wont see such another, not on a summer's day!'

They are all proud of him. Uncle Effingham, as the boy persists in calling George, with half-a-dozen little black-eyed darlings of his own, spoils him almost as much as Grace does. He is not a man of quips and cranks, and such merry conceits; but he has one or two private jests of their own with the little fellow, in which, judging from the explosions of laughter by which they are followed, there must be something irresistibly humorous, apparent only to the initiated. George's beard is quite white now, and the snowy locks which peep from under his beaver form no unpleasing contrast to his coal-black eyes, glittering with fire and intellect, and the swarthy glow on his firm healthy cheek. He is very happy, and obeys Grace implicitly in the most trifling matters. The only fault to be found in his strong sensible character is, that he defers too much to the whims and fancies of his pretty wife. Need we observe she has plenty of them ready for the purpose. The neighbours say she ' rules him with a rod of iron,' that she ' bullies him,' and ' worries his life out,' and ' abuses his goodnature ;' that ' his stable contains a grey mare better than any horse,' &c. &c.; but George knows better. He knows the depths of that fond true heart; he knows that a word of tenderness from him can at any time bring the tears into those fawn-like eyes, which he still thinks as soft and beautiful as ever. What though he does give her her own way in everything? Does he not love her, and is she not his own?

So he works on manfully and fearlessly, doing his duty in that public life to which he has returned. His fanaticism has been disciplined to piety, his enthusiasm toned to patriotism; he is an able statesman and a valuable member of society. Probably little Humphrey is the only person in the world who thinks George Ellingham ' the funniest man he ever saw in his life !'

The young gentleman is an only child; need we say what is his parents' opinion of their treasure? Need we say how his father watches every turn of his countenance, every gesture of his graceful, childish limbs, and loves him best—if indeed he can be said to love him at any one time more than another—when he is a little wilful and a little saucy, when the blue eyes dance and sparkle, and the rosy lip curves upward, and the tiny hand turns outward from the wrist, with his mother's own gesture and his mother's own beauty blooming once more, and radiant as it used to be, long, long ago? He is Sir Humphrey Bosville now, knighted at Whitehall by his Sovereign's hand; for prone as was the Second Charles to forget faithful services, he could not for very shame pass over such devotion as Bosville's unnoticed and unrewarded.

' Odd's fish, man !' said the Merry Monarch, as he gave him the *accolade* with hearty good-will; ' many a shrewd blow have you and I seen struck in our time, but never was one given and received so deservedly as this!'

But Sir Humphrey is all unchanged from the Humphrey Bosville of the Queen's household and the King's guard-room.   He rides maybe a stone heavier or so upon his horse, but he rides him still like a true knight, fearless and loyal to his *devoir*, faithful and devoted to his ladye-love—yes, she is his ladye-love still—as dear, as precious now after years of marriage as when he took leave of her at Falmouth, and watched for the very glimmer of her taper to bid her his tacit farewell from under the cedar at Boughton.   He has got the foolish sleeve-knot still, he has got one or two other equally trifling absurdities; perhaps they represent to him a treasure that is beyond all value here ; that, unlike other treasures, he may peradventure take away with him hereafter.

And Mary, riding by her husband's side with calm contented face, is no longer the proud imperious Mary of the Court—the spoiled beauty, whose intellect no statesman was to overreach, whose heart no gallant was to be able to touch.   She has known real sorrow now, ay, and real exquisite joy—such joy as dries up the very memory of pain with its searching beams.   They have each left their traces on her countenance, and yet it is beautiful still with the placid and matronly beauty of the prime of womanhood. There may be a line or two on the sweet fair brow— nay, a thread of silver in the glossy rippling hair; but there is a depth of unspeakable tenderness in the comely mask through which the spirit beams with more than its pristine brightness; and the love-light in her eyes as she looks in her husband's face is unquenched, unquenchable.

Mary laughs, and says 'she has grown into a fat old woman now;' and no doubt the graceful figure has become statelier in its proportions, and the Court dresses of Oxford and Exeter would scarcely be induced to meet round the still shapely waist; but Humphrey cannot yet be brought to consider her as a very antiquated personage. He says, 'She has always been exactly the same in his eyes;' and perhaps indeed the face he has learned so thoroughly by heart will never look like an old face to him.

She spoils him dreadfully—watches his every look, anticipates his lightest whim, and follows him about with her eyes with a fond admiration that she does not even try to conceal. She is always a little restless and out of spirits when away from him if only for a few hours; but she brightens up the moment they come together again. It seems as if she could never forget how near she once was to losing him altogether. She would not say a wry word to him to save her life; and she is angry with herself, though she cannot but confess its existence, at her jealousy of his lavishing too much affection even on her boy.

With all a mother's fondness she knows she loves the child ten times better that he is so like his father.

So the little fellow shoots out from amongst the group upon his pony, careering away over the upland like a wild thing, amidst the laughter and cheers of the lookers-on; and they too move off at a steadier pace behind him, for the sun is already sinking, and the old trees' shadows are creeping and lengthening gradually to the eastward. They move off, and the old oak stands there, as he did in King James's time, when Sir Giles Allonby was young; as he will when that bright-haired child shall become a feeble grey-headed man; when the actors and actresses in our historical drama shall ·be dead and buried and forgotten.

He is standing there now, though the scenes which we have shifted are scenes of full two hundred years ago. He will be standing there, in all probability, two hundred years hence, when we shall assuredly be past away and gone—past away from this earth and gone elsewhere—Where?

THE END.

THE OLD COALPIT;
OR, THE ADVENTURES OF RICHARD BOOTHBY IN SEARCH OF HIS OWN WAY.
A Story for Boys. By E. J. May. Author of
'Louis' School Days.' 4s. 6d.

SWORD AND GOWN.
By the Author of 'Guy Livingstone.' 7s. 6d.

GEORGE CANNING AND HIS TIMES.
By Augustus Granville Stapleton. 16s.

PELOPONNESUS: NOTES OF STUDY AND TRAVEL.
By W. G. Clark, M.A., Fellow and Tutor of Trinity College, Cambridge. 10s. 6d.

REVOLUTIONS IN ENGLISH HISTORY.
By Robert Vaughan, D.D.
The First Volume, REVOLUTIONS OF RACE. 15s.

SOLDIERS AND THEIR SCIENCE.
By Captain Brabazon, R.A. 7s.

ESSAYS WRITTEN IN THE INTERVALS OF BUSINESS.
The Seventh Edition. 2s. 6d.

HISTORY OF THE LITERATURE OF ANCIENT GREECE.
From the Manuscripts of the late Professor K. O. Müller.
The first half of the Translation
By the Right Hon. Sir George Cornewall Lewis, Bart., M.P.
The remainder of the Translation, and the Completion of the Work,
By John William Donaldson, D.D.
Three Volumes, 8vo, 36s. The new portion, Two Volumes, 20s.

COMPANIONS OF MY SOLITUDE.
The Fifth Edition. 3s. 6d.

THE CLOISTER LIFE OF THE EMPEROR CHARLES THE FIFTH.
By WILLIAM STIRLING, M.P. The Third Edition. 8s.

MAN AND HIS DWELLING PLACE.
An Essay towards the Interpretation of Nature. 9s.

DISSERTATIONS AND DISCUSSIONS, POLITICAL, PHILOSOPHICAL, AND HISTORICAL.
By JOHN STUART MILL. Two Vols., 8vo, 24s.

OF THE PLURALITY OF WORLDS. AN ESSAY.
The Fifth Edition. 6s.

BACON'S ESSAYS.
With Annotations by the Archbishop of Dublin.
The Fourth Edition. 10s. 6d.

EXTRACTS FROM JEAN PAUL RICHTER.
Translated by Lady CHATTERTON. 3s. 6d.

SHIPWRECKS OF THE ROYAL NAVY.
By W. O. S. GILLY. With Preface by the Rev. Dr. Gilly.
The Third Edition. 5s.

THE KINGDOM AND PEOPLE OF SIAM;
With a Narrative of the Mission to that Country.
By Sir JOHN BOWRING, F.R.S.
Two Vols., with Illustrations and Map, 32s.

THE SPANISH CONQUEST IN AMERICA,
And its Relation to the History of Slavery, and to the Government
of Colonies. By ARTHUR HELPS.
Octavo. Vols. I., II., 28s.; Vol. III., 16s.

FRASER'S MAGAZINE

FOR FEBRUARY,

CONTAINS

FRASER'S MAGAZINE FOR MARCH

WILL CONTAIN

LONDON: JOHN W. PARKER AND SON, WEST STRAND.